THE LEGACY OF THE SKY SERPENTS

Published by Silvettica | 2025

FIRST EDITION

For more information, visit: **http://www.authorkevincox.com**

THE LEGACY OF THE SKY SERPENTS

FATES OF GALANOR 2

KEVIN COX

CHAPTER 1

W EKENWILD NEVER TURNED travelers away, it unmade them, one step at a time. To the unmarked eye, the forest was chaos: black trees in endless rows, a tangle of shadows too precise to feel natural, yet too complex to follow. But for Selaina, something had shifted. The power of the Wishing Stone still echoed in her bones, reshaping her sight. Now she could feel the truth behind the illusion.

This wasn't chaos. It was order; brutal in its precision, the kind that made her instincts recoil before her thoughts could catch up.

The trunks of the trees rose in complicated alignments, each like a column placed by unseen hands. Above her, blue leaves shimmered in measured patterns. They didn't shift with the breeze but moved in time, like dancers following a song only the forest could hear. A cadence in the quiet. A pulse beneath the silence.

The tree roots weren't trying to trap her, they were tracing invisible spirals in the stone, weaving the forest into a living hymn. The whole forest wasn't a maze; it was a message. And somehow, she could hear it.

These weren't random threads of light. They twisted and turned with impossible precision, like the weaving of a loom too vast for mortal eyes. It wasn't just music, it was architecture. A language of shapes and movements, older than words, deeper than thought.

She couldn't read it, yet. Only feel it. Like a song written in what wasn't said.

Somehow, she knew. This was how the world itself was

written. Not with ink or sound, but with patterns, geometry hidden in breath, root, light, and will. Her understanding wasn't whole yet. It sat inside her like a seed, buried deep, just beginning to bloom.

When she stepped forward, the land responded with a faint tug, like it had felt her presence and adjusted slightly. A thread of light shimmered ahead, so faint it could be her imagination. Then another. Each step drew more into view. They weren't showing her the way, only answering her, as if her will and the forest's were slowly finding the same rhythm. To walk Wekenwild was not to navigate. It was to attune.

Behind her, the others faltered, struggling against the oppressive sameness of their surroundings.

"We're walking in circles," Garrick grumbled behind her. There was a weight to his tone, a growing impatience that hadn't been there before. "Just say it. You have no idea how to get out of here."

Selaina could hear the scrape of his boot against the ground, the subtle shift of leather as he adjusted his sword strap.

She slowed her pace, turning slightly, her hand brushing against a low-hanging branch that glowed faintly blue to her eyes. "It's not exactly a circle. It's a spiral. The path folds back on itself, but it keeps moving forward."

"That doesn't make sense. Every tree looks the same." Ysadora's voice was tight with frustration. "How can you tell anything apart in this place?"

Selaina turned fully to face them. She gestured vaguely to the air around her. "Because I stopped trying to fight it. There's a pattern. It's almost too perfect to be natural, but it's not random. It's a kind of... rhythm."

"So we're marching to the beat of a haunted forest's drum?" Kadin asked, resting his foot on a rock and inspecting the crossbow he'd recently claimed. He turned the weapon over, his lips curling into a faint smile. "Are you sure whatever was inside the Wishing Stone hasn't affected your mind?"

She moved ahead slowly, brushing her fingers along the bark of a tree that shared the blue glow of the branch. The touch sent a pulse through her fingertips, not warmth, exactly, but a kind of recognition. A sense that the tree had seen her before and remembered her pattern.

The farther she walked, the more the air felt aware, like the forest was listening. The roots beneath her feet weren't random tangles. They curved with purpose, forming fractal spirals, a clear design within nature. Leaves overhead pulsed like breath in a choir, shimmering in alternating patterns, measured, restrained, deliberate.

And the lines, only she could see them, traced through the air like faint ribbons of light, weaving from tree to tree. They moved when she moved, adjusting the structure of the forest ever so slightly, as if improvising around her presence.

Each glowing thread thrummed beneath her step, welcoming her deeper into the song. The forest didn't resist her. It resonated with her progress. Each step struck something under her skin. The forest responded to her, not as an invader, but as an instrument, woven into its pattern.

Behind her, the others stumbled and muttered. Garrick cursed under his breath. Ysadora scowled into the sameness. But Selaina heard the melody rising now, an unseen refrain that changed with every step, each moment adjusting itself around her presence. The forest opened to her. It didn't fight her steps, it followed them.

There was no map, no compass. Just current and countercurrent, like the tides of thought. The way through didn't unfold in a linear fashion. It curved like memory, looping back, drifting sideways, always drawn toward something older than the words that tried to define it.

For the first time since touching the Wishing Stone, Selaina felt not like she was carrying the power, but like it was starting to carry her.

"Rhythm or not, I can't see it," Ysadora pressed, the skepticism in her voice sharpening. "I hope you're not making this up."

Rykan stepped closer, the quiet creak of leather accompanying his movement. "I believe her."

Kadin let out a huff. "Of course you do. If she told us the trees were whispering directions to her, you'd probably believe that too." The exaggerated swing of his crossbow strap made his frustration known.

"What else would you have us do?" Ysadora's sharp tone carried a hint of resignation.

"Maybe if we all hop on one foot while singing to the leaves," Kadin muttered. His smirk was audible.

Faint lines only Selaina seemed to be able to see pulsed with every step she took, a guiding thread through the maze. The forest resisted the others, the glowing leaves swaying without wind, the rows of trees whispering softly in patterns just on the edge of understanding. Garrick's hand hovered near his weapon, as if he was sensing threats around them.

Selaina led them onward, her heart pounding but her steps unwavering. Each twist and turn felt natural to her, like a song she'd always known but had only just begun to sing aloud. Yet beneath the rhythm of her steps, something pulsed, an undertow she couldn't shake. A feeling, quiet but insistent, pulling her attention southward. Toward something distant. Something waiting.

She had felt it first just after absorbing the Wishing Stone's power, a whisper threading through her mind, calling her to a place she had never been but now saw clearly whenever she closed her eyes.

A great mountain rising from the heart of the world. Crags like teeth. A summit lost in sky. And above it all, a golden light, radiant and pulsing, as if the mountain itself held something sacred, just beyond the veil.

She hadn't told them. Not about the mountain calling her. They had sacrificed so much to get here. Elysia had died believing. Darian had stood beside her, fought for her, then betrayed her and fallen. He hadn't wanted power. He'd just wanted something back, something lost: his wife. It haunted Selaina in the quiet spaces, the weight of it, the pattern of it. All that loss. All those choices. And now, this strange power humming beneath her skin.

Her remaining companions deserved more than a nebulous vision. She owed them more than her instincts. More than a direction only she could sense.

And maybe, if she was honest with herself… she was afraid. Afraid that, if she spoke the truth, told them something was calling her, pulling her south toward a mountain none of them had seen, they would look at her like she was lost to madness. Like Myrradin. Like all those who claimed destiny and fell beneath its shadow.

Still… the call of the mountain hadn't faded. It had only grown more insistent.

So she kept walking. Letting the current of the forest guide her steps, and burying the pull deep where no one could hear it.

"The forest doesn't want us lost," she said, her voice low but steady.

"The rows, the patterns, they're not meant for our perception." Her eyes moved to the others. "We should decide what to do next. How do we take on the Iron Flood? How do we fight Vatreus?"

"We're back where we started then," said Garrick, drawing in a sharp breath. "If you don't have the answers, none of us do."

"Just get us out of here first," said Kadin.

For a moment, the group walked in silence. The tension in the air didn't abate, but it shifted. They weren't following the forest's rules anymore, they were following Selaina's.

Just as the forest's rhythm began to change, Selaina stopped. She turned to the others, her voice steady. "We're almost there."

As they rounded the next bend, the careful design of Wekenwild unraveled. The precise symmetry of the trees gave way to uneven, twisting growth. Ahead, a clearing opened, bathed in the first natural light they had seen since stepping into the forest. The air itself shifted, as if the land had exhaled, releasing them from its quiet grasp.

Selaina stepped forward first, tension slipping from her shoulders as she lifted her gaze to the open sky. The sunshimmer danced high above, wild and unfettered, its shifting hues of teal and crimson echoing their release from Wekenwild's tight order.

She turned back, a faint smile tugging at her lips. "See? I told you."

Behind her, Ysadora stepped into the light. The shift from shadow to sunlight revealed the fine chain threaded between her black horns, catching the morning glow. Her dark hair fell like a curtain against the slight iridescence of her blue-tinged skin.

Kadin muttered something under his breath, but there was a begrudging lilt to his voice. Behind him, Garrick exhaled, a subtle shift, but one that spoke of relief. Ysadora's silence lingered longer, and though Selaina didn't meet her eyes directly, she felt the weight of her gaze, something keen and considering beneath it.

The forest thinned, giving way to the rocky desertscape of Nordravin. The rising sun spilled golden light over the horizon, stretching long shadows across the jagged terrain. Rykan stepped out behind her, blinking against the light. In the sun, the sharp lines of his face emerged more clearly, angular and weather-worn, with eyes that always seemed to be scanning the horizon. He moved like someone born in the in-between: part soldier, part survivor, all instinct.

They pressed forward, the weight of their journey settling into every step. The tension between them was different now, no longer the quiet unease of Wekenwild, but something weightier, something unspoken.

Selaina's thoughts turned to the Wishing Stone. She had refused to use it for Myrradin's intended purpose, a decision that still hung heavy in the air between them. Myrradin's betrayal had only solidified her resolve. His hunger for power, cloaked in the guise of righteous intent, had nearly cost them everything. Even Ysadora, his former apprentice, had acknowledged Selaina's choice as the right one. Rykan, steadfast as ever, had never doubted her. But Garrick and Kadin… their distrust lingered like a shadow.

"We should go east," Rykan said as they reached the salt flat. "It's just a few days' journey to Tathara."

Garrick let out a slow breath. "You want to liberate Tathara? Unless you know of a willing army, I don't think the five of us stand much of a chance."

Rykan didn't hesitate. "We don't need an army. We have destiny on our side."

Kadin snorted. "Oh, well, if destiny's backing us, why stop at Tathara? Let's go ahead and topple the whole empire while we're at it."

"Destiny isn't a shield of invincibility," Ysadora said, her voice even. "It's no guarantee. It's a path, one that can either be fulfilled or lost."

"My mother was there when the Iron Flood took the city," said Rykan. "I need to know what happened to her."

"I hope that one day a force rises, capable of defeating the Iron Flood, reclaiming your city," said Garrick. "But right now, it's just a dream."

"You make it sound like we've already lost," said Selaina.

"Haven't we?" asked Garrick. "We were supposed to change the world, and here am I back in Nordravin, worse off than I was before. Elysia died for nothing. I can't do this anymore."

"After everything we've been through together, you would leave things like this? We now have a chance to stop Vatreus," said Ysadora.

"That was what the Wishing Stone was for," said Garrick. "We've failed at everything we set out to do."

Rykan shook his head. "No. Not yet." He stepped forward, his eyes fierce. "Garrick, we can still make this right. Maybe Myrradin failed us, but that doesn't mean we stop. Whether Elysia knew it or not, this is what she was fighting for. So we finish it."

Selaina turned to him. "And how exactly do we finish it? Five people against an empire?"

Rykan didn't hesitate. "We don't need plans. We need pressure. Movement. Break something big enough and the cracks will spread."

"And what about the people caught in those cracks?" Selaina asked, her voice quiet but firm. "You talk like change is a fire, but fires burn. Sometimes the answer isn't tearing things down. Sometimes it's rebuilding what's been lost."

Rykan looked away, jaw tight. "Rebuilding only works if there's anything left to build with."

"There is," Selaina said. "There's us. There's always us."

Kadin let out a slow whistle. "Well," he muttered. "Destiny, fire, rebuilding. All sounds very noble, until it's your name on the stone."

"How Elysia will be remembered rests in our hands," said Selaina. "We can make her death mean something, or we can let it be nothing." She turned to Garrick. "We need your experience, your swordsmanship. None of us can fight like you do."

"You would pass up a chance to follow Zhal Evurah?" Ysadora said. "How often does anyone get that opportunity? Our names would be written into legends."

"Aye, and legends seldom tell of those who were crushed beneath the wheels of destiny. How often do the songs recall their names?" Kadin smirked, adjusting the strap of his gear. "If I've a choice, I'd rather be a surviving footnote than a lauded martyr."

Garrick scratched the side of his beard, eyes narrowing. "The last time someone was hailed as Zhal Evurah," he muttered. "Well, let's just say it didn't go well."

"Who else could make such a claim?" Ysadora asked.

Garrick's gaze shifted to the horizon. He rubbed at his jaw absently, fingers catching in his beard, then let his hand fall to his belt as though grounding himself. "Before we go any further, I should tell you something, something that may change your mind about wanting me with you."

CHAPTER 2

Selaina's shoulders tightened. Something in Garrick's tone, a quiet finality, the burden of something long overdue, set her nerves on edge. What could he have done that would make him think she wouldn't want him here?

The group exchanged uneasy glances.

"Tell us what?" Ysadora asked.

Selaina kept her expression still, though her gaze flicked away for a heartbeat, her stomach fluttering nervously.

"I used to be in the Iron Flood," Garrick said. His voice was steady, but there was a heaviness to it, as if each word carried years of regret.

A chill crept through Selaina, thin and sudden, like a shadow slipping past her thoughts. The Iron Flood. Vatreus's army. The same force that had burned cities, taken prisoners, destroyed lives. And Garrick had fought among them? Had he—?

No. She pressed the thought aside. If Garrick had been the kind of man to revel in conquest, he wouldn't have left. He wouldn't be standing here now, bracing himself for judgment.

"I was a soldier," he continued, his voice quiet. "Fighting for what I believed was truly honorable. Vatreus brought cities together; he claimed he would unite kingdoms and end the wars of the nobles that soldiers and peasants suffer for."

He paused, his eyes scanning their faces.

"It was the first time I ever saw things that way," Garrick

said. "That fighting for your king and country wasn't always about oath and honor, for a just cause, it was often nobles using our lives to settle their personal petty squabbles."

He exhaled heavily.

"I wanted a king who served everyone, not just himself. And for a time, I thought that was Vatreus. But there are no good kings. Once power touches their lips, it leaves a thirst only the wine of corruption can satisfy."

"The wine of corruption," Kadin said, his tone dry. "A vintage that never runs dry, it seems."

Selaina's voice was soft but insistent. "So Vatreus wasn't always like he is now?"

"No, he wasn't," Garrick said. "Unless I was too blind to see it."

"What opened your eyes?" Selaina pressed, though gentler this time.

Garrick's jaw clenched. "I saw the source of his power. The gate where they led men, women, and children to be sacrificed to something... not of this world."

"Azragul," Ysadora whispered, her face pale.

Garrick nodded. "I couldn't be part of it anymore. I deserted and left that life behind."

Selaina forced herself to breathe, her hand brushing briefly over the mark of three stars on her forehead before falling away, as if shielding something unseen. The gate. The sacrifices. The images from the Wishing Stone surfaced in her mind, vivid and inescapable.

Vatreus. Not the warlord, not the butcher of cities, but the boy, thin, trembling, barely clinging to life. She had seen him in those visions, not as an enemy, but as a brother, lost to a fate neither of them had chosen. Could things have been different? If not for his illness, if not for their parents' desperate bargain with Azragul... would he have grown into something else? Someone she could have saved?

Her fingers twitched toward her forehead, brushing the faint glow of her mark before she caught herself. She couldn't let them see her shaken. The whispers of destiny coiled at the edge of her mind. Had Vatreus once believed he was meant for something greater, too? Had he stood where she stood now, convinced he could wield power without it corrupting him?

Once power touches their lips...

If power revealed what Vatreus truly was… what would it reveal in her?

Ysadora stepped closer to Garrick. Her expression was tight, but something passed across her eyes, quick and uncertain, grief, maybe, or something nameless caught in the space between breath and memory.

"I followed Myrradin my whole life. He was the only family I ever had. Not by blood, but by choice. And I thought… I thought I knew him." Her voice wavered, but she pushed on. "I told myself his ambitions were noble, that his hunger for power was just the price of wisdom. I wanted to believe it." She exhaled, shaking her head. "Maybe I still do, in some small, broken way. But if it was always there, if I was blind to what he really was, then what does that say about me?"

Selaina met Garrick's gaze. "If I had used the Wishing Stone to change fate, Azragul would have struck a bargain with Myrradin. The sacrifices would have continued. If we can stop Vatreus, we might finally end this cycle. Garrick, we need you."

He didn't answer. His eyes flicked toward the horizon, his expression unreadable. A muscle tensed in his jaw, and for a long moment, all she could hear was the wind scraping over the rocks.

"And what if we can't stop him?" Garrick's voice was rough, quieter than before. "What if we're just delaying the inevitable? I believed in Vatreus once," he said. "I was wrong. How do I know I'm not making the same mistake again?"

Selaina didn't flinch. "Because this time, you've already seen what he's become."

Garrick looked away, then back, slower this time.

"I don't see much hope," he muttered. "But if there's even a sliver of a chance to end this differently…" He paused, then nodded once. "Then I'm in."

Selaina's breath stilled.

The words struck deeper than she wanted to admit. Did Garrick see something in her that she refused to see in herself? The idea clawed at the edges of her mind. Had Vatreus once believed he was fighting for something noble, only to step off the edge into ruin? And if so, how close was she to that same fall?

She had to believe it was different. That she was different.

She exhaled, meeting Garrick's gaze without flinching. If doubt had a place in her, then so did purpose. She would not be him.

"Is anyone even the slightest bit concerned whether I'm going with you or not?" Kadin asked, breaking the tension with his usual irreverence.

"I figured you'd let us know when we got there," Selaina said with a knowing smile.

Kadin tilted his head, mock considering. "If I said no, would you try to talk me into it?"

Selaina's smile softened. "Kadin, you always seem to live by your own rules. I don't think my words would change much."

"A fair presumption," Kadin said, pausing for dramatic effect. "In case you're wondering, I think I'll come along. At least until I decide not to. And who knows? Maybe we'll find some rarities worth trading."

Rykan snorted, shaking his head. "Always looking for an angle."

"That's why you keep me around." Kadin shrugged, flashing his usual grin. "That, and I make a great decoy."

They walked across the salt flats, the landscape barren and stark, gleaming faintly under the sun's unrelenting gaze. Above them, the sky was alive with the radiant hues of sunshimmer—a cascading display of light that danced and flowed like ribbons of silk, painting the heavens in soft blues, greens, and golds. The effect mesmerized Selaina, a reminder of the world's beauty even in its harshest places.

As they neared the edge of the salt flats, the air grew warmer, and the landscape shifted. The stark white expanse gave way to the vivid hues of the russet forest, where trees with strong trunks and fiery-red leaves cast shadows across the curved road ahead. Selaina paused, her gaze lingering on the sky, where the sunshimmer's light refracted through the edges of the trees, making the leaves glow with a faint ethereal sheen.

Taking a deep breath, she let the stillness of the forest wash over her. But her peace was short-lived. Her eyes flashed to the center of the forest, where she remembered Elysia's body rested. The thought weighed on her, but she pushed it aside, focusing instead on the road ahead.

In the distance, a plume of dust rose above the treetops, a hazy column that disrupted the serene beauty of the scene.

"Something's coming," Rykan said, stepping beside her and breaking the silence.

Selaina's gaze remained fixed on the dust. "Who else would be traveling through this wasteland?"

Garrick's voice was grim. "It's the Iron Flood."

Rykan's jaw tensed. "They're taking more people to the gate."

Kadin inhaled sharply. "Impeccable timing. As always."

Ysadora scanned the horizon. "They can't see us yet."

Selaina continued to watch the dust move. "If we're going to take the fight to the Iron Flood, I can't think of a better way to begin."

Rykan hesitated. "Amera rides with them." His voice was quiet, but weighted. "She's a powerful sorceress. Without Myrradin, it won't be easy."

Selaina lifted her chin. "Who needs Myrradin? We have Ysadora."

Ysadora gave her a sharp look. "I'm not a master, but I should be able to bind her. How powerful can she be?"

"Don't be so sure," said Garrick. "She can do things I've never seen anyone else do. I'm not sure we can win this fight."

Selaina's expression hardened. "What good is destiny if we hide? We can't leave these people to die."

Rykan stepped forward. "She's right." He exhaled. "I was one of those captives once. If not for luck, I would have suffered the same fate. We have to help them."

"I hope I'm wrong then," Garrick said. "Eliminating Amera would be a huge blow to the Iron Flood." He paused. "And a small measure of vengeance for Elysia."

"I suppose I don't want to be left out," Kadin said. "What's your plan?"

"I'll bind the sorceress," said Ysadora. "The rest of you take the soldiers."

"Let Selaina take her down," said Garrick. "We may need your help with the soldiers. Only engage Amera if necessary."

"If I miss, we fall back," said Selaina. "We regroup. No one dies for a single mistake."

"And here I thought we were going in without a plan," Kadin muttered. "Turns out the plan is not dying. Refreshing."

Selaina's heart pounded as she crept into the forest. The serenity of the grove was marred by stark reminders of their recent battle. Bodies of Iron

Flood soldiers lay scattered among the red leaves, their lifeless forms casting long shadows in the morning light. The air hung heavy with the coppery tang of blood and the stillness of aftermath.

"They're moving fast," Garrick said grimly, stepping over a fallen soldier, his boots crunching on brittle leaves.

Selaina's gaze lingered on the bodies, the weight of the fight pressing down on her. She tightened her grip on her bow, the quiver slung over her shoulder rattling softly with the arrows she had left.

"They'll know someone's been here," Ysadora said, her eyes scanning the scattered remains. "This forest tells a story, whether we like it or not."

They spread out, slipping silently into the cover of the forest. The soft crunch of leaves and the occasional snap of twigs were the only sounds as Selaina crouched behind a thick tree trunk. The clatter of wheels and the heavy hoofbeats of ridgebacks shattered the stillness, a reminder that this moment would change her.

Her breath hitched as the first cart rolled into view. The soldiers moved with grim purpose, their hands resting on weapons that would soon be drawn. At the head of the column sat Amera, just as Garrick had said, her dark figure draped in flowing robes that seemed to shift unnaturally in the light. Even from a distance, her presence pressed against Selaina's skin like an unseen weight, suffocating in its intensity.

The power inside her offered no direction. Just pressure, like it was waiting for her to decide how to use it. It did not give her the certainty she had expected. Instead, it left her standing at the edge of a choice, one that belonged to her alone.

Her fingers brushed the fletching of an arrow, her hand trembling. Was it fear? Or was it the power she carried now, waiting, watching, urging her forward? She steadied herself, forcing her breath to slow, her heart to obey. This was the moment when she became what the world expected of her. What she expected of herself.

Her gaze flicked to her companions, their figures hidden among the trees, waiting. They believed in her enough to stand with her. That belief settled into her like a second heartbeat, grounding her. The bodies of the fallen soldiers, who had once stood where these men stood now, echoed in her mind. *If we fail, we join them.*

Selaina exhaled. A single breath, measured, final.

She let the arrow fly, the sharp twang of the bowstring reverberating through the hushed forest. The arrow vanished into the distance, a silent predator seeking its mark. It flew with purpose, clean, straight, and sure. A whisper of sound followed it, cutting across the breathless moan of the wind. For a heartbeat, she believed it would strike.

Amera hadn't moved. She stood still as stone, her black cloak rippling like shadow made flesh. The arrow tore toward her chest.

Time bent.

The arrow slowed in mid air, a leaf frozen halfway to the ground. Even sound thinned, stretching the moment like a note held too long on an unseen harp. Around her, the world stood still.

Selaina's pulse faltered, but she did not stop perceiving.

She had felt this in Wekenwild. The false chaos of perfect structure. The hum of rhythm beneath stillness. She could feel it now, like the forest's silent song echoing through the battlefield.

This wasn't dreamlike. It was deliberate. Archeinor magic. Order.

Amera reached into the stillness, and the air shivered, not like wind, but like a harp string snapped too tight. She plucked the arrow from its path like it had always belonged in her grasp.

Something cracked, not in sound, but in the space behind it. Selaina felt the melody rupture, a discord that rippled back into her bones.

The moment unraveled. The leaf fell. The wind returned. Sound surged back in. Rykan stirred beside Kadin, unaware anything had changed.

Selaina stared at the woman ahead, her heartbeat loud in the returning silence.

Amera held the arrow between two fingers. It hadn't broken. It hadn't missed.

It had been taken.

"Halt!" Amera shouted, her cloak coiling with unnatural life. The ridgebacks jerked to a stop, snorting and stamping in confusion. "There are enemies among us," she said, her eyes sweeping the tree line like a blade. "Find them. Kill them all."

CHAPTER 3

THE MOMENT SHATTERED like glass underfoot. From the trees, Rykan watched the clearing explode into motion. A roar of movement followed Amera's command, soldiers shouted, swords sang from their scabbards, and ridgebacks reared as their riders yanked hard on the reins. Moments ago, the troop had barely breathed. Now it tore itself open, blades, shouts, dust everywhere.

The air cracked with urgency. Rykan ducked lower, the brittle yellow weeds scraping against his arms as he pulled Kadin down beside him. His heart thundered. The scent of dry earth and blood clung to everything.

Beside him, Kadin let out a low curse. "Well, that didn't take long." He dropped lower in the weeds beside Rykan. "You ever get the feeling we just skipped straight to the losing part of the plan?"

Rykan's grip firmed around his sword. "Stay low," he whispered, barely audible over the clamor. "They're coming this way."

Kadin let out a dry laugh. "Fantastic," he muttered. "Remind me why I signed up for this?" Then softer, almost to himself, "Right, because sitting still never kept me alive before."

Rykan didn't answer. His gaze flicked to the others, still concealed in the shadows, waiting. But the plan had already unraveled. Amera's sharp eyes swept dangerously close to where Selaina had taken cover. They had only seconds.

A soldier's shout split the air. "Over there!"

Rykan moved before thought could catch up. The underbrush

tore at his legs as he sprinted, the dry earth cracking beneath his boots. He didn't look back. He just ran, anything to pull them away from the others.

Then his foot caught on something solid. He twisted, barely keeping himself from falling, and his gaze dropped.

The Dreadstorm Knight.

Or what was left of him.

The shattered armor lay in the undergrowth, cracked open like the husk of something long dead. But death had not reclaimed it fully. Ants and carrion beetles crawled through the empty chest plate, swarming the once-imposing armor, giving it the grotesque illusion of movement. The sight of it twisted Rykan's insides. For a second, he wasn't in the weeds. He was back in the moment Elysia fell. Her scream. The light dying in her eyes. He pushed it down, turned it into fire. He'd only need it for one more strike.

A shadow loomed over him.

"I found him!"

The soldier's blade descended like judgment.

Rykan lunged. He feinted left, twisting mid-strike as steel clashed against steel. Sparks flared in the gloom, the force of the impact jarring through his arms. The soldier pressed forward with brute strength, knocking Rykan off balance. He staggered a step, barely dodging the next swing.

No time. No hesitation.

He caught the next blow on his guard, then shoved forward with everything he had, shoulder slamming into the man's chest. The soldier stumbled. Rykan's blade came up and in, driving deep. The man gasped, the shock barely had time to register before he dropped.

Another enemy surged from the right.

Rykan braced, but the sword never landed. Garrick crashed into the clearing like a storm, his blade intercepting the attacker mid-strike.

"This is for all the victims you've brought to that gate!" he growled, blade arcing in a brutal, precise cut.

The soldier faltered, staggered by Garrick's assault. Rykan recovered fast and swept in low, his sword biting deep into the exposed flank. Blood sprayed as the man crumpled.

Before they could breathe, another soldier came barreling forward.

This one didn't hesitate. He swung hard at Garrick, forcing him into retreat. Rykan stepped in, but the soldier was quick, turning to meet him. The clash of blades was rough and uneven. Rykan's foot slipped on a patch of torn earth, and the soldier seized the moment, raising his blade high.

The ground trembled. Roots burst from the soil, thick and writhing, wrapping the soldier's legs mid-stride. He roared, slashing down at them, cutting one, but a second coiled around his arm, yanking him off balance. Ysadora stepped into the clearing, staff raised. Her breathing was already uneven.

The soldier spat a curse and lunged for her before the roots could lock. She recoiled a step, slamming her staff down again. The earth obeyed. The roots surged, pulling the man back and down into the dirt, thrashing.

Another came from the side. Ysadora turned too late. A blur cut past her. The man froze mid-swing, eyes going wide. Then he dropped, two clean slashes across his back.

Kadin stood behind him, blades crimson and breathing hard. "You're welcome," he smirked, but it was thin.

The air changed. Amera stepped forward. Her power unfolded like the tearing of fabric, loud in the soul, silent to the ear. The battlefield froze, as if the air itself had thickened. Her gaze flicked to the lifeless Dreadstorm Knight sprawled in the dust, and for a fleeting moment, something dark crossed her face, horror, sorrow… then fury. Was it grief? Recognition? For the knight, or something else?

"Must I do everything myself?" she muttered.

All at once, the field reacted, grass flattening, leaves tearing sideways, as if chased by something vast and invisible, fast and ravenous.

Kadin spun at the shift in the air. "New plan. Run." He barely had time to react before an invisible force wrenched him into the air, his body snapping rigid as though caught by unseen claws.

Rykan moved, blade flashing, but he didn't make it two steps.

Magic slammed into him like a tidal wave. His body locked mid-stride, sword frozen in the air. Breath ragged, muscles screaming, but nothing obeyed him, not even gravity.

Nearby, Garrick suffered the same fate, his blade inches from a killing strike before his limbs jerked unnaturally, suspended mid-motion like a puppet severed from its strings.

Amera's grip was absolute.

Ysadora's voice cut through the tension. Her staff struck the ground, and the earth obeyed.

The soil split open, thick roots and twisting vines surging upward, reaching for Amera like the hands of the forest itself. They wrapped around her arms and legs, constricting, dragging.

For a moment, just a moment, she struggled.

Then her gaze snapped to the vines. She raised one hand, her fingers tracing two curves, one line, a motion so precise it felt more like geometry than gesture.

The vines stopped. They didn't snap or tear. They just stopped, like their reason for growing had been stripped out of them. They unraveled slowly, curling backward in perfect spirals. Veins collapsed inward. Moisture beaded across their surfaces, then flowed away, sucked into the soil as if gravity had turned sideways. The plants shriveled from the inside out, fading to pale husks, then collapsing into powder before they even touched the ground. Ysadora stumbled, her staff dimming in her grip.

Rykan couldn't move.

He couldn't even breathe.

CHAPTER 4

SELAINA STEPPED INTO the clearing, breath catching, the bow already rising in her hands. Dust clung to the air like smoke after lightning, and the remnants of magic still hummed across the ground, an echo of the chaos she hadn't been fast enough to stop.

She saw them first, Rykan, Garrick, and Kadin, suspended mid-motion, their bodies rigid with invisible tension, like puppets caught mid-fall, frozen while the world kept moving.

Amera stood at the center of it all, shadow-coiled and unmoved. Selaina's gaze locked on her, her steps unwavering, her will honed to a single point. This was the moment. The one she'd felt building since Wekenwild.

She drew in the forest's rhythm, the magic still lingering in the trees. Her breath synced with the pulse beneath the chaos. She wasn't stepping into it, she was already part of it.

Amera smirked. She twisted her hand, and suddenly, Rykan, Garrick, and Kadin were wrenched forward, their bodies pulled between Selaina and her shot.

"Not so confident in your aim now, are you?" Amera's voice curled with amusement, but Selaina caught something off, a tension in her tone, a hint of strain. The sheen of sweat on her brow, the shallowness of her breath, signs that the magic was costing her.

She lifted her other hand, reaching for Selaina, intending to seize her in the same grasp that held the rest of them. But something was different. Her fingers trembled, the magic faltering before it could take hold. Selaina didn't rush. She moved like the spell had already opened space for her.

The world around her dimmed to shadow and pulse, her body attuning to a rhythm older than sound.

Amera's spell reached for her like a grasping hand, threads of force that should have bound her in place. But Selaina stepped through it, through the center of its pattern, as if it were a curtain made of mist and memory. The magic brushed her skin like static, then passed through, failing to tether.

To her eyes, the air between them shimmered, laced with lines of force, flowing like light trapped in a dance. She sensed the structure of it, lines of force rotating like a lattice, something she couldn't have named but somehow understood. As if the magic had a shape, and her instincts knew how to move through it.

It was like Wekenwild again, the dance of lines and stillness, not meant to be dodged but understood. This wasn't power against power. It was permission.

Each note vibrated against her skin. Each heartbeat aligned with the pulse of the earth. She didn't dodge the spell. She sang with it, without a voice, an instinctive harmony that nullified its power.

Amera's eyes widened, as if something was slipping through her grasp. She clenched it into a fist, tried to reinforce the weave, but Selaina was already outside its reach. Already somewhere else. She hadn't vanished, just slipped beyond reach.

For a breathless instant, the battlefield hushed, drawn into the impossible.

The realization sparked across Amera's face, momentary but unmistakable. The moment stretched, tense, as unseen forces clashed between them, neither willing to yield. Selaina's bowstring remained taut, her arrow nocked, the tip gleaming. The air between them was charged and waiting for something to break.

Rykan fell, the magic around him shattering as he hit the ground hard. Selaina saw him roll to his feet without pause, his blade flashing as he surged forward. She saw the weight in his swing: rage, exhaustion, memory. Everything he hadn't said aimed at Amera in that one motion. For a heartbeat, it looked like he might reach her.

Then Amera turned, and the air imploded.

Selaina felt it like a pressure drop, like something massive folding inward around them. The spell lashed out again, worse than before. It wasn't just magic anymore. It was something alive, cruel and grasping. Rykan froze mid-stride, suspended in place, his sword barely a breath from Amera's throat. Selaina could see him straining, every muscle taut with resistance, but the hold didn't waver. His chest barely moved with the obvious effort, as if he were breathing fire just to stay upright.

Selaina fingers ached to release, but she couldn't yet, not with Rykan so close, not with the air still thick with danger.

Then the ground beneath Amera erupted. Selaina glanced to the side, just as Ysadora drove her staff into the dirt, jaw clenched. Shards of jagged stone speared upward toward Amera in a sudden burst of force.

Amera snarled and swung both hands wide. The stones exploded in mid air, showering the clearing with fragments. Selaina ducked as a sharp edge grazed her shoulder. Dust and light spun through the chaos, the world a blur of heat and noise.

But Selaina felt the opening before she saw it.

Her body moved by instinct. She raised her bow, drew the string, and loosed the arrow in one smooth motion. A sharp whistle sliced through the clearing as the arrow burned through the air like light made solid.

Amera turned at the last instant.

Too late.

The arrow struck hard. Selaina saw the woman's body wrench back, heard the cry tear from her throat as the shot buried deep. The spell shattered. Rykan dropped like a stone, the invisible weight released. Garrick and Kadin fell beside him, gasping, their limbs free again.

Amera stumbled, her robes blooming red, one hand pressed tight against her side. Still, she tried to rally, her hand lifting with a final flutter of power. Selaina's fingers drew taut on the bowstring, the strain trembling up her arms. Then came the wave, raw and unrelenting. It flung Rykan backward into the sand like a broken banner.

Amera turned, staggering away, bleeding and disoriented.

Rykan scrambled to his feet. His muscles coiled, ready to chase her down.

"Let her go," Selaina said, her voice cutting through the haze.

He froze, his gaze snapping to hers. The look in his eyes was all fight, every instinct still screaming to finish it. But she held his gaze, firm and still, and didn't flinch.

"We've done what we needed," she said quietly. "A wounded animal is most dangerous when cornered."

Amera disappeared into the swirling gold light, her silhouette fading like a shadow at dusk. Selaina stood motionless, the tension still vibrating through her limbs. The battlefield pulsed with the echoes of spent magic and blood. Silence gathered in the space where Amera had stood, thick as ash.

The fight was over, but Selaina's body hadn't caught up. Her limbs remained coiled, her pulse tight, like she was still listening for the next threat. She wasn't just the arrow anymore. She was what came after.

They moved together toward the road, where the captives still huddled, eyes wide with a hope they didn't dare speak aloud. Some stared into the trees, expecting Amera to reappear and punish them for even thinking they might be free.

Selaina stayed close, her bow lowered but ready. Rykan stepped ahead of the group, sword still drawn, the sun flashing along its edge. The two drivers caught sight of him and froze, tension rippling through their frames.

"You're relieved of duty," Rykan said, his voice sharp enough to cut through the silence.

The men bolted from the carts, crashing into the underbrush with barely a backward glance. It was a second kind of release, one Selaina didn't mind watching. Kadin raised a brow as he watched them flee.

"Let's hope they don't stumble into anything worse than us out there," he said. "Though at the rate they're running, they'll be halfway into the valley before nightfall."

Selaina turned her attention to the prisoners still bound in the carts. Relief hadn't reached their faces yet, only wary silence, as if they weren't sure this freedom would last.

Rykan approached first, his tone gentler now. "Let's cut these people loose."

A young woman with dark hair and umber-toned skin looked up at him from the first cart. Her eyes were clear and sharp. "Who are you?"

Rykan climbed onto the wheel, leaning in to untie her ropes. "We're friends," he said simply, though the words carried a kind of weight Selaina couldn't define.

"Friends might be a bit presumptuous," Kadin muttered from nearby, crouched beside another cart. "Let's see how they feel about us once they're free."

As they worked, Rykan asked, "Were you all taken from Tathara?"

The woman scoffed and lifted her chin. "Tathara? Do I look like one of those prim and proper capital folk? I'm Nadara of Zalorin."

Selaina glanced at her, struck by the pride in her voice. Nadara didn't shrink from the moment. Even bound, she spoke like someone who expected the world to listen.

Nadara smirked, her voice edged with a wry sort of confidence. "You know the type. Fussing over every detail. Everything has to look perfect, everyone has to act a certain way. They care more about the bouquet than the roots."

Selaina watched Rykan pause in his work, clearly intrigued. "What do you mean by that?"

"The part that actually matters, the foundation. The roots," Nadara said, and there was something sharp in the pride behind her words. "Where I'm from, we don't waste time with appearances. Zalorin isn't perfect, but we know what keeps us standing."

Kadin leaned casually against the cart, a smirk tugging at his lips. "Foundations are well and good, but I've found it's often appearances that keep you alive long enough to matter. Hard to stay standing if the wrong people notice you."

Rykan shrugged like the conversation didn't quite stick to him. "I've never been called prim and proper."

Nadara studied him for a beat. "You're Tatharan?"

"Not what you expected?" he asked, lifting a brow. "I was born in the Candasara Isles," he added, almost as an afterthought.

Selaina noted the flare of surprise in Nadara's expression. "Never met anyone from there," the woman admitted, then turned her gaze toward Selaina, and the shift in her demeanor was immediate. Her eyes latched onto Selaina's forehead, the mark of the three stars.

Selaina barely resisted the instinct to step back. Instead, she held her ground as Nadara reached out, fingers brushing the mark on Selaina's head, her touch gentle, but searching. Selaina tilted her head slightly, allowing the contact, even as something tense coiled inside her.

The moment their eyes met, something cracked open inside her.

The visions. What Darian had called the sight beyond seeing.

Pieces of Nadara's memory slipped into her, uninvited, undeniable.

A red stone flickering with unnatural light.

A man in crimson robes, lying motionless beneath the roots of a great tree.

A woman's sobs, low and ragged, as Nadara knelt beside her, offering a scrap of cloth patterned with a strange emblem.

The images struck like sparks on dry kindling, sharp, searing, gone in an instant. Selaina blinked, staggered by their weight. The memories weren't hers, yet they clung to her as if she'd lived them.

She said nothing. Couldn't. But her gaze lingered on Nadara, newly aware of the quiet depths behind her voice, of the grief stitched into every word.

Nadara's breath left her like a prayer as she withdrew her hand from Selaina's mark. "The Whisper Beyond the Stars," she murmured. "How is this possible?"

Before Selaina could answer, Ysadora's voice cut in. "She carries the last remaining destinies of Ethyllion."

Nadara stepped back, her expression unreadable for a long moment. Then, with a slow nod, she turned and strode to the first cart. Selaina watched as her posture shifted, her movements focused, precise. When her eyes landed on something in the pile of stolen belongings, they lit with sharp recognition.

"My weapon," Nadara muttered, pulling free a glaive.

She didn't just retrieve it, she claimed it. Her fingers wrapped around the shaft with familiarity, and in one smooth arc, she spun the blade through the air. The edge whispered as it cut a perfect circle, and a grin curved her lips, feral and proud.

"Still balanced," she said.

Then, as if to test it, she struck the trunk of a nearby tree. The glaive sank deep with a crack that echoed through the clearing. She yanked it free, turning back to the group without flinching.

Selaina felt the tension ripple through the group, Kadin's stance shifting, Garrick's hand brushing his hilt. Nadara wasn't showing off. She was reminding herself who she still was. She planted her feet in a wider stance, as if daring the world to try knocking her down.

"Anyone want to test if I'm rusty?" Nadara asked, half-teasing, half-daring.

No one answered. Kadin lifted a brow but said nothing. Garrick muttered something Selaina couldn't catch.

Nadara only chuckled and rested the glaive against her shoulder, perfectly at ease. Selaina envied the confidence she portrayed. Even the power Selaina had taken in from the Wishing Stone hadn't given her that kind of assurance. She wondered if that was something she would always struggle with.

Selaina watched as Nadara returned to the cart, pulling a satchel from the heap and slinging it over her shoulder like she'd always belonged here. She didn't ask to join them. She simply moved as though the place was already hers.

Selaina understood what Nadara had endured, how it felt to go on after everything familiar had been stripped away.

Rykan leaned against the cart, watching Nadara's display of prowess. "With skill like that, how did the Iron Flood manage to catch you?"

Nadara stopped mid-spin and planted the glaive against the ground. "There is only so much one can do against many," she said. "And their armor is strong."

Selaina stepped closer, something straining behind her ribs. "How far away is Zalorin?"

Nadara's expression shifted, the light fading from her eyes. "Less than a day from here," she said quietly. "But there is nothing to go back to. When I returned, they had burned most of it to the ground. Somehow our sacred tree survived, but everyone who lived there…" She trailed off, her voice rasping with the weight of loss. "Gone."

Selaina's breath caught. The ache in Nadara's voice was too familiar, an echo of all the places Selaina had passed through, all the faces that would never return. The sky above seemed to press lower.

Across the group, Rykan had stilled. Selaina knew he carried his own grief, for Tathara, his father, the uncertain fate of his mother. His silence now said it all. He'd seen it too: what the Iron Flood left behind. Smoke. Silence. Graves with no names.

"The Iron Flood is attacking villages in Nordravin now?" Garrick asked, frowning. "How can they hold the kingdom of Elenior and still reach this far?"

Nadara's eyes burned. Her hands gripped the glaive as if the truth needed something solid to hold onto. "They're spreading like a plague. Whatever sickness has poisoned their leaders, it's infecting others. The desperate, the lost, those who crave power, they're drawn to it, consumed by it. With every village they burn, more join their cause. And with each victory, it becomes harder to stop them."

Selaina gripped the cart's edge, a sick weight settling in her chest.

Nadara's words hit harder than she wanted to admit. The Iron Flood wasn't just winning, it was multiplying.

CHAPTER 5

THE SUN BLED into the trees, painting the forest in copper and rust. Smoke still clung to the clearing where the battle had ended, a haze of ash and magic suspended in the hush that always followed violence. Rykan shifted his weight, his shoulder aching from where Amera's spell had flung him into the ground. Around him, the others moved, quiet, shaken, but alive. A few broken weapons lay scattered in the dirt.

A cart creaked behind him as the last of the prisoners climbed down. Selaina stood a few paces ahead, her gaze locked with that of Nadara, who had already started carving space for herself among them. Nadara. Fierce, composed, even after all she'd lost.

Selaina's voice broke the silence. "What will you do now? Do you have anywhere to go?"

Nadara exhaled, one hand stiffening around the shaft of her glaive like it was the only thing keeping her tethered to the earth. "I don't know." She looked toward the horizon, where dusk draped the world in shadows and long memory. "There's nothing left. Nowhere to return to." Her voice thinned. "I can't let them get away with what they've done."

Rykan watched her closely. He'd seen this look before, burnout beneath bravado, fury fighting back collapse. It was a fragile balance. Loss could hollow a person out from the inside. He'd seen it in the streets of Tathara, in the eyes of soldiers who'd lost more than they could name. But Nadara wasn't crumbling.

"You are Zhal Evurah," said Nadara. "You fight the Iron Flood. I want to fight with you."

The words landed like a flint strike, sharp and sparking. Selaina hesitated, not visibly, but Rykan knew her well enough to catch the shift. The slightest stiffening of her shoulders. The pause in her breath.

He understood why. Trust was no longer a luxury.

But there was something familiar in Nadara's voice. That same fire he'd once seen in Selaina before the Wishing Stone, before the mark, before everything she carried now.

And Rykan found himself hoping, just a little, that fire could still be enough.

"And why should we trust you?" Garrick's voice cut through the moment, steady, unreadable. "You've just lost your home. You've lost everything. What if this is just a thirst for revenge?"

Nadara turned to him, unflinching. "Revenge won't bring back the dead." Her voice didn't waver. "But stopping them will keep someone else from losing everything, like I did."

Garrick studied her for a long moment, then gave a small nod, seemingly satisfied.

Selaina let out a slow breath. "Vatreus has his army," she said, her voice carrying across the clearing. "We need to build one of our own. If he can twist men into fighting for his cause, then we must give people a reason to fight for something greater. This war won't be won by a single sword or destiny. It will be won by those who refuse to kneel, by warriors who stand even when the world tries to break them."

Rykan saw Nadara's jaw tense, something flaring behind her eyes. It wasn't hesitation. It was resolve.

"We'd be honored for you to be our first recruit, Nadara," Selaina said.

Nadara inclined her head slightly, a hint of something like pride in her gaze. "Then I fight with you. For my family. For Zalorin. For all of us."

"Welcome aboard," Kadin said with a faint smirk. "Just be warned, we've a talent for getting into trouble. You might regret saying 'all of us' before this journey's over."

As the last of the captives were freed from their bonds, Rykan leaned against the cart, watching the others organize the group. Garrick and Kadin ushered the former prisoners into one of the carts.

A few paces away, he noticed Ysadora moving beside Selaina, her expression curious and cautious. "What happened back there?" Ysadora asked in a low voice. "Amera's power should've worked on you. Why didn't it?"

Rykan paused, his hands stilling as he listened.

Selaina looked down at the dust stirring in the breeze. "It felt familiar," she said. "The same rhythm I sensed in Wekenwild. Her magic had the same kind of pattern, like music in the ground, in the air. I didn't fight it. I moved through it."

Ysadora tilted her head. "You resonated with it?"

Selaina nodded. "I knew the melody."

Rykan frowned slightly. Melody? He wasn't sure what they meant exactly, but the way Amera's grip had failed, while his own body had been pinned like stone, made him wonder just how much Selaina had changed.

Rykan exhaled, running a hand through his hair as he watched Garrick approach an older man. The man's white hair and weary eyes carried the weight of survival, yet there was a spark of determination there.

"Head south," Garrick told him, his voice firm. "The Iron Flood's grip on the north is tightening. If you stay here, you won't last long."

"Do you know the Welanor Path?" Nadara interjected, stepping up beside Garrick with a confidence that caught Rykan's attention.

The old man nodded. "I do."

"The Welanor Path will take you to the Telaris River," Nadara said, her voice steady as she addressed the older man Garrick had been speaking with. "Cross at the ruins of Stormgait, and stay on the forest trails. It's your best chance."

The old man nodded, gratitude visible in his weary expression. "Thank you," he said, gripping the reins tightly as he prepared to leave.

Rykan watched the cart roll away, the two ridgebacks pulling it steadily as it disappeared down the road. The creak of its wheels and the occasional snort of the ridgebacks faded into the distance, leaving behind an almost oppressive quiet in the forest.

"You think they'll make it?" he asked, breaking the silence.

"They have to," Garrick said flatly, his gaze still fixed on the road. "No one else is coming to save them."

Nadara shifted in her seat, arms crossed as she glanced at Rykan. "And what about us? Where exactly are we headed?"

"We need soldiers," Selaina said.

"We're not going to find any around here," Garrick muttered, adjusting the strap of his sword. "If the Iron Flood has taken hold of this land, we're already too late."

"Tassimun," Nadara offered, leaning forward. "I've heard whispers of a resistance gathering there."

Garrick scoffed. "Tassimun? That cesspit? It's nothing but smugglers and sell-swords. Unless you've got a fortune in aurin, we won't be finding an army there."

Kadin snorted, stretching his legs out in front of him. "Smugglers and sell-swords fight just fine when they've got a reason to. And if they don't, well… that's what persuasion is for."

Nadara smirked. "Exactly. And there are more than just mercenaries in Tassimun," she said. "Warriors. Desert clans. Leaders who still hold sway over the free lands. If you can convince them to fight, you won't just have an army, you'll have warriors across all of Nordravin."

Garrick shook his head. "That may be true, but men who trade in blood rarely shed it for free. You think warriors and clan leaders will fight because it's right? They'll fight when it benefits them, or not at all."

Selaina met Garrick's gaze, her voice steady. "We don't have the luxury of waiting for the perfect fight. If there's even a chance they'll stand with us, we take it." She turned to Nadara. "How far is Tassimun?"

"Not far. We could reach it before dusk," Nadara said.

Rykan ran a thumb along the edge of his sword's pommel, his thoughts turning over the possibilities. "Would they be willing to bring in outsiders?"

Nadara tilted her head. "If you have something to offer… yes. Tassimun runs on trade. Trust never made it through the gates. Alliances, information, survival. If they believe you can give them an advantage, they'll listen."

Selaina met Nadara's eyes for a long moment, then gave a nod. "Show us the way."

The group settled into a quiet rhythm. The weight of the last hours pressed into their bones, but a direction, however uncertain, had begun to take shape. Even movement, even uncertainty, was better than stillness.

"Let's hope they're as eager to fight as we are," Ysadora murmured, as she guided the cart they had commandeered down the road toward Tassimun. The Sunkeeper stone atop the staff on her back flared, casting long, restless shadows across the road.

Kadin exhaled, adjusting his bracers. "Or at the very least, let's hope they don't try to kill us on sight. That'd be a bad start."

Rykan shifted, eyes drawn toward Selaina. She sat quietly, her expression unreadable. She stared into the distance toward the south, like something was distracting her. Something he couldn't see. The faint glow of her mark caught the last golden rays of sunlight filtering through the red trees. Even in silence, she steadied him. She'd changed since the beginning—more than a fighter, more than what she meant to others. Something deeper now, harder to name. And still, she pulled them forward, like gravity disguised as grace.

The ridgebacks picked up their pace, the cart jolting as the path grew uneven. Rykan clutched the side, his fingers flexing against the worn wood. His eyes flicked toward the horizon, where the deepening sky bled into the dunes beyond.

Whatever lay ahead, they were already on the path. There was no turning back now.

CHAPTER 6

THE CANYON KEPT its secrets buried deep, its walls steeped in the hush of old betrayals. The cart jolted over a rise in the road, and Selaina braced herself, fingers clenching around the worn edge of the wooden bench. Late afternoon light painted the canyon walls in gold and rust, the shadows deepening in the crevices of the rock like ink pooling on parchment.

They were all thinking it: Would this place hold what they needed? Allies. Warriors. Hope. Or was it just another mirage in a dying land?

Ahead of them, the valley began to open. She could see it now, Tassimun, cradled in the low basin like a secret the desert hadn't quite buried. From a distance, it looked peaceful. Safe. She'd learned that peace, especially when it came easy, was rarely to be trusted.

Ysadora sat at the front of the cart, reins in hand, guiding the ridgebacks with a quiet focus. Her cloak snapped in the wind. The Sunkeeper stone caught the light now and then where it rested on her back. She hadn't spoken much since they entered the valley. None of them had.

And Nadara… Were they right to trust her? To let her join them, to accept her word about Tassimun? Selaina had seen something when they met, a vision, as always. It happened every time she looked at someone for the first time. It wasn't prophecy, but it brushed close.

But fragments. Glimpses of their path.

She had seen Nadara holding a red stone, rough on one side, gleaming with faceted light on the other. Something about it pulsed, unmoving yet alive, as if fire smoldered at its core.

In the second image, Nadara stood in a shadowed shrine. Sunlight filtered through a break in the ceiling, casting gold across the roots of an old tree. Beneath it lay a man in faded red robes, lifeless. Nadara knelt, rifling through his pockets until she drew out a map.

The third vision: a small, dim dwelling. A woman sat weeping while Nadara handed her a scrap of cloth with a stitched symbol on it.

At first, Selaina thought the man in red robes was someone from the Iron Flood, someone Nadara had fought. But now… she wasn't so sure. The images could mean so many things. And all they had, truly, was Nadara's word that her village had been attacked. What if Selaina had let the enemy walk straight into their ranks?

She drew in a slow breath. Soon enough, Nadara would reveal who she really was. People didn't share their truths with strangers, not right away. Especially not when those strangers could see things they hadn't said aloud.

Selaina would wait. But she wouldn't stop watching.

From a distance, Tassimun looked like a natural formation, mud-brick towers rising like worn stone teeth.

But as they neared, the city's breath shifted. The air stank of dust, sweat, and something metallic, blood not yet washed away.

The guards at the gates wore no matching colors, only piecemeal armor patched from old campaigns. Their hands never strayed far from their swords, and their stares were sharp enough to draw blood.

Inside, the market roared, but it wasn't the welcoming clamor of trade. It was a hum of friction, of wary glances and broken deals. Stalls spilled over with weapons, but no one browsed for long. They moved quickly, furtively, as if they knew the ground might betray them if they stayed too still.

Somewhere in the crowd, a pot shattered. A man shouted, but no one turned.

Wind chimes of hammered metal hung from poles and awnings, clinking softly, out of rhythm but strangely calming.

Brightly colored banners hung above the streets, stretched between rooftops and stalls like faded pennants from old victories. Some bore emblems, spiraling suns, broken axes, a silver hand gripping a flame, but Selaina didn't know their meanings. Clan signs, mercenary brands, trade houses? Maybe all three. Whatever they stood for, they added to the quiet tension that threaded through the market, as if everyone here had drawn their lines long ago and was just waiting for the next bargain to shift them.

Beyond the gates, the city was a maze of tight alleys and wide markets, all converging at a central plaza marked by a circular stone fountain, a rare oasis, its waters glinting blue against the muted palette of earth and brass. Canopies of faded cloth stretched over the bazaar, providing shade for rows of traders, smiths, and mercenary captains hawking their services like common wares.

They rode slowly through the dusty street until a boy appeared beside the ridgebacks, reaching up to calm them. He moved with gentleness that put them at ease, tying a rope from a nearby post to the reins. Then he extended his hand, and Nadara took it, stepping down onto the cracked, sunbaked street. Selaina followed, mimicking her, letting the boy steady her as she climbed down.

He placed his upright hand beneath his tilted chin in a sharp, graceful gesture of salute.

"Welcome to Tassimun," he said. "The meeting of many roads."

Nadara leaned in slightly. "Do you have an aurin?" she asked quietly.

Selaina fumbled in her bag, fingers brushing worn cloth and smooth stone, searching for a coin. Before she found one, Kadin stepped forward and handed the boy two coins from his satchel.

"Keep them watered," Kadin said. "And don't let anyone near the cart."

The boy nodded sharply. "I'll guard it like my own," he said, and with another grin, he darted back to secure the reins more tightly.

They moved through the market, wading through the press of bodies, shoulders brushing silk robes and scarred leather. Steel glinted from every table, a forest of blades meant more for killing than display. Few dared to linger. Eyes darted over shoulders. Voices dropped to wary murmurs. The city hummed with a brittle kind of energy, the sound of deals struck between clenched teeth.

Somewhere deep in the bazaar, an argument flared with a sharp cry, but no one turned to look.

"Can I interest you in something?" said a voice.

Selaina turned. A man stood behind one of the tables, arms crossed, eyes appraising.

"Looks like you could use a better bow," he added, nodding at the one on her back.

She straightened. "I prefer to keep this one."

Jeth had carved it himself with steady hands, sure strokes. It had outlived him. The carved details reminded Selaina of a serpent wrapped around a tree spiraling along the limb, smoothed by years of use. It wasn't ornate, but it was well balanced, dependable. Like he had been.

"What are you doing here then, if you're not looking to buy?" the man asked.

"We're looking for someone," Selaina said. "Someone who might know how to reach those still fighting the Iron Flood."

The merchant's expression shifted. He lowered his voice just enough to be heard over the hum of the crowd. "People who say things like that tend to disappear. Sometimes for good reason."

"We're not looking to stir up trouble," Rykan said, stepping in.

"Then don't ask for war in a city that's tried to live without it," the merchant replied. "We sell to the Iron Flood like we do to anyone else. That's what keeps Tassimun standing."

Selaina stepped back, catching Nadara by the arm and pulling her away from the table. Her voice was low but sharp. "What have you brought us into?" she hissed. "They sell weapons to the Iron Flood?"

"They just want aurin," Nadara said. "That's what merchants do. But not everyone here bows to coin. We need to find the mercenary leaders. The outlaws. That's who we must convince."

Selaina felt it before she saw it, that quiet pull of something watching her, waiting. A woman across the street met her eyes. And the visions came, one beneath a red moon, one over a burning brazier, one high on a wall beneath a sky full of ash. Each carried the weight of goodbye.

"You have the look of someone who is not where they're supposed to be," the woman said, her eyes sharp but not unkind. She stood beside a vendor's cart draped in tarnished silks, one hand resting on the hilt of a curved blade that looked ceremonial... but well used.

Selaina stepped forward, careful not to bump a crate of chainmail leaning precariously against a nearby stall. "It's a beautiful city," she said, eyes scanning the street, "but I've never been here before. None of this is familiar to me."

"That's not what I mean." The woman's gaze didn't waver. "You carry the mark of Zhal Evurah. One chosen for a great path. What would you be doing here?"

A gust stirred the banners overhead. Selaina felt the eyes of her companions behind her, waiting. "We want to fight back against the Iron Flood," she said. "But we are few. We need soldiers."

"You are eager to fight." The woman shifted her weight, scanning the crowd as if half-listening. "But before a warrior can truly fight, they must learn who they are without the blade."

Selaina's voice remained steady. "I know who I am. I'm not a warrior. I never wanted to fight." Her fingers brushed the hem of her cloak. "But we must, if we're going to save Galanor."

"And what would you do with Galanor, if you saved it?" the woman asked, stepping closer. A merchant behind her slammed a box shut; no one flinched.

"I wouldn't do anything," Selaina answered. "The people would be able to live in peace."

"Peace for mortals is not possible," the woman said. "It is in our nature to need, to want, to act to fill those needs, for ourselves and those we love. And everyone else does the same. As long as there is need, there will be conflict. End one war, and another will rise to take its place."

"I don't believe that," Selaina said. "I've seen people connect. We can love, we can help each other. We could build a world that everyone shares in. One of harmony and peace."

The woman studied her. "You're right," she said at last. "It could happen… for a time. But it can never last." She paused, as a pair of armed men passed them, whispering in a dialect Selaina didn't know. "The question becomes: is that brief moment of harmony worth fighting for? Worth dying for?"

Selaina nodded. "Yes. We have to try. Even if success is unlikely. We can't let the world be ruled by fear. We can't let more people die just because we think it's hopeless. What's the point of being alive if we're not meant to try for something better?"

The woman's expression softened. She smiled. "I am Rashiri Al'Zan," she said. "Come with me. I will help you."

Selaina hesitated, eyeing her. The woman's words held weight, but so did her silences. "I'm Selaina. But I don't follow strangers blindly," she said. "If this is a trap, know that we won't go quietly."

"Good," Rashiri said. "You wouldn't be worth following if you did."

Selaina glanced back. Rykan stood a few paces behind her, watching Rashiri with narrowed eyes. Nadara rested her hand on her belt, clearly still deciding whether to trust her. Ysadora remained near the cart, the Sunkeeper crystal catching the light on her shoulder.

"We'll walk with you," Selaina said. "But be wary."

She motioned for the others to join her. Rykan came to her side first, still silent but steady. Nadara followed, Kadin falling in just behind with a shrug and a quiet, "Well, that was intense." Ysadora walked last, casting a long look at Rashiri as they passed. Garrick remained where he was for a moment longer, gaze sweeping the crowd before stepping forward.

Rashiri took them behind the stone structures to where the road ended. The sand dipped into a shallow basin, and as Selaina stepped closer, she saw the hollow was filled with a broad sheet of sparkling, sunlit glass. A few others already stood upon it, murmuring in low voices.

"This is sacred ground," Rashiri said quietly. "Weapons must be left behind."

Rykan tapped the surface with his boot, the glass ringing faintly beneath it. "What is this place?"

"This is where enemies meet not with blades, but with words," Rashiri said. "To make peace. To bargain. Sometimes, to surrender."

Ysadora stepped forward, crouching to press her palm against the glass. Her eyes fluttered closed. "There was fire," she said softly. "So much fire. Panic. A man standing alone. He held up his hands to stop the fighting, but they didn't listen. Then…" Her hand twitched. "Lightning, like the sky split open. It struck here. The ground screamed. And then… silence. All of it turned to glass."

Rashiri blinked. "I didn't realize you knew Tassimun's history."

"I don't," Ysadora said. "I saw it. In my mind."

Rashiri studied her for a moment, then nodded slowly. "You are gifted."

Her gaze shifted out across the glass. "Long ago, a battle between rival clans was halted by an elder who stepped between them. He offered his life to end the bloodshed. They killed him. But the sky struck back. Lightning fell here and turned the battlefield to glass, killing the ones who ordered his death. Since then, no blood has ever been spilled on this ground."

Selaina removed her bow, her knife, and quiver and placed them gently on the sand. The others followed suit, laying down their weapons in a growing line near the edge.

They stepped onto the glass.

Rashiri's voice rose to address the others already waiting.

"Allow me to introduce Selaina, Zhal Evurah."

Laughter rippled from the gathered leaders, rough, dismissive. But as Rashiri stepped aside and Selaina came fully into view, the laughter faded. One by one, their eyes locked on the faint glow of her mark. It tingled under their gaze, warmth blooming beneath her skin.

Rashiri gestured toward another woman with a nod. "Vireya Valis, Blade Broker."

The sharp-eyed woman didn't move, arms still crossed. Her fingers, however, tapped the empty sheath at her belt. She gave Selaina a slow, measuring glance, as if judging if she was flesh and blood like everyone else.

As their eyes locked, a glimmer of steel rang through Selaina's mind. A younger Vireya, blood on her knuckles, standing alone over the body of a man twice her size, his blade still in her hand. A deal made in whispers beneath a desert moon. A broken promise sealed with fire.

"Ashoun Dar," Rashiri continued, "Voice of the Sand Clans."

The man in sand-colored robes gave a subtle incline of his head, his eyes veiled, expression borrowed from the same stone as the canyon walls. Another quick flash hit Selaina: Ashoun as a boy, kneeling beside a dying elder, lips pressed to the sand in apology. A council chamber, his voice rising in protest while the others turned away. Then silence, years of watching, waiting, choosing when to speak.

"And Zorath Jek," Rashiri finished, turning toward the massive man half-shadowed by a cracked stone pillar. "Hand of the Oathless."

Zorath gave no signal of acknowledgment, just a calm demeanor and quiet strength. Selaina saw flashes of his memories. A battlefield at dusk, tinged not with glory but with grief. Zorath kneeling beside a slain comrade, hands pressed to his chest, swearing an oath to no one but himself. Another image: Zorath walking away from a burning village, carrying a child who would not stop crying.

Ashoun spoke first. "You stand in Sal'Zharin, the Circle of the Sacred Sands," he said. "A place where rivals speak as equals. If you're here, you must have a proposition."

Selaina stepped forward, her boots whispering against the glass. "We're seeking allies. Warriors willing to stand against Vatreus and the Iron Flood."

Vireya raised an eyebrow, unimpressed. "My warriors are loyal to aurin," she said. "Your clothing, your bearing…" she gestured with a flick of her fingers "…speak little of wealth. Do you truly believe you can afford our blades?"

Before Selaina could speak, Garrick moved beside her, arms tense at his sides. "They've already taken Elenior," he said, voice clipped and low. "If no one fights, there won't be any aurin left to chase."

Ashoun's eyes slid toward him, then back to Selaina. "If you are Zhal Evurah, we have not heard your name. Nor your deeds. The sand clans do not stir lightly. We trade with the Iron Flood. They leave us in peace." His tone never wavered. "We will not break that peace on words alone. If stories of your victories reach our ears… perhaps then we will listen."

"What peace?" Nadara stepped forward, fists clenched. "They destroyed Zalorin. My home. They didn't offer us peace, they offered only fire. And it will come for you, too."

A breeze stirred dust across the surface of the glass. One of the leaders shifted.

Zorath, who had been silent, finally raised his head. His voice was rough, weathered, deep as the stone beneath them. "There has been much debate among the Oathless. The burning of even one village cannot be ignored forever." He looked directly at Selaina. "You've brought your message. I will carry it. If they answer, I will return with word."

"Thank you," Selaina said, meeting his gaze.

"How long?" Nadara asked, quieter now. "How long before we know?"

"We ride for Kheshar's Wake at sunrise," Zorath said. "Three days, if the winds favor us."

Selaina inclined her head. "We're grateful you're willing to carry our words. And the risk that comes with them."

No one spoke as Rashiri turned. The others followed, silent, retrieving their weapons in solemn rhythm. Selaina picked up her bow last, brushing dust from the worn grip.

As they moved toward the edge of the market, the quiet press of the city swallowed them once more. Traders called out. Somewhere, a woman shouted in another tongue.

"Though they don't speak of it openly," Rashiri said as they walked, "unease is spreading. The Iron Flood grows, and they all feel it. But they will not move yet. Not until the fire touches them directly."

She paused beside a faded banner overhead, its cloth fluttering weakly.

"I fear you've come too soon in your journey…" she murmured. "Or perhaps too late."

Selaina frowned. "I don't even know where I need to be. How can I possibly know when?"

Rashiri narrowed her eyes. "Zhal Evurah walks the path of where and when. Once you see it, you will know."

That night, Rashiri found them shelter in a narrow clay-walled hut tucked behind the market corridors. Blankets were spread across the floor, and the roof creaked gently with the breath of desert wind.

They lay close together in the dark, wrapped in stillness.

Selaina stared at the low ceiling. Sleep came slowly, held at bay by the strangeness of the place, the weight of what had not yet happened, and the quiet, rising fear that maybe she wasn't strong enough for what the mark of destiny demanded of her.

But at last, her thoughts softened. Her breathing steadied. And the dark began to open.

Selaina half woke to the sensation of fingers in her hair, gently combing across her scalp, smoothing strands behind her ear. The touch was slow, rhythmic, nearly hypnotic, but not right. At first, it felt like tenderness, something familiar. Maybe Rykan, watching over her while she slept.

But her limbs wouldn't move. Her breath wouldn't deepen. Her body remained still, heavy, quiet, too quiet. Her eyes stayed closed, too heavy to lift.

The fingers continued, parting strands, tracing behind her ear. The touch was careful in the wrong way, like someone who had seen comfort but never offered it.

A breath touched her cheek, warm, too close, just before a voice whispered beside her ear, soothing and soft.

"You shouldn't have done that, my dear…"

CHAPTER 7

OLD FINGERS SLID down Selaina's neck, slow and deliberate, then rose to her forehead. They hovered for a moment, then pressed gently against the mark.

"You shouldn't have used the Stone. Now it is you that he needs."

Selaina's consciousness stirred against the veil of sleep, but her body remained locked, cradled in the hush of paralysis. She couldn't move. Couldn't breathe deeper. The world pressed close, thick as wet linen and just as smothering.

And then came the sense of presence. It didn't rise from thought or memory, it came from something else entirely. A second space unfolded behind her closed eyes, layered over the dream like oil poured across glass. The edges didn't match. The light was wrong. She felt herself falling sideways into it.

It was a chamber, not one she'd ever seen, but one that felt ancient, like the breath of something that had been waiting too long.

The firelight inside was too warm, flickering with a slow, unnatural rhythm. The air smelled of ash and resin and something older than both. Gwenna sat at its center, cross-legged in a hollowed-out circle of bone, strands of long white hair, and twisted roots. The floor beneath her seemed to breathe, pulsing gently.

Before her, a basin was filled with liquid that did not ripple, it shimmered, like silvered oil stitched with veins of shadow. Something inside it moved with Selaina's breath.

Around it, Nadrok silhouettes crouched, unmoving, their eyeless gazes turned inward, into the liquid, as if anchoring its reach. Gwenna's fingers hovered just above the surface, stirring it without touching.

"Myrradin broke our tether," Gwenna murmured to someone unseen, "but I still have remnants of her. We can find her."

At her side lay a small dish carved from onyx. Inside it, coiled like a curse, lay strands of white hair, fresh and virile, as if she'd been waiting for this moment since the day she took them. Gwenna plucked one between two fingers and let it drift into the basin. The surface flared, then calmed.

A ripple moved across the firelight, and from its edge, a figure emerged.

He didn't step into the room so much as unfold from the shadows, a tall man draped in silver-threaded robes that shimmered like silk woven with frost. His expression was unreadable, carved from stillness. On his finger coiled a ring of black stone, dull and heavy like a weight pressed against the world. His eyes held no light. Just calculation.

"So this is the one who holds the Stone," he said, peering into the basin. His voice was smooth, clinical. "She doesn't look too impressive to me."

The shadows at his side thickened. A second figure moved within them, her presence like cold breath on glass. A young woman in a low-hung hood stepped into the circle, shadows clinging to her like a second skin. Her eyes flashed beneath the hood, too bright. Too sharp. Her voice flowed like silk caught on thorns.

"They never do, Arathain," she said. "Until they burn."

Gwenna's lips curved faintly, but her gaze stayed on the basin. "Careful, Syra. She might be aware of us."

Inside the dream, Selaina strained. The air thickened, viscous and heavy. Her heart slammed against her ribs, but her body refused to answer her commands. This was more than a dream. It was a gate, opened from the far side. And Gwenna wasn't just speaking through it.

She was inside it. Watching.

The basin shimmered brighter as Arathain leaned closer. His eyes flicked across the vision like a hunter reading tracks. "Clay walls. Market drapes. She's somewhere dry, a desert border."

"Good," said Gwenna. "She hasn't left Nordravin. But there are many villages and camps. I need more."

Syra tilted her head, eyes glittering. "The roof is redgrass. It only grows near the Telaris River."

"That narrows it," Gwenna said. "But I need something unique. A symbol. A name. A scar in the land."

Selaina focused her thoughts, remembering the songs of Wekenwild, the way she had felt the forest's rhythm, the way she trusted it. She reached for that same rhythm now, claiming the dream as her own.

Light cracked through, radiant, like morning breaking over frost. It bloomed within her, surging and searing outward. The basin in Gwenna's circle shattered. The Nadrok figures recoiled, their forms unraveling into smoke.

Gwenna screamed. Selaina rose within the dream.

She stood at the edge of a sky stripped of earth, where only wind and starlight remained. A vision she'd had before, but clearer now. Ahead, a mountain loomed, its crags jagged as teeth, its summit lost in clouds roiling with color.

Circling it were three serpents, vast and coiled, one gold, one emerald, and one sapphire. She heard their names in crystalline rhythms: Auronia, Verantis, and Zaryneth. The Sky Serpents from Jeth's book. They moved in wide, impossible arcs, gliding like celestial rivers, like constellations come alive. Their scales shimmered with ancient symbols that danced just beyond comprehension, as though language itself had been woven into them before civilization existed.

Their eyes, each the size of a small moon, turned toward her. Their gaze didn't rest on her, they peered through her, as if reading something hidden in her soul.

A deep chord thrummed through the sky, vibrating in her chest like the breath of the world itself.

Then they spoke with gravity.

Zhal Evurah.

The words did not echo. They rooted.

Her breath deepened. Her limbs relaxed. In that moment, she carried more than her own name. She bore the weight and memory of all who came before. She was river and stone, wind and memory. Her body glowed with the faintest light, like the edge of a dawn still unborn.

She opened her mouth to speak, but only a sound emerged, a low, choral tone that seemed to complete the serpents' chord.

Behind the mountain, the world cracked open, revealing a path, raw and trembling with possibility. A choice laid bare. A path she had not yet walked, but had always been awaiting.

The serpents vanished into the clouds, her surroundings changed, but the weight of their gaze remained.

She saw Tassimun in her dream, quiet beneath the stars. The market slept, its banners stilled. But then Iron Flood soldiers slipped through the streets like vipers, heading toward one of the stone structures near the rear of the city.

Ashoun stepped out to meet them, his robes trailing in the night breeze.

"General Grethos," he said. "Why have you come while the city sleeps?"

"It's time to decide," Grethos said, his voice low and firm. "Will you join Vatreus, or not?"

"We can't afford to take sides," said Ashoun. "You know that. It's bad for business. Why ask again?"

"We're not asking," Grethos said. "We're giving you a choice. Kneel… or burn."

Ashoun stood tall. "The sand clans kneel to no one."

Grethos stepped back. "We can't allow you to aid our enemies." He raised his hand, then let it fall to his side.

Soldiers stepped forward, carrying large crates. They set them down near Grethos and tipped them, pouring a thick, syrupy substance onto the cobbled streets.

Ashoun's brow furrowed.

"What is that?"

Grethos turned and disappeared into the shadows beyond the light.

Then everything erupted in fire.

Selaina's eye twitched.

Her body jerked, and she gasped for air.

She sat bolt upright in the hut, sheets tangled around her legs, her skin slick with sweat. The smell of smoke still clung, but this time, it wasn't dream-born. It was real.

"Rykan!" she called urgently, shaking him. "Wake up!"

He stirred, groggy. The others began to rustle awake.

Ysadora jolted up, already alert. She scrambled outside without a word.

Selaina grabbed her bag and bow, Rykan doing the same, and they pushed through the hut's flap into the night. Outside, the horizon was glowing red and green, fire licking the market's edge like it had been waiting all along.

Garrick, Kadin, and Nadara burst out behind them, all of them blinking into the firelight, confusion giving way to horror.

"The pen!" Ysadora shouted, already untying the ridgebacks.

Selaina and Rykan sprinted to help her. The animals thrashed in panic, but Ysadora calmed them with gentle hands, guiding them away from the encroaching blaze. The cart was nearby, its wheels half-sunk in the ash-dusted sand.

Selaina and Rykan leaped aboard as the ridgebacks reared, and Ysadora cracked the reins.

The flames moved unnaturally fast, sweeping over stone and sand as if the city itself had turned to tinder. The fire gave off a green hue at the base, and its scent was wrong, acrid and metallic, not wood or cloth, but something engineered to destroy.

As the cart lurched forward, a familiar voice rang out through the fire:

"You don't have to do this, General!" Ashoun's voice cracked with desperation. "We can make better blades! Cheaper too! Anything you want, any kind of weapon or armor!"

Garrick, Nadara, and Kadin leaped into the cart and Ysadora snapped the reins again. The ridgebacks surged forward, hooves kicking up fire-lit sand. The flames tore through the dwellings, chasing screaming figures through alleys and tents.

As they barreled away from the fire, Selaina turned back, and froze.

On the rooftop of a burning structure, Rashiri stood alone, framed by fire. She raised one hand and waved to Selaina. She didn't run. She didn't cry out. She stood in the light of the flames, motionless and unshaken.

The ridgebacks smashed through the fence. Wood splintered. Sand burst upward.

Selaina looked back once more, but there was only fire.

She exhaled, relieved they were free, but heavy with grief. She didn't know if Rashiri would survive, but as the flames swallowed the rooftop, Selaina clung to the hope that some truths burned brighter than fire.

CHAPTER 8

THE ROAD AHEAD bent gently southward, as if the land itself remembered the way to the mountain in her vision. Selaina sat near the back of the cart, her legs tucked beneath her, feeling each uneven jolt as the wheels bumped along the worn, winding road.

"Is there nowhere safe?" Nadara asked, her voice tight. "The Iron Flood are everywhere."

"We need to go south," said Garrick. "As far as we can, places that haven't even heard of the Iron Flood yet. If we don't warn them, Galanor as we know it will become nothing more than a memory."

Selaina looked out over the horizon, where the road disappeared into the folds of hills and fading sun. The weight in her chest, that quiet pull she had felt since Wekenwild, rose again.

She hesitated, then spoke. "Last night, I saw a mountain in a dream. It rose above the clouds, and three serpents came down from their roost, coiling around its peak. They looked at me, not like a dream. Like they really saw me. And they were calling me."

As the others reacted, she kept her voice steady, but inside, her thoughts churned. She had known from the moment she woke that this was where she had to go, whether the rest followed her or not. The feeling hadn't faded. It had only grown stronger, rooting itself deeper into her bones.

She didn't want to walk this path alone. But if no one else believed her, she would go anyway. Still… she hoped they would choose to follow.

"Kylinshan…" Ysadora turned her attention from the road, her brow furrowed. "That would make sense. It's always been part of the Zhal Evurah path, those who seek the Sky Serpents' blessing."

Rykan straightened, eyes bright. "Yes! I've always wanted to see Kylinshan. If we keep heading south, we can get there."

"The Sky Serpents are just a story," Garrick muttered. "How is chasing a dream supposed to help us fight Vatreus?"

Selaina turned to him, her voice calm but unwavering. "They're not a story. Not to me. That dream wasn't my imagination, it was a call. I felt it through the Wishing Stone's power. And I know… I know they're real."

Garrick didn't respond, but his silence was heavier than denial.

"I've seen enough in the last few days to believe anything at this point," Kadin said, adjusting the strap across his chest. "What's one more impossible thing?"

Nadara took a scroll from her pouch, unrolling a map. "Kylinshan… If we're heading south anyway, we may as well find out." She added, "And if what Selaina says is true, we're not chasing a myth, we're answering a summons."

"Kylinshan is sacred to all of Galanor," Ysadora said. "If Vatreus laid a hand on it, that might be enough for the other kingdoms to unite and rise against him."

"It's not undefended either," Kadin added. "The mountain villages around there are full of warriors, disciplined, territorial. Vatreus would gain little and bleed plenty. He'd be a fool to push that line."

⸙

It had only been a few days since they left the scorched valleys of Nordravin, but the change in the land was undeniable. The dry wind was gone, replaced by thick, humid air that clung to their skin and curled their breath. Green had returned to the world, vivid, unruly, and everywhere.

The forest rose around them like a wall, dense with ferns and twisted roots, the canopy overhead so thick that sunlight reached the ground only in dappled shards. Vines hung from towering trees, some with blooms as large as shields. Insects buzzed in a constant chorus, and now and then, a distant call echoed through the trees, something not quite bird, not quite beast.

Their path had narrowed to a trail barely wide enough for the cart. Every step forward felt like trespass.

Selaina sat near the back, her hair damp with sweat, the cart creaking beneath her. The air smelled of moss, wet bark, and deep, hidden things. She couldn't explain it, but the farther they traveled, the more she felt the pull of the mountain from her dream. Not just a vision now, but a presence. Waiting. Watching.

She glanced toward Garrick, who sat across from her, sharpening his blade with slow, methodical strokes. His expression, as always, was unreadable, though the tight set of his shoulders betrayed an undercurrent of tension. The rasp of metal against stone was the only sound he made, a steady rhythm that seemed to echo the weight of his thoughts.

In the back corner of the cart, Kadin was fiddling with a handful of trinkets he had collected along their journey, a tarnished coin, a shard of polished crystal, and what looked like a bent nail. He examined each item with exaggerated seriousness, turning them over in his hands as though they were priceless treasures.

Rykan leaned against the side of the cart, his hand resting idly on the hilt of his sword, eyes scanning the trees as if he expected an ambush at any moment. His posture was relaxed, but his gaze never stopped moving, a predator always ready to strike.

Beside Rykan, Nadara unrolled her scroll with quiet purpose, her hands steady, her gaze sharp. Selaina watched, long enough to feel that quiet unease stir again. She still hadn't forgotten the visions from their first meeting: the red stone, the dead man, the weeping woman. Just fragments. But they clung to her, stubborn as burrs in the dark.

Nadara glanced up then, just briefly, as if sensing Selaina's attention. "We're close," she said, matter-of-fact, her eyes turning to the trail ahead.

Selaina gave a small nod, masking the twinge of guilt that rose in her chest. She looked away, focusing on the motion of the trees sliding past. Her suspicion hadn't vanished, but for now, it slipped back beneath the surface.

Her thoughts churned with fragments of the past and guesses about what lay ahead as the forest began to thin, giving way to open hills. When the village of Haughlen appeared in the distance, her heart lifted momentarily, until she saw the banner.

The trident and shield of the Iron Flood flew high above the town square, its presence stark and foreboding against the gray sky. Her stomach twisted at the sight, a cold weight settling over her chest. What should have been a place of safety was now a stronghold for their enemy.

"We can't go through there," Selaina said, her voice low but firm.

"I see it," said Ysadora as she pulled the reins, slowing the cart as they all took in the sight.

The road ahead was no longer an option. Without waiting for a debate, Ysadora turned the cart sharply, guiding it back toward the tree line.

The path they took was rough, little more than a clearing among the woods, and the cart lurched violently as the wheels hit exposed roots and rocks. Selaina winced at each jolt, her grip locking on the wooden edge. The sun hung low, casting long shadows through the trees as the faint colors of sunshimmer played above the canopy. But even the beauty of the sky couldn't soothe her unease.

"They're spreading faster than I thought," Selaina murmured, more to herself than anyone else.

Nadara turned her head, her expression unreadable. "The Iron Flood doesn't waste time."

Selaina didn't respond immediately. Her mind churned with questions, each one heavier than the last. How many more villages like Haughlen had fallen? How many more would follow? She leaned back against the side of the cart, the rough wood pressing against her spine, trying to focus on the steady rhythm of the wheels. But the silence gnawed at her.

She glanced at Garrick. "What do you think this means? Why take these smaller towns?"

Garrick's jaw set, his gaze distant. "Supply routes," he said finally. "They're laying the groundwork for something bigger."

"Where do you think they might target next?" asked Selaina.

"That's harder to say," Garrick admitted, shifting. "Now that they've moved into Sybara, I'd assume they're positioning for Virelda. But taking Haughlen... it could mean they're planning something further south."

"South?" Selaina repeated, her voice edged with worry. "What is his goal exactly? Can anyone truly hold this much territory?"

"Hard to guess without knowing the full scope of their forces." Garrick's voice carried a hint of frustration. "Vatreus always played the long game. He might be planning something we won't see coming."

Selaina's fingers stiffened even more on the cart's edge, this time in an attempt to balance her mind as well as her body. Could they stop the Iron Flood before they consumed everything?

Eventually, they rejoined the path past the village and rolled into a low basin, lined with moss-covered stones half-swallowed by the earth. Selaina leaned forward as the mist thickened, something in the air shifted. Not magic, not quite. But close. The others said nothing, but she felt it like a presence bracing behind the hills. Waiting.

Ruins emerged through the haze, stone pillars rising like sentinels, archways cracked and leaning. Their jagged tops disappeared into the low-hanging mist, as if the sky itself had been carved away. Crumbling structures dotted the valley, immense and monolithic, hewn from single pieces of stone. No decoration. Just scale. Authority.

The cart slowed as they entered the valley proper, Ysadora guiding the ridgebacks carefully over the uneven ground. The sound changed first, birdsong vanished, replaced by a quiet so dense it pressed against the skin. The air cooled under a leaning arch, and a faint mineral tang settled on Selaina's tongue. Old water, cracked earth, the scent of things buried and forgotten.

Even the ridgebacks hesitated, their steps slowing, hooves striking stone with a cautious rhythm. Selaina felt it too, a prickling at the base of her spine, not fear exactly, but reverence. Like she was trespassing through someone else's memory.

Selaina couldn't stop looking. Even where the buildings had collapsed, arches caved in, towers split, the lines of the fallen pieces still aligned. It was like seeing a shattered mirror whose cracks had chosen where to fall. The buildings weren't just broken. They were still remembering how they had once stood.

Something in her responded to that. It wasn't awe. It was recognition. The mark on her brow pulsed faintly, like a whisper brushing through old stone. This place hadn't just been built. It had been designed. Not to impress, but to mean something.

She didn't understand the message. But part of her wanted to.

The silence pressed in, thick and expectant. The air felt charged with memory. She scanned the base of a tower across the square, and for a breath, it was as if the ruins were looking back at her.

Then something moved. Her heart skipped. A figure, or more of a shadow, slipped out of sight beneath one of the towering arches as she blinked, her eyes still adjusting to the misty light.

The Nadrok.

She glanced at the others, her pulse quickening. No one else seemed to notice. Selaina steadied herself, afraid that Gwenna was lurking nearby.

"What is this place?" Selaina murmured, more to herself than to anyone else.

"Stormgait," Garrick replied, his tone heavy with history. "Ruins of one of the cities of the giant races."

Selaina forced herself to focus on the conversation, but her attention kept drifting to the edges of her vision. Shadows shifted there, always at the periphery, just out of focus. A prickling sensation crawled along her skin. She could feel them watching.

"Giants?" Selaina repeated, her gaze sweeping over the remnants of the strange architecture. The sheer scale of it was daunting, like standing in the shadow of forgotten gods.

"Six thousand years ago, the world was filled with them," Ysadora said, her voice carrying a scholarly cadence. "For a time, there was peace between them and the smaller races, our ancestors."

Selaina considered this. The Nadrok were not known to harm anyone, but she had seen what Gwenna could do with them. Could Gwenna be watching them now, through Nadrok eyes? Could these silent watchers be preparing a dark gateway, as Gwenna had done before?

"What happened?" Selaina asked, her voice tinged with both curiosity and dread.

"As their population grew, the giants needed more room to expand," Garrick explained. "That expansion often came at the expense of villages belonging to what they called the lesser races."

"And our people joined together to fight them off," Rykan added, his tone tense.

"Possibly the worst war this world has ever seen," Ysadora said, her voice quieter now, as though the weight of those ancient battles lingered even in memory. "The giants were unmatched in strength and size. Entire armies were obliterated trying to stop them."

"Sounds like a brilliant plan," Kadin said dryly. "Throw everything you have at something twice your size and hope it flinches."

A shiver climbed Selaina's spine. Not from the cold, but from the weight of presence. Not human. Not giant. Something quieter. Observing. The Nadrok were still out there.

"How were they defeated?" Selaina asked, her voice barely above a whisper, as if speaking too loudly might awaken the ruins around them.

"Zhal Evurah," Ysadora said, her gaze distant, as if recalling a legend. "He had the power and the knowledge to defeat them. Through his strategic brilliance, he led our kind to destroy their cities, proving that intellect could triumph over brute strength."

"According to Elysia, his name was Ardalion Guvallus," Garrick added, his voice tinged with reverence. "One of her direct ancestors."

Selaina glanced at him, her breath stuttering in her throat. Even now, Elysia's name carried a weight that was hard to bear. She let her gaze drift back to the towering ruins, her thoughts heavy. If this place had been built for giants, what sort of power had it taken to bring them down? And what would it take to defeat the forces they faced now?

"I didn't realize her family had such a legacy," Selaina said softly. "Where did the giants go after their defeat?"

"Unfortunately, they refused to submit to what they considered lesser creatures," Ysadora replied. "The war dragged on until they were driven to extinction."

Selaina shook her head, trying to imagine a world where such enormous beings roamed freely. "They should have preserved their kind, we could have shared the world, if only they had been satisfied with the territory they had," she murmured.

"Evil comes in all shapes and sizes," Nadara interjected, her tone sharp but steady. "It wasn't just giants they fought, it was tyranny and brute force. Just as we are now."

Selaina shifted, eyes flicking again to the edges of the mist. The sense of being watched hadn't faded. The Nadrok didn't attack, but Gwenna had used them as her eyes before. Was she watching now, behind some ruined pillar, waiting for the right moment to act?

Selaina's gaze drifted toward the towering remnants behind them. The mist had swallowed most of the valley, but the weight of it lingered in her chest. The stillness. The scale. The silence that felt too full.

Garrick gave a slow nod, the furrow between his brows deepening. "It did take something immense. Maybe that's why Vatreus carries what he does." He glanced ahead, as if picturing the man. "That sword he wields, it's said to be giant-forged. Made for hands bigger than ours. And he swings it like it belongs to him."

"I can believe it," Rykan said. His voice was flat, but Selaina saw the change in his grip, the way his knuckles whitened around his sword. "I've seen him use it, it's long enough to skewer several men in a single strike."

She didn't ask what he'd seen. The shadows in his eyes told her enough. That sword had taken something from him, and the weight of that memory still sat in his hand.

Selaina turned to Garrick. "How well did you know Vatreus?" she asked, her voice steady, though inside she felt anything but. There was curiosity in her question, but also something deeper, a need to understand the brother she had never truly known, the man whose choices loomed over her like a shadow she couldn't escape.

Garrick paused, his sharpening stone hovering over his blade. "Know him? Not personally," he said, glancing up at her. "We crossed paths often enough, but I was never formally introduced, if that's what you're asking."

"What was he like?" Selaina pressed, her voice quieter now, almost hesitant.

Garrick resumed his work, the rasp of stone on steel filling the silence for a moment. "Charismatic. Commanding. He had a way of making people believe in his cause, even when they shouldn't have." He frowned, the edge of a memory sharpening alongside his blade. "But there was always something... calculated about him. Like every word, every gesture, was part of a plan. And looking back... maybe it was." Garrick stopped working for a moment. "The man had a way of making you feel like you knew him. But I'm not sure anyone really did."

"You almost sound impressed," Selaina said softly, tilting her head as she studied him.

The sharpening stopped mid-stroke. Garrick set the blade aside and leaned back, meeting her gaze. "I was, once," he admitted, his voice low. "He could inspire loyalty like no one I'd ever seen. You wanted to believe him, even when you knew better."

Selaina's frame tensed at his words. "Why do people still follow him?"

"Because they believe he can give them what they've lost," Garrick said, his voice almost bitter. "Safety. Purpose. Order. He's good at making you think that's all he wants. But trust me…" He leaned forward, his tone heavy. "Vatreus never does anything without a reason. And those reasons?" He clenched his jaw. "They're never what you think."

The ruins fell behind them, swallowed by mist. Selaina turned forward, and only then noticed the sound, low and steady. Water. A wide river sprawled ahead, a bridge rising from its banks like a spine of stone.

The ruins stood silent, broken and still, but something in the fog lingered too long. A shape that didn't quite belong. Watching. She didn't mention it. But her fingers drifted toward her mark, just to feel that it was still quiet. Ahead, the river awaited.

The bridge loomed above the water, carved from colossal stone blocks, weathered smooth by six thousand years of river and rain. The cart jolted as they crossed it, the worn slabs shifting under the ridgebacks' hooves. Selaina gripped the railing, marveling that each stone was as large as the cabin she once called home.

The width of the bridge was such that several of these carts could pass each other while crossing. Reinforcing the stone blocks were the colossal trunks of old trees and metal was used in places as well. Piers of the great blocks towered above them as they went through, supporting the spans of the bridge.

"We are crossing the Taleris River," said Nadara, as if noticing the wonder in Selaina's eyes. "Possibly the sturdiest bridge in the world, it was built six thousand years ago."

"This bridge has stood for six thousand years?" asked Selaina.

"Just as the mountains have," said Ysadora. "This bridge was made from them."

They passed the river into dense jungle, the canopy thick and damp with recent rain, until they came to a small wooden bridge spanning a ravine. As Ysadora slowed the ridgebacks, a sharp whistle cut through the air, followed by the solid thunk of an arrow striking the right side of the cart.

"Down!" Garrick barked, yanking Selaina as he leaped from the cart.

Ysadora, Nadara, Rykan, and Kadin followed in quick succession, crouching behind the left wheels for cover as a volley of arrows rained down.

But then more shafts came whistling in, from the other side.

A jolt of awareness raced through her. They were surrounded.

Selaina pressed her back against the cart, heart pounding, and swiftly notched an arrow. Her eyes darted through the underbrush, searching for movement.

Kadin crouched nearby, his crossbow loaded. He fired twice, both shots missing their mark before his third bolt found its target, dropping an archer from the trees.

"Got one," he muttered, reloading.

Selaina noticed movement from behind the trees, masked marauders loosing another barrage. She exhaled, steadying her aim, and released her arrow. It struck true, embedding itself in the chest of a bandit, who collapsed with a choked gasp. On the right, more archers moved from their positions, weaving through the trees to outflank them.

Garrick unsheathed his sword with a sharp rasp, a growl in his throat. Without hesitation, he charged toward the advancing bandits. Selaina pivoted, notching and loosing another arrow in rapid succession. Her shot took down a bandit mid-draw, clearing Garrick's path as he closed the distance.

Ysadora raised her staff, summoning vines and roots from the forest floor. They snaked upward, wrapping around a struggling bandit and pulling him to the ground, entangling him completely.

On the other side, Nadara spun her glaive with ease, her blade gleaming in the light. She joined Garrick, moving fluidly to intercept another assailant. Garrick's sword arced downward, splitting the bandit's guard, while Nadara's wide swing forced the remaining marauders to retreat. The last three turned and bolted into the jungle, their cries echoing through the trees.

"Don't let them go!" Garrick barked, his tone sharp with urgency as he sprinted after them. "They're only falling back to regroup!"

Selaina turned back to the left as Rykan cut down an archer before he could notch his next arrow. Kadin fired his crossbow a heartbeat later, striking another bowman who had taken aim at Rykan. Then, in the deeper shadows of the forest, Selaina spotted a final figure, a bandit half-hidden, drawing his string with slow, steady intent.

She raised her bow and fired on instinct. The shot flew wide, sailing too high. Her stomach dropped. It wasn't fast enough. Wasn't true. The bandit had already lined up his target, Kadin, and there was no time to nock another arrow. Panic surged, but beneath it, something else stirred.

A pressure that had been building for days, subtle, electric, rose to the surface. The mark on her forehead tingled. The memory of the Sky Serpents, the strange current that had coursed within her since the Wishing Stone, everything converged in that single heartbeat. Her breath caught, and without knowing why, she thought, *lower... faster.*

The arrow twitched.

Her focus narrowed. The world shrank to that one piece of wood and feather, cutting through the air. A soft shimmer of blue light trailed behind it as the arrow tilted mid-flight, obeying a will she hadn't known she was shaping. She didn't fully understand what was happening, only that she needed it to strike.

The arrow corrected its path and drove straight into the bandit's chest. He staggered back with a strangled cry, his own bowstring loosing uselessly as his arrow flopped to the ground. He fell.

Rykan dispatched the last of the attackers, and stillness settled over the clearing. Kadin turned slowly, staring at Selaina, wide-eyed and unblinking.

She stepped toward the fallen bandit. Kneeling beside him, she wrapped her fingers around the shaft and pulled the arrow free. A faint blue haze still clung to the wood, trailing from the fletching like smoke that hadn't quite decided to fade.

Ysadora's gaze lingered on the tingling mark at Selaina's brow, then drifted to the quiver slung over her back. "Fascinating. Untrained power often surfaces through habits, actions your body already understands. That kind of instinct isn't random. Magic responds to intent, and yours was sharp. Focused. You tapped into something deeper."

Selaina turned the arrow slowly in her hands, its shaft still warm where the light had gathered. "You think I could do it again?"

Ysadora gave a rare, thoughtful smile. "With practice, and a little guidance? Yes. And next time, you won't need to rely on instinct alone."

Selaina glanced at the ground and stooped to pull another arrow from the earth, checking it for damage. Kadin joined her, muttering about wasted bolts, but her mind was already elsewhere, turning over Ysadora's words like a spark waiting for kindling.

Nearby, Garrick, Nadara, and Rykan moved among the bodies of the marauders, their movements deliberate. Garrick crouched beside a fallen bandit, turning over a ragged tunic to check for insignias or clues. "Nothing that tells us who they are," he muttered. "Just opportunists, by the look of it."

Nadara's glaive glinted as she used its tip to shift a pouch on one of the corpses. "A few coins," she said, tossing the pouch to Garrick. "Barely worth their lives."

Rykan bent over an archer, pulling free the man's quiver and inspecting the arrows. "At least their gear's in decent shape," he said, handing a few arrows to Selaina.

Selaina slipped the arrows into her quiver. Her gaze lingered on the forest edge, where the bandits had been running to. "Do you think there might be more of them?"

"If there are, we'll be ready," Garrick said, rising to his feet. "But for now, we've sent a clear message."

CHAPTER 9

A S THE GROUP finished gathering what they could, Selaina spotted Rykan wiping his blade clean on a fallen bandit's tunic. She walked toward him, each step measured, the weight of the fight still in her bones.

He looked up as she approached, and the tension in his shoulders eased. "You well?" he asked.

"I am now," she said. Her eyes lingered on his for a moment before dropping to the blade in his hand. "You didn't hesitate back there."

Rykan gave a tired half-smile. "Neither did you."

Selaina stepped closer, near enough that the heat between them settled into something steady. She wanted to reach for his hand, but hesitated.

"I thought for a moment you…" She trailed off, shaking her head. The image of the bandit taking aim at him before she could turn, still repeating in her thoughts. "Never mind."

Rykan's voice was low, honest. "I'm still here."

She nodded. Fortunately, Kadin had intervened, when she hadn't been fast enough.

They stood there for a beat longer than necessary, not in an embrace, but in understanding. Then Rykan looked down, brushing dirt from his glove, and the moment passed.

From a short distance away, Garrick cleared his throat. "If we're finished brooding over the bloodshed, we need to get moving."

Selaina exhaled through a faint smile. Rykan gave her a small nod before they both turned toward the cart, where Ysadora was already soothing the ridgebacks with quiet words and a handful of berries.

"Looks like we're done here," Garrick said, motioning for the group to load up. They rode on, the cart creaking as it rolled down the uneven path. The jungle thickened again, the humid air oppressive and clinging. But after a time, the trees began to thin, giving way to a clearer road.

Ahead, a large gate loomed, blocking their path. Soldiers stood in front of it, their postures rigid and their faces shadowed by the guard towers on either side. Archers perched above, their bows resting loosely in their hands, but their readiness was unmistakable.

Ysadora slowed the ridgebacks to a stop, her gaze fixed on the guards. The silence pressed in, broken only by the faint creak of the cart.

Selaina clutched her bow tightly, her eyes scanning the soldiers. "What now?" she asked softly, glancing at Garrick.

"No Iron Flood banners," Garrick said as he rested a hand on his sword, his voice steady but low. "We'll see if they're friend or foe."

Rykan's gaze swept the gate. "I'm ready for just about anything at this point."

One of the guards stepped forward, a stocky man with a weathered face and close-cropped hair. His leather boots crunched on the gravel road as he stopped before them, posture stiff with authority. "From where do you come, and what business brings you to Thalindor?"

"We've traveled far," Ysadora replied smoothly. "Most recently from Elenior, passing through Sybara."

"What brings you here?" the gruff guard pressed, eyes narrowing.

"The Iron Flood," Ysadora said grimly. "We seek a haven to start anew."

The man's expression hardened. "The Iron Flood is moving on Sybara?"

"They are," she confirmed. "And no one seems able to stop them."

Another guard, leaner, younger, with sandy hair tucked beneath his helm, shifted uneasily beside him. "We've heard rumors," he said in a lower voice. "A large force moving south through Drymara. Some say they're heading toward the borderlands."

The older guard grunted. "Rumors. We'd know if they were that close."

"Would we, Fergus?" the younger one countered. "The roads are a mess, and half the outposts haven't reported in for weeks."

Ysadora leaned forward, her tone sharp and urgent. "If those rumors are true, you should be rallying your forces. The Iron Flood doesn't stop. Once they're here, it'll be too late."

The older guard, Fergus, shook his head. "That may be," he said coldly, "but it doesn't change the toll. Ten aurin each."

"Sixty aurin?" Ysadora repeated, brows furrowing. "We don't have that much between us."

Fergus folded his arms. "Then those who have ten may enter. The rest will have to earn their way."

Before Ysadora could respond, the younger guard stepped closer, his gaze fixed on Selaina. His eyes widened.

"Wait… that mark, could it be?"

"The Whisper Beyond the Stars," Nadara said, stepping forward, voice steady. "I follow her."

"Let them in, Fergus," the younger guard said, gesturing. "She is Zhal Evurah."

Fergus remained unmoved. "Zhal Evurah is a myth. I'm not letting anyone in without the toll."

"But look at her forehead!" the younger guard insisted, pointing. "She bears the mark!"

Fergus scoffed. "If she's Zhal Evurah, why isn't she fighting the Iron Flood instead of running from them?"

The guard's words stung more than they should have. *Why isn't she fighting the Iron Flood?*

Selaina held her expression steady, but inside, something recoiled. She didn't need to ask why he said it, only why it struck so close. She wasn't fighting the Iron Flood. And sometimes, even she questioned if she ever truly would.

Not because she lacked the strength.

But because this wasn't a mantle she'd earned. It was one she'd taken from the Wishing Stone, not out of confidence, but out of fear.

Not because she believed she could carry it, but because she feared no one else would.

And that was more terrifying than failing, watching the world fall apart while she did nothing.

"Maybe because she's smart enough to know that one hero against an army isn't a story with a happy ending," Kadin said dryly. "But we are recruiting, if you're interested."

Selaina finally spoke, her voice calm but unwavering. "I'm here with a purpose, not to waste lives in fruitless battles. The Iron Flood is a tide, and tides are turned by more than brute force."

The younger guard nodded eagerly. "And they're heading toward Kylinshan. The Sky Serpents will appear to Zhal Evurah at the mountain summit."

Fergus's scowl deepened. "Hundreds have climbed that mountain and seen nothing."

The younger guard leaned in, voice low. "Do you really want to be remembered as the gatekeeper who denied Zhal Evurah her path? Especially if the rumors are true?"

Fergus hesitated, his jaw clenching. He glanced between Selaina and the empty road stretching behind them. The younger guard's words seemed to settle on him like dust. Finally, he let out a sharp breath. "Fine. I'll lower the toll. Five aurin each."

Ysadora reached into her robes, producing the coins with a faint smile. "That, we can manage."

The gates groaned open, heavy doors creaking on iron hinges. As the cart rolled forward, Ysadora gave Fergus a sly glance. "You'll be remembered for this," she said, her tone dancing between jest and promise.

As the cart passed through the gates, the heavy wooden doors creaking shut behind them, Selaina felt the weight of the guards' gazes lingering on her. The mark on her forehead had once been a symbol she hardly understood, but now it seemed to speak for her before she even opened her mouth.

Rykan leaned closer, his voice low enough for only her to hear. "Your mark will open up so many things. It will signal allies and draw them to you."

Selaina glanced at him, her lips curving into a faint, uncertain smile. "I hope you're right."

But even as she said it, a knot of doubt twisted in her chest. The mark was no longer just a strange gift, it was a banner others followed, a weight others expected her to carry. It frightened her how easily people listened now, how quickly they attached meaning to a glowing sigil on her skin. What if they were wrong about her? What if she wasn't ready?

She lowered her gaze for a moment, her thoughts turning inward. She hadn't asked for any of this. And yet, she couldn't imagine turning away from it, either.

The group fell into a quiet rhythm as the cart rumbled onward, the shadow of the gates giving way to the bustling streets of Thalindor. Around them, the sounds of life returned, merchants haggling, children's laughter, and the distant clang of a blacksmith's hammer.

But Selaina's thoughts remained on the whispered rumors of the Iron Flood's movements. Their enemies were close, closer than she'd expected. She placed a hand over her quiver, the memory of her guided arrow still fresh, the faint blue light of its flight repeating in her mind. If this really was her destiny, then whatever lay ahead wasn't just her path to walk, it was her burden to bear.

Above the crowded streets, the distant peaks of Kylinshan loomed like guardians, shrouded in mist. The summit waited, and with it, answers she wasn't sure she was ready to face.

For now, she could only move forward.

CHAPTER 10

THE MOUNTAINS WATCHED in silence, their flanks scorched by the touch of unwelcome hands. After several more days of travel, riding by day and resting under the stars, the cart groaned as its wheels jolted over a protruding stone, and Rykan steadied himself with a hand on the edge. He glanced at Ysadora, her grip confident as she guided them forward, eyes sharp on the uneven road ahead.

The climb grew steeper, the air cooler, carrying the crisp bite of mountain chill and the sharp, clean scent of pine. Rykan barely noticed the faint trickle of water whispering somewhere among the ferns or the occasional cry of a hawk overhead. His focus stayed fixed on the horizon, where the low sun cast long shadows over Kylinshan's towering peaks, their jagged edges cloaked in an ethereal mist that clung to the ridges like a shroud.

The cart creaked as it rounded a bend, the trees thinning ahead. Through the break in the canopy, the village of Alisaran emerged, its curved tile roofs nestled into the mountainside, half-swallowed by greenery, like part of the land itself. For a moment, something in Rykan's chest let go. But the feeling didn't last. As they drew closer, a darker weight returned.

Smoke rose in thin, dark plumes where no chimneys stood. The air carried a faint, acrid tang. Even the forest's colors seemed dimmed, leeched of life by something unseen. Rykan leaned forward, his hand brushing the hilt of his sword.

"Something's off," Rykan muttered, eyes narrowing.

Garrick, seated beside Nadara, squinted at the distant gate. "That's not the work of nature," he said grimly.

Ysadora eased the reins, her posture stiffening as the village came into view.

From the bench behind her, Kadin leaned forward, one arm resting loosely on the cart rail. "Nothing says warm welcome like boarded windows," he muttered.

Rykan, seated nearby, caught the glance Kadin cast sideways, not toward the village, but toward Ysadora. It was brief, but unmistakable. He wasn't just watching the road. He was watching her. He narrowed his eyes. Whatever passed between them, it wasn't just about the mission. But whether it was admiration, wariness, or something else entirely, Rykan couldn't say.

As they neared the gate, its once-beautiful archway, crafted of dark wood and stone, came into view. Blackened scorch marks marred its surface, and crude red symbols were scrawled across it. Rykan recognized the markings immediately. The Iron Flood.

"Look what they've done," Garrick said, his tone sharp with disapproval. "Even this place is not immune."

Selaina shifted in her seat, her gaze darting between the defaced statues flanking the gate. "They've been here." Her voice dropped.

Nadara's eyes narrowed. "That smoke's fresh."

The cart came to a halt at the edge of the village. Smoke hung faintly in the humid air, curling into the canopy above and carrying the tang of burned wood and ash. The road ahead was lined with lanterns on delicate wooden posts, their vibrant silk coverings tattered from battle. The trident-and-shield banners of the Iron Flood hung over the arched gates, clashing with the serene architecture of the village.

Rykan crouched against the side of the cart, scanning the village. The curved, tiled roofs of the buildings peeked out among the lush greenery, their intricate carvings and painted eaves damaged but still beautiful. A soldier stood in the distant streets, his black armor gleaming dully in the midday light, while villagers moved, clearing debris or rebuilding walls. Likely under watchful eyes of more soldiers they couldn't see.

"Do you think they've taken the mountain?" Rykan asked.

"The defenders of Kylinshan are too well entrenched," Ysadora replied. "It would take months to control the heights."

"So what do we do now?" Rykan asked, glancing toward the path that vanished into the cliffs beyond.

"We can't just stroll in," Garrick said, quiet but firm. "They'll stop us before we make it ten paces."

"This village marks the start of the mountain trail," Ysadora said. "If we're going to reach the summit, we have to get through somehow."

Rykan's jaw twitched as his gaze swept over the damaged buildings. "The villagers might still be resisting."

"The battle is over," said Garrick. "Any villagers left have given up for their own survival."

"Agreed," Nadara said, adjusting her satchel. "But sneaking past an entire garrison is a tall order."

"We have to help them somehow," said Selaina.

Kadin scoffed quietly, leaning back with a smirk. "And how do you suggest we help? Take on an entire garrison? Last I checked, we're not exactly an army."

The group fell quiet as Garrick led the ridgebacks into the thick underbrush beside the trail. Ysadora followed, murmuring to calm them as she untied the harnesses.

"We're leaving the cart?" Selaina asked.

"We can't take it with us," Garrick said. "Too noisy, too slow. If we're going to sneak past a garrison, we go light."

He unclipped the last buckle, and the ridgebacks shifted restlessly.

"They won't wander far," Ysadora added. "Not if they're trained well enough. Better that than risking their lives, and ours, dragging a cart through occupied streets."

Selaina stroked one of the ridgebacks' necks. Its ears stirred at her touch, nervous but willing. "It feels wrong leaving them."

"They'll be safer than we will," Rykan said, adjusting his blade.

"We'll have to sneak in and get to the trail," Kadin said, his fingers twitching as though eager for a challenge. "Lucky for you, I've got a knack for this sort of thing."

"Isn't there a better plan?" Ysadora asked in a dry tone, her eyes scanning the village from their hiding spot. "Anything other than sneaking through a village occupied by soldiers and hope we don't get caught?"

Rykan leaned forward. "We may not have a choice. The mountain trail is on the other side. Unless you know of a way to make the Iron Flood disappear, this is what we may have to do."

Nadara's gaze flicked to him, her lips pressing into a thin line. "If we get caught, I'm not dying with my back turned."

Kadin grinned, adjusting his cloak with exaggerated confidence. "Stick with me, and you'll live to see the summit of the mountain."

Garrick snorted. "If your mouth doesn't give us away first."

They crouched behind a thicket near the gate, Kadin leading the way. Rykan's hand hovered near his sword, every sound sharpening his focus.

The group slipped through the gate's shadows, staying low. The wide main road was flanked by elegant buildings with lacquered wood and delicate latticework windows, but their beauty was marred by scorch marks and debris. The air was unnaturally still, broken only by the occasional bark of orders or the distant clang of rebuilding efforts. Even the smallest sounds felt exaggerated in the hush, each step threatening to betray them.

Kadin paused near a broken section of fencing, motioning for the others to stop. "There," he murmured, pointing toward an alley partially obscured by the collapsed remains of a building. "That'll get us closer to the trailhead."

Rykan crouched beside him, eyes scanning the alley and the plaza beyond. Two soldiers lingered nearby, their helmets gleaming faintly in the torchlight. Their posture was relaxed, but their weapons hung ready at their sides.

"How do we get past them?" he whispered.

Kadin grinned faintly, pulling a small pouch from his belt. "We get creative."

Before anyone could object, he tossed the pouch toward a pile of crates. The faint jingle of coins broke the silence like a hammer on glass. Both guards stiffened, their heads snapping toward the sound.

"What was that?" one muttered, already moving.

The other stayed at his post, squinting into the dark. "You see anything?"

The first guard bent down, plucking a coin from the dirt. "Oh-ho," he said with a grin. He started scanning the ground, spotting another glint just beyond.

"What'd you find?" the second called, suspicious now, but curious.

The first didn't answer. He knelt, brushing dirt aside as he reached for the pouch. That was enough to draw the second guard in. "Seriously?" he muttered, stepping away from his position.

As they clustered around the pouch, Kadin waved the group forward, his grin fading into a face of focus.

Rykan led the way, his sword drawn low, every step a heartbeat.

"Hey, you need to share some of that," the second guard was saying as their voices trailed off.

"Who says? I found it," the first shot back.

The alley swallowed the group in darkness, the packed dirt soft beneath their feet. Every shadow felt alive, every silence stretched, fragile and sharp.

Rykan's fingers curled hard around the leather-wrapped hilt of his sword. They weren't safe yet.

As the group crept closer to the village square, the hush of the alley gave way to the low murmur of gathered soldiers and the heavy silence of fear. Rykan motioned for them to stop and pressed against the wall of a collapsed structure, peering through a splintered window toward the plaza.

A line of villagers knelt in the dirt, hands bound behind their backs. Soldiers flanked them on either side, tense and unmoving. At the center stood a figure cloaked in dark crimson, his armor scorched black around the edges and polished to a dull gleam. Covering the lower half of his face was a mask of dark iron, unadorned, as if hammered into shape for utility rather than symbolism.

He didn't speak. He didn't move.

"It's him," Garrick muttered, his voice flat.

Selaina glanced at him. "Who?"

"Kallus." Garrick said the name, like it tasted wrong in his mouth. "General Kallus, if he still bothers with titles."

Selaina's breath caught. "Why does he wear a mask?"

Garrick grunted. "Because monsters look better with their faces covered."

In the square, one of the villagers, a man with a weathered face and blood on his sleeve, looked up and spat into the dirt.

"Do what you will," he said. "The mountain will turn against you."

Kallus didn't react. He simply lifted his hand.

A nearby soldier obeyed without hesitation, driving a blade into the man's chest. The villager slumped forward.

Selaina flinched. Rykan clenched his jaw. He'd seen enough executions to know what fear could make a man say, but this was different. This wasn't fear. This was defiance.

"We can't stop this," Garrick said quietly. "Not here. Not now."

"But we can make sure it ends somewhere," Selaina murmured, her voice tight.

Another soldier dragged the next villager into place.

Kadin gestured toward the far side of the square. "We move now. While their attention is fixed."

They pulled back from the window and slipped into the next alley, the sound of sobbing and steel echoing behind them. Garrick was the last to leave, his eyes lingering on Kallus's unflinching figure in the firelit square.

"I left that uniform behind," he said under his breath. "But that man… I never stopped fearing I'd see him again."

Even the air seemed to hold still, thick with smoke, silence, and the weight of what they couldn't stop.

Rykan glanced at Selaina. Her expression had shifted, still, focused. Whatever she felt, she didn't speak it.

Then came the sound, a slow rasp of metal on stone.

A Dreadstorm Knight moved with a measured, deliberate gait, his blackened armor gleaming faintly with an otherworldly sheen. Through the gaps in its plates, an eerie blue mist swirled, flashing like trapped lightning. The air around him seemed heavier, colder, as if the knight carried a piece of the abyss with him. Regular soldiers scattered from his path, their faces pale, their eyes averted.

Rykan's knuckles whitened around his sword's hilt. "One of the knights," he whispered, his voice barely audible. "We can't fight that. Not here."

"We won't have to," Kadin said, though his voice lacked its usual confidence. His gaze darted between the knight and the alley's exit. "We just need to stay quiet."

The knight stopped abruptly, his helm turning as though he had sensed something. Rykan froze, his breath caught in his throat. The blue glow within the armor pulsed outward, like a storm trapped in a vessel, brushing the seams as if testing its confinement. A cold dread settled over the group, the oppressive silence broken only by the faint, mechanical rasp of the knight's breath.

Kadin led them on, moving quickly but carefully through the narrow alley, their breaths shallow as the Dreadstorm Knight's boots echoed ever closer. Blue mist drifted from his armor. The shadows quivered in time with his breath, like the very alley had begun to breathe with him.

They were almost past the mouth of the alley when a sharp voice called out, too close. "Hey, did you see that?"

Rykan's heart stopped. One of the guards was looking straight toward the alley. His companion followed his gaze, squinting into the dark.

"There," the first one muttered. "I swear something moved."

The second shook his head. "Probably rats. Come on, move. You want to get the Knight's attention?" He nodded toward the Dreadstorm Knight.

But the first guard didn't look away.

Rykan's fingers traced the hilt of his sword. He didn't draw it, but every muscle in his body was ready.

There was nowhere to run, no corner to slip behind, no stall to duck beneath. Only a weathered wooden door half-hidden by crumbling stone.

"Inside. Now," Kadin hissed.

Rykan moved first, reaching for the handle and pushing the door open just enough for them to slip inside one by one. As the last of them entered, he pulled it shut just as the faint glow of the knight's flame crept around the edge of the alley wall.

They pressed themselves against the walls, hearts pounding. The dimly lit room was cramped, a single lantern casting dancing light across the space. Near a low table, a family huddled together, a man gripping a carving knife with trembling hands, his wife holding their young daughter close. The girl couldn't have been older than twelve.

The way the family looked at them, with fear in their eyes and weapons born of desperation, struck a familiar chord in Rykan. It was the same haunted expression he'd seen outside Tathara, the faces of those lined up and loaded into carts bound for the mountain gate. Fear. Hopelessness. He hated it, but he couldn't fault them for it.

"Please," Ysadora whispered, her voice gentle but urgent. "We mean no harm. Just let us stay until the streets are clear."

The girl's eyes widened, her gaze caught the soft glow on Selaina's brow, and she stilled. "Mama, look," she whispered, pointing. "The Whisper Beyond the Stars."

The woman held her daughter more closely, but her expression softened as her gaze settled on Selaina's brow. "Is it true?" she asked, her voice trembling. "Are you… Zhal Evurah?"

Selaina hesitated. Rykan could see the doubt spark in her eyes, the instinct to deny, to step back from the title that had followed her like a shadow since Wekenwild. But then something shifted. Her posture straightened, just slightly. She met the woman's gaze.

"Yes," Selaina said, her voice soft, but unwavering. "I am."

Rykan felt a tightness ease in his chest. She had claimed her title. She wasn't hiding anymore.

That mark of Selaina's… it was like a beacon, impossible to hide. It gave people hope, but it also painted a target on her back. How could he protect her from something she couldn't control?

The man's grip on his knife faltered as he exchanged a glance with his wife. Finally, he nodded toward a storage room at the back. "Hide in there. Quickly."

As they moved toward the small room, the girl tugged at her mother's sleeve. "She'll save us," the child whispered.

The mother knelt beside her, smoothing her hair. "Hush now, little one."

Inside the cramped storage room, the group crouched among sacks of grain and bundles of herbs. Selaina's glowing mark was faint but visible even in the low light. Rykan kept his hand on the hilt of his sword, his ears straining to catch the sounds of soldiers outside.

The man came near the doorway, lowering his voice. "My name is Brali. There is something I feel I need to tell you," he said, looking at Selaina.

Rykan's hand hovered over his sword. He didn't know what the man was about to say, but Selaina was already listening.

Selaina hesitated, but only for a moment. "What is it?"

Brali lowered his voice. "A month ago, I went to the hot springs beyond the village, the ones said to hold ancient power. I hoped for clarity, maybe even healing. But something else happened."

Selaina tilted her head, her interest piqued. "What did you see?"

"A lone wolf stood beneath a silver moon. It howled once, and the moon cracked like glass.

The shards fell, glowing as they tumbled, And where they struck, two rivers of light were born.

The wolf followed them until they met. But their light had turned to blood.

The wolf howled again. And the river split back into two.

The blood faded. Their light returned."

Rykan's hand clung to the hilt of his sword. He kept his eyes on the door, but his thoughts weren't on the danger outside. Something about the vision, it pulled at him. Like it knew more about Selaina than Brali ever could.

He glanced back and caught her watching him.

Not looking for protection. Not asking anything aloud.

Just unsettled. Searching.

He gave her a small nod. Nothing more. Letting her know he had heard it too.

Her gaze lingered a second, then dropped. But Rykan stayed with the silence.

Whatever that vision meant, it had shaken something loose in both of them.

Selaina frowned, her brow creasing. "What does it mean?"

Brali shook his head. "I don't know. But when I saw your mark, I felt it was meant for you to hear. Perhaps it will make sense as your path unfolds."

Ysadora, standing near the doorway, crossed her arms and murmured, "Or it could just be the remnants of a dream. Visions like that can be... unreliable."

"Unreliable or not, it doesn't mean they're meaningless," Nadara countered sharply, her gaze flicking to Selaina. "What if it's a warning?"

Selaina's voice was quiet but strong. "I don't know what it means, but… something about it feels important."

CHAPTER 11

BOOTSTEPS ECHOED DOWN the street outside, making Rykan focus on every breath he took.

"Have the Iron Flood taken control of the mountain?" Garrick asked.

"I haven't seen any of them go up the path," said Brali. "Many of them left, but they were headed south."

The tension in the room hung heavy until the sound of boots echoed down the street, halting all conversation. Everyone froze, muscles tight with waiting. The noise stopped near the house. For a long moment, the only sound was the pounding of Rykan's heartbeat in his ears. Then the boots moved on, fading into the distance, and the village fell silent once more.

Brali left, and a moment later, returned. "They're gone," he whispered. "For now."

Emerging from the storage room, the group found the family still gathered near the table. The man looked weary but resigned as he put down his knife. "You must be heading to the mountain, there's a trail behind the old shrine," he said. "It's hidden, but it'll take you past the guards."

"The old shrine," Rykan repeated, nodding. "Thank you."

The woman stood, her gaze lingering on Selaina. "The mountain will be cold," she said, moving to a chest near the wall. She opened it and pulled out several cloaks lined with thick fur, holding them out. "Take these. They're all we can offer."

Selaina stepped forward, accepting the cloaks with a grateful nod. "Your kindness won't be forgotten," she said softly.

The girl moved closer, her small hand reaching out to touch Selaina's. "Will you come back?" she asked, her voice quiet but hopeful.

Selaina crouched to meet the child's gaze, her expression gentle. "If I can, I will."

The mother quickly pulled the girl back, her expression apologetic. "Go now. Before the soldiers return."

As they slipped out the back, Rykan glanced over his shoulder. The girl stood watching Selaina. She wasn't afraid. She wasn't even curious. Just waiting, like someone holding on to a promise no one had made.

The towering peaks of Kylinshan loomed ahead, shrouded in mist. As they moved toward the hidden trail, Rykan glanced at Selaina, her mark still visible beneath the cloak's shadow. Every step closer to the mountain felt like they were walking into something far bigger than any of them. He just hoped he was strong enough to stand beside her when the time came.

The group moved cautiously through the narrow alleyways, guided by Kadin's sharp eyes and Brali's directions. The faint glow of lanterns from the main streets barely reached them, casting long shadows that seemed to stretch and shift with every step. Rykan gripped the hilt of his sword, his muscles tense as his gaze darted between every glint of movement. The Iron Flood's banners loomed in the distance, their crimson symbols glowing faintly in the torchlight.

"We'll need to stay low near the shrine," Kadin whispered, his voice barely audible over the muffled sounds of soldiers patrolling nearby. "There's no telling how close the guards might be."

"Let's not waste time," Garrick said, his tone clipped. "The longer we stay, the more likely someone spots us."

As they rounded a corner, the old shrine came into view. Hidden among a grove of ancient trees, the structure had weathered centuries. Its roof sagged under the weight of moss and time, but the intricate carvings of celestial figures along its stone walls were still visible, glinting faintly in the moonlight.

"Over there," Nadara murmured, pointing toward a narrow gap in the foliage behind the shrine. "That must be the path."

Rykan led the group closer, his heart pounding as they approached the clearing. The air was colder here, carrying a faint tang of mountain stone and the earthy scent of damp leaves. They paused behind a crumbled wall, waiting for Kadin to scout ahead.

After a few moments, Kadin returned. "Two guards at the shrine's front entrance, but they're distracted. We can slip around them if we stay quiet."

"Let's move," Rykan said, motioning for the others to follow.

One by one, they crept through the shadows, their footsteps muffled by the soft earth beneath them. The guards' voices were a low murmur in the distance, their torches casting a rippling light that barely touched the group as they slipped behind the shrine.

As they reached the hidden trail, Rykan exhaled, feeling a bit of relief. The path was narrow and overgrown, winding its way into the dense trees that cloaked the base of Kylinshan. The sounds of the village grew fainter with every step, replaced by the rustle of leaves and the occasional call of nightbirds.

When they were far enough from the Iron Flood's reach, Garrick spoke. "This'll do. We can't risk going further tonight."

They found a small clearing off the trail, shielded by thick underbrush and a canopy of ancient trees. The air was cold, biting through their cloaks, but they set about making camp quickly. Garrick and Kadin scouted the perimeter, their footfalls muffled by the soft forest floor. Ysadora knelt near the center of the clearing, her staff planted firmly in the ground as she coaxed a faint glow from the Sunkeeper stone embedded at its top. The golden light spread softly over the group, bright enough to illuminate their work but not so much as to risk detection.

Nadara glanced up from the supplies she was unpacking, her gaze settling on the glowing stone. "How does that thing work, anyway?" she asked, her voice curious but tinged with skepticism. "How do you control something like that?"

Ysadora sighed, brushing a speck of dust from the shaft of her staff as though the question barely warranted the effort of a reply. "Technically, anyone can activate a Sunkeeper. You just channel a bit of energy into the crystal, and it lights. Simple enough."

She lifted the staff, letting the faint golden glow dance over their faces.

"But keeping it like this, low, steady, just enough to see without drawing every creature in the dark to our doorstep, that takes finesse."

Her eyes settled on Nadara with a faint, practiced smile. "Most let it burn too bright, drain it within hours. Then, when the sun doesn't show itself for a week, like it often doesn't in the mountains, they're left with nothing but regret and shadows."

She lowered the staff again, letting the glow dim to a warm pulse.

"You have to understand the crystal. Feel how much light it's holding. How fast it's giving that light away."

"Sounds like you have it all figured out then," Nadara replied.

"Kadin, I've gotta hand it to you," said Garrick. "I had doubts you could lead us through all that."

"Doubts? Garrick, I'm wounded," Kadin said, his grin cutting through the cold air. "Though I'll admit, sneaking through a village swarming with Iron Flood wasn't exactly on my list of ambitions. But," he added with a mock bow, "it's nice to have my skills appreciated for once."

Rykan knelt beside Selaina as she unrolled her cloak, her hands moving with a steadiness that didn't match the firelight in her eyes. She hadn't said much since Brali's story, but the way she held herself, like the words had taken root, said more than her voice ever could.

"Everything well?" he asked softly.

Selaina nodded, though her voice was quiet. "That vision… it felt like it wasn't just his. Like I've somehow seen it before."

Rykan placed a hand on her shoulder, his grip steady. "We'll figure it out."

She reached up and placed her hand gently over his.

As the others began to settle in for the night, Rykan kept watch from beneath the shadows of a bent pine. His eyes swept the tree line, but now and then, they flicked toward Selaina and Ysadora. The two sat a little apart from the others, the faint pulse of the Sunkeeper crystal casting blue warmth across their faces.

Ysadora made a small, shaping gesture with her fingers, and Selaina mirrored it. Nothing happened at first, then there was a flicker of light, like fireflies drifting through air too cold for them. Rykan noticed the way Selaina's eyes narrowed, the way she held still.

He couldn't hear their words, but it didn't matter. He knew from her face what she was feeling. Focus and frustration, but also wonder. Whatever they were doing, it wasn't idle talk.

Rykan paced away from the camp while the others slept, keeping his distance by choice, though the quiet had grown heavy. The cool night air wrapped around him, and the steady drone of insects buzzed like a lullaby he couldn't let himself listen to. More than anything, he wanted to lie back beneath the stars, let his thoughts drift to anywhere but here. But he couldn't, not with the weight of the day still on his shoulders, and the unspoken trust the others had placed in him. Someone had to stay alert.

After a time, he heard a shift behind him. Someone else was awake.

Nadara rose from her bedroll and crossed the clearing. Her steps were quiet but purposeful as she made her way to where Rykan stood watch.

"You should get some rest," she said, her voice softening but still firm. "I'll take watch now."

Rykan hesitated. He didn't know her well enough to trust her completely. There was something unreadable about Nadara. She moved like someone who had learned to hide more than she shared.

"My watch hasn't ended yet," Rykan said, keeping his voice low. "The moon is still low."

"I know," Nadara said. "But I can't sleep anyway. You may as well get some rest."

He didn't move. "Something troubling you?" he asked. "I imagine you still carry the images from Zalorin. Everything falling apart. Your people dying."

"I didn't witness any of that," Nadara said. "When I returned home, it was already done."

"Doesn't make it any easier," Rykan murmured.

"No, it doesn't," she said. "But I was too late. All that was left was ash… and silence." Her eyes narrowed. "Sometimes I think I should've died with them. But I didn't. And now I have to make that mean something."

"When the Iron Flood attacked Tathara," he began, slower now. His shoulders rose slightly, like he was bracing for a blow. "Maybe I should've fled. Found others. Brought help. But I didn't. I stayed."

Nadara watched him, but didn't interrupt.

"Vatreus struck down my father," he said. "I saw it happen. Stood there and watched him fall. And when Vatreus left, I went to him. He was still breathing."

A pause. "Then the Iron Flood came for me. I killed two before they brought me down."

Nadara's voice softened. "They took you alive?"

Rykan nodded. "I was too angry to think. Too hurt to run. There were just too many of them."

She looked away. "Grief didn't make me stronger. Just angry. Alone. With no plan and no one left to listen. I thought maybe the world would turn me into something it feared," she said. "But it didn't. If I wanted justice… I'd have to shape it myself."

They were quiet for a moment.

"We have that in common," she said.

Rykan didn't look away, but his hand rested a little more tightly on his sword.

"It was fortunate you weren't there when Zalorin was attacked," he said carefully. "If you had been… you might've died too. Do you think it was fate that sent you away?"

"It wasn't fate," she said. "I was sent away on a journey. A stranger died in our village. I was told to find out who he was, where he came from. My elders thought it was nothing. But I wasn't sure."

Rykan's gaze drifted to her hands, one resting near the flap of her satchel. He thought he saw the edge of something dark and jagged. She didn't seem to notice.

"Did you find what you were looking for?" he asked.

"I found his family," she replied. "And more questions."

"How did he die?" Rykan pressed. "What was unusual about it?"

She turned toward the dark. "There were signs. Ones my elders ignored. That's why they sent me, so I'd stop asking."

"And did you find answers?"

"Not all of them," she said. "But I'm starting to piece it together."

He gave the satchel a long glance, the silence between them widening, filled not with distrust exactly, but with everything unspoken.

"You should get some rest," she said again, her voice quieter but still firm. "I'll take watch now."

He studied her a moment longer, her posture rigid, her eyes drawn to more than just the path. Whatever was coming next, she was already bracing for it.

He nodded, settling against the earth. But his fingers stayed near the hilt of his blade, just in case.

CHAPTER 12

ENTLENESS HUNG IN the forest air, though something deeper stirred under the leaves. Verdant grasses and ferns spilled across the path, framing a brook that babbled over smooth, time-worn stones. Selaina slowed, her gaze catching on clusters of pink and white blossoms clinging to the tangled undergrowth, their petals trembling in the soft breeze. The growth nearly obscured the narrow trail, as if nature itself were trying to reclaim it.

Beams of golden light pierced the canopy of vine-covered trees above, painting the brook with shifting patterns of warmth and shadow. The air smelled faintly of wet earth and flowering herbs, sweet but sharp. The beauty of the moment struck her like an unexpected melody, yet a quiet unease coiled in her chest. How many more scenes like this would they encounter before the hardships overtook them?

Ysadora knelt by the brook, the strands of silver woven between her antler-like horns catching faint reflections as she leaned forward to drink. Selaina followed her lead, uncertain how plentiful water would be as they ventured deeper into the mountains. The water showed her face, warped, as if even the stream wasn't sure who she'd become.

Moving her hair aside, she studied the glowing stars marking her forehead.

Was this really her? She was no longer the girl who had once hidden away in the forest with Jeth and her mother. Though she was happier with who she had become, more self-assured, more comfortable meeting strangers, she couldn't help but worry. It felt like the girl she used to see reflected back at her was slipping away.

Kadin crouched nearby, rinsing his hands in the current. He glanced sideways at Ysadora, who was shaking the water away in the same way she did everything, sharp, efficient, and without wasting a motion.

"Careful," Kadin said lightly. "You're setting a high standard for wilderness elegance."

Ysadora didn't look at him, but a faint smirk ghosted across her lips. "Try not to fall in."

Selaina, still crouched beside them, noticed the exchange. It was small, almost nothing. But the edge in Ysadora's posture had softened, and Kadin looked… quietly pleased.

"Selaina?" Rykan's voice broke into her thoughts, low and familiar, like a hand on her shoulder.

She turned to see Garrick and Nadara beginning to walk ahead, following the brook upstream.

"I'm coming," she said, rising quickly and adjusting her bag. He waited a beat for her to fall into step beside him before moving on.

The forest thickened around them, the trail dissolving into a tangle of vines and tall grass. The growth pressed in from all sides, wild and unrelenting.

Selaina slowed, scanning ahead. They wouldn't get far without clearing a path.

Her eyes shifted to Nadara, who walked a few paces behind, her glaive slung across her back, long-bladed, curved, and sharp.

"Nadara," Selaina said. "Would you mind clearing us a way through?"

She was careful that there was no edge to her voice, but she watched warily for the response.

Nadara gave a curt nod, unslinging the glaive without protest. "Of course."

She moved forward, blade swinging with controlled efficiency, slicing through vines and overgrowth with practiced ease.

Selaina watched her a moment longer, thoughtful. She had wanted to see how Nadara responded, how she moved under direction. So far, she was doing well. But trust would take more than that.

Selaina began to focus on the sounds of the forest, listening to the songs of birds as they called out overhead. They were layered together, but as she concentrated, she could pick individual calls.

One of the birds made a series of melodic chirps, rapidly shifting in pattern and tone. Another let out a sharp clicking rhythm that echoed off the trees, too steady to be wind, too irregular to be comforting. Somewhere deeper in the canopy, a high-pitched note rose and fell in a haunting loop, like a call waiting for an answer. Her favorite was a flurry of fast chirps with a twinkling, bell-like cadence. Selaina wasn't sure if it denoted joy or alarm, but she hoped the former.

She had grown up with familiar bird calls that signaled changes in the day, shifts in weather, warnings of predators. But these voices were different. New. Across Galanor, the birds had their own languages, and somehow, hearing them helped her feel more rooted in herself.

Garrick tapped her shoulder.

She turned, expecting to see more wildlife. Instead, he pointed to a shadow between two trees. At first, she thought it was only the light shifting, but then she saw it: a group of dark-feathered birds stepping cautiously across the forest floor. Large, elegant, but wary.

She glanced at him, and he gave a small nod. A silent instruction.

Selaina slid her bow from her back and nocked an arrow. She lifted her hand, feeling the drift of the wind against her fingers, adjusting her angle to match the natural rhythm. The others kept moving ahead up the slope as she crouched low, breathing steadily. Her eyes tracked the largest of the birds, studying its pattern of movement. It bobbed and paused, too cautious to follow a predictable rhythm. She exhaled slowly and released.

The arrow struck. The bird dropped. The others scattered into a cloud of wings, graceful, startled, gone.

Garrick retrieved the prize quickly, wrapping the bird in cloth and tossing a glance over his shoulder as they resumed walking.

"That's a nice sephant," he said. "They can be quick. Your instincts are getting better."

She looked down at her bow, her fingers still tingling. "I felt the wind shift. I didn't think, I just… acted."

Garrick gave a short nod. "That's the difference between prey and predator." He glanced at the trees ahead. "Prey reacts. Predator anticipates."

Selaina looked where he did, but saw nothing, only trees and dappled light.

"Something's been tracking us for the last half mile," Garrick said quietly. "I haven't told the others yet. No need to panic them. But listen, tonight, when we camp, you'll help me set the trap."

Selaina's chest tensed. "What is it?"

"I don't know," he admitted. "But it moves like it knows what we are. Watches from just far enough away. That's what predators do. They wait for weakness." His eyes swept the trees behind them, lingering a second too long on a patch of shadow.

They reached a clearing near sundown. Garrick marked the edge of the camp with subtle signs, scratches in bark, angled sticks in the underbrush. While Selaina cleaned the bird, she glanced often at the tree line.

The feathers shimmered, blue, purple, green, when turned in the light. She slipped a few into her bag.

Predator. Prey. Maybe tonight, she'd be both.

Kadin made a fire pit and Garrick fashioned two tree limbs into forked stakes that he put into the ground on either side of the pit. They held another horizontally to roast the bird over the flames. As Selaina removed the innards from the bird, she glanced up at Rykan, who was clashing swords with Nadara. She seemed to be showing him something he was doing wrong.

Once the sephant had finished roasting, they gathered around the fire to eat. The others claimed stones around the fire as seats. Selaina stayed in the grass. There had been things swirling in her mind ever since hearing that Garrick was in the Iron Flood. Perhaps it would be better to ask certain things in private, but they rarely got moments alone with anyone.

"Do you mind if I ask more about the Iron Flood?" Selaina asked, glancing at Garrick.

"This feels like the kind of topic that might end in heated words. Should we get some water ready to douse the fire?" said Ysadora.

"What do you want to know?" Garrick replied, his expression cautious.

"I just want to understand them better," Selaina said. "How did you first hear of them?"

"It was during my time with the Sybarran army," Garrick began, "fighting for Lord Calden and the town of Mirus. We were at odds with a lord in Derenhold, but it was in the Kingdom of Elenior, so all cities in Elenior became our enemies.

He paused, as if marshaling his thoughts. "They said Elenior threatened our borders. We believed them. Said we had to protect our people. So we struck first. Tore down banners. Burned their armory. Thought we were sending a message, but it turned into war."

"When it ended, we signed a treaty. Celebrated. But it felt hollow," he said, jaw tensing. "Later, I heard it was all over a marriage dispute. A noble's pride."

Selaina frowned, her stomach knotting. "That's… awful."

He let out a dry, humorless laugh. "You don't learn things like that until it's too late. We thought we were defending our homes. Turns out we were pawns."

"And that's when you found the Iron Flood?" Selaina asked.

Garrick nodded. "In small towns, people whispered about Vatreus like he was a savior. Said he'd unite the people, tear down the lords, build a city where no one bowed to anyone."

Nadara's voice cut through the smoke. "You were one of them." Her voice was still sharp, almost disbelieving.

"I was," Garrick said. "Until I wasn't."

Her fists clenched in her lap. "And how many Zalorins did your brothers kill before you'd had enough?"

"They're not my brothers," he said, his voice low. "They became what they claimed to hate. I left before it turned into slaughter."

Selaina's gaze flicked between them. Nadara's fists were tight in her lap, her eyes locked on the fire, breathing steady, but shallow.

Nadara didn't speak again, but her silence said everything. A fracture had opened.

"Death and fear, just like the lords they hated," said Ysadora, grimly.

Rykan nodded. "But worse."

Selaina spoke softly to Garrick. "I can see how it would seem appealing at first. To someone who's lived through what you did."

"Nobles are not always like that. I grew up in Tathara," Rykan said. "It's not perfect, but it's strong because of its laws. Because its people respect them. My father died defending it. My mother believed in it. And I still do."

"Rules? Or chains?" Kadin asked. "Depends where you're standing. From the top, it looks like order. From the bottom… it's just a cage."

Garrick gave a quiet nod. "That's the point. I understand why you believe in it, Rykan. I believed in crown and realm too. Until I saw how easily it serves the few."

No one spoke. The fire filled the pause with its slow crackle. Selaina's gaze flicked from Garrick to Rykan, her thoughts churning. "It sounds like defeating the Iron Flood is only the start," she said softly. "Galanor needs leaders who can serve all its people."

She thought of Garrick's words, that Vatreus had once only wanted to unite people, to bring change. Wasn't that what she wanted too? To heal what was broken? To end the cruelty? It was a noble desire… until it twisted. Until it made monsters of men.

Maybe it wasn't ambition that corrupted the world, but desperation. Maybe those who tried the hardest to fix everything were the ones most at risk of losing themselves.

CHAPTER 13

Selaina's fingers rang along her bowstring, and she intentionally slowed her breath. A branch twitched beyond the firelight, seemingly for no reason. The wind was still.

"And where do we find those leaders?" Ysadora asked.

Selaina had no intention of becoming like Vatreus. But how could she know if that path was already taking shape beneath her feet?

She turned, her gaze settling on Ysadora. "Did you ever have any inclination that Myrradin was using us for his own purposes?"

Ysadora paused mid-bite, her fingers hovering over the food. "As I told you before, I never had any reason to believe he wasn't telling the truth."

"There must've been something," Selaina said, her voice quiet as she rested her elbows on her knees. "Some clue we overlooked. Something that could've alerted us to his true motivations."

Ysadora let out a slow breath and set her food down. "And if there was? Anything I pointed to, you'd all blame me for not warning you earlier."

Selaina shook her head, her hands clasping together. "It's not about blame, Ysadora. I want to make sure I don't make the same mistakes again."

The words came too quickly, too deliberately. What she didn't say, what she couldn't say aloud, was that the person she was really afraid of trusting too blindly… was herself.

She remembered the way Myrradin used his wisdom to justify control. How easily power had disguised itself in purpose. He'd meant to change the world. Vatreus had meant to save it. And both had been consumed.

What if the same thing awaited her?

Ysadora leaned back slightly. "He could be arrogant at times, but many mavins are," she said. "Some might say he was self-absorbed. We all have our flaws. I never thought much of it."

Selaina's hand drifted to the fabric at the edge of her cloak, bunching it unconsciously. "If we can't see any signs, how can we trust anyone?"

"You can't," Kadin said, tossing a twig into the fire. "That's why I usually work alone. The only time you should work with anyone else is when you have common goals, mutual advantages."

"There has to be some measure of trust," Nadara interjected, shifting to face him directly. "Without it, a group falls apart."

"Even if Myrradin used us, we won," Rykan said, adjusting the strap of his scabbard.

"Did we?" Selaina asked, her voice barely above a whisper as she stared at the ground. "Sometimes it doesn't feel like it."

Rykan leaned forward. "Of course we did. Myrradin didn't get what he wanted, and you have the power of the Stone."

Selaina's eyes lifted to meet Ysadora's. "Do you think he was ever good?"

"I have to believe he is still good in some way," Ysadora said, her hands resting loosely in her lap. "I thought of him as a father. When I was a child in Veladralis, he saw potential in me, brought me out of the orphanage, and cared for me like his own. He told me, all the time, I would be a great mavin one day."

"I didn't know you were an orphan," Selaina said, tilting her head.

"I never knew my real mother and father," Ysadora said, her gaze shifting to the flames. "I was told they both died when I was very young, but… sometimes, I wonder. Sometimes it's easier to tell a child their parents are dead than to tell them they abandoned you."

Selaina hesitated before speaking. "I can see why you would still care for him."

Ysadora's shoulders stiffened. "Care for him? You say it as though you question my loyalty! I didn't go running after him—I followed you. I believe in you, Selaina. Zhal Evurah. There is love for him that I cannot erase, but I cannot justify his choices. If someone in your family did the same, would you not still love them? Care about them, even as you fought against them?"

Selaina's gaze lowered as she intertwined her fingers, rubbing them back and forth. Her mind circled back to the Wishing Stone, to the boy who had become Vatreus, her brother. What would the others say if they knew?

"I'm sorry, Ysadora," Selaina said finally. "I don't doubt your loyalty to our cause. I can see why you would care for him, even love him for what he did for you. This must be very difficult. I just wonder if at one point he genuinely wanted to stop Vatreus for the good of everyone, instead of taking his place."

"Power is one of the greatest temptations," Kadin said, stretching his legs out toward the fire.

Selaina looked away, her fingers brushing against the edge of her quiver.

Somewhere in the trees beyond the firelight, another branch shifted. No wind stirred it.

She froze.

The others continued talking, unaware. But her breath had stilled. That sound, soft, deliberate, too measured to be natural, echoed in her chest like a whisper from the forest itself.

"Power," said Selaina. "That's what scares me."

But the thought lingered in the space between her breaths: *What if I grew to want the Sky Serpents' gifts for the wrong reasons? What if I already do?*

It wasn't about greed, or conquest. It was subtler than that. A need to prove herself. A hunger to make things right, so strong it might become something else. Something darker.

Even here, surrounded by those who trusted her, the question lingered, a secret ache she couldn't name. She couldn't be Vatreus. But what if the path that shaped him was already forming beneath her feet?

"You can't fear power if you want to wield it," Nadara said. "It's what you want to do with it that makes it right or wrong."

Another step. Soft, then stillness. Just beyond the circle of firelight, something waited.

Selaina didn't turn her head, but she knew. She knew the way a hunter knows when it is no longer the hunter.

"I've felt real goodness before, it was beautiful," Selaina said, her voice soft but steady. "I've seen it in people. In all of us. It may be fleeting, but I dream of it spreading across Galanor."

As she spoke, she shifted her weight. Her posture changed into one she could hold, shoulders relaxing. In her stillness, there was readiness.

Garrick noticed. Their eyes met for only a moment.

She nodded once. He returned it.

She kept talking. "Not long ago, I would have said my greatest wish was to return to the forest and for my mother to return so we could live as we did before she was taken. But now…"

Another movement. Closer. She listened to its steps, timing them with the cadence of her own breath.

"…Now, I want more, for each of us. I want us to have the lives we deserve, free from the Iron Flood's shadow. I've seen too much beauty and wonder beyond my little forest to ever go back to what I was. There is goodness in the world, and I want to see it. I want to live it."

Garrick's hand moved to his sword. Quietly. Almost reverently. "Wanting that kind of future is what sets you apart. It's easy to fight for survival, but fighting for something better, for others, that takes real courage."

"I've never seen a drop of selfishness in you, Selaina," Rykan said. "I wouldn't fear the power in you."

Selaina smiled faintly, though her heart still bore the weight of their journey. Her eyes flicked toward the trees, not breaking the conversation, but tracking the rhythm of danger.

The predator was real. But so were her fears.

And neither would control her. Not tonight.

Selaina glanced at the others, each lost in their own thoughts. Garrick, the seasoned soldier seeking redemption. Ysadora, torn between loyalty and disillusionment. Nadara, still something of a mystery. Hardened by loss, yes, but whether it was resolve or something else beneath her guarded exterior, Selaina couldn't yet tell. Kadin, ever the opportunist but proving himself time and again. And Rykan, steady and unwavering, her anchor in this storm of uncertainty.

For a moment, the silence spoke louder than words. The towering peaks of Kylinshan waited, shrouded in mist and mystery, promising answers and dangers in equal measure. Selaina looked up, the faint glow of her mark reflecting in Rykan's eyes as he met her gaze.

The doubts, the fears, they were still there. But so was hope. And for now, that was enough.

One by one, they all lay down to rest. The fire burned low, crackling softly as the last of the wood surrendered to ember. Garrick rolled onto his side, his back to the flames, but Selaina knew he wasn't planning to sleep. He had heard it too.

The quiet that followed the group settling wasn't natural. It was the hush of something watching.

Selaina lay still, her body calm but alert. Her fingers hovered near her bowstring, breath slowing. A faint scuff broke the silence, one footfall, weight distributed to muffle sound. Then another. She pictured it: low to the ground, lean, patient. Not rushing. Waiting for stillness. For isolation.

It was hunting.

Her pulse didn't race. She thought of Jeth, how he'd taught her to breathe with the forest, not against it. How to become a part of the world so completely that nothing noticed you until it was too late.

A soft, rhythmic click of claw on stone. Just outside the circle of light.

Selaina shifted, her movement disguised as someone curling in sleep. Her fingers brushed the arrow at her side, drawing it slowly. She didn't look at Garrick, but she felt him move too, the quiet tug of a knife leaving its sheath.

The plan didn't need words.

Another step. Closer now. Its breath rasped low, guttural. It didn't know she was awake. It didn't know its presence had been detected.

Selaina waited.

Another pause, just before the edge of the fire's glow.

Now.

In one fluid motion, Selaina rolled and rose to one knee, loosing her arrow into the dark. It struck with a wet thud and a sharp cry, a creature's voice, animal but intelligent, pierced the night.

Garrick was already moving, knife in hand. The shadows bucked as the creature lunged, wounded and wild. It burst into the firelight, feline in shape, but warped, stretched, like a child's drawing come horribly alive. Its limbs were too long, its back too arched. Dusky fur shifted in the light like smoke, and twin eyes glowed a pale green, set too wide on a face marked with jagged whisker lines that pulsed faintly like veins.

Its paws made no sound on the forest floor, even in pain. Garrick didn't wait for it to charge. His blade sank into its side, angled up between the ribs. The beast hissed and slumped into him with one last rattling breath.

Around the camp, rustling started, blankets shifting, weapons reached for. Rykan ran to Selaina's side.

Garrick leaned close, voice low. "You chose the wrong prey."

A final thrust, and it was over. Selaina let the air ease from her lungs, unaware she'd held it so long. The predator was gone, but her resolve remained.

"What in all of Galanor was that?" Kadin muttered, crouched low, crossbow drawn but now unnecessary.

"A shavarra," Garrick said, still crouched by the body. "Forest stalker. They hunt by sound, not movement. I haven't seen one since the ridgelands."

"It's horrifying," Ysadora said softly, "but strangely beautiful."

The creature's hide shimmered faintly in the firelight, a pattern of subtle markings, vaguely resembling thorned vines or coiling shadows, slithering beneath the surface of its fur like a reflection disturbed by wind.

Selaina stood beside Garrick, the tension still in her limbs, the bow heavy in her hand. The adrenaline left her slow to speak, but her gaze was steady.

Garrick stood beside her, wiping his blade.

Rykan came up next, a crooked grin tugging at the corner of his mouth. "You're terrifying," he said, voice low and full of a kind of awe. "Beautifully terrifying."

Selaina shot him a look, but the faintest smile betrayed her.

"That was impressive," Garrick said. "You did well tracking it in the dark."

"You taught me what to listen for," Selaina replied, her voice low, almost reverent.

He nodded. "And you trusted yourself."

They stood there a moment longer, watching the forest reclaim its stillness. Then Garrick crossed his arms loosely over his chest and gave her a rare, quiet smile, more respect than praise. "You're not just surviving anymore. You're starting to understand what it takes to protect others."

Selaina exhaled, the tension finally leaving her limbs. There was no glowing mark, no prophecy guiding her. Only instinct.

She wasn't Vatreus. She was Selaina. And she would hunt the darkness, one step, one arrow, at a time.

Later, while the others slept, her thoughts danced with the shadows. Somewhere beyond the horizon, answers waited. She only hoped she would be as ready to face them when they finally arrived.

CHAPTER 14

THE NIGHT PRESSED heavily upon the forest, its oppressive darkness broken only by the pale glow of a gibbous moon, its light filtering weakly through the tangled canopy like fractured silver. Beneath the gnarled, ancient trees sprawled an overgrown graveyard, its weathered tombstones jutting at odd angles, crooked relics to forgotten lives. Vines, thick and sinewy, coiled around the crumbling stone mausoleums, their iron gates hanging ajar, stained orange with rust and flaking in jagged edges. The air hung heavy with damp and cold, laden with the mingled scents of moss, decay, and something older, something steeped in ancient magic, sharp as ozone and elusive as a dream slipping away at dawn.

The forest had long since forgotten the dead, only the Sullen remembered where to feed. They moved like phantoms through the graveyard, their wraithlike forms shimmering faintly as they glided among the graves. They did not disturb the brittle leaves underfoot, their ethereal presence barely a whisper in the still night. The structure was unassuming, its stone walls weathered and cracked. Inside, the shadows deepened, a chill emanating from within. A simple iron gate, rusted and hanging ajar, offered no resistance as they slipped through.

The interior was cramped, the air dense and stale. Only three niches adorned the stone walls, each holding the remains of long-dead wizards. Their bones rested in silence, surrounded by small tokens of power: a staff, an amulet, and a collection of scrolls. The faint glow of ancient runes lingered in the cracks of the stone, casting the chamber in an eerie blue light.

One of the Sullen hovered over a niche, its clawlike hand extending toward a skeletal figure. The remains clutched a staff, its surface etched with faded sigils of protection. The wraith's fingers glowed faintly, and as it touched the staff, magic seeped from the artifact, spiraling into the Sullen's shadowy form. A low hiss escaped, the wraith shuddering with satisfaction as it absorbed the residual power.

Another Sullen turned its attention to an amulet lying among the scattered remains of another wizard. The amulet shimmered faintly, its once-potent magic reduced to an ember of its former strength. The wraith reached for it, drawing the power into its body with a sound like wind rushing through hollow stone.

The third wraith lingered near the scrolls, its skeletal hand brushing over their brittle surfaces. As it lifted one, the dormant runes flared briefly before fading, their magic drained in an instant. The faint crackle of disintegrating parchment filled the small chamber before falling into silence once more.

Then, without warning, the Sullen near the staff froze. Its form began to ripple unnaturally, a rasping gasp escaping from the darkness that obscured its face. The others turned, their forms recoiling as the afflicted wraith convulsed violently.

"Dazurel, what is happening to him?" one of the Sullen whispered, his voice a thin, ghostly rasp.

The convulsing Sullen collapsed to the ground, its form writhing and twisting grotesquely. Bones cracked and reshaped beneath its dark shroud, its limbs jerking unnaturally. A sickly blue mist poured from its body, rising like smoke to swirl in the stagnant air. The remaining Sullen shrank back, their shadowed forms trembling with unease.

Only one remained still: Dazurel.

Taller than the others, his form was more solid, anchored. The air bent subtly around him, as if recognizing something older. His voice, when it came, was low and layered. "The boundary's been breached."

The mist thickened, swirling faster, as the writhing Sullen let out a final, guttural wail. Its body split apart, the shadows of its form unraveling like torn fabric. From the center of the wraith's remains, a crimson portal erupted. The edges of the portal pulsed with chaotic energy, bathing the chamber in an ominous red light.

The Sullen cowered before the portal, even Dazurel's form dipping slightly in deference. Within the swirling depths of the portal, a dark shape stirred, vast, malevolent.

Even the boldest among them dared not draw closer. Not a door, but a wound in the skin of the world. A window into the chaos beyond, where their master's voice bled through.

"Did you truly believe you could escape my sight?" The voice boomed from the portal, discordant and layered as though a thousand anguished souls spoke in unison.

The remaining Sullen sank lower, bowing before the voice that seemed to press the very air around them.

"You were tasked with finding the Wishing Stone and bringing its power to me. Yet you failed," the voice thundered. "The stone's energy has been stolen by a mere girl!"

Dazurel did not bow fully. He lifted his head just enough to speak. "We sought the Conclave members as you commanded. The girl's interference was… unforeseen."

Lightning lashed out from the portal, striking the stone walls and leaving a jagged scorch mark. "Unforeseen? You dare speak of failure as if it excuses your incompetence? I was so close, so close to an artifact that would have allowed my manifestation into the mortal world. Your failure is unacceptable."

Another wraith knelt lower, its shadowy form trembling. "Great one, please! Give us another chance. We will find her and bring her to you."

The portal pulsed, its crimson glow deepening as the voice grew colder. "You do not deserve my mercy. Yet I will grant you one final chance. Know this: you are not alone in this hunt. My other servants now share your task. Only those who succeed will earn my favor. Fail me again, and your fates will be worse than oblivion."

The Sullen exchanged glances, their forms dimming briefly as they nodded in unison.

"We will not fail you, great one," one of them vowed.

Dazurel turned his head toward the others, but his tone remained steady. "We understand the stakes. We won't allow another failure."

A beat of silence followed, thick with expectation. Then the voice came again, deeper, colder.

"The girl now carries the power of the stone. Bring her to me, and you will return to my favor."

Then, as if offering them a final truth before departing, Nociferon's voice shifted, less command, more doctrine:

"No beginning. No end. Only will."

The words struck deeper than threat, something absolute. Final. Even the air seemed to recoil. The chamber fell still. A sigil flared beneath the fallen Sullen, pulsing once before the portal collapsed inward.

Without a word, the remaining Sullen retreated from the mausoleum, melting into the graveyard's shadows. The forest whispered with an unnatural wind, the pale moon casting cold light over the forgotten tombs. Somewhere beyond the graveyard's boundaries, their hunt began anew.

CHAPTER 15

A SOUND JOLTED RYKAN out of the dream, wood cracking on wood. Sitting up quickly, he found Garrick and Nadara engaged in a duel. They were practicing, moving slowly and more deliberately than they would in a real fight.

The dream faded, but something lingered, a faint metallic taste on his tongue, the scent of charred bone hanging in the air. Distantly, as if underwater, he could still hear whispers, words he didn't know, spoken in voices not entirely human. It wasn't the first time he'd seen the Sullen this way, like shadows burned into memory, but this time, the feeling clung to him longer, like frost on skin that refused to melt.

Ever since he had touched the faint glow coming from the withered tree in the mountains, since the energy had marked him, these visions came unbidden.

Not just dreams, but warnings.

They had spoken of her. Not with urgency, but with certainty. They were looking for Selaina.

He sat against a tree as pale light began to touch the horizon, the air still heavy with the weight of the dream. Across the fire, Selaina slept, her face more peaceful than he'd seen it in days.

His fingers dug lightly into the moss beside him. She was already juggling the pressure of destiny, the memory of what Myrradin had done, the fear that she might one day become like him, or worse, like Vatreus.

He couldn't be like Myrradin, hiding truths "for her own good."

Rykan ran a hand over his face, the bark rough against his back. He would tell her, just not yet.

His gaze returned to Selaina. She stirred, pulling the edge of her cloak more tightly around her shoulders, but didn't wake.

Rykan made his way over to Garrick and Nadara, watching as they sparred in the early morning light. Both were armed with wooden sticks, selected to be the closest approximation to their usual weapons. Nadara's was a longer, tapered staff, mimicking the reach and weight of her glaive. Garrick's was a shorter, heavier rod, shaped like a training sword.

Nadara lunged forward, thrusting her staff in a calculated strike toward Garrick's midsection. Her grip shifted effortlessly as she kept the staff moving, maintaining control over its longer reach. Garrick sidestepped, his wooden stick coming up just in time to deflect the blow with a sharp crack.

Garrick stepped to his left, just outside the staff's path. Nadara extended fully, her momentum carrying her forward and putting her slightly off balance. Unable to immediately retract her weapon, Nadara left herself open as Garrick executed a precise cut, his makeshift sword tapping lightly against Nadara's ribs.

"You overcommitted," Garrick said with a grin as he stepped back.

"I don't usually have to worry about moves like that," she conceded, a small smile breaking through her focus. "Let's go again."

Off to the side, not far from the dying embers of the fire, Rykan caught a glimpse of Selaina and Ysadora walking together in the clearing, but they quickly came to a stop. Selaina held her bow loosely, her stance relaxed but attentive, while Ysadora spoke low and deliberate, gesturing with one hand, the other hovering near Selaina's quiver. Rykan couldn't hear their words, but the air between them seemed charged, like the breath before lightning strikes. Selaina raised her bow, and as she released the arrow, Rykan swore he saw it shift in its flight, its angle subtly corrected in mid air. Ysadora nodded, her expression unreadable, but Rykan could tell by the way Selaina held herself afterward, shoulders lifted, breath caught, that something important had clicked. Magic, maybe. Or confidence. Or both.

Nadara and Garrick circled each other nearby with wary eyes and ready stances. Garrick sprang into action with a series of aggressive thrusts.

"Let's see how good your defense is," he said.

Nadara deflected his stick expertly with the shaft of her staff, using the length to keep him at bay.

"You're keeping your distance," Garrick remarked, circling her slowly. "Afraid I'll get inside your guard?" He rolled his shoulders and shifted his stance, his weight centering like someone always ready to react.

"I'm not afraid of anything," Nadara shot back, swinging the staff in a low arc.

Garrick blocked it with a deliberate parry, the impact vibrating through the air but neither losing their grip.

"You won't have the luxury of pulling strikes in a real fight," Garrick said, pressing forward with a series of short, controlled swings.

Nadara retreated a step to regroup. Each parry was controlled and precise, maintaining her balance.

"And you won't have the luxury of catching your breath," Nadara quipped, spinning the staff and driving him back with a quick jab to the chest.

Nadara initiated a feint, making a deceptive move as if to strike at Garrick's left. As he moved to block the expected attack, Nadara swiftly changed her angle, swinging the glaive in a wide sweeping motion to his right side, which was now less defended.

Garrick attempted to adjust, stepping back to regain his posture, and readied his wooden sword for a counter-strike. Nadara's reach and the speed of her adjustment gave her a fleeting but crucial advantage. As Garrick stepped back, Nadara advanced, shortening the arc of her swing to maintain pressure. With a swift, fluid motion, she lightly tapped Garrick's shoulder with the flat of her staff.

"See that coming?" Nadara teased.

"Now that's what I call artistry," Kadin said, clapping. "Though if this were a real fight, I'd suggest throwing in a bit more flair, maybe a backflip or a battle cry. Keeps the crowd entertained." He flipped a coin from one hand to the other, watching it spin as if gauging the odds of a rematch.

Garrick laughed heartily. "How long have you been fighting?" he asked his opponent.

Nadara paused, her gaze drifting to her glaive leaning against the tree. "Since I was very young," she replied, a small smile playing at her lips.

"When your mother forges weapons from dawn till dusk, you can't help but try them out as soon as you can lift them. She once told me: a good weapon doesn't flinch when the fight comes to it. She forged blades for warriors twice my size, but she always made me my own."

Garrick nodded, intrigued. "What made you choose a glaive, then?" he asked, gesturing towards the imposing weapon.

Nadara's eyes lit up with pride. "I was taught that your weapon should be like a part of you," she began, her voice taking on a reflective tone. "An extension of your body and spirit. For me, nothing else felt more right." She stepped toward the tree and took the weapon in her hands. "The first time I picked it up, it was almost magical. I knew it was my calling. It balanced perfectly with my own rhythm."

"Magical, huh?" Kadin mused, crossing his arms. "I once had a calling too. Turns out, it was to avoid anything sharp coming my way."

Rykan cleared his throat. His fingers ran along the hilt of his sword, a familiar gesture he did more out of thought than readiness. "You two sparring or trying to settle an argument?"

Garrick grinned, lowering his weapon slightly. "Depends. You want to join in?"

Rykan raised an eyebrow. "Why not? Might be worth reminding you both what real speed looks like."

Nadara smirked, stepping back to give him room. "Bring it on."

Rykan searched for a suitable limb from beneath the trees. Once he found something that would work, he stood ready, then launched into a whirlwind of movement as he darted forward with rapid slashing attacks. His stick moved in quick arcs, each swing followed by a sudden change in direction. Garrick maintained a tight defensive stance. He parried with minimum effort as he watched Rykan.

Increasing his intensity, Rykan unleashed a flurry of feints and high energy strikes, each faster than the last. His breathing grew heavier, his attacks a display of impressive speed. Garrick continued to defend, stepping back slightly with each of Rykan's advances, leading him on and making him extend further.

Rykan launched into a flurry of slashes and feints, his stick darting through quick arcs. Garrick parried with minimal effort, stepping back just enough to draw Rykan forward.

As he executed a particularly aggressive overhead strike, Rykan's muscles tensed up. Garrick seized the moment, stepping inside Rykan's reach, his stick sweeping low to tap against Rykan's leg.

Breathing heavily, Rykan stepped back, nodding in acknowledgment of Garrick's hit. He took a moment, hands on his knees, catching his breath.

Walking up to him, Nadara offered some advice, her tone constructive. "Your attacks are hard to predict, but you're not pacing yourself. Unpredictability isn't just about speed and power or where your attacks land, it's also about when they happen."

Frustrated, Rykan wiped the sweat from his brow. "Then how do I break through?"

"You don't, not by force," said Nadara. "Watch him. Wait. Even the best make mistakes, but only if you let them."

"He never makes mistakes," Rykan countered, his tone a mix of respect and irritation.

Selaina, who had been standing nearby, stepped closer. "We're wasting daylight," she said. "We should get moving."

"She's right," said Garrick, tossing his stick aside.

Rykan turned, unsure how long Selaina had been watching the match. His eyes met hers for just a moment, searching. She tilted her head, the faintest smile touching her lips, and gave a small nod. A quiet confirmation.

He didn't need her to say anything. That look said enough.

After covering the embers of the campfire, they gathered their things and set out through the forest. As they walked up the sloping terrain, Rykan wished that he had not expended so much energy practicing swordplay. The grassy forest began to give way to more rock and stone the further up they went.

The dream lingered, a dull pressure at the edge of his thoughts. Selaina drifted ahead slightly, her bow slung across her shoulder, eyes scanning the terrain. Rykan quickened his pace to fall into step beside her. His stance shifted unconsciously, standing a little taller, arms looser, face softer, until he noticed it and tucked the feeling away. The others were just behind them, close enough to hear if anyone shouted, but far enough for a bit of privacy.

"Selaina," Rykan said, keeping his tone steady, "I've been thinking about what lies ahead. We need to be ready for anything."

She glanced at him, a curious expression crossing her face. "What do you mean?"

"Our enemies won't sit idly by while we climb this mountain," he said. "We can't afford to let our guard down."

Selaina slowed her pace, considering his words. "You think Vatreus knows we're coming?"

Rykan's hand found the hilt of his sword. "It's not just Vatreus. We don't know who or what else might be watching. We need to be prepared, for anything."

Selaina adjusted the quiver on her back, her steps steady. "You're probably right. But we've faced dangers before, and we've made it this far."

Rykan nodded. "Just don't let your guard down. The closer we get, the harder they'll try to stop us."

She glanced at him again, more slowly this time. "I'll be careful. And I trust you to watch my back."

They walked in silence for several steps, the trail narrowing between rising stone.

Then, more quietly, Selaina added, "None of this is what I expected."

She paused, her gaze drifting toward the ridge ahead.

"When I left the forest, I was just trying to find my mother. I thought that would be the end of it, that everything would make sense once I found her. But things keep changing. The Wishing Stone. Darian… Elysia…" The name caught in her throat. "I still see her face sometimes. Just… how she looked at me. Like I mattered, even before any of this."

Rykan glanced toward her, but stayed quiet.

"I thought carrying this mark would mean I had answers. She let out a breath. "And then you."

Rykan looked over but still said nothing.

"I used to carry everything myself," she said, voice low. "But lately… it feels a little lighter when you're near."

Rykan's hand lifted halfway between them, then stopped. He curled it into a loose fist at his side instead, as if steadying himself.

His fingers flexed once, resisting the urge to bridge the small space between them. "Then I'll keep walking with you."

Their eyes met again, something quiet and steady passing between them.

Neither of them said another word as the trail twisted onward. The moment had passed, but it lingered, like warmth after the fire fades.

As they continued further up the mountain, the dense forest around them gradually began to change. What was once a thick carpet of fallen leaves and soft earth now showed signs of bare rock across the terrain. The air grew crisper, the scent of earth and moss shifting to a cooler, sharper bite.

The shade of the trees above them thinned, allowing more direct light from the sun. Signs of harsher conditions lay ahead, evidenced by the gnarled and twisted trees and exposed roots clawing into cracks in rock searching for soil. Large boulders, layered with moss and lichen, were strewn across the forest floor in patterns that indicated they had tumbled from the cliffs above.

Underfoot, the gravelly stone required more careful navigation as the ground became rougher and more challenging. Occasionally, the path would narrow dramatically, skirting dangerously close to sudden drops where the granite of the mountainside was exposed, like bones of the earth in jagged outcrops.

Their conversation quieted as they adapted to the changes with caution. Moving more slowly, they concentrated their attention on the terrain. At times they came to a stop to help each other on a particularly tricky section of the path or to take in the view that opened up through the thinning trees.

Garrick and Nadara helped point out less obvious trails or shortcuts through the rocks. Nadara's glaive proved useful for testing the stability of stones before stepping on them. Garrick's experience enabled him to predict shifts in the path or to find easier passage.

As they climbed higher, the sound of the wind changed. Whispers through pine needles and the hollow echo off stone replaced the rustling of leaves. The light grew harsher, the shadows sharper, and the smell of pine resin blended with the damp earthiness of the forest floor.

Nadara paused briefly, pulling a parchment from her bag. She unrolled it, scanned it quickly, then rolled it back up and tucked it away. Rykan had seen her look at it before, but curiosity finally got the better of him.

"Is that a map of the mountain?" he asked, falling into step beside her.

Nadara glanced at him. "It's a map of Galanor."

"May I see it?"

She hesitated, her hand tightening around the parchment in her bag. After a long moment, she took it out and unrolled it again, holding it open with care. Rykan leaned closer, his brow furrowing as he studied the intricate details.

Circles were marked across the map, scattered in seemingly random places but forming a loose pattern he couldn't quite decipher.

"What are these circles?" he asked.

"I'm not sure yet," Nadara replied. "But there's one here, on Kylinshan."

Rykan's gaze lingered on the mark. "You think Kylinshan holds the answer?"

Nadara nodded. "That's the plan."

"Where did you get this?"

"The stranger I told you about," Nadara said. "The one who died in my village. He was carrying this map."

"You said there was something unusual about him," Rykan asked. "What was it?"

"He avoided everyone, kept to himself, even skipped the markets and artisans. Strange enough for a traveler. Then one day, he was found dead under an old tree in the ruins of an ancient temple. No wounds, no marks. Just… dead."

"And this map was all he had?"

"Not all." Nadara reached into her bag, pulling out a jagged red crystal. The sunlight struck its many facets, casting shards of fractured light onto the ground.

The crystal seemed alive. Its surface shimmered, shifting subtly as though it were coated in molten fire. A faint hum emanated from it, low and steady, like a pulse that resonated in Rykan's chest. He took an involuntary step back.

"I've never seen anything like it," he said, his voice low.

Nadara's grip curled around the crystal. "Neither have I. But whatever it is, it's not something you want to hold for long."

As she tucked the crystal back into her bag, Rykan noticed the faintest trace of heat lingering in the air, as though the stone had been burning. The light that had danced on the ground moments earlier seemed slow to fade, leaving behind a ghostly glow that only added to its mystery.

"So you think this stone, and whatever happened to that man, are connected?" Rykan asked.

"A puzzle that I haven't quite pieced together yet," Nadara admitted, her voice quieter now. "I did learn that the stone is called Embryss. Whatever it is, it must be important."

A bend in the trail revealed a cluster of low brush clinging to the mountain's edge. Just beyond it, the terrain dipped and widened again, but the silence was broken before they could take another step.

"Careful where you place those boots, young one!" a wavering voice exclaimed. "You nearly trampled a patch of skyroot!"

Startled, Rykan halted, his eyes locking on the elderly figure up ahead. The man was short and stocky, his frame sturdy even with age. His hands, calloused and thick-fingered, moved deftly as he adjusted the soil around the delicate plants. The coarse gray tunic he wore was patched in places, layered with a sleeveless vest made of rough wool that had clearly seen many seasons. His boots, scuffed and cracked but solid, hinted at a lifetime spent navigating the rugged terrain.

The man's face was deeply lined, his weathered skin resembling the craggy cliffs of the mountain. A neatly trimmed gray beard framed his square jaw, and his dark eyes, sharp and piercing, had the look of someone who noticed every detail. A broad leather belt around his waist held an assortment of tools, small knives, pouches, and a wooden mallet, all practical and well used. His presence seemed as rooted and enduring as the mountain itself, as though he had sprung from its very stone.

Rykan could only stare, the old man's sudden appearance as improbable as the plants he so carefully tended.

The man straightened, brushing dirt from his hands. "You've got sharp eyes for a cliff trail, but none at all for what's under your feet. That's a rare trait, dangerous, depending on where you're headed."

Rykan exchanged a glance with Nadara, uncertain whether to apologize or ask a question.

The old man squinted at them for a beat, then gave a small, knowing nod. "Hm. You're not from these parts, I take it. But the mountain's watching you anyway."

He turned back to his plants. "Be mindful where you walk, boy. The roots remember more than you think."

CHAPTER 16

THE MOUNTAIN SOFTENED here, as if bowing to something older than stone. As the old man knelt among the jagged rocks, his gnarled fingers deftly worked the soil, loosening it around the base of a sturdy, green-stemmed plant crowned with serrated leaves. Selaina watched him intently, her hand resting lightly on the string of her bow, the taut fibers humming faintly with the tension of her grip.

Tension that coiled in her fingertips as her gaze tracked the shadows beneath the overhanging rocks. Each of the man's movements was slow but precise, the kind of deliberate care honed over a lifetime. With a careful tug, he drew the plant free, its bulbous roots emerging from the earth, still clinging to strands of damp soil. He paused, brushing the roots clean with methodical patience, as if handling something precious. Then, with a measured breath, he placed it in his satchel, the quiet rustle of fabric the only sound breaking the stillness.

The man had a slightly elongated face with high cheekbones and a silver beard. His eyes were a light golden brown, with a narrow upward tilt at the outer corners. He finished plucking the plants in one area and then came closer to them. He stood still for a moment, looking at them as he tapped the fingers of one hand against his opposite elbow.

The man's gaze caught hers, and something shifted behind her eyes. Her strange gift of seeing others' thoughts… It was like being pulled gently beneath the surface of still water.

At first, the images were grounded in the present—his weathered hands cradling a clay jar, etched with flowing water patterns. His steps, deliberate, tracing worn paths through a village. Whispers of Shadal's people passed around him like wind. His thoughts were weighted with worry, fading water, uncertain days.

Then, something shifted. The faint rustle of leaves deepened into a low, rhythmic sound, steady and resonant. Selaina glimpsed the shimmer of sunlight rippling across golden scales and felt, for a fleeting moment, an ancient sorrow of impossible depth.

"Well… aren't you going to move?" the old man asked as he reached toward a cluster of leafy plants growing between the rocks. The words were casual, almost absentminded, but there was a sharpness just beneath them, a cold glint buried in the gravel of his voice.

Selaina and the others instinctively stepped back, giving him space. She glanced at the others, half-expecting someone to question him, but no one did. Maybe they were as caught off guard as she was. Or maybe they simply respected the quiet authority in his voice.

As they moved to continue up the trail, his voice followed them. "You could help me, you know?"

Selaina paused, turning back slowly. "Help how?"

"You see an old man on his knees gathering skyroot, and you have to ask?" he replied, not unkindly, but with the dry bite of someone used to being ignored.

Rykan took a step toward her, folding his arms, not protectively, exactly, but present.

Selaina studied the man for a long moment. She didn't know him, or this plant, or this place. Part of her wanted to move on, to stay focused on the summit. They had a purpose. A path.

But something in the quiet steadiness of his hands, the way he treated the root like something sacred, made her pause. She didn't understand its significance, but she knew what it meant to tend something fragile. To be asked for trust with no explanation.

Her boots shifted on the stone. Then, with a breath, she stepped forward. "I suppose you want me to pick the rest of these for you."

"Only one more," the man said, standing slowly. "But skyroot requires a delicate hand. You must keep everything intact. If you break it, it won't keep… not that most notice such things anymore."

Selaina glanced at the other stalks, their jagged leaves rustling faintly in the breeze. "I'm not sure I can," she admitted. "But I'll try."

"If you cannot pick skyroot," the old man said, "how do you expect to reach the summit?"

Selaina knelt beside the plant, brushing away loose soil. The earth was cool and soft beneath her fingertips. Her thoughts quieted, not in fear, but in focus.

The old man knelt beside her. "Grasp the stem firmly, but gently. You mustn't force it. It's about guiding it. Respecting it."

Selaina nodded, her brow furrowed. "Like guiding someone who doesn't yet know they're ready."

He didn't respond. But his silence felt like agreement.

She let her fingers move slowly, tracing the root's shape beneath the soil. There was a pattern to it, soft, subtle. A rhythm. A melody. Not as mesmerizing as the pulses in Wekenwild, but more… harmonious. Balanced.

Her breath steadied. She loosened the earth in gentle spirals until the root shifted beneath her touch.

Then, slowly, she lifted it free.

The roots came up whole, fine and delicate, glistening with moisture and clinging strands of rich soil. She held the plant in her palm, surprised at how light it was… and how much it felt like something important.

"Good," he said. "You listened. At least you did that. You respected its path. Remember this, young traveler: the way you treat the smallest root may reflect how you handle the steepest mountains."

"Who are you?" Selaina asked as the man began to make his way up the sloping terrain.

"My name is Oran," the old man said. "I come from the village of Shadal."

"Village?" said Selaina, following him as he passed by the others. "Are they friendly? Do they welcome outsiders?"

"We are as friendly as you are to us," Oran said, with a tone that wasn't unfriendly, but not open either. "If you need rest, I will take you there."

"Thank you," said Selaina. "That would be most kind of you."

"Many come up this path with hope on their faces," said Oran. "Most leave in silence… If they leave at all."

"Is it that dangerous?" Selaina asked.

"The path to the summit of Kylinshan is challenging," said Oran. "If you come seeking the blessing of the Sky Serpents, it would not be worth the trouble."

"It's already been dangerous," said Selaina. "When we got to Alisaran, it had been taken over by the Iron Flood. Their banners fly over the town square. It's a stronghold now."

Oran paused, his brow furrowing, then shook his head dismissively. "The lowlands burn with their own wars. The mountain remains. That's always been enough, for those who know its true worth."

"But what if they do come?" Selaina pressed. "If they gain full control over the area, they could cut off access to the mountain entirely, or worse."

"The mountain is not so easily claimed," Oran said, his tone calm but firm. "Shadal has stood for centuries, hidden and protected by Kylinshan itself. The Iron Flood will find little of interest here."

"Little of interest?" Selaina's frustration seeped into her voice. "They've already seized Alisaran. Do you really believe they'll stop there?"

Oran regarded her for a long moment, his expression unreadable. "Perhaps. Perhaps not. But the concerns of the lowlands are not ours. The mountain has its own ways of dealing with threats."

A flare of heat rose in her chest. She looked away, jaw clenching. His indifference stung, but she reminded herself that his life and worldview were deeply tied to the mountain.

"I hope you're right," she said quietly. "Because if you're wrong, Shadal could be next."

"Is that why you have come to Kylinshan?" Oran said. "To persuade us to join your fight?"

"I was called here," Selaina said, removing the hood of her cloak. "I have the mark of Zhal Evurah."

Oran stared at the mark. His silence stretched a beat too long. He lowered his head just slightly, his gaze narrowing, not in skepticism, but as if weighing something vast and unseen. "Many have believed themselves destined. That has always been the mountain's favorite jest. Since Ethyllion's fall, none have left these heights with a light heart. The mountain keeps its own counsel, and the serpents… they don't bestow the Crown of Breath lightly."

"Sounds like a polite way of saying we're wasting our time," Kadin said, crossing his arms as he glanced at the looming peaks.

Selaina didn't flinch. "I didn't come with a light heart," she said quietly. "I carry the hopes of Galanor with every step I take. If the serpents truly see into a person's heart, then they already know why I'm here."

"What would it take for the Sky Serpents to return?" asked Rykan

Oran paused, his eyes scanning the horizon as if searching for an ancient truth hidden among the peaks. "Perhaps something that was lost long ago, perhaps nothing can," he replied slowly. "But if they do come… it will not be because they were called."

As Oran took the lead, guiding the group through the increasingly rugged terrain, the journey up the mountain intensified. The path wound precariously along the outer edges of sheer cliffs, occasionally breaking into gentle upward slopes. Below, the once grassy landscape transitioned into stark, rocky terrain enveloped by a thick, swirling mist that seemed to whisper secrets of old.

Above them, imposing granite formations jutted out like the spines of some great beast, casting long shadows over the narrow pathways. The group maneuvered carefully between massive boulders, their surfaces slick with moisture from the mist, which clung to everything with a cold persistence.

As they progressed, the air grew cooler and the path less forgiving. They came to a wider open space where Oran made his way near the edge of a cliff wall. Most of the others found boulders to sit on and rest, while Selaina followed him. He brushed debris from a great statue of a man carved out of one of the granite formations. The old man bowed his head for a moment and closed his eyes.

Selaina waited for him to open them again before she spoke. "Who is this?"

"The first of those who carried us," he said. "Ordained through Ethyllion to balance the world between order and chaos."

"You mean Zhal Evurah?" Selaina asked.

"Yes, his name was Marduron," said Oran. "Like you, he was a lith. He was known as a splitter of winds."

"What does that mean?" Selaina asked.

"I am not certain," said Oran. "It is said that, nine thousand years ago, the world was overrun with beings called tyrasaurs, who began to destroy the ecosystems of the world. Their population grew as they needlessly slaughtered, bringing many races to extinction. The celestials could not intervene. Through Ethyllion, they appointed an emissary to act on their behalf. Sadly, the tyrasuars had to be wiped out to allow the world to flourish again. Marduron led the war against what seemed impossible odds, but he prevailed, and we stand here now, because of what he and those allied with him did so long ago."

"How does this happen in the first place?" Selaina asked. "If there is supposed to be order in the world or a balance, how is all this darkness and chaos allowed to flourish?"

"Because we are allowed to choose what paths we take," said Oran, "and many times, we don't choose what we need, but what we want."

"If people keep choosing things that lead to the suffering of others… maybe they shouldn't get to keep choosing," Selaina said, then hesitated. "I know that's not fair. I've made choices too. But there has to be a point where someone says, enough."

Oran looked blankly in the distance as if searching his thoughts. "In the times long forgotten, there were two rivers flowing from the sacred peak of Mount Sianyu. The first river meandered slowly through the lush valley, nurturing the earth and the communities along its banks. It was deliberate and kind, bringing life wherever it flowed. The second river ran swiftly toward the plains, its course wild and untamed. Often it would flood the lands, destroying crops and homes in its impetuous rush."

Selaina listened, her brow furrowed as she absorbed the imagery.

"The sage of Mount Sianyu, a man of great wisdom, observed these rivers from his high retreat," Oran continued. "He taught his followers, saying, 'Behold the rivers, for they are like the hearts of men. One river reflects the soul that tempers its strength with wisdom, enriching the world around it. The other, while powerful and majestic, often acts without foresight, leading to turmoil and loss.'"

Oran glanced at Selaina and pressed on.

"A young disciple once asked this sage if they should build a dam to restrain the reckless river, to prevent its floods. The sage responded with a gentle shake of his head, and said, 'To control it fully is to deny its nature. It must find its way, learning from its sister river, yet we cannot hasten its journey. For who are we to decide its path? Who among us is so virtuous that he can judge the river without first understanding the source of its rush?'"

Oran paused as if allowing his words to sink in.

"This is the essence of free will," he explained softly. "Every soul must choose its path, and while some choices lead to hardship, the freedom to make these choices is sacred. Just as with the rivers, people must learn from their journeys, guided, but never forcefully controlled."

Selaina pressed her lips together, her gaze drifting to the mist-veiled cliffs. She remembered the vision of the world Myrradin would have created if he had acquired enough power. A world of complete order where no one had their own will. They would go about performing tasks as drones. It may have been more efficient, but there was a huge price to pay for that.

"But then, that history shows that their choices lead to needing to send someone to destroy them in order to save the world," Rykan said.

"On rare occasions, yes," said Oran. "But we must allow everyone to make choices, it is the only way to learn and grow. If they do not learn, they sometimes must be removed."

Near the cliff's edge, Selaina looked out over the world below. Galanor stretched wide before her, vast and humbling. Living in her secluded forest, she never imagined the world was this big. Through the mist clinging to the mountain, Selaina spotted a pattern of objects in the yellow plains below.

As she watched, the objects seemed to move slowly across the field between distant trees. "What is that?" she asked.

"An army," said Oran. "Moving in formation."

Garrick and the others came over, taking a look for themselves. "The Iron Flood is on the move," he said. "Heading further south."

"You see," said Oran. "The army is moving away from Kylinshan. We have nothing to fear."

"Likely soldiers that stopped in Alisaren for the night," said Garrick. "They're not leaving it."

"So you'll ignore the rest of Galanor," said Selaina. "As long as the trouble stays beyond your borders?"

"That is not what I mean," said Oran. "If we leave Shadal behind for another's war, we may save no one. Not them. Not ourselves. We have resources to manage and protect, our own people have expectations. If our warriors leave, the Glissarans would take our village. You're asking us to abandon everything we value."

"By the time they come for you," said Selaina, "you might be standing alone."

"Where were they when Glissara came down from the peaks?" Oran asked. "When they took our water? Left us with so little to grow crops that we have to hunt for every bit of food."

"Who is Glissara?" Selaina asked.

"The village farther up the mountain," said Oran. "They'd use any weakness to their advantage."

"Their numbers look larger than I thought," Nadara said, eyes on the valley.

"Either they have grown, or they are risking the defenses of the territory they hold," said Ysadora.

"Where do you think they're heading?" Rykan asked.

"There are many cities in the south," Garrick replied. "It seems Vatreus has grown impatient. Like Ysadora said, if he's throwing his full force south, this could be his fatal mistake."

Rykan clenched his jaw. "If he leaves Tathara undefended, the people could rise up and retake it. We need to be down there with them."

"The six of us wouldn't make much difference," said Kadin. "But Selaina acquiring the power she needs? That could turn the tide."

"They are using my home for weapons and supply," said Nadara. "We could pull that out from under them."

"Vatreus wouldn't make that kind of blunder," Garrick said. "They wouldn't abandon their new territory without making it difficult to retake."

The wind tugged at Selaina's cloak as she stepped forward. "We need to be patient If we rush in without thinking, we risk everything. Climbing this mountain as planned gives us the best chance to make a real difference. But we won't take unnecessary risks to get there."

Garrick nodded. "She's right. Rushing south now could play into Vatreus's hands."

Rykan sighed. "It feels wrong to just stand here while they suffer."

"I understand." The mist curled at her ankles as Selaina turned toward him. "But sometimes the biggest advantage is waiting for the right moment."

"Then let's get moving," Kadin interjected, his voice breaking the tension. "Every minute we linger, we fall further behind."

"I was ready before you started looking at the view," said Oran as he moved away from the statue, crossing the stony field.

As Selaina began to follow Oran across the uneven ground, the group fell into a slow, careful rhythm, picking their way between moss-covered stones and patches of loose shale.

Kadin walked a few paces ahead of Ysadora, idly flipping a dagger between his fingers. Her staff struck a steady rhythm against the rock, weaving through the steps of their boots. "If you ever want tips on how to look intimidating with a stick," he said over his shoulder, "I do offer private lessons."

After a moment, Ysadora said flatly, "I imagine most of your students end up stabbed."

"Only the slow ones," Kadin replied, flashing a grin.

From behind, Selaina caught the faintest twitch of a smile at the corner of Ysadora's mouth, gone in an instant, but real.

The field of jagged rocks gave way to a staircase carved into the mountain itself. Some steps were smooth and precise; others looked careless, hacked in haste or worn by time.

As they climbed, Oran leaned against the irregular rock formations that flanked the staircase, his hand tracing the cool, weathered surfaces. Selaina found herself mimicking his actions, using the rocks for support where the steps grew perilous. The air thickened with a dense, swirling mist that clung to their clothes and skin, cloaking the path ahead in a ghostly veil. Visibility dwindled to a few feet, and the world reduced to the immediate roughness of granite beneath their hands and the eerie silence interrupted only by the distant call of a hidden bird or the soft whisper of the wind.

Towering spires of granite rose like the petrified trunks of an ancient, titanic forest, silent and immovable.

Lichens and small, hardy bushes clung to their crevices, and in some places, the rock faces were smoothed by centuries of wind and rain, reflecting a silvery sheen that rippled with the movement of the mist.

Above them, the steps continued to ascend, disappearing into the thickening fog that seemed to hold secrets as old as the mountain itself. Each step taken on the uneven path took them deeper into the heart of a landscape shaped by time, elements, and the hands of forgotten ancestors. After reaching a plateau, they saw another statue standing nearby. A man raising a sword above his head in triumph.

"Who is that one?" Selaina asked.

Oran glanced at the statue but didn't slow his pace. His mouth drew into a tight line, and his eyes barely lingered on the stone figure before flicking away, dismissive.

"Voreth," he said, the name dropping from his lips like something bitter. "One of the first to come to Kylinshan after the three celestials were changed into Sky Serpents, allowing them to bless Zhal Evurah with the power they needed to balance the world."

He gestured vaguely toward the statue, but didn't look back.

"There were pockets of energy left over from the formation of the world. Raw creation. Chaotic, and in need of order. For reasons we may never know, it began to erupt again, violently. Voreth came forth, chosen from those beyond the stars. Wielding the power gifted by the serpents, he was to bind those forces, stabilize them. Restore peace to Galanor."

The bitterness in Oran's voice didn't match the reverence of his tale. Was it betrayal? Shame?

"Why do you say his name like that?" Selaina asked quietly. "With such... disdain?"

"He may have saved the world," Oran said. "But in time, he became one of its greatest threats. His rise to fame led to selfishness and arrogance. Voreth wanted all kingdoms to bow to him. He had a great palace built in his honor, as well as a grand throne where he demanded everything be made to serve him. As the kingdoms began to rise up in opposition, even his own army turned against him. We honor him for saving Galanor, but his fall is held as a lesson to anyone seeking power."

"That sounds familiar," said Rykan. "But I didn't think Zhal Evurah could become something like that."

"He was not the only one to become an enemy," said Oran. "But he was probably the worst."

"How many others?" Selaina asked.

"Five or six that I can think of," said Oran. "Maybe more, not all agreed that they turned to selfish ways. Some helped their kingdoms in disputes and wars afterward. Those kingdoms would say they were only doing what must be done."

"What made them become like that?" Selaina asked. "What should they have done differently?"

"They forgot the glory was never theirs," Oran said. "They were only the vessel. That's what every Zhal Evurah must remember."

The wind shifted, carrying a biting chill as the group stood in silence. Selaina traced a finger along the cold granite at her side, but her thoughts remained with Oran's words. She couldn't help but feel the weight of the destinies she had taken on, were they truly hers to claim? The trail ahead seemed steeper now, its dangers not just in the climb but in what awaited her at the summit. Would the Sky Serpents see her as an imposter, or something worse?

CHAPTER 17

T HE MOUNTAIN DID more than test, it measured them. Longing to rest his weary feet, Rykan picked his footing with increasing care, each step a deliberate choice on the unforgiving terrain. The mountain offered no comfort, only distance and silence. The uneven ground tugged at muscles he hadn't strained in years, sending dull aches radiating through his calves and knees. The carved stairs, though a welcome reprieve in places, were treacherously uneven, some barely rising above the path, others demanding a full climb. Beyond the edges of the trail, jagged rock spires pierced the misty clouds, looming like solitary mountains crowned with slender evergreens.

Voices echoed faintly down from the stone steps ahead. A group of weary travelers appeared through the mist, their cloaks ragged, their faces drawn with exhaustion. One of them, a broad-shouldered man with a frayed scarf wound tight around his neck, raised a hand in warning.

"Turn back," he said. "There's nothing up there."

Selaina narrowed her eyes. "You came seeking the Sky Serpents?"

"We came, we waited, we prayed," a woman muttered beside him, her voice brittle with frustration. "Three days in the summit caverns, calling to the sky, and nothing but silence. If they were ever real, they've long since turned their backs on us."

Another traveler spat to the side. "They say the serpents favored only one village. That the blessing was meant for a man who betrayed them. That's why they stopped coming."

A third traveler leaned on his walking staff. "They weren't celestials at all. Just mortals like us, transformed, some say punished, others say blessed."

Another shook his head. "No. They weren't punished. They rose above. They chose to become more than mortal."

Selaina's jaw tensed. Rykan noticed it immediately. "We'll decide that for ourselves," he said.

The group passed them without another word, descending the way Selaina and the others had climbed. Their footsteps vanished into the mist, leaving only the distant sound of falling stones and fading disbelief.

"What if they're right?" she murmured. "What if the serpents are gone, and all I have is… this mark?"

"None of them were Zhal Evurah," Rykan said. "You are. That's the difference."

The trees stood improbably tall, their roots clutching the sheer stone as if defying gravity itself, their dark-green needles shimmering faintly in the pale light.

Fierce-looking birds glided near the peaks. Watching them, Rykan felt heavier, bound by gravity and flesh. Their calls echoed commandingly across the jagged mountain walls. Sounds of gathering rocks rolling and sliding down gave Rykan pause. He covered his head as the larger pebbles bounced off the steps into the mist below.

As the trail rose into thinner air, Rykan's ears clogged with pressure, leaving him uncomfortably off balance. Below, the world vanished into swirling mist, and the mountain stretched onward, bare and exposed. A sudden wind sliced through his fur-lined cloak, and he instinctively drew it tighter, silently thanking the woman in Alisaran for offering it to him.

The stone stairs ended abruptly, giving way to a plateau of hardy grasses and scattered boulders. Ahead, a walled village stood nestled against the base of an imposing cliff wall, its wooden gate open. Shadal crouched in the mountain's shadow, not humbled, but hardened by it.

As the group approached, Rykan could make out the compact, sturdy buildings clustered within the walls. Stone block foundations supported tall, narrow wooden structures with steep, shingled roofs designed to withstand the mountain's harsh weather. Shadal's buildings were solid and practical, built with function in mind. Many structures were two or three stories high, their upper levels adorned with simple carvings that hinted at the strength and pride of their people. But even pride bore the wear of waiting too long.

The villagers were short and stocky, their frames hardened by the mountain itself. They moved with the quiet confidence of people who labored not for show, but because survival demanded it. Most wore practical, heavy clothing in muted earth tones, reinforced with leather accents. A man hoisted a bundle of firewood over his shoulder as if it were kindling, his steps steady and unhurried. A group of children darted by, laughing as they hauled water from a nearby hole. Even joy here moved with purpose, built for steep roads and cold wind.

As Rykan's gaze wandered, he caught sight of several warriors stationed at key points along the village's perimeter. They stood still as statues, their postures exuding a quiet vigilance. Each was armed with a long spear tipped with blackened steel, the hafts carved with intricate patterns that seemed to ripple in the light. Their dark leather armor blended almost seamlessly with the rugged terrain, making them seem like part of the mountain itself. Though their expressions were calm, Rykan noted the way their sharp eyes tracked every movement, scanning the horizon as if expecting trouble. Not nervous, not afraid, just certain it would come.

One warrior's gaze flicked toward their group, pausing momentarily on Rykan before shifting away. Rykan felt tension in his shoulders, the unspoken acknowledgment of being watched by those who took their roles seriously. He found himself instinctively adjusting the strap of his scabbard, his hand brushing the hilt of his sword as if to remind himself of its presence.

"You have a lot of soldiers for a village that isn't concerned about the Iron Flood," Selaina said, her tone probing but measured.

Oran didn't break his stride, his gaze fixed ahead as he replied. "As I told you, our battles are not with those in the lowlands," he said calmly. "But with the Glissarans of Kylinshan. Though we have a truce, our quarrels go back a few thousand years and skirmishes crop up from time to time, even now. Our soldiers are more of a deterrent than anything else, a reminder that, if they try to take our village, their losses would be devastating. I have long held hope for a lasting peace, but we must remain vigilant."

Rykan frowned, glancing between Oran and the stationed warriors. The spears, the watchful eyes, everything about their readiness seemed like overkill for a truce.

Bright blue and yellow flowers adorned some of the windowsills, their cheerful hues standing in contrast to the village's otherwise rugged appearance. The faint clang of hammers echoed from a smithy, where two burly workers pounded red-hot iron into shape. The scent of wood smoke and freshly turned earth filled the air, mingling with the distant tang of pine.

The cobblestone street wound through the village like a forgotten stream, and Rykan followed it in quiet thought. Nadara paused to speak with a woman carrying a wooden bucket of water, her arms flexing under its weight as if she carried it every day without thought. Selaina and Oran stopped to talk to a passerby, but Rykan's attention was drawn to the subtle details of the village. It was as if every corner of Shadal spoke of resilience and strength, a place built to endure whatever the mountains threw at it.

"The steeply sloped roofs of your buildings," Nadara said, gesturing toward the structures around them. "Do they have a particular significance?"

"We get heavy snow here during the later seasons," the woman replied. "The slopes help it slide off so it doesn't collapse the roof."

"Snow," Nadara repeated, her tone thoughtful. "I've never seen it."

"Neither have I," Rykan added, glancing at Nadara.

"You'll see plenty of it if you keep heading higher," the woman said with a faint smile. "It snows year-round further up the mountain. Safe travels."

Nadara thanked her and continued studying the buildings around them.

"Impressive, I'll give them that," Kadin remarked, tapping one of the stone walls with his knuckles. "But I can't help wondering, do they build this way because they're strong, or because they're stubborn? Sometimes, survival's just a matter of knowing when to leave."

Further into the village, the cliff wall opened into a monumental stairway, stone steps carved directly into the mountainside. At its summit stood a vast archway flanked by unlit torches. The structure looked less built than unearthed, its stone columns echoing the cliff's natural striations. A vaulted interior loomed just beyond the threshold, hinting at a space meant not only for shelter, but for legacy.

As they continued, Rykan noticed how the villagers carried themselves. Every movement was precise, efficient, not rushed. As if the mountain had taught them how to survive one gesture at a time.

Rykan and Nadara exchanged a glance, then moved forward together, drawn on by the sheer scale and purpose etched into the stone. This wasn't just a building, it was a statement of who the Shadalans were.

"Wait," said Oran. "If you are going to the Stonehold, allow me to take you. We do not take kindly to outsiders in certain places unless they are accompanied."

Rykan turned to Nadara. "Oh, I just wanted to look," he said.

Oran shook his head. "The Stonehold is sacred to our people. It's a place of both governance and protection. Outsiders showing up without a local guide might be seen as a challenge, or worse, a threat. This is our history. Some things are irreplaceable."

His gaze lingered briefly on Selaina, eyes narrowing, not with suspicion, but with a kind of careful calculation. Almost as if he were measuring something only he could see. Then he gave a small nod to himself and turned back to the path.

"Then by all means, lead the way," Nadara said, her tone measured but curious. "I'd rather not make enemies before we've even said hello."

Selaina nodded, glancing at Oran. "We're grateful for your help. We don't want to make this any harder than it needs to be."

Oran gestured for them to follow, leading them toward the carved stone steps that ascended toward the imposing structure in the cliff. As they went past, villagers paused their work to watch, their guarded expressions underscoring Oran's warning.

Rykan slowed to allow Oran to pass him. He watched Selaina's eyes widen as she took in the sight. Garrick, Ysadora, and Kadin moved in line with them as well, eager to see this wonder more closely. They stepped through the archway into cool, dim light. The scent of old stone mingled with faint traces of incense. Flickering torches lined the corridor, shadows dancing across bas-reliefs etched into the walls, scenes of mountain life, celestial myths, and seasons of harvest.

The passage opened into a grand antechamber. At the far end, two statues stood in solemn contrast. One, pristine and broad-shouldered, bore the resolute expression common to the Shadalans. The other, a tall, slender woman, was cracked and worn by time. Her arms stretched outward, not in command but in welcome, an ancient gesture of peace, worn soft by centuries of wind and silence.

Around the chamber's edge stood a small group of elders, their robes simple but marked with silver thread. They didn't speak, only watched, present not as guards, but as witnesses. Their solemn presence gave the space a quiet weight, as if they were keepers of memory more than ceremony.

One of the villagers eyed Rykan as he came closer to the statues. The man looked past Rykan at Oran, then on to the others before looking back at Rykan. With questions filling his head, Rykan felt he should vocalize them as if to explain his interest in the statues.

"What happened to this one?" Rykan asked as he stood before the statue of a tall slender woman.

One of the villagers approached. "That is Talia. Once beloved in Shadal... until she forgot who she was."

Selaina glanced at the statue. "Forgot?"

"She was born in Glissara, married Doran, a man of iron will and clearer eyes than most," the man continued. "Together, they brought peace between Shadal and Glissara. And when the Sky Serpents came, they honored both of them for their unity. But Talia... she didn't stay balanced. She favored Glissara. After Doran died, she ruled from their temple."

Another voice, an elder's, cut in, low and bitter. "While Glissara built shrines in her name, we rationed water and buried sons and daughters. Her children abandoned Shadal entirely. Left us dry while they carved rivers through their gardens."

"Just as her statue has been neglected to time and decay," said Oran. "The bond she fostered has thinned to myth, hardly remembered at all."

Another elder spoke, voice gravelly. "But we still honor Doran. The Sky Serpents favored his strength. They say Verantis wept when Doran died. Not out of sorrow, but respect."

Selaina stood still, staring at the statue of the woman. One wrist had broken clean through, the outstretched hand missing entirely, as if history had severed her offering mid-reach, leaving only the ache of what was meant. Something about the way Selaina looked at it made Rykan uneasy.

Not afraid, just… solemn. As if she was seeing something in the crumbling figure that the others couldn't.

Her hand rose slowly to her brow, brushing just above her eyes where the mark rested, still hidden by the edge of her hood.

Rykan watched her, caught in the quiet gravity of her gesture. For a moment, her eyes flicked to his, just briefly, but it was enough. There was no fear in them, no doubt. Just the ache of someone wondering if they'd be remembered the right way. If they'd leave behind something more than fractured stone.

He gave her the smallest nod. It wasn't quite reassurance, more like solidarity. He didn't know what she was thinking, not fully. But he understood the weight of what she carried. He saw it, even when she didn't say a word.

Garrick stepped forward, gesturing to a smaller statue tucked near the rear wall, less central, worn nearly smooth by time and weather. "And who's that?" he asked.

An elder turned his head, his face softening with quiet reverence. "Few ask about him anymore. That was the last Zhal Evurah," he said. "He's not remembered for speeches or battles, but for a single act that saved us all."

"What did he do?" Rykan asked.

"He was the first to use the Wishing Stone," the elder replied. "He moved backward through the order of time and prepared the Chamber of Facets, where Ethyllion once stood, deep in the mountains of Nordravin. He wove powerful magic into its walls. So when Azragul shattered Ethyllion and crossed into our world, the trap was already waiting."

The elder paused, brushing dust from the statue's shoulder with unexpected care. "He changed fate to give Galanor a chance."

Oran's gaze lingered on the worn edges of the carving. "And who knows what he set into motion," he said quietly.

"I don't know about everyone else, but I for one am exhausted," said Kadin. "Where might we find comfortable accommodations?"

Oran stepped forward. "You can stay with me. My home has space for you all, provided you honor the hearthshare."

"That is very generous of you," Rykan said. "But what is hearthshare?"

"We don't ask for coin from travelers if they need to stay the night,"

Oran said, turning on his heel. "But we do ask them to be one of us for a time. Working alongside us, sharing effort and skills. That is hearthshare."

"A fair charge," Kadin said, his tone wry. "Though I'd prefer if it doesn't involve mucking stables. Perhaps a tale or two would suffice?"

"You may offer what you will," Oran said, turning to lead them onward. "But remember, your choice will show not only your skill, but the shape of your spirit."

CHAPTER 18

Rykan and the others followed Oran out into the heart of the village. The bustling streets hummed with quiet purpose. Villagers moved with efficiency, their work precise and unhurried. Scanning the scene, Rykan watched for any sign of someone in need of help, but the people seemed to anticipate one another's needs, their actions flowing seamlessly together.

Some of the smaller shops had missing shingles, and other buildings showed signs of wear, damaged boards weathered by years of mountain storms. Rykan wasn't an expert carpenter, but he had learned enough in his schooling to handle basic repairs. This seemed like the perfect opportunity to leave a positive mark on the village.

"Garrick, do you think we could make some repairs on those buildings?" Rykan asked, pointing to the damaged structures.

"I don't see why not," Garrick replied. "I've done my share of rebuilding."

"You'll need me for this too," Nadara said, stepping closer.

Rykan nodded. "Glad to have you." He noticed Selaina surveying the area as well, likely searching for her own way to help.

Rykan stepped into a nearby shop. The air inside was rich with fragrance, a blend of earthy, floral, and spicy scents. Two long worktables dominated the room, each lined with glass jars labeled in a neat but unfamiliar script. Some jars were dirty, their contents obscured by residue, while others gleamed as though freshly polished.

To his left, a group of villagers sat quietly, waiting as a man pressed handfuls of herbs between two thick wooden boards. Across the room, a large hearth bubbled with open jars of boiling water, the steam curling into the air.

"Good day," a woman said from behind one of the tables. "Welcome to our sanctuary of healing. It's not often we see lowlanders here on Kylinshan. What brings you to us?"

Rykan hesitated only briefly. "We noticed your roof is missing shingles, and some of your boards need replacing. We'd like to help with the repairs."

The woman blinked, clearly surprised. "You don't have to do this. There are surely others in greater need."

"Then perhaps you can direct us to them after," Rykan said. "But right now, we'd like to help you."

She smiled, her expression softening. "You are kind, but resources are limited. Gathering lumber and preparing it is no small task."

"Which forestland do you use for lumber?" Garrick asked, stepping in.

"The southern forests," she said after a pause. "But as I said, this isn't necessary. We planned to repair it ourselves, eventually. Priorities have been elsewhere."

"The southern forests," Garrick repeated with a nod. "Thank you. We'll take it from here."

"If you insist," she said with a sigh. "There's a mill in those woods. They'll prepare the wood for you and already know the measurements we need. You're welcome to use the axes leaning against the back. But be warned, there has been talk of strange creatures moving about. Some say maugwins and other shadowy things have wandered closer to the village than they usually do. It would be best to stay together."

With two axes behind the shop, Nadara stepped forward and took one, while Rykan took the other. As they left the shop, they found Ysadora standing alone, scanning the area as if searching for something.

"Would you like to come with us, Ysadora?" Rykan asked. "We're going to gather wood to repair the shop."

"I suppose I could," she replied, stepping toward them.

They made their way through the village and across the main road to a forest near the mountain's edge. The tall, slender trees loomed overhead, their bluish-green needles swaying in the light breeze. Garrick retrieved a hatchet from his bag and approached a tree, inspecting its width.

"Where did you get that axe?" Ysadora asked, tilting her head.

"I think it came from, well… Myrradin's things," Garrick said after a pause.

"I thought it looked familiar," she murmured, her tone neutral.

Garrick swung the hatchet at the tree's base. With its short handle, he couldn't use his full strength, but he managed to make a decent notch in the trunk. After a few swings, he moved aside looking to Rykan.

"Your turn," Garrick said.

Rykan moved in, bracing one hand against the trunk for balance as he adjusted his grip. He aimed for the cuts Garrick had already made but found his swings awkward and inefficient.

"Use both hands," Garrick suggested. "Gives you better control."

Rykan took the handle with both hands but hesitated before swinging again.

"You're still too horizontal," Nadara said, observing him. "Swing downward, let the axe's weight do the work."

Taking their advice, Rykan swung again. The blade bit into the wood with a satisfying thunk. He swung again, each downward motion feeling more precise and powerful.

"My turn," Nadara said, stepping forward.

Rykan stood back as she went to work with a different style, quick, measured chops that sent small chips of wood flying. After a while, she slowed, wiping the sweat from her brow.

"Want to give it a try?" Nadara asked, holding her axe out to Ysadora.

"I don't normally do this sort of thing," Ysadora said, taking the axe with some hesitation. "But I'll help however I can."

She glanced at the tree, then let the axe drop into the grass. Reaching for her staff, she pointed its end at the trunk, her expression sharpening with focus. The air around them seemed to shift, the chopped wood at the tree's base creaking and snapping. The tree swayed, its top leaning ominously.

"Move!" Ysadora called, her voice tight with concentration.

The group scattered as the tree gave a final groan and toppled. Branches cracked and splintered as it fell, crashing into the forest floor with a resounding boom.

Nadara stared at the fallen tree, then turned to Ysadora with wide eyes. "You mean to tell me that, this whole time, you could've just done that?"

"Not exactly," Ysadora said, brushing dirt off her sleeve. "It helps if there's already a cut in the trunk."

Garrick picked up the hatchet, scanning the surrounding trees. "We'll need more than one, and I'd rather not rely on magic for every single one."

The steady rhythm of Garrick's axe filled the silence, and Rykan found himself studying the swing pattern. For a moment, he considered asking Garrick for more pointers, but a faint rustling in the grass behind him drew his attention.

The sound was coming from a dark corner of the forest, the thick canopy completely shading the light of the sun. It was subtle at first, blending with the natural noises of the forest, the rustle of leaves, the occasional chirp of birds, but then it grew more distinct. The crunch of dry grass and snapping twigs suggested movement, deliberate and unhurried. Whoever it was didn't seem to care about masking their presence. Rykan turned, his curiosity spiked.

He glanced over his shoulder at the others. Garrick was still focused on chopping, Nadara was examining another tree, and Ysadora stood a short distance away, leaning against her staff. None of them seemed to have noticed. Perhaps it was Selaina, coming to check on their progress.

The footsteps slowed and then stopped, leaving an uneasy silence. Rykan paused, the rustle in the trees pulling him off the path and into the shadows. The dense trees and underbrush quickly obscured his view of the others, but Garrick's rhythmic chopping was still audible, reassuring him that the others weren't far off.

The sound of footsteps gave way to something stranger, a low vibration that seemed to hum through the trees. It resonated in Rykan's chest, faintly at first but growing stronger with each step. He paused, his senses on edge, as the vibration deepened into a guttural, snarling growl.

He froze, scanning the shadows ahead. Between two towering pines, a figure emerged, a beast unlike anything Rykan had ever seen. Its hulking form was covered in black fur that bristled like razor-sharp quills, dark smoke curling from its body as though it were aflame. Its glowing green eyes fixed on Rykan with a predatory intensity, and its wide, toothy maw curled into a snarl that sent a chill down his spine.

A growl tore through the woods. Instinct took over. Rykan's hand found his sword. Whatever this thing was, it wasn't natural, and it wasn't friendly.

Rykan's boots slid on the stones as he stepped back, sword rising. His pulse hammered like a drum in his ears. The creature moved slowly, each step deliberate, its claws digging into the earth and leaving faint wisps of smoke that dissipated into the air. Its body seemed less solid than shadow, shifting unnaturally with the dim light. Rykan extended his blade, keeping it pointed at the beast, a silent warning to stay back.

The creature growled low, a guttural sound that vibrated through the trees, then lunged. Rykan braced himself, thrusting his sword forward in a desperate attempt to stop it. The blade grazed its side, but the beast's momentum was unstoppable. It slammed into him, knocking him to the ground with bone-rattling force.

Rykan struggled, his breath driven from his lungs as the beast's weight pinned him. Its green eyes bored into his, and its wide, snarling maw snapped down. The beast's jaws closed on his arm, fangs like burning iron. Smoke hissed from the punctures, curling into the air like a living thing. He gritted his teeth, trying to twist free, but its grip was unrelenting.

A sudden, ear-splitting crack echoed through the forest, followed by the thunderous crash of falling wood. The ground trembled beneath them, and the beast's head jerked toward the sound. With a snarl, it released Rykan, darting back into the shadows with unnatural speed, its smoky form vanishing into the trees.

He staggered to his feet, blackened residue dripping down his forearm. The smoke didn't just linger, it pulsed, alive, as though something inside it watched him. His arm was numb, but his chest ached, with more than pain. Something had entered him. And it was waiting.

Branches rustled behind him, and Garrick and Nadara emerged, their axes in hand. They stopped, staring at the massive fallen tree nearby.

"What happened to you?" Garrick asked, his tone already hardening.

Rykan turned his arm, studying the wound. "Some kind of wild beast attacked me," he said, trying to keep his voice steady. "It came out of nowhere."

Ysadora appeared moments later, her staff brushing against the underbrush. She looked at the bite. One hand hovered near the delicate chain coiled around the base of her horns as she frowned. "That doesn't look like an ordinary bite."

"Is it some kind of poison?" Rykan asked, his gaze narrowing as he glanced between his wound and Ysadora.

Without answering, Ysadora took her staff, aiming its tip at his arm. A faint hum emanated from the wood as energy gathered at its end. "Hold still," she said. "This might hurt."

"What are you—" Rykan began, but his words cut off with a sharp gasp as a searing blue spark ignited in the blackened wound. Pain shot through his arm, so intense it knocked the air from his lungs. He clenched his teeth, a low, breathless groan escaping.

The spark fizzled out with a hiss, leaving his skin raw and throbbing. The pain drove him back a step, hand clamped tight over the wound.

"What was that?" Rykan demanded, his voice tight.

Ysadora lowered her staff, beads of sweat forming on her brow. She exhaled heavily. "I can't remove all of it," she admitted. "But I've stopped it from spreading. That should buy you some time."

Rykan's eyes widened, his fingers pressing against the wound. "What do you mean, 'buy time'? What is this thing?"

"It's a curse," Ysadora said, her tone measured but grim. "It's not a crafted spell. It's something wild, a raw manifestation of chaotic energy. I've suppressed it, but... I'm not skilled enough to purge it entirely."

Rykan's stomach sank as he looked at her. "So, what happens now?"

"It should fade in a few days," Ysadora said. "But until then, it might attract attention."

"Attention?" Rykan's voice rose. "What kind of attention?"

Ysadora met his gaze, her expression grave. "Creatures that normally hide in the shadows, unusual sensations, visions... Be mindful."

Rykan muttered under his breath, running his hand through his hair. "Great. That's just what I need."

Nadara, who had been watching in silence, stepped closer, her gaze sharp. "Maybe Selaina could do something to remove it all."

Ysadora hesitated. "Selaina wouldn't know the intricacies of removing a curse. If she could even summon that kind of power, she would do too much damage without control."

Rykan flexed his arm, wincing. The sharp edge of pain remained, but the eerie numbness had faded. That, at least, was something.

"Fine," he said, resigned. "Let's just get this wood and get out of here. The last thing we need is another surprise attack."

The shadows pressed in around them. Something unseen tugged at the edges of Rykan's awareness. A faint rustling drifted through the trees, low, deliberate, and distant. It barely registered. Too faint for the others to notice. But Rykan heard it as clearly as a whisper. Maybe it was the curse heightening his senses… or maybe the thing in the dark was calling only to him.

The pain in his arm might fade in a few days. But what else might find them before then?

CHAPTER 19

As Selaina moved through the village, she couldn't help but notice the quiet rhythm of the place. Every motion, from the blacksmith's steady hammer to the baker's careful stacking of bread, was practiced, almost rehearsed. People worked in silence, their eyes downcast, their movements efficient. It reminded her of the forest, where labor was lonely but necessary. Here, the stillness didn't feel like solitude, it felt observed.

And she was being watched.

Elders, like those in the cliff temple, lingered at street corners and terrace landings, their gazes following her as she passed. They didn't speak or smile, just watched. They watched everyone, not just her. A boy refilling his mother's wood basket, a man tying bundles of herbs along the eaves. Always the same: silent observation, like gardeners inspecting for signs of blight.

Selaina followed a narrow trail past homes and bristling trees until she came upon a shallow water hole, nestled in a basin of cracked stone. A thin stream trickled from higher ground, metallic in scent, barely filling the hollow. Nearby, an old man stood beside a cart, his weary-looking ridgeback drooping with age.

Their eyes met. And suddenly she had a vision. Sight beyond seeing. The old man's memories.

He gripped the worn handles of a plow beneath a cloudless sky, dust thick on his tongue. A woman knelt by a dry well, a child clutching her skirt. Another vision came over her: the man, younger now, lifting stones with bloodied hands as a ragged group climbed a half-built mountain path. Then she saw him again: a firelit winter night, neighbors eating while he quietly went without. The vision faded.

Children scurried to and from the water hole, filling small pails. Several full buckets already sat in the man's cart. As he stooped to lift another, his hands trembled. Selaina approached.

"Here, let me help you," she said.

"You're kind," he replied, voice strained, "but I can manage."

Selaina offered a faint smile. "Isn't this what hearthshare means?"

After a pause, he stepped aside. She hoisted the heavy bucket, it was no easy task, and carried it to the cart. The weight felt like more than water.

"Why's the water hole so far from the village?" she asked.

"This was a river once," he muttered. "Until the Glissarans dammed it. Used to feed the valley. Now it barely keeps us alive."

As Selaina handed a fresh bucket to one of the children, she noticed the boy staring into the trees. "Is something wrong?" she asked.

"We heard something," he said quietly.

Another girl piped up, clutching her pail. "It was growling and it wasn't the wind."

Selaina kept her voice calm. "Could've been an animal. Wind through branches. Easy to mishear."

"I don't think so," the boy said, glancing back at the shadows. "It sounded like a maugwin."

Selaina's gaze narrowed. "You've seen one?"

"Not me," he admitted. "But Renlow said he did. Then he disappeared."

"My brother says they hunt people who go too far into the woods," the girl whispered.

Selaina crouched beside them. "You're safe here. If there's something out there, I'll find it before it finds you."

One boy looked up. "Are you a hunter?"

Selaina smiled. "I've hunted before." She took a step toward the forest but glanced back at the children. "Stay here and finish filling your buckets. I'll make sure there's nothing out there."

After they were finished, the old man guided the mule back toward the village with the children following. Selaina wandered near a hunter's clearing where some were carrying several rabbits and a pair of larger animals slung over their shoulders. Her attention was caught by a soft ripple of laughter nearby. She turned to see Kadin crouched near a group of children, a faint smile playing on his lips as he mimed an exaggerated sword fight with a stick. The children giggled and cheered, their wide eyes reflecting pure delight.

Kadin's movements were playful yet skilled, each swing of the makeshift weapon accompanied by a dramatic flourish. One child, emboldened by the show, stepped forward with their own stick, declaring, "I'll defeat the great Kadin!"

"Oh, you think so?" Kadin replied, his voice light but carrying a trace of something deeper. "Well, let's see what you've got, young warrior."

Selaina lingered, watching as Kadin allowed the child to land a triumphant "strike." His grin was genuine, but there was a trace of something else in his eyes, a shadow of memory, perhaps. His tone held more than playfulness, there was care in it, a remnant of someone who had once known what it was to protect and nurture.

For a moment, Selaina wondered what story lay beneath that shadow. Had he once played like this with his own siblings? Or perhaps with children he'd vowed to protect but couldn't save?

Her gaze fell on a young hunter, struggling with the process of cleaning the animals they had killed, his cuts hesitant and clumsy. She walked over, settling near him.

"Could I help with that?" she asked, gesturing to the partially skinned animal.

The hunter looked up, startled. "You know how to do this?"

Selaina smiled. "I've prepared plenty of game back in my forest. It's not much different."

The hunter stepped aside, handing her his knife. "Let's see what you can do."

Selaina knelt by the carcass, working with practiced hands as she explained what she was doing. Teaching him the same way Jeth had taught her. Her movements were smooth and confident as she made precise cuts, separating the hide and removing the meat with care.

Kadin wandered over, watching from a safe distance. "So, this is what you did in your forest?" he asked.

Selaina glanced up briefly. "Among other things. Want to help?"

Kadin chuckled nervously, shaking his head. "I think I'll pass."

"Oh, come on," Selaina said, raising an eyebrow. "I've seen you fight grown men with daggers. Don't tell me a little blood makes you queasy."

Kadin hesitated, his face twisting with a mix of reluctance and pride. "Fine. What do I do?"

Selaina handed him the knife and motioned to the animal. "Start by making a cut here," she said, pointing to a spot near the hind leg. "Then peel the hide back carefully."

Kadin took the knife, his movements stiff and hesitant. He grimaced as the knife sank into the flesh, the smell of blood wafting up. "Killing is one thing. This is a bit… sadistic, don't you think?" he muttered.

Selaina suppressed a laugh. "You're doing fine. Just don't think about it too much."

"Easy for you to say," Kadin grumbled as he struggled with the slippery hide.

After a few minutes, Kadin dropped the knife and stepped back. "I think I'll stick to fighting things before they end up like this."

Selaina shook her head, smiling as she resumed the work. "Not everyone has the stomach for it. But it's important to know how to make use of what the land gives us."

As she worked, she set aside strips of sinew in a small bundle near her knee.

One of the hunters, broad-shouldered, with a worn leather apron and a crescent-shaped scar under his eye, paused and tilted his head. "What are you keeping that for?" he asked, gesturing to the sinew.

"The sinew?" Selaina glanced at the pile. "It's good for bowstrings, cord, stitching. I usually dry it and twist it while it's still pliable."

The man gave a short grunt of surprise. "We burn most of that with the scraps. Never thought to use it for cords."

Selaina smiled. "Jeth, my old teacher, used to say everything in the forest has another use if you're patient enough to find it."

He crouched beside her, inspecting her work. "You cut clean," he said, nodding. "But you're fighting the hide a bit. Try this."

He pulled a hooked blade from a sheath at his belt, short, thick, and curved like a talon. The handle was wrapped in pale twine, worn smooth from years of use.

Selaina took it, testing the balance. "What is it?"

"Split-hook," he said. "We use it when the hide's still tight. Gets under without tearing the meat. Here, start there, then roll the edge back with your palm."

She tried it, the blade gliding beneath the hide with surprising ease. Her eyes widened. "That's… clever."

The man chuckled, folding his arms. "Took me a few years to stop butchering like a lumberjack."

"I'd like to make one," Selaina said, handing the blade back. "If somcone could show me how."

He gave a nod. "We'll trade. You teach us how to use the sinew, and I'll show you how to shape and edge one of these."

They worked side by side, exchanging quiet tips and occasionally dry humor. Kadin, hovering near the edge of the clearing, watched with one eyebrow raised.

"You warm up quick to people who hand you weapons," Kadin said, eyeing the knife.

Selaina smirked. "That's what trust looks like, Kadin. Try it sometime."

"It didn't work out so well with Myrradin. Or Darian," he added, more softly.

"I haven't forgotten," she said quietly, meeting his eyes now. "But if I stop trusting everyone, then I become like them."

Kadin gave a small grunt and looked away, kicking at the dirt. "That's the thing about trust, never holds up under close inspection."

By the time she finished, the meat was neatly prepared, and the hunters expressed their gratitude. Kadin, still pale, leaned against a nearby post, clearly relieved the task was over. Selaina wiped her hands on a rag, satisfied with the work but eager to see what the others were up to.

She found them repairing a building, and her eyes swept the scene. Garrick was on the ladder, Nadara handing up boards, Rykan steadying the frame. But something made her slow.

Rykan's movements were slightly off, his posture tighter, his left arm close to his side. When he shifted, she caught a glimpse beneath his sleeve: dark fabric, and something beneath it that didn't look right.

He hadn't noticed her yet. But as if sensing her attention, he looked up. Their eyes locked. He didn't smile. Didn't flinch. Instead, he simply pressed his hand against his arm, subtle, guarded.

Selaina's stomach churned.

She changed course and approached. "Rykan," she called, her voice firm but not loud. "What happened to your arm?"

He hesitated, then exhaled slowly. "Something bit me. In the woods. Ysadora healed it."

Selaina stepped closer, eyes narrowing at the bruised, blackened flesh. "It doesn't look healed. It looks like what Gwenna did to me."

"I told you, she handled it," Rykan said. "It's not spreading."

"I've seen something like this before. We should ask someone here. There might be someone who knows how to treat it completely."

"I'm fine," Rykan replied flatly.

Ysadora, who had been nearby, turned. "I suppressed it," she said. "It was a wild curse, raw, unshaped. Not like Gwenna's. I did everything I could."

"And if that's not enough?" Selaina asked, her voice rising.

Rykan stepped between them, his voice tired. "We don't have time to chase answers that don't exist. Let's finish the repairs."

Selaina sighed and turned away, her thoughts still racing. The patch on Rykan's arm was more than an injury, it was a warning. She couldn't shake the feeling that it would draw something far worse than beasts in the forest.

Above them, the sky deepened into shades of gold and purple, the first signs of twilight stretching across the mountains. Whatever was coming, Selaina knew they wouldn't have the luxury of ignoring it for long.

CHAPTER 20

Selaina steadied a ladder, hauled logs, and accepted sore muscles as payment for peace, a rhythm of shared purpose the villagers called hearthshare. She and the others were guests in Oran's home, repaying his welcome with service instead of coin, giving back to the place that had taken them in.

As the sky deepened to shades of indigo, a quiet shift rippled through the village. One by one, the villagers began drifting toward the plaza, their tools set aside and their expressions expectant. A man and woman passed by, their faces lined with the warm weariness of the day. They beckoned to Selaina and her companions with a simple gesture, no words exchanged, as if the gathering was as natural as breathing. Together, they followed, the sound of footsteps and hushed voices rising to meet the cool embrace of the evening air. The sky was cloudless save for streaks of fire-pink near the horizon.

Behind her, she heard the sharp clap of sawdust being brushed from hands. Rykan caught up to her a moment later, falling into step beside her.

A woman turned toward them, sunlit face reverent. "We celebrate Aelara," she said.

"The first star of the evening," a man added. "She was the first of the celestials."

The woman's expression darkened. "Unless you count the Fallen Star," she said, her voice cutting through the calm.

The sudden tension prickled at Selaina. The crowd seemed to shift uneasily, as if the woman had uttered something forbidden.

The man's shoulders sank as he let out a heavy sigh. "Why even bring that up?" His hand moved absently to scratch his chin.

Selaina's thoughts churned. She'd never heard of that before. "What Fallen Star?" she asked, her voice cutting through the murmurs.

The man straightened, his discomfort plain in the way he looked past her. "A legend," he said too quickly. "One better left to silence."

But the woman pressed on, undeterred. "The celestial with great promise, that was to bring splendor and beauty to the world but instead defied his station, and nearly destroyed it," she said, her tone sharp.

Selaina's gaze met the woman's, and in an instant, the woman's memories unfolded.

A candlelit room.

A child crouched beneath a curtain.

A heavy old book open in her lap.

The pages fluttered.

And the girl's eyes filled with tears, though she didn't stop reading.

Selaina's mind raced, piecing fragments of old stories together. "Defied? Like the Sky Serpents?" she asked, her voice edged with uncertainty. If the Fallen Star was another outcast, why hadn't she heard of this before?

The man shook his head, his words deliberate. "Not really. The Sky Serpents defied their creator and accepted their punishment, so they were allowed to endure. The Fallen Star hid from judgment, within a realm without shape or reach."

The explanation left Selaina hollow. Beside her, Rykan hadn't said a word, but when she shifted, unsettled, he turned just slightly, watching her instead of the sky.

Her gaze flicked to his, uncertain.

He gave a small, firm nod, like he was anchoring her in place. As if reassuring her that whatever haunted her in that story wouldn't reach her tonight.

She exhaled, her shoulders loosening a bit. Just knowing that he noticed her unease helped.

Selaina glanced at the horizon, wondering what it meant to lose purpose entirely. She thought about her own path, her mark, and her mission. Had the Fallen Star begun with the same determination she had now, only to lose his way? If even celestials could fall, what chance did she have?

"There it is," the man said, pointing midway up into the sky. "Aelara, the first star of the night."

Selaina followed his gaze, and after a brief search, her eyes found the sparkling star. She had never before considered the first star of the evening, and for a moment, it was a comforting constant in an ever-changing world.

"I don't know why we do this every night," the woman muttered, breaking the silence.

"We're supposed to reflect on the day," the man replied. "Think about what help we brought to others, what we learned, and how we can improve tomorrow."

"That's what we're supposed to do," the woman said. "But does anyone actually think about those things? Or do we just do it out of habit?"

Selaina considered the woman's words. Forest life had been nothing but routine, each day a quiet echo of the one before, until everything changed.

"Sometimes routine feels dull," she said. "But if we pay attention, it can remind us why we started. Meaning slips away when we stop noticing."

The woman gave a slow nod. "I'll take that as the new thing I've learned today."

Selaina blinked, surprised the woman credited her with the thought. Had the woman already known it deep down, waiting for someone to say it aloud? It was humbling, and it made Selaina wonder what other truths she might find in unexpected places, or people.

The man gave a small nod. "Even if it's just for tradition, Aelara reminds us to pause. That alone has value."

Selaina wondered how often that happened to her. Could all the answers be right in front of her, and she just couldn't see them? As the village darkened, she stood watching the skies as the other stars appeared. The cool night air passed over her, and for a moment, she felt like a distant version of herself was watching, remembering this moment as the one when everything changed.

The mark never pulsed with pain, but it hummed, softly, like distant thunder beneath her skin. A reminder. A presence. Something had awakened when she touched the Wishing Stone, something ancient and vast that still stirred quietly within her.

She had felt it before, in the heart of Wekenwild, where the forest's order had seemed impossible to navigate. But in that stillness, something inside her had known the way. Something without thought, but rhythm. Trust. As though the power she'd taken on didn't just live inside her, it was leading her.

Sometimes, she could almost hear it: not words, but impressions, emotions that weren't hers. A sense of timing. A pull toward certain paths. Her body reacted before her mind understood why, moments of clarity so finely tuned they unsettled her. Like the way she resisted Amera's power.

Was it newfound intuition? Or something more?

She didn't know what she was becoming. And that frightened her more than she wanted to admit. But tonight, watching the stars brighten above a village caught in its own quiet rhythms, she felt… apart. As though she were observing herself from a distance, from some far-off future. Remembering this moment not as it was happening, but as the moment everything shifted.

And maybe it had.

"There you are," said a voice close by.

Selaina turned. Oran stood with Rykan, Garrick, Ysadora, and Nadara.

"Since you are my guests tonight," Oran said, "I wanted to invite you all to dinner."

"Thank you," Selaina said. "I am getting rather hungry."

Oran led them away past the row of shops to an area with small houses clustered closely together, where the scent of hearth smoke and flowering vines hung in the air, hinting at a quiet life beyond the village bustle. As they passed a modest garden, Rykan asked, "Is this your garden? Why do you walk so far to get skyroot?"

"We don't grow skyroot in the village," Oran replied. "It tends to overtake everything. But it's still useful."

Inside Oran's home, a long table waited, already set with containers brimming with meats, plants, and fruits. Oran stood behind the head chair while the others entered. Kadin dropped into a seat quickly, then motioned for Ysadora and Nadara to join him. Rykan hung back, offering Selaina the next choice. She sat near Oran, across from Nadara. Garrick and Rykan took the remaining seats.

"This table is yours tonight," Oran said. "But remember, even meals can teach us, if we let them."

Everyone leaned over the table, filling their plates. Selaina picked what looked familiar: long-sliced potatoes, green bushy vegetables, and a soft grain dish. Three kinds of meat lay in the center, some fatty, others lean. She chose modestly.

Just as the group was preparing to eat, Oran raised a hand. "Not yet," he said. "You must follow our way."

Garrick paused. "What do you mean by your way?"

"You must exchange plates with the person across from you," Oran said.

His voice carried both gentleness and gravity. As the group hesitated, Selaina felt the meaning of the ritual. It was more than just as a custom, it was a quiet act of trust. She glanced at her plate, then at Nadara's, wondering what pieces of the other woman's story were contained in those bold flavors. For a moment, it felt less like dinner and more like stepping into someone else's skin.

"To live among others is to taste what they carry," Oran explained.

There were murmurs, but they complied. Selaina and Nadara swapped plates. The food now before her was bright in color. Its scent was bold and richly spiced.

She glanced across the table. Did Nadara love these intense flavors, or simply not fear discomfort? Either way, it made Selaina curious.

"I see you have a taste for meat," Kadin said, eyeing Garrick's former plate.

"I lived alone in the wilderness," Garrick replied. "You eat what you catch."

Ysadora, picking at Rykan's plate, wrinkled her nose. "I don't usually eat this much meat either. Why do we have to do this?"

"To taste someone else's choices is to glimpse their world, memories, comforts, even grief," Oran said. "It's not just a meal. It's a mirror."

Kadin raised a brow. "So the lesson here is Garrick eats like a starving wolf."

Oran offered a faint smile. "Perhaps. Or perhaps you'll learn something about your own reluctance."

Selaina took a bite, thoughtful. The spices lingered—unfamiliar, intriguing—like the edge of an idea forming on her tongue. Nadara's choices spoke of boldness and contrast, and for a moment, Selaina felt herself transformed, not by the food, but by the willingness to understand someone else's world through it. Nadara's plate was adventurous, much like the woman herself. Selaina decided to honor it with the same openness.

The clinking of spoons faded as firelight softened the edges of their faces. Oran leaned forward, his voice gentle but clear. "Who were you kind to today?" he asked her. "Whose day did you make better?"

She hesitated. "I helped a man at the water hole. He was loading buckets onto a cart. The children were trying to help, but it was too much for them. I helped them finish. And later, Kadin and I came across two hunters. I showed them how I clean a kill. We shared what we knew with each other."

Oran nodded. "That is the spirit of hearthshare. Why those tasks?"

"They were things I knew. Carrying water, preparing food, my mother taught me those things. It felt right."

"And what did you learn from them?"

"That people do things differently. And there's always something to learn. Even small help can mean something."

"And how do you think they saw you?"

Selaina thought for a moment. "Hopefully, as more than just someone passing through. I tried to be present. To see how they live."

Oran looked down, brushing grains off his plate. "Sometimes the quietest moments tell others the most."

Selaina sat back, her gaze distant. She thought of the man with the worn hands, the quiet hunters, the children. Could that same attentiveness help heal more than a village?

"Do you believe presence is enough to bring peace to a fractured world?" Oran asked.

"No," Selaina said. "We have to stop Vatreus. Him and the Iron Flood."

Oran studied her. "And if you are Zhal Evurah, why seek the blessing?"

She touched her forehead. "Wasn't I called here? Why else would I have this mark? Why do I feel this fire?"

He asked gently, "Are you trying to convince me, Selaina… or yourself?"

Her answer stalled in her throat.

"If the Sky Serpents give you the Crown of Breath, what will you do when they ask for it back?" he asked.

"I'll return it," she said.

Oran's voice held a quiet challenge, his gaze steady on Selaina. "Then remember, this task never ends. Even if you stop Vatreus, another need will rise. He thinks he's filling one now. How are you different?"

CHAPTER 21

THE FIRE CRACKLED in the silence, casting slow shadows across the table. Selaina's hand rested near the edge, her fingers tense with the weight of Oran's question.

"I've lived without power," she said at last. "I earned what I have. Vatreus was handed his strength and never learned to go without. I have friends who won't let me forget who I am."

Oran's eyes passed over them all, pausing at the fire. "You speak of earned strength. But strength isn't always enough." He turned to Rykan. "And you? What would be your undoing?"

"Impatience," Rykan answered, shifting uncomfortably in his seat.

As the firelight danced, he looked down at his hands. Selaina, watching, gently brushed her fingers near his. Rykan glanced up, his tension easing.

"I act before I think," he said. "My mother warned me about it, but it still happens," he admitted, eyes lowering to his hands again.

"Fire burns bright in need," Oran said. "But it also consumes." He looked into the fire. "Do you know why the Sky Serpents fell?"

Selaina shook her head.

"They were celestials once. Ordered never to interfere. But they saw two mortals, Doran and Talia, whose love had united feuding villages. When famine struck, and shadow beasts came down from the mountains, the celestials had a choice: let the couple die, or break their vow."

"They saved them?" Selaina asked quietly, leaning forward.

"They gave them the breath of the stars," Oran said. "It amplified their strength, awakened their magic. With it, the lovers survived. But the celestials were cast down, stripped of their divinity. They became the Sky Serpents."

Selaina frowned, her voice low with disbelief. "They were punished for mercy."

Oran's gaze dropped to the fire. "They chose the cost," he murmured. "Love is the most powerful force in existence. But fear of losing it… that's what makes even the wise act without foresight. That was their undoing."

Selaina's thoughts caught on the word *love*, tangled in the gravity of Oran's voice. She didn't move. But across the table, Rykan had stilled completely. His elbow rested on the wood, his head bowed, fingers running once, slowly, along the scabbed bite on his arm.

She watched him. His movement and the tension behind it. The way his jaw clenched when he didn't speak.

Then, perhaps sensing her eyes on him, he lifted his gaze and met hers. In that look, he asked a question she wasn't ready to answer.

She didn't offer one. Instead, she inhaled, and exhaled, just deep enough for him to see she'd felt it too.

They looked away at the same time.

Kadin's voice cut in, quieter than usual. "Love's a tricky thing. Makes you braver than you should be. Or maybe more foolish. Either way, it always leaves its mark."

Selaina glanced at him, surprised by the uncharacteristic gravity in his tone, but he didn't elaborate, his gaze fixed on the dancing fire.

Beside her, Selaina saw Rykan go still. His hand, which had been absently tracing a knot in the wood, froze mid-motion. His expression didn't change much, but there was a shift, a quiet straining around the eyes, a shadow of thought behind them. She followed his gaze as it dropped to the table, his shoulders drawing inward, as if he was weighing something unspoken.

She wondered what he was thinking, what choices he feared, what lines he might cross if it meant keeping someone safe. The thought unsettled her more than she expected. Because she wasn't sure if she could say she'd act any differently.

The celestials had acted out of love, yet even their compassion had carried a cost. She thought of her own companions, of Rykan's loyalty, Kadin's wit, and Garrick's steady presence. Her bond with them was her strength, but could it also become her weakness?

Could her love for her friends, the need to protect them, lead her to make the same mistakes as the celestials? Would she sacrifice too much, or take a step too far, and pay a price she couldn't foresee?

Her fingers gripped her cup, the weight of her destiny pressing more heavily against her heart.

Oran leaned back, his gaze turning distant, as if looking beyond the walls of the house to the mountain itself. "The summit of Kylinshan has long been a place of power. It is where the celestials first touched Galanor, shaping the world as we know it."

Selaina's brow furrowed. "Touched Galanor? How?"

"Reaching into molten fire, they interacted with the primal ingredients of creation to form the Dawnstone," Oran said, his voice quieter now, reverent. "It once rested at the mountain's peak, blazing with the combined essence of the celestials. When the Dawnstone was formed, Kylinshan rose from the molten surface of the world, a bridge between the heavens and the earth. The stone carried their light, their unity… and their purpose. A charge of power gathered around it, and mortals would journey there to connect with the Azsh Rozaht, the all-encompassing thought."

"What happened to it?" Rykan asked, leaning forward.

"Mortals began to demand rather than ask," Oran replied, his tone heavy with regret. "Their communion became selfish, focused on power instead of reverence. Then came the great avalanche that sundered the Dawnstone. Even now, remnants of its energy linger at the summit, gathering over centuries. But only the Sky Serpents can channel it, and only to bless the rightful Zhal Evurah."

"I've never heard that version of the story before," Rykan said, breaking the thoughtful silence.

Ysadora tilted her head back ever so slightly, the faintest trace of skepticism masking her keen attention. "Neither have I," she admitted.

"The stories originated here," Oran said. "You won't find a more detailed account of the history anywhere else."

Selaina furrowed her brow. "The tale of Doran and Talia. Are you saying that love can be perilous?"

"Anything worth having is," Kadin said, his voice unusually quiet. He traced the edge of his cup, avoiding the others' gazes. "But sometimes, you don't get to choose whether it's worth it, or whether the cost comes first."

Oran tilted his head, his gaze thoughtful. "A mountain by itself isn't dangerous. Leaping from one of its edges, that is dangerous. The same is true of love, power, or anything else we hold dear. They are forces, neither good nor bad on their own. The danger comes from how we act upon them, and whether we lose sight of the consequences."

Kadin looked up, his smirk faint but sharp. "And sometimes, you don't see the edge until it's too late."

"Perhaps," Oran said, his tone calm but probing. "But even then, you have a choice, to fall, or to climb back up."

Selaina's gaze moved between them, sensing an unspoken weight behind Kadin's words. "But what were the celestials supposed to do?" Selaina pressed. "Just let Doran and Talia die?"

"They were ordered not to interfere with mortal affairs," Oran said, his voice measured. "To do so is to alter the Prime Sequence. It's the purest form of arrogance to believe one knows better than the Azsh Rozalit."

"And what insights did you glean from Rykan's food choices, Ysadora?" Oran asked, glancing at her with a hint of amusement.

Ysadora lifted an eyebrow, eyeing Rykan's plate. "He doesn't like much that's green."

A ripple of laughter passed through the group. Rykan made a mock-offended face and glared at his plate protectively.

Kadin gave with a crooked grin, nudging Ysadora's elbow lightly. "Careful. That was dangerously close to charm."

Ysadora raised a single brow, a rare, secretive smile tugging at her mouth. "Don't get used to it."

Selaina caught the exchange, small, almost nothing. But for a moment, the tension in Ysadora's shoulders seemed to slip away, like someone had loosened a knot she hadn't noticed was there.

Oran let his smile linger. "Perhaps so," he said, reaching for his cup, "but even the strongest need more than one kind of strength to thrive." He took a slow sip, then added casually, "Sometimes, the things we avoid say just as much as the things we reach for."

Rykan leaned back, crossing his arms. "I'll try and remember that."

"You should," Oran said, his gaze steady. "Especially when the path ahead will demand more from you than comfort and habit. In the face of chaos, balance is what keeps us whole."

"Balance, huh?" Kadin tapped his fingers lightly on the table. "Funny thing about balance, sometimes it feels like it's just a fancy word for juggling. One wrong move, and the whole act comes crashing down."

Oran's gaze settled on him. "And yet, the act continues. What does that tell you?"

Kadin smirked faintly, though his tone carried a rare seriousness. "That maybe the trick isn't balance, it's learning how to catch what falls."

Oran set his hands on the table in front of him. "Perhaps. But true balance is not in catching, it's in knowing when to reach, and when to let fall. Not all that slips from your hand is meant to be held."

Selaina's eyes lingered on Oran as their words settled in. She thought of her own choices, the risks she'd taken, and the power she now carried. Balance. She would need to find it, not just for herself, but for everyone depending on her.

Through the window, the first star of the evening sparkled, its light a quiet reminder of the vastness of the journey ahead.

After the meal, Oran asked each of them what they had learned that day. Most of their answers were simple observations, moments that felt small and fleeting. Selaina wondered if they truly understood the weight of his question. Perhaps they didn't yet see how the smallest lessons could shape a path in ways they couldn't yet imagine.

As the night deepened, they cleared their plates and stacked them neatly by the hearth. In the main room, Selaina spread out a blanket, the same one Myrradin had once given her. She paused for a moment, her fingers brushing the edge of the fabric, and wondered if something good could still remain from someone so full of contradictions.

The group crowded onto the floor, each finding their place in the shared space. Nadara blew out the last candle, plunging them into pitch darkness. For a while, the silence felt heavy, punctuated only by the faint whistle of wind through the cracks in the stone wall.

Tomorrow, the mountain would demand more of them. Tomorrow, they would climb higher, leaving the safety of this village and stepping closer to whatever awaited them at the summit. Selaina lay awake for a time, staring into the black void of the room, the word balance whispering through her thoughts.

The room was quiet, save for the wind outside and the occasional shift of someone settling into sleep. Selaina, wrapped in her blanket, stared at the ceiling as her thoughts drifted to the space beside her. She couldn't see Rykan in the dark, but she felt when his breathing slowed to match hers.

There was comfort in that simple rhythm. In knowing, without needing to ask, that she wasn't alone. Without a word, Selaina rolled slightly toward the sound. Just close enough for the silence between them to feel full, not empty.

A star, no longer alone, in an endless sky.

Her destiny still shrouded in mist.

And tomorrow, the mountain would call once more.

CHAPTER 22

RYKAN FOUND HIMSELF standing in a place he had never seen before, yet it carried a disturbingly familiar weight, like the echo of a nightmare half-remembered. The air pressed in around him, thick with unnatural fog that coiled and shifted as though it had a will of its own. Faint whispers slithered through the haze, circling him like fragments of a forgotten language, their meanings just beyond his grasp.

Tall, jagged stones encircled the clearing, their slick surfaces catching the dim, red glow emanating from a gnarled, lifeless tree at the center. Its twisted branches clawed upward, pulsing with a light that beat like a heart, casting shadows that moved as if alive.

At the base of the tree stood a figure cloaked in shadowy robes. Rykan watched from a distance, unsure if he had form or substance in this place. He felt no weight in his limbs, no breath in his lungs. The figure did not look his way, perhaps could not see him at all, but Rykan felt the pull of his presence, like gravity bending toward something malevolent.

Around the tree, more figures appeared, some blurred, some sharp. They did not arrive; they were simply there, as though drawn from distant corners of the world through mirrored flames. In the waking world, they might have stood far apart, but here, they circled one vortex, their wills stitched together across the roots of the old tree.

Within the hollow of the tree, a convulsing red vortex churned. Black and crimson energy crackled like lightning across its surface, humming with a low, dreadful resonance. It pulsed like a wound torn open through root and stone, bleeding chaos into the stillness around it. The vortex churned with a hunger that felt disturbingly alive.

The figure spoke in a low, reverent tone, his words trembling. "Lord Nociferon, I bring news from the shadows."

A voice spoke with the sound of a choir of discordant harmony. "Arathain, your words had better be worth the burden of dragging my mind into this confining state of time. Speak, before the weight of this temporal world tests my patience further."

"I have found the girl you seek," said Arathain, the man wearing robes like a mavin or sorcerer. "She ascends the mountain of Kylinshan."

Rykan's arm began to hurt. He looked down to find the dark area surrounding the animal bite growing.

"She seeks the Crown of Breath. Who among you can reach her?" said the voice of Nociferon. Soon the vortex hummed with greater resonance. "She must not find her way to the temple. "Even now, the energy of the Wishing Stone overwhelms her mortal form. She will lose her mind to it. The power of Archeinor will consume her as it has so many others. Time cannot contain her. It never could. There is no beginning. No end. Only will."

The vortex pulsed, making his words echo through the roots and stone.

"It will take time to get there, my lord," said Arathain. "But fiends of shadow lurk everywhere. They will find her and delay her until we arrive." He paused, then added, almost with relish, "Already, there are those on the mountain cursed with Bloodshadow. Their wounds will fester and bleed. The maugwins will scent it, follow it like wolves to prey. And where the cursed bleed… the shadows will gather. From there, we can open the way."

The familiar voice of Gwenna spoke next. "I will commence immediately, my lord. I still command the Nadrok across Galanor. When they find the girl, I will employ them to slipstream directly to her side."

Another figure stepped out of the gloom, tall, draped in robes that shimmered like smoke, her face mostly hidden beneath a bone-pale hood.

"Do you want me there as well, my lord?" asked Syra, her voice like silk drawn over glass, elegant, but edged with something sharper.

"No. Stay where you are. Until the girl is in our possession, your task remains unchanged, and should stay unnoticed," said Nociferon.

"The Sullen will begin making our way to the mountain as well, my lord," said Dazurel, speaking for them. "There will be no escape."

"I cannot afford for her to be harmed," said Nociferon. "She must remain alive and intact until we can use the essence of the Wishing Stone in her body."

"She won't be harmed, my lord," said Arathain.

The bite on Rykan's arm burned with an uncontrollable rage as the darkness spread further.

"Your services will not go unrewarded," the voice declared. "In the new world I shall forge, powers beyond your comprehension will be yours to wield. Embrace the future I offer, and you will ascend to heights you could only dream of."

"I can see it already," said Gwenna. "What Galanor could be if we tip the scales of balance toward chaos. Time no longer a prison. The cycle of life and death, broken. And at last… I will see my sister again. The illusion of choice binds us. But true freedom is the absence of structure. That is what Nociferon offers."

"To even *imagine* it," said Syra. "A world unshackled by Archeinor's cruel symmetry, no decay, no end, only becoming."

"I shall remake the mortal realm into its rightful state," said Nociferon. "Perpetually transforming, endlessly evolving… This is what creation was before it was caged," he said. "No beginning. No end. Only will. The world was not born of order, it was shaped by it. But it longs to return to its wild breath."

The words curled like incense, slipping through Rykan's ears and down his spine. For one terrible moment, he believed them. He wanted to turn and run, but he was surrounded by nothing more than the darkness of the unknown in all directions.

A low whisper surged past his ear, whether from the vortex or his own imagination, he couldn't tell. That was enough.

Rykan bolted into the dark unknown, the abyss around him alive with shadows that lunged and clawed at him, their formless tendrils tearing at his mind as much as his body. The oppressive darkness seemed to close in from all sides, a suffocating void that threatened to consume him whole.

His heart pounded with a primal terror, each breath ragged as he pushed himself forward, desperate to escape the unseen horrors pursuing him.

But no matter how fast he ran, the shadows kept pace, whispering ancient secrets that he felt deep in his bones, but couldn't understand. They gnawed at him, leaving him feeling exposed and vulnerable. The ground beneath his feet seemed to dissolve into nothingness, and for a moment, Rykan feared he would be lost forever in this nightmare.

Suddenly, as abruptly as it started, the terror ceased. He awoke with a gasp, his body drenched in cold sweat. His heart still raced, but he was back, back in the room, surrounded by the others. The familiar sight of the dimly lit space anchored him to reality, though the lingering dread from his dream still clung to him like a second skin.

He couldn't keep this from Selaina any longer.

Rykan sat up slowly, scanning the room until his gaze found her. She lay peacefully, her face serene, untouched by the horrors that haunted him. Her breathing was steady, calm, so different from the chaos still thrumming through his veins. For a moment, he envied that peace.

He hesitated. Maybe now wasn't the time.

Rykan ran a trembling hand through his damp hair, trying to steady his nerves. The images from the dream flashed in his mind, dark, twisted, and all too vivid.

What if they were right? The thought gnawed at him. The images from the dream flashed in his mind. Whatever power Selaina had taken from the Wishing Stone, what if it was destroying her from the inside out? The idea chilled him to the core. Would they even realize it before it was too late? After all they had been through, he couldn't bear the thought of losing her.

But as much as he tried to push the dark thoughts away, the voices and their promises began to worm their way into his mind. The voice on the other side of the vortex spoke of the unordering of time, where death no longer mattered. It was a concept so alien, so tantalizingly impossible, yet Rykan couldn't help but contemplate it.

What if it were true, he wondered, his mind racing. Could this Lord of Chaos really accomplish this unraveling of time? Did he mean that they could rewrite fate without the Wishing Stone? That he could have his father back? Perhaps their original plan could work after all, maybe they could still create a time where the Iron Flood never existed.

If this were true, Selaina wouldn't need to carry the burden of the Wishing Stone's power. She could be that girl again, unburdened, unmarked by the crush of destiny. Rykan's heart ached at the thought, Selaina, smiling again, unburdened by the fate of the world. That towering destiny, always demanding more, could finally be left behind.

They could both be free.

If time unraveled and the Iron Flood never rose, would the path that brought her to him simply… disappear? What was the difference between their plan to change time with the Wishing Stone and unraveling it altogether? Would he live out his days in a Tathara never overtaken by the Iron Flood, waiting for something he couldn't name? Or would he even exist at all in this reordered world?

He didn't know.

And that uncertainty sank deeper than the promises Nociferon had offered.

Taking a few deep breaths, Rykan forced himself to calm down. He knew he needed rest, but the thought of closing his eyes again filled him with dread. Still, he couldn't afford to be weak, not now. Not when they were so close to their goal of reaching the summit, and danger lurked around every corner.

With a final glance at Selaina, Rykan gathered the courage to lie back down. The bedroll felt cold against his skin, but he closed his eyes and willed himself to relax. As the darkness of sleep began to pull him under once more, he could only hope that this time, the shadows would remain at bay.

⌘

As dawn broke through the windows of the main room, Rykan tried to ignore the others as they stirred from their slumber. Nadara groaned softly, pulling her blanket tighter before finally sitting up with a resigned sigh. Kadin rubbed the back of his neck, squinting toward the light. Ysadora was already on her feet, repacking her satchel with a quiet efficiency that irked Rykan for no good reason.

He wasn't ready to move. Even more so, he wasn't ready to gather his things and start the journey again. But it was no use, he wasn't going back to sleep.

Rykan rubbed his eyes and rose, leaving his blanket where it was. He joined the others as some bundled their bedding and others secured their weapons. Selaina offered him a tired smile as she adjusted the strap across her shoulder.

A few moments later, Garrick handed him a rolled blanket, his own, already packed tight. Rykan accepted it with a quiet nod of thanks.

Oran stood nearby, watching their preparations with calm attentiveness. He stepped forward, holding a small basket. "I prepared something for you," he said. "Dried fruits and oats. It should keep well."

"Thank you," said Selaina, stepping closer. "You've been so kind to us, Oran. I hope we can make it up to you one day."

Oran smiled gently, his eyes filled with the depth of many years. "Kindness is given without demand. But ask yourself, if you could walk through a single moment again… what would you change? What would you carry differently?"

The room grew still. Even Kadin, who had been fussing with his boot, paused to glance up.

Oran's words hit Rykan harder than expected. He'd always lived like there'd be time later, to fix, to mend, and to speak. But people left. Moments passed. And sometimes, the chance never came again. Still, Oran's words lingered: Today is always a new beginning. Maybe he couldn't undo the times he'd let someone slip away, but he didn't have to keep repeating the pattern. He could be more present. More intentional.

He looked around the room, at Selaina tightening the straps on her pack, at Garrick checking the edge of his blade, at Nadara winding her long hair into a braid, and silently promised himself not to miss the next chance. Because whether you had a thousand tomorrows or only one, the time to change was always now.

"Before you leave," Oran said, "you should come to the spring basin. Everyone will be there. We purify ourselves before the day begins. It is quite refreshing."

They passed through the main square, the morning quiet broken only by soft footfalls and the low hum of villagers heading in the same direction. Kadin yawned and stretched dramatically. "You think this place has bitterroot brew?" he muttered.

Nadara gave him a look that shut him up faster than a command.

When they reached the basin, it was already teeming with people. Some waded knee-deep, others submerged fully and returned dripping to the stone edges. Steam rose where the cold met early sunlight, rising like breath from the earth.

Selaina removed her cloak and boots, dipping her toes into the shallows. "It's freezing!" she said with a shiver, hopping backward.

Oran passed by without hesitation, walking into the water with steady purpose. He showed no expression of discomfort as he sank to his shoulders and then beneath.

"I think I'll warm up just watching him," Kadin said, but Ysadora was already at the edge, unfastening her gloves. "It's a ritual," she said simply. "There's value in it."

Garrick was pulling off his outer layers. "If nothing else, it'll wake us up."

Rykan stepped forward, the cold mist curling around his calves like fingers. Each step into the water was a quiet dare. The deeper he went, the colder it bit, but he welcomed it. It grounded him, cut through the dream-fog still clinging to his mind. Maybe this was what he needed. Something real and pure.

Selaina was ahead of him, chest deep now. She paused, took one breath, and slipped beneath the surface. When she came back up, the water rolled off her like silk. She didn't say anything, just kept moving through the shallows with a quiet grace.

Rykan didn't wait any longer. He took a final step and plunged under.

The cold wrapped around him with all the welcoming of stone. His breath vanished. For a second, everything stopped, no mountain or prophecy, no voices clawing at the edges of his mind. Just the silence of water. The hush of the world held at bay.

Down there, eyes closed, he tried to release the thoughts that stalked him in the dark: the dream, the bite, the promises whispered through blood and shadow. He tried to believe he still had choices. That he wasn't already tethered to something he couldn't see.

When he rose, he gasped. Air rushed back in, sharp and clean. The morning light caught the surface of the pool, and around him, others were already wading back to shore.

Nadara's braid shed water as she whipped it back over her head. Garrick was wringing out his tunic. Even Kadin, swearing and shivering, had gone under.

But Rykan stayed a moment longer, water dripping from his hair, his chest heaving. It wasn't just the cold anymore, it was clarity.

For now, that was enough.

"Water shapes the earth just as hardship shapes life," said Oran. "Resist it like stone, and you may face a deluge rather than a trickle."

Rykan used his cloak to dry the dampness off his feet before putting his boots back on. He grabbed his gear as the others prepared to head out.

"Pay close attention when you reach the Serpent's Tear," said Oran. "The path upward is not always visible at first glance. Look closely, and notice the subtle ways water has carved its path through the earth."

Rykan frowned thoughtfully at the words but didn't have time to linger.

Nadara, rummaging through her pouch, stepped forward with a focused urgency. "Oran, before we leave, may I ask you something?"

Oran arched a brow. "Of course."

Nadara pulled out the map of Galanor, its edges worn and creased from travel. "I've been trying to figure out these markings." She smoothed the map on a flat rock, pointing toward the inked circles. "There's one here at Kylinshan. You seem to know so much about the mountain, I was hoping you might recognize what these mean."

Rykan shifted his weight, folding his arms across his chest as Oran leaned in. The older man's eyes moved over the map with the kind of attention Rykan had come to expect from him, slow, deliberate, as if pulling threads from a tangle.

The circles dotted different parts of the map. Rykan had seen them before, but without any rhyme or reason to their placement, they felt like meaningless ink on parchment.

Oran traced his finger to Kylinshan first, then slowly moved to another point. "These markings… they remember," he muttered. "They trace paths the world has tried to forget."

Nadara leaned in. "What do you mean?"

Oran didn't answer immediately. Instead, he began to draw invisible lines in the air above the map, connecting the circles one by one. "They aren't symmetrical, no… but look closer. See how this one here," he pointed to Kylinshan, "connects to this circle in the south?" He drew an imaginary line. "And then this one to the west…"

Nadara leaned in, eyes narrowing. "They're forming something."

"Yes." Oran's voice sharpened with growing certainty. "It's subtle, too subtle for someone just glancing at a map, but the circles align along natural nexus points. Places where the boundaries between the mortal realm and the realms of Archeinor and Pandemora are weakest." He looked up. "That's where the Dreylith Wards were planted. Ancient sentinels created to anchor the boundary between worlds."

"Are the wards inside the temples?" Nadara asked.

"Temples were built around the wards that were known," said Oran. "Most of them are mistaken for ordinary trees."

"Trees?" Nadara echoed. "The Dreylith Wards are trees?"

"Ancient, powerful ones," Oran confirmed. "Far stronger than stone. They cannot be felled or burned."

"It wasn't the temple," said Nadara. "It was the tree inside the ruins that the stranger came to see."

Rykan glanced at her, brow furrowed. "Why? What would be his interest in the Wards?"

"I don't know," Nadara admitted, her expression shadowed with thought. "But if these points mark where the boundaries are weakest, that stranger must have had a reason to tamper with them."

Oran inclined his head. "Whatever their intent, it's troubling. If any nexus point is disturbed, it could open a path for influence—Archeinor at best… Pandemora at worst."

A cold weight settled in Rykan's chest. *Pandemora.* Nociferon's name echoed there like the bite wound that hadn't healed, quiet, festering, always just beneath the surface. Maybe the Iron Flood wasn't the only storm gathering. Maybe it wasn't even the worst one.

He remembered the tree in his dream, the red vortex churning inside it. The way Arathain and the others had spoken, like they were already moving, already tearing at the world's seams.

He should speak. Tell them what he'd seen. Warn them. But what would he say? That chaos itself had whispered to him? That something he barely understood was drawing monsters from the dark? That he felt the storm inside him, and couldn't tell where it ended and he began?

They had enough to carry. Especially Selaina.

So he said nothing. But his gaze lingered on the map. The markings no longer looked like harmless circles. They looked like fractures waiting to spread.

CHAPTER 23

RYKAN CAUGHT THE look Garrick sent him, a silent agreement that they needed to move.

"Thank you, Oran," Nadara said, quiet resolve in her voice.

With a final wave of farewell, the group turned their backs on the village of Shadal, their path bending toward the river.

The wilderness swallowed them almost immediately. Towering trees, some older than memory, formed a living canopy overhead, their branches whispering softly as the wind tugged through them. Shafts of golden light pierced the shadows, revealing carpets of moss and ferns spread like blankets over the ground.

Rykan kept close to the river, its cool breeze brushing his skin as its white-crested cascades crashed over smooth stones. The sound was a steady guide, soothing yet relentless, like time itself carving its path. Ferns and flowers lined the banks, their vibrant colors standing out against the muted greens and browns of the forest. He took a deep breath, the earthy scent of moss and pine grounding him for a moment.

Behind him, the others moved in silence. Footsteps muffled by pine needles. Occasional rustles. No one spoke, but the quiet felt heavy rather than calm, like something unsaid was building between them.

Selaina's gaze was distant, locked on the light shifting through the branches overhead. Ysadora moved beside her, eyes half-lidded in thought, fingers brushing the bark of each tree they passed as if searching for something.

Rykan looked forward again. The trees stretched on, tall and endless. The forest breathed with them, and around them, it watched.

Some time passed like that. No one measured it. Only the sound of the river marked their progress.

Eventually, the trees began to thin, not all at once, but subtly, like the land was giving them room to breathe. Rykan noticed more sky between the branches, the ground sloping upward into clusters of rock. He stepped through a veil of mist and paused.

Before him, stone pillars rose like ancient giants, their surfaces worn smooth by wind and rain. Mist clung to the rocky outcrops, swirling lazily in the soft breeze, casting the mountain in a surreal, dreamlike haze. The sight was beautiful, but his unease lingered, pressing at the edges of his mind.

The sun climbed higher in the sky, drying the dampness clinging to them from the morning's cool air. The trail steepened, forcing Rykan to focus on every step as jagged rocks and narrow ledges demanded his attention. He gripped his sword, the strain in his legs growing with each incline. As they climbed higher, the view opened up. For a moment, he paused, taking in the sweeping valleys below and the mist-wrapped peaks ahead. The vastness was humbling, but it only made him feel smaller, more distant from everything he wanted to protect.

"What do you think the Iron Flood's doing right now?" Rykan asked when they stopped to rest under the shade of a leaning pine tree. He leaned back on his hands, tilting his face toward the sky as though the sun might burn away the tension in his chest.

Settling onto a flat rock, Garrick pulled out his sharpening stone and unsheathed his blade, inspecting it. "They were using Alisaran as a staging area," Garrick said. "Gathering supplies, assessing their troops, planning their next attack."

Rykan picked up a small pebble and tossed it idly toward the edge of the trail. "What if they've already taken half of Galanor by the time we make it to the top of the mountain?"

Garrick paused mid-stroke, glancing up at Rykan with a faint smirk. "He can't move that fast. Supply chains, wounded men, territory to hold. That'll slow him down."

Rykan frowned, turning his gaze to Selaina, who sat nearby, her elbows resting on her knees. He couldn't help but notice how calm she seemed, so certain of their path, even as doubts gnawed at him.

"Why do you continue to doubt that this is the right journey?" she asked, her voice steady but pointed. "I thought you believed in me."

"I do believe in you," he said, shifting under her gaze. "I just... I can't help but imagine that he's growing stronger by the day. That each day we aren't out there ahead of him feels like a day wasted. I fear for my mother. If she's alive, she's still in Tathara under Iron Flood rule."

Selaina nodded slowly, her expression softening. "I understand how you feel, Rykan. My mother is missing too. For a long time, finding her was everything to me. I still ache not knowing where she is."

She looked down, fingers lacing together tightly in her lap.

"But the moment I touched the Stone, everything changed. I felt it, something vast and old moving through me. I saw a path, not just for me, but for the world. This mark... this destiny... it isn't a title. It's a burden. One I didn't ask for, but one I carry now. And I carry it because of him, Vatreus. I know what he's doing, what he's become. And I know... I'm the only one who might be able to stop him."

She turned toward Rykan, her eyes catching his.

"If I turn away now, if I chase my own answers instead of stopping him, then everything he's done, everyone he's taken, keeps happening. That includes your mother. And mine."

Rykan was silent for a moment, his gaze drifting to the edge of the cliff. He crouched near a loose stone and picked it up, rolling it between his fingers. "Does it ever feel like the rules we're given, these paths, these destinies, are just cages with better names?" he asked.

Selaina didn't flinch. "Fate doesn't save us. It offers us the chance to save each other."

Rykan looked down at his hands. "What if that's not enough?"

Ysadora frowned. "Fate isn't something you just rewrite because it's inconvenient."

A breath caught in his throat. He didn't tell them what else he'd seen. In dreams. In whispers. The Chaos Lord's voice, coiled like smoke around his thoughts.

What if time could be undone? What if beginnings and endings were illusions? What if you could stand with your mother again, whenever you chose?

He swallowed hard. "I don't want to watch the world fall apart just because it followed the rules." He looked back at Selaina, eyes burning. "Maybe we need to stop waiting for permission. Maybe we need to break something, to make space for something better."

Selaina stepped closer. "You think the world needs to be destroyed and rebuilt? I think it needs to heal." Her voice was steady, but her gaze was soft. "You tear at the walls because you're afraid they'll close in. I try to hold them up, because I know what happens when they fall."

"I'm not afraid," he said.

"You're not reckless either," she replied. "But you're hurt. And chaos always rushes in through wounds."

He looked away, jaw tight.

"You're not wrong," she said after a beat. "Sometimes the system fails. Sometimes it traps people instead of protecting them. But you can't save the world by burning it down."

Rykan's voice was low. "And you can't save it by pretending the fire's not already burning."

They stood there, not as enemies or even opposites, but as the tension between two truths.

Then Selaina reached out, her fingers brushing his wrist.

"We'll find a way," she said. "Believe me."

He rubbed the back of his neck, glancing uneasily at her. "Well, it's enough to make anyone wonder," he said defensively. "What if we're looking at everything all wrong?" He turned toward Selaina, his expression more searching. "If you had used the Wishing Stone, you said Myrradin would have used the powers of Azragul, a being of Archeinor, to enslave everyone. What if the destinies of Archeinor are enslaving us as well?"

Selaina stiffened, her hand brushing instinctively against her forehead. The movement struck Rykan as odd, hesitant, almost fearful.

Ysadora interrupted before she could answer.

"If time wasn't ordered, we would not exist," she said, rising to her feet. "We need both Pandemora and Archeinor, but without Archeinor, we would have no guidance, no form. We would all be clouds spinning in nothingness with no coherent thoughts to make us distinct from one another. Without the ordering of time, there could be no space, and then we are still in the eternal thought, without a Prime Sequence chosen, without actualization."

Rykan frowned, her words like puzzle pieces that didn't fit together. "Then why do some people want to unravel it?" he asked, his voice tense. "They must know something we don't."

Ysadora's tone softened, though her conviction remained firm. "Many have pursued chaotic magic out of greed and lust for power. And every one of them has failed. By its very nature, chaos resists control. It's a delusion, a trap, for those arrogant enough to think they can wield it."

Rykan stilled, his hand resting on his knee. His voice dropped, more thoughtful now. "And yet they keep trying. Maybe… maybe it's because they're tired of being told there's only one way forward. Maybe they're tired of destiny being dictated to them."

Selaina straightened, her voice steady as she spoke. "Destiny isn't a chain. The path is there, but we're the ones who decide how we walk it. That's the difference between Archeinor and Pandemora, structure versus chaos, not enslavement."

Rykan leaned back, his gaze lifting toward the sky. Her words settled over him, heavy with meaning. Above, the sunshimmer sparkled, like distant flames in the sunlight, as if the heavens themselves breathed them into the air high above them.

Rykan's gaze lingered on the distant shimmer of light. Somewhere, beyond the horizon, answers waited, but so did the shadows.

CHAPTER 24

SELAINA LED THEM onward as the trail veered gently away from the river's edge. The rush of the currents grew softer with each step, fading into a muted murmur that barely reached her ears. The sound of water lapping against smooth stones was all that lingered, a quiet backdrop to their progress. Yet, the river's path revealed glimpses of its wilder past. Carved stones lined the distant banks, their ancient grooves and eroded edges bearing witness to a time when the waters roared far higher and stronger. The exposed rock, streaked with mineral stains and etched with the passage of centuries, stood as a monument to what the river had once been. Selaina cast a final glance over her shoulder at the glint of sunlight on the calm waters. They were leaving behind a piece of forgotten history.

The group emerged from the thick forest into a secluded glade, a tranquil oasis where the river pooled into a wide, shallow basin. Trees, ancient and towering, framed the clearing, their arched branches forming a natural canopy that filtered sunlight into delicate, shifting patterns. The light danced on the surface of the pool, reflecting the sky and trees like a world suspended beneath the water.

Rykan crouched by the bank, running his fingers along the smooth stones at the water's edge. "This river must've been enormous once," he said, his gaze tracing the worn edges of the rocky channel.

"It was," Selaina said, glancing up toward the mountain. "Oran was right. The Glissarans dammed it upstream. This is all that's left for Shadal now."

Nadara frowned, studying the dry, cracked earth along the broader sections of the riverbed. "It's no wonder they're struggling. They must've depended on the full flow."

"It appears that dependence doesn't matter to the Glissarans," Kadin said. "They built their dam and claimed the water as theirs."

Selaina felt the weight of Kadin's words as she looked back at the diminished river. It was more than a flow of water, it was life itself, stolen from one place to enrich another.

And here she was, meant to bring balance. But what if she was more like this dried-up river than she wanted to admit? Carrying something vital, but already cracked and hollow beneath the surface.

The glade was lush with greenery, ferns, mosses, and delicate wild-flowers growing in quiet abundance. The air was cool and fragrant, filled with the earthy scent of the forest and the faint, sweet perfume of blooming flowers. The occasional rustle of leaves in the breeze mingled with the gentle flow of the water, as if the glade itself whispered secrets to those who ventured into its hidden sanctuary.

But as Selaina's gaze traveled along the water, she noticed how the river's path told a story of decline. The smooth stones and grooves in the surrounding rock marked a time when the river must have been much larger, its currents once carving a powerful route through the land. Now, it was a pale shadow of its former self, a dwindling stream that had surrendered its strength upstream to the Glissarans' dam. The edges of the rocky channel, dry and cracked, framed the flow like an old memory, faint but still lingering.

At the center of the pool, a small island rose, covered in smooth stones and crowned with a single, twisted tree. Its branches were heavy with faintly glowing blossoms, like they cradled the last remnants of a forgotten world. The tree stood alone, its beauty otherworldly yet touched by an ineffable sadness, as if mourning the river's former glory.

As Selaina stepped closer, a quiet melancholy settled over her. The glade was undeniably beautiful, but the diminished river and the stillness here felt like a place left behind, its vitality siphoned away. She felt a deep, inexplicable connection to it, as though this forgotten place was a mirror for something in her own journey, a fading beauty, like a dream you can't quite remember.

She lingered there, leaning against a large stone just ahead of the muddy banks. The others continued on the trail, their footsteps fading. But she noticed Rykan making his way toward her.

"Mind if I join you?" he asked.

She didn't answer at first. Then she spoke, not even realizing what it might sound like. "Do you think we're doing the right thing?" She hesitated. "Am I?"

Rykan glanced at her, then at the slow-moving stream. "You're not sure?"

"I thought about what you said. Destiny being a cage," She climbed onto the stone, knees drawn in, arms wrapped loosely around them. "In Wekenwild, everything was so clear to me. But lately… it feels like I'm just being carried along by something I don't understand."

Rykan leaned forward, elbows on his knees, eyes fixed on the slow-moving water. "You ever wonder if… maybe the world does need to be undone?"

Selaina turned slightly, startled.

"I don't mean like Nociferon," Rykan said quickly, running a hand through his hair. "Not tearing it all down just to watch it burn. But… when I look at the way things are, people starving, rulers hoarding power, whole cities crushed under the weight of someone else's dream. It's hard not to wonder if the whole thing was broken from the start."

The wind stirred the grass around the glade. Neither of them spoke.

"I don't *want* to think that way," he added. "But it creeps in sometimes. When I feel like we're bleeding just to keep the pieces from falling apart."

Selaina's gaze softened. "You're not the only one."

"I always figured destiny meant having answers," he said, his shoulders rising. "Knowing the next step instead of stumbling through it."

Selaina didn't look at him, but her fingers traced along her knees, like she was following the edge of a thought. "Everyone thinks I'm strong because I keep going. What if it's just that I don't know how to stop?"

He fiddled awkwardly with the wrist wraps near his sword hilt, not quite meeting her eyes. "That still counts," he said gently.

A hush swept through the glade, the wind curling around them like it was leaning in to listen.

She turned to him at last, her voice softer. "I was hoping you'd say something that made it all make sense."

Rykan's mouth curved into a small, wry smile. "I was hoping you'd figured it out so I wouldn't have to."

She gave a quiet huff, half a laugh, half surrender. "You're not as helpful as you think."

"No," he said, tilting his head, "but I'll be here when you need reminding. Of who you are. Even if you don't have the words for it yet."

Something close to certainty stirred in her. A door left ajar. She didn't speak. Her fingers brushed his, tentative and unsure.

For a heartbeat, nothing moved. Then Rykan's hand turned, sliding around hers, warm and steady. Selaina's chest ached. She hadn't realized how much she'd needed that small, silent anchor until it was there, holding her without demanding anything at all.

His hand turned, sliding around hers. He offered no pressure, only his presence.

"I don't know what's ahead," she said. "But in this moment… it doesn't feel quite so impossible."

"You've already done the impossible," he murmured. "From here on, it should be easier."

CHAPTER 25

SELAINA WANTED TO stay, to sit under the tree and watch its reflection in the water, as if it might help her hold onto that fleeting feeling. But the sun, though lower now, still hung high enough to remind her there was too much daylight left to waste. Reluctantly, she turned to follow the others.

As the shadows between the trees lengthened with the descending sun, a melodic whistle entered the quiet. She recognized the whistle as one of Garrick's signals. Selaina stopped and turned, searching the underbrush until she spotted it, a pronghorn with gray fur nibbling on low-hanging leaves. It was a distance away, and Selaina knew any sudden movement toward it would send it fleeing into the shadows.

Selaina slipped her bow from her shoulder and drew an arrow from her quiver. Rykan and the others stood back as she took aim. It was outside her normal accuracy range but would make for a good test. Without accounting for the force of the arrow or the wind, she fired. Focusing on the arrow as it hurled out of sight, Selaina felt its path. It would fall short, landing in the dirt in front of her prey.

With concentration, she bent the path of the arrow, guiding it upward. The arrow climbed, too high, rising toward the canopy of trees overhead, trailing blue energy as it flew. Selaina forced the arrow back downward until its aim was true. It struck the pronghorn in the back with enough force to go through its heart and out of its chest.

"That was… amazing," said Garrick. "How?"

"I feel connected to something greater," said Selaina. "I don't know if I can explain it better than that. Maybe Ysadora can."

"Tapping into Archeinor's power manifests itself in different ways for different people," Ysadora said. "I suppose it makes sense for Selaina's to be about setting her will on the arrows she uses."

Ysadora stepped beside her, eyes narrowing thoughtfully. "When you loosed that arrow," she said, "did you will its path, or did it respond to your need?"

Selaina hesitated. "Both, maybe. It felt like it was listening. Or… like I was listening to it."

Ysadora nodded. "Then you're not merely guiding arrows. You're shaping potential, refining possibility. That takes discipline. We'll work on it. Tonight, if the forest stays quiet."

Garrick darted into the brush, quickly wrapping the pronghorn in cloth before draping it over his shoulders. The group pressed on, twilight closing in, heavy and stifling.

The forest thinned out as they continued, leaving behind only the oldest, tallest trees, their gnarled branches stretching skyward. The air grew colder, and the bright underbrush gave way to a thick carpet of decaying leaves that crunched softly underfoot.

As they set up camp, Selaina couldn't shake the growing sense of unease gnawing at her. Rykan and the others busied themselves with building a campfire, while she and Garrick worked on preparing the pronghorn for cooking. The fire crackled, its warmth spreading, but Selaina could still feel the chill that crept into her bones. It was far colder than the night air.

"I'm not sure I like this place," Kadin murmured, picking at his food with little appetite. His voice was hushed, as though speaking louder might invite something unwanted. "We should've made camp a few miles back, where it was nicer."

"This is as good a place as any," Garrick responded, though his voice held an edge, as if he, too, felt the unease they all tried to ignore. "We're not here to enjoy the scenery."

Selaina glanced up from her plate, her gaze drifting to the distant peaks. The mark on her forehead tingled, as if responding to her thoughts. She pressed her hand to it absently, as if that might silence it.

Vatreus's name lingered, silent and suffocating. He was her brother, though none of them knew that. The secret settled in her chest like a stone, growing heavier with each day.

What would they say if they knew? Would they pull away? Would fear take the place of trust?

Would they still believe she was the one meant to save anything at all?

The idea of becoming like him gnawed at her soul, a fear she dared not voice. There were quiet moments when, in her mind, the line between them blurred.

She inhaled deeply, steadying her nerves, though her hands were curled tight in her lap.

"Who do you think Vatreus really is?" she asked, turning to Garrick. Her voice was calm, but the question burned in her chest. "Is there a heart in there somewhere?"

"When I first heard him speak," said Garrick as the sharpening stone stilled in his hand, "there was a fire in him, not anger, not ambition, but something pure. He talked about justice, about making the world better for people like us. He called us the forgotten. The ones sent out to die for someone else's pride. Those who hungered for any scraps they could get for a hard day's work. I think, in the beginning, he wanted to do something good. Maybe he even thought he could. I don't think so many people would have followed him if there wasn't something real behind his words."

"But that wasn't enough for him," said Selaina, straightening, her fingers curling again on her knees. She stared ahead, nails pressing into her knee, afraid that meeting his eyes might reveal too much.

"Once we took over one of the lord's houses… the town became ours," Garrick said. He nodded, his voice hardening. "That was his first taste of power and slowly he grew addicted to it."

Selaina's pulse quickened. Was this where the mark would lead her—into the same hunger for control? "What were the first signs of this change?"

"He started seeing people as tools, pieces in some grand design only he understood," Garrick said, resuming the slow scrape of the blade. "And the more you tried to question him, the less he trusted you. By the time I left, he was unrecognizable. He may have had a heart once, but I'm not sure anyone could find it now."

Her voice dropped to a whisper. "Was it Azragul's power that turned him into this?"

The question she asked wasn't the one she feared most. What had their mother seen in Vatreus, all those years ago? He had been a boy, sick, fragile, and yet… she had left him. Presumably, she fled with Selaina in her arms and never looked back.

Selaina had never fully understood it. How a mother could abandon a child. Had her mother sensed what Vatreus would become? Or had the darkness only taken root after that day at the gate? But maybe it was to save Selaina, as the other child.

She remembered the vision the Wishing Stone had given her, the mountain groaning, the gate pulsing like a wound. Her mother had stood beside a man, Lucianis. She had never known him, but something inside her whispered that he was her father.

They had begged Azragul to save their son. His price: a mortal life for each year Vatreus would survive.

Selaina had watched them obey. Watched them push a man, perhaps a friend, perhaps just a desperate stranger, into the darkness beneath the gate.

How many more had followed?

How many lives had they sacrificed, how many years had they carved out for him? At some point, it must have gotten out of hand. It always did. And now… Vatreus was sending sacrifices by the cartload.

She imagined her mother trying to bear it, standing at the threshold again and again, watching faces vanish into shadow. Feeling her son grow stronger with each offering, each life snuffed out like a candle.

And then… she had run. With Selaina.

But Lucianis must have stayed.

Selaina blinked at the firelight, drawing a slow, shaky breath through parted lips, her fingers curling into the dirt. Her father had stayed, with Vatreus. Had he believed he was doing the right thing? That Vatreus could still be saved? Or had he simply accepted that they had gone too far to turn back?

She would never know. The silence he left behind was part of her now. Another unanswered question. Another shadow she carried.

She hadn't only inherited destiny, she'd inherited the wreckage her parents left behind.

"It sure didn't help." Garrick sighed, setting the blade aside and meeting her gaze. "But I don't think anything can justify the choices he made."

The weight of his words pressed against her ribs. "So there's no hope for him then?"

Garrick's gaze was steady but somber. "He's too far into it. No one could convince him to stop now. He'd have anyone who tried… killed."

Selaina looked away, her eyes tracing the jagged peaks silhouetted against the darkening sky. The mountain loomed, its sheer scale matching the burden of her thoughts.

Across the fire, Rykan shifted. "Hope for Vatreus?" he asked as his gaze flicked toward her, then quickly away again. She caught the brief sputter in his eyes, restlessness, maybe even unease. "He killed my father. You really think there could be hope for him? We must have justice. Galanor demands it." His hand tensed where it rested near the hilt of his blade.

Selaina didn't answer right away. A tightness crept into her chest. She pressed her lips together and made her face unreadable.

He didn't know what she carried. The blood in her veins. The memory of what her parents had done. And the part of her that still, somehow, wanted to believe her brother wasn't completely lost.

Was that care… or denial?

The mountain loomed, its sheer scale matching the enormity of her thoughts. Was she destined to stand against her brother? To end what he had become?

And if she failed, what would that mean for the power she carried?

Her eyes drifted from the fire to the shadows beyond. The usual hum of the forest, birdsong, rustling leaves, was gone, replaced by something far more sinister. A low, guttural noise echoed from the darkness, followed by a resonant growl that sent a shiver down her spine.

"What was that?" Rykan asked, his eyes darting nervously into the trees.

"I don't like this place either," Ysadora added. A rhythmic scratching noise began to circle them, the sound growing louder, more insistent. "Something isn't right."

Selaina's heart quickened, her eyes narrowing as she tried to pinpoint the source of the sound. The oppressive stillness in the air felt like a warning, a sign that they were not alone.

"You should have said something sooner," Garrick snapped, his frustration barely concealing his own discomfort. "It's too dark now to find another campsite."

Rykan suddenly stood, rubbing his arm, his face twisted in discomfort. He stepped away from the fire, moving toward the shadows that seemed to pulse at the edge of their camp.

"Rykan?" Selaina called, rising to her feet. Concern bloomed in her chest as she watched him pace, his hand still clutching his arm. "What's wrong?"

"Nothing," Rykan replied, though his voice lacked conviction. "My arm… it just hurts sometimes."

"You mean the bite?" Selaina insisted, stepping closer to him. "Let me see it."

"It's fine," Rykan muttered, backing further away, toward the darkness that seemed to close in around them.

"Come back into the light," Selaina urged. "If it's hurting again, there must be something causing it."

Reluctantly, Rykan moved back into the glow of the campfire, and Selaina reached out to roll back his sleeve. But before she could inspect the wound, another low, menacing growl reverberated through the trees, closer this time. The fire snapped hard, flaring at the sound, and the shadows around them seemed to ripple and grow.

"It's fine," Rykan muttered, but his voice faltered as he clutched his arm more tightly. "It's just… different sometimes. Like it's alive."

"Alive?" Kadin interjected, stepping closer but keeping his distance from the darkness. "That's not exactly the reassuring answer we're looking for, Rykan. What are you hiding under there, a second head?"

"Kadin you're not helping," Selaina said sharply, but her eyes didn't waver from Rykan. "Let me see."

"It's nothing!" Rykan snapped, his frustration laced with a hint of fear. "Just leave it alone."

The fire dimmed. Cold crept in, swallowing the warmth. Selaina's eyes widened as she noticed the shadows lengthening, creeping toward them like living things. Eyes pressed in from the dark, unseen, but felt.

"Do you see that?" Ysadora's voice trembled, her eyes wide as the shadows began to inch closer, darker and more substantial than before.

The low growl came again, this time accompanied by the rustling of leaves and the snapping of twigs. Selaina spun around just in time to see pairs of glowing eyes emerging from the darkness, their cold, predatory gaze fixed on the group.

"Maugwins," Rykan whispered.

The creatures stepped into the faint light, their dark, sinewy forms blending with the shadows that clung to them like a shroud.

As the maugwins advanced, the shadows slithered closer, stretching into long inky tendrils. Selaina felt a sudden, icy grip on her ankle, and she looked down to see a tendril of shadow coiling around her leg, tightening like a noose. The cold was unbearable, seeping into her bones, making it difficult to move, to think.

The maugwins circled the campsite, their movements slow and deliberate, like they could taste the fear radiating from the group. The fire shimmered weakly, its light barely holding back the encroaching darkness. Selaina could feel shadows crawling up her limbs, draining the fight from her.

Ysadora found her staff, rubbing the Sunkeeper crystal to ignite its energy, blinding in the dark. The shadowy tendrils around Selaina's ankle began to writhe and convulse as the light from the crystal grew brighter. The shadows reacted as if burned, twisting and jerking in spasms of pain. A faint hissing sound filled the air, like steam escaping a boiling cauldron, as the dark tendrils blistered and bubbled under the radiant glow.

As Ysadora reached her staff further toward the shadows, they began to wither, their inky blackness peeling away in layers of oily, translucent filth. Selaina stood close to Ysadora as the long claws of the shadow split open along their length revealing a pulsing, rotting core that oozed a thick, tar-like substance. Frayed edges tore apart dripping with vicious, foul-smelling ichor as they disintegrated into the light.

With a sickening wet sound, the remaining shadows retreated as if they were being sucked back into the earth itself, dragging along with them the remnants of their own decay. With one last quiver, the darkness was yanked back violently into the maugwins as their eyes gleamed with some unnatural strength.

The maugwins began circling again, stalking, as if looking for a weakness in the group's defenses. Selaina and the others crowded around Ysadora, trying to keep close to the brightest of the stone's light. Kadin fired shot after shot, planting himself just ahead of Ysadora.

"Don't get noble," she snapped, half-glancing his way as she focused the light into a beam.

"Too late," he muttered, reloading. "You've already ruined me."

Once the maugwins completed a circle, they spread out, surrounding the group, ready to attack from all sides. Selaina readied her bow as the others brandished their weapons.

"I can't let this happen again," Rykan said, as he dashed away from the group.

"Rykan, wait!" Selaina shouted, her voice cracking as he slipped between the maugwins and vanished into the dark.

Kadin stepped closer to her, blade raised. "If that was supposed to be a distraction, it didn't-"

One of the maugwins twisted its head sharply. Its eyes tracked the shadows where Rykan had gone. Then, like a beast catching the scent of fleeing prey, it lunged, leaping into the trees after him.

A second one paused, its body tense, but stayed behind, its eyes still locked on the group.

"What is he doing?" Selaina whispered.

The maugwins moved forward slowly, continuing to stalk the group huddled around Ysadora's light. Then, with a sudden burst of speed, one of them lunged, crashing into Garrick and knocking him to the ground. His weapon clattered to the side as he hit hard, his breath knocked from his chest.

Selaina barely had time to turn before another maugwin charged straight for Ysadora, its eyes locked on the glowing crystal atop her staff.

Garrick gritted his teeth and forced himself up, slashing at the creature's side with his recovered blade. It hissed but did not retreat, circling warily just beyond the staff's glow.

Selaina spun, loosing an arrow at a third maugwin that lunged at Nadara. Nadara met it with her glaive, slicing a deep gash into its shoulder before it slunk back, snarling.

The chaos of the attack was overwhelming. The maugwins came from all sides, yet never all at once.

They weren't just attacking, they were driving them. Cold crept up Selaina's spine. This wasn't a frenzy. It was a plan. They were being positioned. Worn down.

Kadin fired relentlessly into the shifting dark, bolts thudding into flesh and shadow. Nadara spun her glaive in wide arcs, keeping them back for now.

Selaina's bow string snapped again and again as she loosed arrow after arrow into the maugwin harassing Ysadora. Even wounded, the creature did not lunge, it waited. Watching. Flinching only when the Sunkeeper's glow seared too close.

Then it moved.

From Ysadora's blind side, a second maugwin struck, not at her, but at the staff.

Its claws slashed in a swift, brutal arc. The wood snapped with a sharp crack, and the upper half of the staff spun away, the Sunkeeper crystal tumbling loose.

The light wavered as the broken staff clattered to the ground, the Sunkeeper crystal tumbling just out of reach.

Ysadora lunged for it.

Tendrils burst from the maugwins' limbs, slithering across the ground like vines grown wild in the dark. Freed from the crystal's burn, they whipped around Ysadora's arms and legs, yanking her backward. She shouted, fingers just inches from the stone.

Selaina reached toward her, but it was too late.

The shadows swallowed Ysadora whole.

All around them, the maugwins hissed in unison. Their eyes gleamed with sudden triumph. Darkness bled from their limbs, thick and alive.

The power that had been contained now unfurled with monstrous strength. Selaina stood frozen.

What was giving these creatures such power?

Ysadora had been taken by the shadows. The light was dying.

CHAPTER 26

RYKAN TORE THROUGH the trees, boots thudding over the forest floor, scattering leaves and snapping brittle twigs beneath his pounding feet. The shadows twisted, creeping at the edges of his sight like they knew he was watching. He didn't slow. Somewhere behind him, one of the maugwins had broken away from the others, he'd felt it, the way its presence shifted and locked onto him like a scent it couldn't shake. It was following him.

The cool night air burned in his lungs as he pushed onward, navigating by memory, retracing the narrow route they'd taken earlier. The mountain sloped steeply here, the ground uneven with jutting roots and loose stones. He had to stay ahead, had to move fast, but not so fast that he lost control and pitched into the ravine below. It took everything he had to steady his breathing, to resist the wild beat of panic rising in his chest.

Every part of him screamed to turn back, to return to the others. To Selaina. But he didn't. He couldn't. The memory of his father, bleeding, falling, helpless, burned behind his eyes like a wound that never fully closed. He hadn't been fast enough then. He hadn't known what to do. He'd watched death take the man who had raised him, and he hadn't stopped it. That failure lived inside him like a curse.

He wouldn't let it happen again. Not to her.

When the trees thinned just enough to open a small clearing, Rykan stopped. The ache in his legs surged into sharp pain as he dropped to a crouch and pressed one hand to the bark of a nearby tree, forcing himself to listen. Behind him, the forest was quiet. Not safe, just quiet.

He slid his blade free.

The wound on his arm, scabbed and knotted with dark scar tissue, pulsed as if recognizing what was coming. He hesitated only a moment before lining his sword up against it and drawing the edge across. The sting was instant and fierce, sharper than he'd braced for. Blood welled up quickly, thicker than it should be, darker. It hissed when it hit the leaves, and the smell of it turned his stomach.

He remembered Arathain's voice, drifting through that twisted dream, how the blood of the bitten could summon the maugwins like wolves to a trail. Maybe they thought it would lead them to Selaina. Maybe it would. But not if he could draw them away first.

Rykan held his arm out, letting the cursed blood drip freely. The sizzle faded as the ground soaked it in, smoke curling above the leaves. He strained to hear something, movement, a growl, a rustle of underbrush, but only the wind answered at first, brushing through the trees like a warning in a held breath.

He knew at least one had followed him. Had felt it break away from the others the moment he ran. It was out there now, near, watching, waiting.

Fear coiled in his stomach, sharp, taunting him with how easily it could end for him here, alone and unseen. Still, he held his ground. He hadn't been enough to save his father, but maybe this time, he could be enough to give Selaina a chance.

A branch snapped beyond the clearing.

Rykan turned toward the sound. The maugwin crept into view, tall, angular, its limbs bending in unnatural ways as it stepped into the faint moonlight. Its eyes shimmered with oily darkness, and when it opened its mouth, the growl that followed sounded less like a beast and more like the grinding of bone against stone.

He didn't wait.

Rykan moved first, swinging the blade low toward the creature's legs. The maugwin leaped sideways with shocking speed, claws slashing toward his chest. Rykan twisted away just in time, but the force of the counter drove him backward into the moss-covered ground. He rolled to his feet and struck again, landing a blow to its shoulder that split the hide, but the wound only oozed a dark, foul-smelling ichor and made the thing snarl louder.

Rykan circled, breath ragged, keeping his back to the trees. As the maugwin advanced again, something strange pulled at the edge of his awareness.

A whisper.

It wasn't the maugwin. It came from behind him, soft and pulsing, like breath through smoke. He caught the barest glimpse of the ground where his blood had fallen. It was steaming more now. Not just steam, something was rising from it.

He almost turned to look, but the maugwin lunged again, and he was forced back into motion.

Rykan ducked under its claws and drove his sword up through its ribs. The blade hit something solid, bone maybe, but he pushed harder, teeth clenched. The maugwin shrieked in his ear. It thrashed on his blade, claws raking his back. Then, finally, it dropped, collapsing like a puppet with its strings cut.

Rykan staggered away, panting, his hands slick with the maugwin's blood. He bent over, steadying himself on one knee, trying to catch his breath.

For a moment, the creature lay still, its body twisted and twitching. Then the blood steaming across the leaves began to smoke, and the maugwin's limbs curled inward. Cracks spidered across its form as if its flesh were turning brittle, and with a sound like dried leaves crumbling underfoot, the corpse broke apart.

Dust scattered on the wind. Everything that had made it monstrous, gone.

Behind him, the hissing sound began to rise again, growing steadily louder. The sound transformed into whispers, as if carried on the wind, speaking in an unintelligible language that sent a chill down his spine. Rykan turned to find dark red and black smoke curling up from the leaves where his blood had fallen. Perhaps this is the beacon that would call the maugwins to it. The smoke writhed and twisted, as if alive, but Rykan forced himself to turn back toward the direction the maugwins would come from. He couldn't afford to be distracted.

But the swirling clouds of smoke behind him continued to hiss, growing louder and more insistent. Unease gnawed at him until he could no longer ignore it. When he turned to look again, his breath caught in his throat, as a dark figure was taking shape within the shadowy mist.

Rykan nearly dropped his sword as the figure glided through the smoke, too smooth, too silent.

The form solidified, revealing a man cloaked in darkness, his features carved from shadow and malice. An aura of wrongness emanated from him, heavy and cold.

"Bloodshadow," came a low, breathy voice. "I've been waiting for this moment."

Rykan froze as the figure solidified from the shadows. Arathain. A being straight out of his nightmares now stood before him, flesh and shadow entwined, his presence radiating malevolence.

Shadows rippled outward from Arathain's feet, stretching like living tendrils across the forest floor. Even from the clearing, Rykan could hear distant cries, Selaina shouting, Garrick grunting with effort.

Arathain's voice slithered through the air. "She is burdened by a power that will consume her. But you, Rykan, you could save her. Free her."

Rykan imagined raising his sword to stab Arathain as he moved toward the campsite, but Arathain continued, his voice seeping into Rykan's mind like poison.

"Where is the girl?" Arathain asked.

Rykan said nothing, still stunned. The sounds of maugwins cried out in the distance, drawing Arathain's attention. He moved through the forest toward the sound, his steps crunching through the leaves.

"Come, my bitten one," he said to Rykan. "I will show you the ways of the shadow."

A whisper drifted behind Arathain's words, Nociferon's voice, slipping like oil through Rykan's thoughts. *No beginning. No end. Only will.*

The shadows shivered as if affirming it. Rykan's legs moved before his thoughts could catch them. Rykan followed, the forest tilting as his legs moved without him willing them. Somewhere in the back of his mind, the whispers returned, the ones he'd tried to forget.

"The unraveling of order… breaks the cycle… brings back what was lost…"

He remembered Arathain and Gwenna in the dream, speaking of time like thread, and death like a rule, just one among many.

For a heartbeat, Rykan had believed it. Had imagined the world turned inside out, the river of time split open where nothing aged toward death, only transformed.

If chaos could do that… wasn't that worth something? A world where time bent, where nothing truly ended, where his father might…

The thought came unbidden, as if it had always been his own:

No beginning. No end. Only will.

He blinked, startled. Had he thought that, or only remembered it?

But then he saw the camp. Selaina stood in the fading light, bow in hand, hair tangled and face streaked with soot, eyes burning with defiance. Garrick fought to rise, bleeding, his weapon half-buried in the ground. Nadara screamed something, he couldn't hear what.

Ysadora was completely entangled. The tendrils had her arms pulled high, legs bound at sharp angles, her staff gone, her body limp in the air like a broken doll suspended in webbing. Shadows wrapped around her neck, her waist, her mouth. Only her eyes were free, wild and terrified.

Something inside Rykan broke loose.

The dream's lies fell away like ash in the wind.

This was real. This was the cost.

In that moment, the whispers didn't sound like hope anymore. They sounded like poison.

Arathain moved toward Selaina, cloaked in shadows that pulsed and coiled like living extensions of his will. The maugwins hissed in unison, their glowing eyes snapping to him as though acknowledging their master. Their movements synchronized, and their tendrils surged forward with newfound strength.

Rykan's shout rang out, cutting through the rising fog. "Get away from her!"

He charged forward, sword flashing in the dim light, but Arathain raised a single hand, and shadow coiled through the air like smoke turned to stone. It didn't strike Rykan like a weapon; it invaded him. Cold and disorienting, it locked his limbs and stole the strength from his muscles. The world tipped, and he hit the ground hard.

He could still move, slowly. Could still speak, but barely. The shadows dulled him, pinning him at the fight's edge like a discarded pawn. Worst of all, he could still see everything.

Arathain lifted his hands. The forest answered. Smoke bled from the ground and trees, thickening into rotting vines and ribbons of shadow that coiled across the clearing like a living net.

Selaina loosed another arrow. Its glow lit the chaos for a heartbeat before slicing into the tendril on Nadara's arm. The shadows recoiled, hissing, but then surged back, thicker, faster, wrapping around her legs and yanking her to one knee.

Garrick's blade flashed, severing a black coil with a hiss of inky mist. He cut through one, then another, moving with brutal precision. But they just came back faster. Tendrils wrapped around his ankles, then his wrists, dragging him back step by step.

He bellowed and tore one free with sheer force, only for more to lunge in, coiling around his chest and shoulders, pinning his arms tight. He dropped to one knee under the weight, shadows crushing down like stone. For a moment, he disappeared beneath the writhing dark.

Then Garrick roared. He surged upward, shadows tearing as he broke through, his hand snatching his fallen blade from the earth.

Arathain's eyes flared.

Garrick charged. Each step cracked frozen earth beneath his boots as he barreled forward, sword raised, teeth bared. He came within arm's reach, close enough to see the twitch of surprise in Arathain's expression.

But the shadows moved faster.

Tendrils struck from every side, slamming into Garrick's body, wrapping around his throat, his sword arm, his legs. He fought them even as they coiled tighter, lifting him off his feet.

The sword slipped from his hand.

Arathain raised a single finger. The shadows slammed Garrick down, the impact shaking the ground. He didn't rise again.

Nadara swept her glaive in wide arcs, snarling, cutting through the dark. But the shadows regrouped, winding up her legs and dragging her down.

The shadows closed in, swallowing what little light remained.

Selaina fired one last shot, straight at Arathain. He raised a hand, and the shadows armored him while the arrow was still in flight. It turned to dust on impact.

His laugh rolled through the clearing, low and mocking.

Rykan's dread hardened as the tendrils caught Selaina. They snaked around her waist, slithered under her arms, curled tight around her throat. Her bow slipped from her grasp and disappeared into shadow.

Nearby, Rykan struggled to rise. His sword trembled in his hand, his strength still sluggish, poisoned.

"What have you done to them?" he gasped.

Arathain tilted his head. "I've shown them the price of resistance. And now, I will show you your place."

The shadows obeyed his outstretched hand, jerking Rykan's body forward like a puppet on tangled strings.

"I have need of your wound again," he said, and raked open Rykan's scarred arm.

Blood struck the earth with a hiss, coiling into smoke. Shadows stirred at the edges of it, rising and writhing. Arathain shoved Rykan aside like a discarded rag. He hit the ground hard, air knocked from his lungs, vision dimming at the edges.

Behind him, the corrupted blood frothed where it soaked the ground. Smoke surged upward in a spiral, slow at first, then faster, sharper—no longer smoke, but structure. A seam in the world began to open, threaded with veins of shadow and glistening red light. It pulled inward, collapsing and expanding all at once, folding reality around it like a wound torn into the fabric of the forest.

A gateway formed, opened, bled into being.

Selaina was being drawn from the others, her limbs bound by ribbons of living shadow. Arathain ran a finger along her jawline, slow and precise, like he was memorizing something he intended to take. He guided her toward the bloodgate.

Rykan clawed at the ground, dragging himself forward. His fingers struck something solid beneath the leaves, a wooden cylinder, warm and smooth. He curled his hand around it, and there at the top, set in the broken wood, was the Sunkeeper stone.

It flared at his touch, blinding and golden. Light exploded across the clearing, and the shadows screamed. Strength surged through him, sharp and sudden as a lightning strike.

Rykan stood, raising the light high.

Arathain flinched as the Sunkeeper's radiance spread through the clearing. Selaina broke free of the shadows, snatched up her bow, and nocked an arrow. It glowed with the stone's light as it flew, piercing the weakened shadows wrapped around Arathain. He staggered, the tendrils at his feet recoiling.

"This is not over," he growled, voice like thunder on the horizon. "You cannot escape me."

He fell backward into the swirling bloodgate, vanishing into smoke and shadow.

CHAPTER 27

THE REMAINING MAUGWINS faltered, then broke. Rykan surged forward with the light, scattering the tendrils that held the others. One final maugwin lunged, only for Garrick to meet it with a clean strike, dropping it in a spray of shadow.

"A shadowmancer…" Ysadora murmured, shivering as she wiped the dusty remnants of shadow from her skin and stared at Rykan. "There aren't supposed to be any of his kind still around. He used your corrupted blood to escape." Her gaze sharpened. "Is that how he found us?" she snapped, her voice rising as she snatched the Sunkeeper stone from his hand. "What were you thinking, running off like that? Selaina was almost taken because of you!"

"I was trying to draw the maugwins away from you," Rykan shot back, breath still ragged. "I didn't know he could actually follow."

"You didn't know?" Garrick's voice cut in, cold and hard. He wiped blood from his blade, eyes burning into Rykan. "And you still risked all our lives?"

Rykan clenched his jaw, guilt flaring in his chest. "I was leading them off. I was trying to help."

"You're cursed," Ysadora said bitterly. "That bite's drawing them to us. You're a threat, Rykan. Maybe you should've stayed in Shadal, where at least you couldn't get the rest of us killed."

"Cursed, huh?" Rykan snapped. "You said you removed it. So which is it?"

"I said I *suppressed* it," Ysadora bit out. "There's a difference."

Rykan's voice rose. "Funny how that didn't stop you from letting me come along. What was it? Your pride? Couldn't admit you didn't know how to fix it?"

Ysadora shouted. "I didn't anticipate this level of exposure—"

Selaina stepped between them, her gaze flicking from face to face. "Enough. He made a mistake, but Arathain is the one who attacked us. He's the real enemy, not Rykan or anyone else."

Silence followed, strained and fragile.

She turned slightly, meeting Ysadora's furious glare. "And you, you know better than anyone how quickly shadows twist people. Rykan fought to save us when it mattered. You saw it."

Ysadora's mouth opened, but Selaina held up a hand. "We can't afford to fracture. Not now. Pandemora is after me, and if we splinter, it'll make it easier for them to take all of us." She turned to Rykan, her voice softening. "You were trying to protect us, I believe that. But if you're going to be with us, you can't go off on your own again, not without telling someone. We face this together, or not at all."

Rykan gave a reluctant nod, eyes lowered.

Selaina looked to the others. "We don't have to trust each other blindly. We only need to stay together long enough to reach the summit and stop the Iron Flood. None of us can do this alone."

A beat passed. Then Garrick gave a small grunt, sheathing his blade. Nadara folded her arms but said nothing. Kadin exhaled, tension draining from his shoulders.

Finally, Ysadora turned her eyes toward the darkened forest and muttered, "Fine. But if he pulls something like that again, I'll bind his feet myself."

Selaina didn't smile, but her voice carried strength. "Then let's make sure none of us has to make that choice again."

Garrick's eyes moved to the path ahead. "We need rest, but I'm not sure we're safe here."

Selaina nodded. "You're right. We need to move. Find another camp."

Ysadora adjusted her grip on her broken staff, the Sunkeeper crystal glowing faintly in her other hand. "We can travel by its light, but we need to use it sparingly," she said, casting a pointed look at Rykan. "His less-than-practiced touch drained most of it."

Rykan shifted, brushing dirt from his sleeve. "Next time, I'll get your permission before saving everyone…"

He turned away, jaw tight, heart still pounding with a mix of anger and shame. Why did they only see the mistake? The failure?

And then, like breath sliding through a crack in the dark…

No beginning. No end. Only will.

The words weren't his. But they felt… steady. Certain. And that scared him most of all.

"How far do we need to go?" Kadin asked, his voice low.

"Somewhere high," Nadara said, her tone matter-of-fact. "A place with a view of the area around us. We can't risk being blindsided."

Rykan bent to gather his blanket, movements brisk. Selaina had said he'd made a mistake. Maybe things hadn't gone exactly as planned, but he'd drawn Arathain out. Driven the maugwins away. That had to count for something. They should've seen that. They should've thanked him.

Garrick crouched by the fire, covering the embers with dirt. Kadin grabbed the remains of the pronghorn.

"Leave it. No time to waste," Garrick said. The scent of charred prong-horn lingered as they moved on, the faint glow of the Sunkeeper lighting their way.

The forest leaned in around them, the river's murmur their only guide as they followed its winding path. Rykan kept his gaze forward, but the prickling sensation at the back of his neck refused to fade.

The silence hung heavy in the cool night air. Rykan clenched his fists, but said nothing. Selaina turned, eyes drifting to the shadowed peaks on the horizon.

"What about there?" Kadin pointed to an area where large boulders jutted up through the ground.

"Looks good to me," Garrick replied. "Better than being out in the open."

"That will do," Selaina agreed. "We all need to get some sleep before dawn."

They lit a small fire between the tall stones and settled in to rest. Rykan leaned against one of the mossy boulders, the cool stone pressing into his back as he tried to quiet his thoughts. But his mind raced, each moment replaying the events of the night: Arathain's shadowy figure, his whispered promises of chaos, and his insidious offer of protection for Selaina.

Chaos, a better solution? Rykan shook the thought away. Arathain's words had been crafted to deceive, to manipulate. He'd seen too much tonight to believe Arathain had anyone's best interests in mind, least of all Selaina's. But the doubt still gnawed at him, a subtle, nagging voice that wouldn't be silenced.

The destinies Selaina carried, were they a gift or a curse? Could they destroy her as Arathain claimed? He didn't know. But even if chaos held answers, Rykan vowed he wouldn't turn to it. He wouldn't let Arathain win.

He drifted off to sleep, but only for a short time. His thoughts were restless. Rykan leaned against a mossy boulder, the fire's quivering light casting faint shadows that seemed to dance in time with his thoughts. Selaina's steady breathing beside him was a quiet anchor in the wake of the chaos. But sleep felt impossible. Arathain's words, and the sting of his wound, gnawed at him like rot beneath the surface.

He stood and scanned the camp. Kadin was sprawled out like he didn't have a care in the world, while Garrick's snoring could probably scare off any wild beasts in the area. Rykan's gaze shifted to the edge of the clearing. It must be Nadara's turn to keep watch.

Following a faint trail through the trees, Rykan found her leaning against a trunk, her face lit by the faint glow of the distant fire. She looked up as he approached, her eyes sharp even in the low light.

"You should be getting some rest," she said, her tone neutral.

Rykan shrugged, running a hand through his hair. "There's too much going through my head for that."

Nadara studied him for a moment, then glanced away. "For what it's worth, it's obvious that you care for Selaina. I don't think you should go back to Shadal."

"Do you think I'm putting everyone in danger?" he asked, his voice quieter than he intended.

Nadara's expression softened, though her gaze remained steady. "No, it's not you. If this shadowmancer is after Selaina, the best way for him to succeed is to make us all lose trust in each other."

Rykan let out a breath he hadn't realized he'd been holding. Nadara's quiet certainty steadied him in a way his own doubts couldn't. He nodded, then hesitated.

"About that map you showed me earlier, the one Oran said marked the Dreylith Wards, did that help you at all?"

"It did. Let me show you something. In addition to the map, Embryss, and some coins, there was this."

She pulled a small pendant from beneath her cloak, the chain glinting in the moonlight. The pendant's design was intricate, an oblong with a smaller circle within it, resembling an eye. At the center of the eye was a five-pointed star.

Rykan frowned. "What is it?"

"The necklace the stranger was wearing when he was found dead," Nadara admitted. "While I was in Itharun, I found someone who recognized it. He said it was the symbol of a secret sect, the Brotherhood of the Silent Star."

Rykan leaned in, curiosity sharpening. "What are they supposed to be?"

"They were rumored to be safeguarding the world from magic," Nadara said.

"And this stranger?" Rykan pressed. "Do you think he was part of the Brotherhood?"

Nadara nodded slowly. "I think so. But something changed. The family I found in Kyrahza said they didn't know much about his younger days, but that he had been hardworking and dependable. Things changed after he was visited by someone from his past, a man who left him shaken and consumed by guilt. He told his wife he'd made a terrible mistake, that he thought he was helping the world but had instead left it vulnerable to destruction."

Rykan looked down, her words sinking heavy in his chest. The man had made a mistake and so had Rykan. At least in the eyes of Selaina and everyone else. She hadn't said it with cruelty, but the words still echoed. Just like this man, he'd believed he was doing the right thing.

Rykan frowned, firelight catching the edge of his blade. "Did he tell her what he meant?"

"No," Nadara said, her voice quieter now. "But he left their home, saying he had to fix it, whatever it was, or he'd be doomed for eternity. Then Oran helped me see that the map marks the locations of these Drey-lith Wards. The stranger must have been trying to find a way to undo what had been done to the tree near my village."

"So, he didn't know he was weakening them?" Rykan asked.

Nadara shook her head. "Not until it was too late. And now… now I wonder if the Brotherhood was behind it all, whether they poisoned the Wards deliberately or out of ignorance."

Rykan studied her, noting the tension in her jaw, the way her hands fidgeted with the edge of her cloak. She wasn't just telling it, she was wrestling with it, assembling the truth as she went.

"If they were supposed to protect the world from magic, why would they weaken the boundaries?" Rykan asked.

"That's the question I'm trying to answer," Nadara said. "But whatever their intent, it seems the stranger realized too late that he'd been used."

They stood in silence, the night pressing close. Rykan glanced back toward the camp, where Selaina lay sleeping. Her peaceful face was a life-line, a quiet reminder of what they were fighting for.

"You should get some sleep," Nadara said, her tone softer this time. "We'll need all the strength we can get for what's ahead."

Rykan nodded, turning to leave. But as he walked back to camp, he couldn't shake the weight of her story, or the realization that their fates were more intertwined than he'd thought. The fire crackled softly, casting dancing shadows across the stone. Rykan rolled onto his side, the moss cool beneath his hand. He closed his eyes, willing sleep to hush the storm in his mind. But in the hush, the shadows crept closer, heavier, as if Arathain's whispers lingered just out of reach.

CHAPTER 28

THE PATH WOUND steeply upward, forcing Selaina to navigate carefully between hulking boulders and along narrow ledges that jutted out like the jagged teeth of a snarling beast. The river's roar had faded to a murmur. Only gravel crunched underfoot, and the wind whistled through the crags.

The dense forest that once enclosed the trail had given way to stark, unforgiving slopes, their rocky surfaces splintered and sharp, like the mountain itself had been clawed apart. The air grew thinner and colder, carrying the faint metallic odor of stone, while the horizon stretched wide and empty, a stark contrast to the tangled greenery she'd left behind.

Morning had come after a long, restless night, the sun hanging low in the sky and casting long shadows across the rocky landscape. The pale light didn't reach the shadows clinging to her mind. Each breath she took was sharp as the air grew colder. Signs of snow lingered in patches, clinging stubbornly to the shaded crevices where sunlight rarely reached.

Kadin trudged behind her, wiping sweat from his brow despite the chill. "I'll never complain about climbing stairs again," he muttered.

Selaina gave him a faint smile, though her focus remained ahead. The events of the previous night clung to her thoughts like a heavy fog. The maugwins, shadowy and relentless, creatures of chaos they barely understood. And Arathain, his cryptic warnings left an unease she couldn't shake.

She glanced back at Rykan, walking in silence. His expression was distant, his movements slightly off since the bite from the maugwin. But it wasn't just the wound that had changed something between them.

She remembered how he'd run off. Not in fear, but in reckless courage. He thought he was protecting them, protecting her. And yet it had almost cost them everything.

Selaina wasn't really angry. She understood the kind of desperation that came from wanting to undo failure. She lived with that feeling, too. But Rykan had acted alone, without trust, and that wounded her more than she wanted to admit. Did he not believe they could do it together? Did he not believe she could stand on her own?

"Selaina," Rykan said suddenly, breaking the quiet. He nudged her gently, motioning for them to drift a little away from the others, and for now, she obliged.

She slowed beside him. "What is it?"

He looked toward the others, then back at her. "I… should've told you sooner. The nightmares, they're getting worse."

Concern twitched in her eyes. "Rykan, I trust your heart. But sometimes you make it hard to trust your judgment." She softened the words with a glance. "What are you seeing?"

Rykan didn't answer right away. He looked down, jaw tight, his fingers flexing once at his sides before falling still.

He drew in a slow breath, eyes still fixed on the ground. "I keep seeing them. Gwenna, Arathain, the Sullen. They're searching for you. Not just to stop you… to take what you carry. And their master, Nociferon, the Lord of Pandemora, he wants it too. And I think… he knows you have it."

Selaina stopped walking. She had seen Arathain, Gwenna, and Syra in her own vision in the desert, but hearing Rykan confirm it now, seeing the fear behind his eyes, made it feel all too real.

But more than anything, it was his secrecy that stung. "Why didn't you tell me sooner?" she asked, her voice low but sharp. "How am I supposed to trust you if you won't talk to me? My mother kept things from me, my whole life. I can't go through that again." She looked at him, eyes narrowed not with anger, but with hurt. "That's what made you different. Or so I thought."

Rykan's shoulders sagged. "I know." His voice cracked, rough as splintered bark. "But every time I see you struggle… it feels like I've already failed you. I didn't want to add to what you're already carrying."

Her jaw set. "You don't protect someone by keeping them in the dark. That's not safety, it's distance."

He didn't argue. He just looked at her, weariness etched into the lines around his eyes. "I don't want distance," he said. "I want to be near you. To help with what I can. But I don't know how."

"You thought pulling the danger away would protect us," Selaina said. "But it just left us weaker. We survived, barely. But maybe if you'd stayed, we wouldn't have had to."

Rykan's mouth twitched, frustration flaring just beneath the surface. "When the maugwins came, I saw how fast everything was unraveling, how close we were to being overrun. We were going to lose someone." He looked away, jaw tight. "I know the plan was to stick together. But I've seen too many plans crumble while everyone stood still. In Tathara, we had a plan for when the Iron Flood came. We defended the city together. And it didn't matter. We still lost everything." His voice dropped. "So when I saw it happening again, I didn't wait. I acted. Maybe it was the wrong choice. But I'd rather do something and be wrong than stand still and watch every-thing fall apart."

Selaina was quiet for a moment. The wind stirred her cloak, brushing pale strands of hair across her cheek.

"I get it," she said finally. "You saw the cracks and ran to stop the col-lapse. Maybe that *was* the right call." She looked at him, not angry, but steady. "But the rest of us were still inside that crumbling plan, Rykan. We were holding it up, hoping it might last just long enough. And when you left…" Her voice caught briefly. "It didn't feel like you were saving us. It felt like you were giving up on us."

Selaina was quiet for a moment, her eyes tracking the curve of the path ahead. Then she looked back at him. "It's not about anyone being right," she said. "I know you care." She took a breath. "But while we're climbing, while people still believe in me, I can't afford to feel you drifting. I can't wonder if the person I trust most is fighting beside me… or deciding when to fight without me." Her voice dropped, tight with emotion. "I can't have you against me, Rykan. Not now."

He stared at her, eyes narrowing, as if the very idea stung. "I would *never* be against you."

Selaina's hand moved before she could think. She reached for his arm, his left, the one wrapped in cloth and shadowed with lingering magic. Carefully, she peeled the edge of the sleeve back. The skin beneath still glowed faintly, marbled with crimson threads like veins of molten glass.

She traced her fingers near it, not quite touching. "Does it hurt?"

Rykan's breath stopped. "Not in the way it used to."

Her hand hovered there, brushing the edge of the shadowed skin, and she felt him tremble, not from pain, but something more human. She didn't pull away.

"It doesn't seem to be healing," she murmured. "The curse doesn't want to leave."

"It probably would if I hadn't opened it," said Rykan.

Selaina's throat caught. She looked up at him, and for a moment, everything else, their friends, the coming storm, the weight of prophecy, fell away.

"Does this," she said, resting her hand over the curse mark, "feel like something you carry alone?"

Rykan's breath shuddered out of him. He closed his hand lightly over hers, anchoring it there. "Not as long as you are near."

And in that quiet exchange, without vows or declarations, something between them solidified, unspoken, but no less real.

Selaina looked down at where her hand rested over his curse-marked arm, and a weight settled in her stomach. She realized she couldn't hold his silence against him. Her fingers curled against her palm, the guilt of her own silence pressing deeper.

She hadn't told him everything either, her darkest secret: that Vatreus was her brother. The truth wrapped itself around her heart like a vine, constricting. How could she ever say it aloud? Vatreus had killed Rykan's father. If Rykan ever knew, if he ever looked at her and saw the blood of the man who had shattered his life…

He'd never see her the same way again. Maybe that was why his silence had cut so deep. Because she knew what it was to carry something too heavy to say, and still need someone to share it. Her frustration with Rykan slipped beneath the guilt of her own silence.

"We have to be strong for each other," she said at last, and then, slowly, lowered her head to rest against his shoulder.

His arm wrapped around her, gentle but certain. They stood like that for a long moment. Without urgency or promises, just the quiet presence of each other. When they finally turned to rejoin the others, their hands stayed linked.

The path ahead was dark and uncertain, but at least, for now, they weren't walking it alone.

CHAPTER 29

SELAINA WATCHED THE others in silence as they walked, the chill wind tugging at her cloak and her thoughts still heavy from the attack of Arathain and the maugwins. Ysadora walked behind Rykan, carrying the broken piece of her staff that held the Sunkeeper stone. She angled it toward the light, letting it drink in the sun's energy for later. Nadara picked at a wound she had received from maugwin claws during the attack. Ysadora had removed any remnants of shadow, and it looked much cleaner than the bite on Rykan's arm.

Garrick moved up beside Selaina, his eyes tracing the rocky outcrops ahead. "We're getting close," he said. "I hear it."

As soon as he spoke, the distant thunder of rushing water returned. Relief stirred in Selaina—at least they were still following the river, even if it was unseen. Rykan seemed to perk up as well as the sounds touched everyone's ears.

"We're on the right track at least," said Ysadora.

Selaina's steps were bolder as they continued ahead with this knowledge. The terrain grew less forgiving, sloping wildly with loose gravel underfoot, making the path treacherous. It forced them to a ledge that cracked into the stone surface, angling downward beneath the rocks overhead. They passed the opening of a massive cavern where either water or molten lava had long ago carved through the massive stone formations of the mountain itself.

On their right side, a steep cliff wall descended into the

opaque mists. Tufts of grass and small flowers clung to the cracks along the edge. As Selaina looked closely, she saw tiny insects crawling along the leafy growth without a care that they were thousands of feet above the rest of the world.

They came to a separation in the rocky path, where patches of moss clung to the jagged stones, revealing a glimpse of another ledge below. The path, which had seemed solid and reliable, now appeared hollow, with a hidden alcove beneath. The sight of the rocky surface below made Selaina acutely aware of how thin the ground beneath her feet really was. The ledge below felt too close, more real than the clouds beyond the mountain's edge.

Her hands grew clammy. The sudden awareness of the drop sent a shiver up her spine. The firm ground she had trusted now seemed fragile, and the weight of the mountain above them pressed down on her in a way that made her knees weak. A wave of anxiety gripped her as she imagined the ground giving way, the stones crumbling under her feet, leaving her to drop onto the ledge below. She stepped back fast, boots scraping rough stone.

"What is that?" Rykan said behind her, his voice breaking through her spiraling thoughts.

Selaina glanced over her shoulder to see Rykan, Garrick, and Ysadora kneeling at the lip of the gap, peering intently into it. The sight made her stomach flip.

"I don't know," Garrick muttered, narrowing his eyes as he leaned a little closer. "Some kind of strange reflection of light?"

"I've never seen anything like it," Ysadora added, tilting her head as she tried to get a better angle. Her staff hovered close to her side, its faint glow casting eerie shadows over the rocks.

Selaina's breath quickened. "Stand back," she called sharply, her voice trembling. "You could fall."

Rykan smirked, brushing off her concern as he shifted on his knees. "If I had some way to climb down there…"

"What would you want to go down there for?" Selaina snapped, taking another step away from the gap. "It's too dangerous."

"Selaina, look," Rykan urged, motioning for her to come closer. His expression, unusually serious, piqued her curiosity despite her unease.

"I don't want to look," she said firmly. "We need to keep going."

"You have to see this," Rykan insisted, his tone tinged with excitement.

Reluctantly, Selaina edged closer, her steps cautious as if the ground might betray her at any moment. She crouched near the smaller end of the gap, leaning forward slightly to peer over the edge but still keeping her distance.

"You can't see it from that angle," Rykan said, gesturing impatiently. "You'll have to come over here."

With a deep breath, she eased around the edges as Rykan stepped back to make room for her.

"Don't let me fall," she murmured, crouching lower. She hesitated, glancing at Rykan's outstretched hand. Part of her wanted to take it, remembering what they'd shared, the way his voice had trembled when he told her the truth. But the fear was still there, not of him, but of what might pull him under again. She turned to Garrick instead. "If you'll hold onto me, Garrick."

Rykan's face hardened, his brow furrowing. "Why him?"

Selaina's lips pressed into a thin line. "Both of you, hold me," she said quickly, not wanting to argue.

Garrick moved without hesitation, grasping her tunic firmly, while Rykan gripped her left hand. She braced her right hand on the rocky ground, feeling the cool, rough surface steady her as she leaned over the edge.

Amid the dark gray moss-covered rocks, a large stone was embedded in the alcove below. It glinted, as though it pulsed with its own inner light. Iridescent colors shimmered across its surface, shifting with an otherworldly rhythm the longer she stared at it. The sight sent a chill down her spine.

"What is it?" she whispered, her voice barely audible.

"That's what we're trying to figure out," Ysadora said, stepping closer to the edge but keeping a safe distance.

"Do you think it's important?" Nadara asked, her voice carrying a mix of curiosity and caution.

"It has to be," Rykan said firmly, his grip locking on Selaina's hand as if he could anchor her to his conviction.

"Either way, we can't get to it from here," Ysadora noted, her analytical gaze scanning the surrounding ledge.

"It appears the path ahead might take us closer," Kadin said, his tone clipped as he gestured toward the narrow trail winding around the cliff.

Selaina exhaled, forcing herself to let go of her lingering unease. Whatever the stone was, it seemed to hum with intent, as if waiting for them to uncover its secrets

"Let's go see," Rykan said, gently pulling back on Selaina's arm.

Still holding his hand, she used Garrick for leverage as she stood. Rykan led the way down the path ahead, which soon became too rugged to descend standing up.

He turned around, climbing down the rocks in a backward crawl. Selaina followed, her foot searching for a place to support her as she carefully made her way down. After climbing a short distance, Rykan leaped to the flatter surface below.

"Step there," said Rykan, guiding her over to a crevice between the rocks.

"I can't reach that," she said as she peered down.

"You can," he said. "It's not as far as you think."

If she reached her foot that far, she risked losing her grip on the rocks she was holding onto. Garrick was just above her, waiting for her to clear out of his way. Not wanting to hold up the group, she stretched her foot toward the spot, sliding her right hand with her as her fingers gripped another ledge.

She was nearly down, but no foothold remained to descend safely. Leaping off the slope, her feet hit the ground faster than she expected. Rykan steadied her as she nearly lost her footing.

His arms were warm, familiar, and for a moment, she let herself rest in them. For a moment, she forgot about all the ills in the world, Vatreus, her destiny, and the growing uncertainty about Rykan. She steadied herself and he let go, smiling as he stepped aside. He climbed over a ridge of stone beside them, leaping down into the alcove they had seen from above.

After helping Garrick and Ysadora down, Selaina peered over the ridge to find Rykan leaning over the strange stone. It glowed with a dim radiance in colors of violet, blue, yellow, and orange. Eager to get a closer look, Selaina climbed over the ridge, stepping down onto the slick wet rocks of the ledge below.

Rykan rubbed his hand across the surface of the strange stone. "It's so smooth," he said. "Like glass."

"What do you think it is?" she said as she approached.

"It's hard as any stone," said Rykan. "But it doesn't feel like stone."

CHAPTER 30

SELAINA EXTENDED HER hand, her fingers trembling as they met the radiant surface of the stone. The moment her skin brushed against it, a surge of energy coursed through her, and the world around her vanished in an explosion of white light. The brilliance consumed everything, leaving no shadows or edges, only endless blinding light. It was as if her very self was unraveling, then rethreading into the source.

Then, slowly, the blinding intensity began to dim, giving way to a profound stillness. Darkness enveloped her, vast and silent, broken only by faint, swirling embers in the distance. She found herself standing on shifting ground, the terrain beneath her feet alive with change. It alternated between jagged shards of solid rock and molten streams of fiery liquid, each pulse of the earth vibrating through her being. The air shimmered with heat, laced with the sting of sulfur and raw creation. Above her, the sky churned violently, a tempest of smoke, ash, and piercing flashes of lightning that illuminated the chaos.

In the midst of this primordial storm, a brilliant light descended, piercing the shadows. It was not like the white light that had consumed her earlier, this was warm and alive, a star descending from the heavens. Its surface pulsed with an intricate dance of gold and white, tendrils of energy stretching out like seeking fingers. As it neared the chaotic surface of the forming world, its light met the molten fires, and the two forces intertwined in a violent, breathtaking fusion.

The star's tendrils sank into the molten core of the land,

drawing forth something extraordinary. From the raging inferno emerged a glimmering shard, a fragment of perfect solidity amidst chaos. The shard glowed fiercely, its surface a kaleidoscope of color, shifting and alive with the energy of creation. Selaina's spirit lifted as the shard rose higher, pulled upward by the star's light.

Then more stars descended from the swirling heavens. Each was unique, their lights casting varied hues of gold, blue, silver, and red. Their combined energy reached down, converging on the shard, pulling it upward with a power that shook the unstable earth. Together, the celestial lights shaped the fragment, coaxing it into a massive, towering form. Granite, obsidian, and crystal interwove as if spun by the stars themselves, forming an immense mountain that pushed ever skyward.

The peak of the mountain shimmered like no other stone. Its surface radiated with an otherworldly glow, suffused with streaks of orange and blue, as though it still carried the essence of the stars. Around its base, the boiling chaos calmed, transforming into flowing valleys and rugged hills. Rivers of molten fire cooled, hardening into vast plains of dark stone. Galanor's chaos stilled, hardening into a land of power and strange beauty.

Kylinshan stood alone, vast and still, a monument to the harmony the celestials had forged. At its heart was the fragment they had pulled from the fires: the Dawnstone, the source of the mountain's radiant energy, an artifact of divine creation.

As the vision faded, Selaina felt herself drawn back to the present. The chaotic heat of the primordial world ebbed, replaced by the cool stone beneath her hand. She gasped as the world returned, and the stone's glow greeted her once more.

But now, she understood. The mountain's peak was no ordinary formation, it was the very bridge between the chaos of Pandemora and the order of Archeinor, a pillar of creation itself, forged in the union of opposing forces.

The world around her sharpened as her senses returned, the faint rustle of wind and the distant cries of mountain birds grounding her. What she'd witnessed settled on her mind like a stone, leaving her unsteady. Her knees gave out, and she caught herself just before hitting the rocks.

"Selaina?" Rykan's voice broke through the haze, sharp with alarm.

He was already moving, his hand catching hers just in time. She gripped it tightly, her bewildered gaze meeting his.

"I saw them," she whispered, her voice trembling. "The celestials… the forming of the mountain… everything."

The others were circling closer now, Garrick stepping forward with narrowed eyes, Nadara tense at her side, Kadin looking genuinely unsettled.

"You went still," Garrick said quietly. "Like stone."

"I called your name three times," Ysadora added, eyes flicking between Selaina and the glowing rock.

Kadin knelt beside her, his usual sarcasm nowhere in sight. "You looked like you weren't even breathing."

Selaina swallowed hard. "I wasn't… here."

Rykan's brow furrowed as he studied her expression, a mix of awe and lingering confusion.

Before he could respond, Nadara stepped closer, her voice calm yet curious. "Could it be the Dawnstone Oran spoke of?" she asked, gesturing toward the radiant stone.

"Maybe it's just a fancy way of reminding us mortals how small we are," Kadin said.

"Yes, it is the Dawnstone," said Selaina, ignoring Kadin's comment.

"But he said it was destroyed," Rykan said, his gaze shifting to the shimmering surface, doubt glimmering across his face.

"Maybe this was a piece of it," Garrick offered, his tone measured as his hand rested on the hilt of his sword, as though expecting something to happen.

"You saw all that from this stone?" Ysadora said, climbing briskly over the ridge, her gaze fixed on the glowing surface. Without waiting for an answer, she stepped forward. "Let me try."

Leaning over the strange stone, she placed both hands firmly on its surface. Her eyes fluttered shut, and her jaw clenched as if she were bracing herself. For a long moment, she stood perfectly still, the tension in her posture palpable. Then, with a sharp exhale, she stepped back abruptly, breaking contact with the stone. Her eyes flicked toward Selaina for the briefest moment before she turned away.

"What did you see?" Selaina asked, her voice soft but insistent as she watched Ysadora retreat.

Ysadora didn't answer right away. She climbed back over the ridge, her movements sharper than usual, and returned to the path. Selaina hurried to catch up, her concern growing. She noticed the rigid set of Ysadora's shoulders and the way her silence seemed to hum with unspoken tension.

"Will you tell me what you saw?" Selaina asked quietly, her tone careful.

"I didn't see anything," Ysadora said curtly, her words clipped and final. She lingered at the edge of the path, her fingers tensing around her staff. With a heavy sigh, she added, almost bitterly, "I guess it only works for you."

Selaina frowned, sensing the tension behind Ysadora's words. Her instinct was to ask more, to dig into what Ysadora wasn't saying, but she hesitated. Ysadora had always been the one with answers, the one who could touch an object and unearth echoes of its past. That ability had been their key to so many mysteries. Yet here she was, unable to glean anything from the stone that had revealed so much to Selaina.

"Ysadora…" Selaina began cautiously, stepping closer, "are you—?"

"Don't," Ysadora interrupted, her voice sharper than she may have intended. She exhaled deeply, avoiding Selaina's gaze. "I'm fine. Let's just keep moving."

Selaina held her tongue, uncertain what would help or make it worse. Ysadora had always been the steady one, the voice of certainty. It unsettled her, Ysadora didn't usually go quiet when things got hard. Selaina realized Ysadora's frustration wasn't with the stone, it was with herself.

She took a slow step beside her, not speaking at first. "You know… it doesn't have to mean anything."

Ysadora didn't respond, but her grip on the staff loosened slightly.

"I didn't ask for this," Selaina added gently. "I'm still figuring it out myself."

That got a faint snort from Ysadora. "You always seem to figure things out."

Selaina glanced sideways at her. "Only because I have you yelling at me when I don't."

For a second, Ysadora's mouth twitched, almost a smile. But it vanished just as quickly. "Let's keep moving," she said, though her voice had lost some of its edge.

As they walked, Selaina hoped this was the first crack in the wall between them.

Kadin glanced back as they walked. When his eyes met Selaina's, he offered a faint, knowing look, part sympathy, part amusement. The kind of expression that said, *Yeah, that's just Ysadora… don't let it get to you.* Then he gave the smallest nod, barely perceptible, and turned back to the path.

Selaina exhaled, the tightness in her chest loosening just a little. Nothing needed to be said. The glance had said more than enough.

Her muscles tensed as the ledge sloped upward. Selaina was glad to find the pathway widening as it returned them to a more expansive area. Further ahead, trees and grass returned, though now many of the leaves and foliage bore a pale blue color.

The roaring of the water grew louder as they approached the jagged ridges of sharp rocks that had hidden it from view. The path twisted and turned, the sharp edges brushing against their boots, until the landscape opened to reveal the river once more.

Selaina's breath caught as the waterfall came into view, spilling over the cliff like a silver ribbon unfurling from the sky. Above it, the sunshimmer flowed in brilliant streaks of sapphire and rose, framing the falls like a celestial crown, radiant, but sorrowful, as if mourning all that had been lost. It was beautiful, but her eyes lingered on the uneven flow. The water fell in fragmented streams, leaving streaks of bare rock visible. Smooth grooves cut into the cliffside hinted at a time when the waterfall had been a mightier force, carving a deeper path into the rock below.

Selaina knelt near the river's edge, running her fingers through the cool water. Its surface rippled gently, carrying fragments of sunlight that danced like liquid gold. The pool beneath the waterfall churned where the streams met, but it was smaller and shallower than she had imagined. She couldn't help but picture how it must have looked before, full and overflowing, the kind of river that would have fed fields and forests far beyond this mountain. Now, it seemed restrained, as though it held back its potential.

"This must be the Serpent's Tear," Selaina said softly, gazing up at the cliff.

The others gathered near her, their voices hushed in the presence of the cascade. Twisting trees with silver and purple leaves framed the scene, their branches bending toward the pool as if drawn to its allure. The air was thick with mist, cool and heavy, carrying the faint tang of minerals. Rainbows gleamed near the base of the waterfall, where the water crashed into the pool, sending up plumes of shimmering spray.

The sight of the subdued river and waterfall carried a sadness that matched the name of the place. Serpent's Tear, a monument to both the Sky Serpents' defiance and the consequences of imbalance, now seemed to mirror the struggles of those who lived below.

"Is this where we're supposed to go?" Garrick asked, breaking the silence. "I don't see any path forward."

"There's no climbing those cliffs," Kadin added, shaking his head.

"Oran said the way wouldn't be obvious," Selaina replied, her brow furrowing. "There must be something we're missing."

"Why didn't he just tell us?" Rykan grumbled. "Would've saved us a lot of time."

"Oran never gave answers easily," Nadara said. "He wanted us to find them ourselves."

"Selaina," Ysadora said, stepping closer, her voice a touch sharper than usual, "you could see the way out of Wekenwild. Can't you see something here?"

Selaina's fingers twitched at her side, her gaze flashing rapidly over the cliffs before settling again, water streaming down the cliffs, roots twisted in the stone, the slope of the earth too steep to climb. She reached inward, calling to the sense that had once shown her the path through Wekenwild, the rhythm of the forest's breath.

But nothing answered. No shimmer behind her eyes. No whisper from the stone.

The world stood silent. Indifferent.

She kept still, hoping some pulse would break through the hush—to reveal the hidden path in time. But the longer she waited, the more the silence thickened, not just quiet, but hollow, like an empty room behind a locked door.

Her breath caught in her throat as the others waited behind her. She felt Ysadora's gaze on her, sharp and expectant. Selaina forced her voice to remain steady.

"Nothing's coming to me," she admitted, avoiding Ysadora's gaze.

For a moment, silence hung between them, heavy and uncomfortable. Selaina glanced up, catching the faint twitch of Ysadora's lips, the way her fingers gripped her staff more tightly than usual.

"Convenient," Ysadora muttered, just loud enough to be heard.

Selaina wandered away from the others after the camp began to take shape, her gaze fixed on the thin streams of the waterfall. She lifted her hand, letting the faint glow of her mark guide her. She tried to focus, on the water, the mountain, on anything, but nothing stirred. The silence in her power felt... hollow.

"You're too tense," Ysadora said behind her.

Selaina turned, surprised.

Ysadora didn't meet her eyes at first. "You're expecting something to happen. Magic like yours doesn't shout. It listens."

"I don't know what it's listening for," Selaina admitted. "I barely know what I'm listening for."

Ysadora stepped beside her, hesitated, then reached up and lightly pressed two fingers to Selaina's brow, just beneath the mark. "Close your eyes. Feel where the water touches the rock. It's no different than the way you feel your arrow. Don't think. Just... follow."

Selaina did as Ysadora instructed. Her breathing slowed. For a moment, nothing changed. Then the sound of the waterfall deepened, not louder, just fuller. She could almost feel the stone beneath it, like a heartbeat echoing through the rock.

Her eyes opened, a spark in them. "I... felt something. But I still can't see a path."

This wasn't like Wekenwild. That had been pure structure, pure pattern. It made sense to her, even if she couldn't explain how.

But this... this was nature. And nature wasn't just order or chaos. It was both, tangled together. Alive. Moving. Sometimes contradictory. She could feel its rhythm, but not read it. It didn't respond like magic did.

She was starting to understand magic. But this... this wasn't magic. This was the mountain, alive and inscrutable.

"It's getting too dark," Garrick shouted toward them. "We should make camp."

Ysadora gave a small nod. "Good. Try it again tomorrow." And with that, she turned and walked away.

Reluctantly, Selaina nodded. Yet as she turned to help set up their camp, her gaze lingered on the fractured cascade. The waterfall's mournful descent echoed the fractures she felt deepening—not just in the mountain, but within herself, and between them all. Somewhere in the mountain's shadows, the answers waited. They only needed to find the light that would reveal them.

CHAPTER 31

RYKAN STOOD ADRIFT in a void that writhed with restless shadows, their movements like a silent storm. Cold air pressed against him, heavy with murmuring voices just beyond understanding. Beneath his feet, the ground shifted in a maddening rhythm, as if the void itself were caught in an endless struggle between form and chaos. Each breath was sharp, laced with a metallic tang that hinted at dread and something ancient.

The voices echoed in the void, their sources revealed as spectral forms drifting in and out of focus. Threads of shadow linked their hollow forms in a pulsing web of darkness. The strands hummed faintly, whispering between forms. At first, the whispers blurred at the edge of hearing. Then they sharpened into pleas, warnings, something darker.

A low chant began to rise, and as it grew clearer, the shadows twisted and converged.

The illusion of space collapsed. Though each speaker remained physically apart, communing from far-flung corners of the world, each bound to a different portal, the vision brought them together around one central flame.

The flaming red portal pulsed at the center, its heat casting no warmth, its light warping their shapes like shattered reflections. It was the same gash in the world Rykan had seen before, bleeding chaos through root and stone. Not a doorway, but a wound. A voice was speaking through it.

Arathain stood tall and sharp, his edges wavering like a blade caught between realities. Beneath the gnarled branches of a dead tree, his tattered cloak whispered against the broken earth, shadows rippling from his boots like oil.

To his left, Gwenna appeared amidst a tangle of roots, their ends rising like fingers to clutch at her feet. Her black and silver hair stirred in a wind no one felt. Malice shimmered in the eyes beneath her hood. The bones at her belt clicked softly, in rhythm with the pulse of the flame.

Syra stood farther back, veiled in drifting ash. Watchful, unreadable. Her hands were folded behind her like someone awaiting a verdict.

Dazurel was nearest the flaming heart of the portal, his form dimming and warping in its glow. His ghostly face was partly hidden under a torn shroud, anxious, his eyes darting between the others.

The voice cut through the haze like a blade. "Your recent attempts to seize the girl were… disappointing," it said. "You were given a simple task, and yet you let her slip through your grasp again."

Arathain stood beneath a lifeless tree in the center of ancient, crumbling ruins. "There was nothing simple about it," he replied. "Might I remind you that Gwenna had no better luck than I did."

"Casting blame should be beneath you," said the voice, colder now. "I granted my servants power beyond all mortal measure, and yet you falter."

Arathain's eyes flicked toward the darkened sky. "Because our power was never meant to move freely under the eye of the sun."

There was a pause, long, tense.

"You speak of weakness."

"I speak of truth," said Arathain. "One of them carries a shard laced with celestial fire. The world has not forgotten what we are, and beneath the sun's gaze, our shadows thin."

"Gwenna already learned of their instrument," said Nociferon. "I expected more of you."

"The maugwins stripped them of the shard, and still they recovered it," he added, voice sharpening. "That stone must be destroyed completely, or we may never succeed."

"The Sullen are not affected by celestial light, Lord Nociferon," said Dazurel. "We are heading toward the mountain, but progress is slow."

"If Arathain had waited, my lord," Gwenna interjected, shadows curling through her voice, "my Nadrok are also gathering on the mountain. I will reach them soon. I'll correct his error."

"My lord," Arathain said, stepping forward. "The girl is making swift progress. I cannot wait for the bloodshadow to fester and bleed. If there is a path, any path, that will take me further up the mountain, ahead of her, I will not fail you again."

"I must be at full strength when I re-enter the mortal plane," said Nociferon. "One chance more is all I will give."

The air trembled.

"Yes, if you would grant a pathway," said Dazurel, "the Sullen could reach the mountain more quickly and—"

Dazurel flinched as something unseen seized him. His body convulsed, as though his bones were breaking from the inside. Then, with a deafening snap, he was wrenched into the air, dragged toward the flaming portal.

"My lord, please!" he shrieked, thrashing, his feet skidding across the stone. "I have served you! I—"

The rest dissolved into a howl of agony as his limbs began to stretch, long and thin, like melting wax beneath a black sun. His jaw unhinged. His scream went silent.

The portal pulsed hungrily.

Dazurel's last shreds vanished into the churning red, devoured by the chaos beyond.

"One life given," Nociferon intoned, his voice now devoid of breath or warmth. "To bind the roots. Blood will open it. Blood feeds more than the gate. It feeds the wild breath that came before the woven cage of order."

Gwenna flinched as Dazurel's final shreds vanished into the chaos. The portal's light shimmered, casting red veins across her face. She turned away sharply, as if the sight had scorched her vision.

When she spoke, her voice was low and frayed. "My lord… was that necessary?"

Syra didn't look up. "You already know the answer to that."

Nociferon did not respond at first. The silence stretched, long and unnatural, as if even the void itself recoiled. Then, his voice returned, darker, deeper, as though echoing from beneath the world.

"Your failure," he answered, "made it necessary. His essence is now rooted in the heart of the wards. A path may form, but it will be thin, brittle. You must strengthen it."

The gate trembled. Nociferon's voice returned, lower now, almost reverent. "No beginning. No end. Only will."

The portal's once-flaming heart convulsed, then began to twist inward, the light folding in on itself like molten metal sucked into a vacuum. Where before it had flared like fire, now it deepened, thickened. Rootlike tendrils of shadow unfurled from its edges, anchoring into the stone with slow, deliberate hunger. The surface of the gate no longer danced, it churned. Like a bruise opening across the world, it revealed glimpses of other roots, other hollows, echoing with distant cries and red flashes, as though roots of ancient trees had momentarily bled into one. What once was a voice speaking through a wound had become the wound itself, opened wide enough for passage.

Arathain bowed low, but his eyes dared a quick look at the scorched earth where Dazurel had vanished, and a shiver passed through his shoulders despite the stillness.

His voice was steadier than he looked. "The maugwins…"

"Yes. Let their bloodshadow soak the roots," said Nociferon. "Chaos born in blood will awaken the gate fully."

Gwenna stared as the portal beside them groaned softly, its surface slick and roiling like coagulating blood. Thin tendrils of shadow reached outward, brushing the ground as if searching for something to anchor them.

"And once opened, can it hold?" she asked.

"Only for a time," Nociferon said. "The binding will fray."

Syra gazed into the red gate. "Then we must choose our moment carefully."

"Do not fail me again," said Nociferon.

Rykan's body shook as he awoke, but the waterfall's roar steadied him. The stars twinkled down at them, the night still holding its breath as everyone else remained asleep. He lifted his arm; the maugwin's bite had scabbed over again. Nociferon's words echoed in his mind as his eyes drifted to his sword.

Rykan's eyes traced the jagged scab on his arm, the wound from the maugwin still raw and itching beneath the surface. The memory of Nociferon's voice lingered, twisting in his mind like the cold mist around the waterfall.

The memory of Dazurel's scream coiled inside him, less for what it meant for the Sullen, and more for what it proved: Nociferon would stop at nothing.

His hand hovered over the hilt of his sword, the weight of it a comfort and a curse. Selaina's face came to him in flashes, the determination in her eyes, the quiet strength she carried despite the overwhelming burden placed on her.

He exhaled slowly, gripping the hilt more tightly. The stars above seemed distant, unreachable, as though mocking his uncertainty.

The night seemed to slow to a stop as he stared into the darkness. He wasn't a hero, but maybe that didn't matter. Maybe becoming a hero was a choice.

The wind picked up, gusting through his hair. Rykan lay back on his blanket, staring up at the stars. He was nearly certain he wouldn't be able to sleep again anytime soon. His mind raced with half-formed ideas.

The night's stillness shattered with a chill that crept through Rykan's body. It wasn't only the mountain air, it was something deeper, more sinister. He bolted upright on his blanket, the jagged scab on his arm itching like a silent alarm. The howling wind rushed through the camp, carrying an eerie sound that sent shivers through his core.

Then he heard it, a desperate cry for help. Selaina.

Rykan sprang to his feet, drawing his sword in one swift motion. His eyes darted around the darkened camp. Selaina's blanket lay empty, and a strange, glowing tempest tore across the ground, whipping up debris as it moved. Its unstable, erratic light pulsed like a heartbeat.

"Selaina!" he shouted, sprinting after the storm.

The vortex stabilized, rising above the trees. Rykan's stomach sank as he caught sight of her, Selaina, caught in its grip, her figure silhouetted against the fluttering glow. She reached for him, fear carved across her face, then vanished. The storm coalesced into a shadowy form, a Windwraith, and soared above the waterfall, disappearing into the night.

"Myrradin!" Ysadora's voice cut through the chaos, her staff gripped tightly in her hands.

The name struck Rykan like a blow, and he immediately knew she was right. Myrradin had taken Selaina.

"She's gone," Rykan said, his voice barely above a whisper. His hand trembled around the hilt of his sword until his knuckles turned white. After everything they'd faced, after everything she had endured, she was gone. Fire rose up through the despair. "We have to get her back!"

"There's no point chasing him now," Ysadora said. "He moves faster than us. We'd never catch him in the dark."

"Why would he take her?" Kadin asked, his voice laced with frustration. "Revenge?"

Ysadora didn't answer immediately. Her hand gripped her broken staff, the Sunkeeper crystal catching faint glints of starlight. Rykan noticed how Kadin glanced at her then, not with sarcasm, but something quieter. Concern, maybe. A trace of it flashed in his eyes, and for once, he didn't press her for an answer.

Instead, he muttered, "We've all got our ghosts, I guess." As he spoke, Kadin's fingers toyed absently with the frayed cloth tied around his wrist, a nervous habit he didn't seem to notice.

Ysadora replied, her expression grave. "Myrradin doesn't act out of spite. Whatever his reason, it's calculated."

Nadara crossed her arms, her voice low and tense. "What do you think he'll do to her?"

"I don't know," Ysadora admitted, "but Myrradin wouldn't harm her outright. He wants something. That much is clear."

Garrick slammed his fist against a nearby rock. "So that's it? Everything we've been fighting for, climbing for, gone in an instant."

Rykan's jaw tensed as he remembered Gwenna and Arathain's warnings. "They said this would happen," he muttered. "They said someone else was hunting her, that they could protect her. I didn't listen."

Ysadora stepped forward, her tone sharp. "You're not seriously entertaining the idea of trusting them?"

"I don't trust them," Rykan snapped. "But I can't help wondering if they could have stopped this from happening."

Ysadora's eyes softened, though her voice remained firm. "Myrradin is no ally, but neither are they. Whatever his plans for Selaina, she's better off with him than in Arathain's hands."

Rykan's voice dropped to a whisper. "I should have done something. I should have stopped this."

"We were all caught off guard," Garrick said, his voice steady but weary.

Kadin gave a short, sharp laugh, louder than the moment called for. "Maybe this destiny nonsense isn't real. Maybe we've been chasing a lie. I would think something destined would be a lot easier."

Nadara's gaze hardened. "Destiny isn't easy, Kadin. The greatest destinies are forged through the hardest trials. The stories make it sound glamorous, but those people suffered before they succeeded."

"The way they are regarded, you would think they lived as kings," Garrick said.

Ysadora tilted her head, one of the small charms between her horns catching the light. "Nadara is correct," she said. "The only ones that lived as kings after they fulfilled their destinies were the ones who started using their power for themselves. They became enemies and were hunted down."

"We're wasting time," said Rykan. "We have to get up these cliffs and find her!"

"And we will," said Garrick. "But now we all need to get back to sleep. We'll begin at first light."

"You think you're in charge now?" Rykan said. "Myrradin already has a head start on us. I don't care what the rest of you do, I'm going now!"

"Rykan, it's too dark," said Nadara. "Your mind is unsettled. Sit down and breathe. Prepare yourself for the journey tomorrow."

"The maugwins grow stronger in the dark," Ysadora added. "We're safe here for now, but the shadows will claim you if you go alone."

Rykan stared at them, his shoulders heaving with ragged breaths. Finally, he turned away, returning to his blanket. He dropped to the ground, his sword still clutched in his hand.

As he lay there, staring up at the stars, his thoughts churned. Selaina wouldn't understand if he had let Arathain near, but at least she might have been safe. Safer than in the clutches of Myrradin.

And yet, deep down, he knew the truth. Safety had never been part of their path.

CHAPTER 32

Tʜᴇ ᴡɪɴᴅ ʜᴏᴡʟᴇᴅ, clawing at the night's edges, its icy fingers slicing the air. Selaina felt its relentless bite against her skin, sharp as shards of glass, her hair lashing around her face like untamed ribbons. Jagged cliffs cut the dark below her, their edges stark and menacing, vanishing into a swirling blur of shadow and storm. Far beneath, she glimpsed the shimmer of water catching moonlight before it, too, was swallowed by the void.

She twisted, kicking and clawing at the Windwraith's grasp, but there was no flesh to strike, no body to push away. The spectral form around her writhed like smoke and storm, cold and unyielding. Myrradin's voice echoed faintly in her ear, distorted by the wind: "This is for your own good, Selaina. You have no idea what's coming."

She gritted her teeth. "Let me go!"

Drawing from the energy that still pulsed within her like a buried flame, Selaina thrust her hands outward, summoning a flare of power. The Windwraith recoiled. In that instant, her body twisted free from the current, and they both plummeted.

The sky ripped past her. Myrradin's form unraveled above, half mist, half man, grasping at the air as he fell beside her.

Impact. The snow cracked beneath her like a frozen lake giving way. Her body tumbled across the crusted plateau, coming to a stop near a jagged outcrop of rock. Her lungs burned. Her vision swam.

The wind had gone still.

For a long moment, Selaina lay on her back, blinking up at

a churning sky. Then she forced herself up, every muscle aching, and staggered to her feet.

Nearby, the old man emerged from the mist, Myrradin, now returned to mortal form. He sat hunched on a stone, his breath visible in the frigid air, weariness clinging to him like frost.

"I was trying to fly you to the summit," said the old man. "But if you prefer to walk, we can still reach it from here."

Selaina rose to her feet, staring back at Myrradin. She reached for her bow, but realized it was not on her back. She had placed it beside her blanket to sleep.

"I'm not going anywhere with you," she declared.

"You'll make it to the summit," Myrradin replied. "One way or another."

"I don't need your help," she shot back. "I have friends to help me, which is more than can be said for you." She moved past him, toward the ledge behind.

Below, the terrain fell away in jagged ridges and glinting ice. A silver ribbon of water carved through the valley, the Serpent's Tear.

"From here, there is no path that will lead back to them," he said, as her hope began to deflate. Her eyes scanned the mountain below, realizing she was cut off from her friends.

"You may be Zhal Evurah," Myrradin said, his tone shifting, almost conspiratorial. "But your insight is still lacking. I had to get you away from them. Their intentions may be true, but their faith will wane. One by one, they will abandon you, some will even turn against you. Rykan especially has made choices that will make your journey impossible."

"You don't know anything about Rykan!" Selaina spat.

"But how do you think the maugwins found you?" Myrradin countered. "His connection to Pandemora is too strong. He is confused now; soon he will call out to the shadows, and even I may struggle to protect you."

"I don't believe a single word out of your mouth!" Selaina shouted, fury blazing in her eyes. "You've deceived us once already. I will never trust you again."

"I'm not asking you to trust me," Myrradin replied, his gaze cold and calculating. "As I said, I'm here to ensure you succeed."

"How am I to succeed?" she challenged. "You leave me with no friends and no weapons."

Myrradin's eyes glinted with a cold amusement. Without a word, he stood, unfurling his cloak to reveal her bow and quiver, the wood gleaming in the moonlight. He tossed them onto the snow near her feet. Selaina glanced at the bow for a moment before looking back at him. Her heart pounded in her chest. Was this another one of his tricks? She hesitated for only a moment before deciding that it didn't matter, she needed that bow. She stepped forward, eyeing Myrradin as she grabbed the bow and quiver from the snow. Taking a deep breath, she took one of her arrows from the quiver, examining it carefully. Then, in one swift motion, she nocked the arrow and drew the bowstring back, aiming directly at Myrradin's heart. Her breath caught as she released the arrow, sending it flying straight toward him.

Myrradin didn't flinch. With barely any urgency, he extended his hand, and a blue translucent sphere formed around him, his Aedavaris shield. The arrow struck the shield with such force that it shattered on impact, shards scattering like sparks against the blue barrier.

"So eager to strike—anyone in your way is a target," Myrradin said, low and mocking. "You're more like Vatreus than you care to admit."

Selaina stood frozen by his words. "You know nothing about me…"

"Your family was key to what I needed to save Galanor. I studied them, your mother and father, trying to find who was there the day the bargain with Azragul was made," Myrradin said. "Did you know your father sought out drunkards, orphans, those who had been forgotten? He led them to the gate in the mountain, giving Azragul the flesh and blood required to keep Vatreus alive."

"I'm sure that's why my mother left," Selaina replied, unable to hide the bitterness in her voice.

"She couldn't bear the guilt," Myrradin continued. "Not even keeping her son alive could justify what they did."

"If you're trying to make me feel responsible," Selaina shot back, "don't bother. I'm going to set things right."

"You had the chance to do that," said Myrradin. "Instead you chose to take Ethyllion's power for yourself."

"Because I saw you!" she exclaimed. "Giving orders, being pampered, you made mindless servants out of the world."

"As usual, you misinterpreted what you saw," Myrradin retorted. "What I wanted with the power of Azragul was to bring the world together for one purpose... to save it. There is something far more dangerous than Vatreus coming. A force that doesn't belong in this world, one that was never meant to return."

Selaina faltered, something inside her paused. Her hands flexed at her sides, fingers briefly curling before she forced herself to still.

Could it be true? Another force, worse than Vatreus? The Sullen, Gwenna, even the Nadrok... all echoes of something deeper?

She hated the way Myrradin's voice steadied when he spoke of it. Hated how it sounded... reasonable.

For half a breath, she wondered, what if she had made it worse? What if stopping him had opened the door?

But then the memory came, sharp, inescapable. The silent streets. The blank eyes. The endless lines of people moving in perfect obedience. A world without chaos... but also without soul. Without choice.

Was that what he meant by saving it?

"Then maybe the world needs strength, but not the kind that shatters it, only to rebuild it in chains." Her stomach turned. His calm unraveled, and underneath it was what it had always been, control, pretending to be salvation. "Let me guess," Selaina said, sarcasm returning like a shield. "You have a new plan, and once again, you need me to do your bidding."

"Oh, this isn't *my* plan anymore," Myrradin replied coolly. "It is yours. When you failed to use the Wishing Stone as I instructed, when you took its destinies for yourself... This is the choice you have left us with."

"Why wouldn't you just tell us from the beginning?" Selaina demanded.

"I told you what you were ready to hear," Myrradin answered, a hint of frustration creeping into his voice. "Vatreus and the Iron Flood are immediate threats. Would you have listened if I had warned you of dangers you've never heard of?"

"How can I answer that? You didn't give us the chance!" Selaina responded.

"Your bloodline is tainted. How could I trust you to do the right thing?"

Myrradin pressed, his tone cold. "Look at everything you've done. You couldn't even follow my simple plan, all because you wanted power as your own."

"Don't try to turn this around on me, Myrradin," Selaina said, her voice strengthening. "You are the enemy here and a threat to Galanor."

"You'll understand eventually," Myrradin said, voice calm, but there was a quiet satisfaction curling beneath his words. "I only hope it isn't too late for the rest of us."

He moved a step closer, his gaze never leaving her. "Your father… he reached the point where he couldn't take another life. After giving so many to the gate, after watching what it made of Vatreus, he finally saw the truth of it. He'd created something he could no longer control."

He studied her reaction.

"By the time your brother was a young man, he'd consumed a hundred lives for a hundred years. But it wasn't enough. The hunger had changed him. Twisted him. So Lucianis walked to the gate alone." Myrradin's voice dropped. "No tricks. No captives. Just himself. Maybe he thought giving himself would undo it. Maybe he hoped it would jolt Vatreus out of his madness. Or maybe—" he let the words hang, just long enough to sting, "he just wanted to understand what it felt like, to become the sacrifice."

He offered no comfort in the silence that followed, only the faintest shadow of a smirk.

"But it didn't change anything. Vatreus wanted more. He always will."

This information overwhelmed Selaina, but she fought to maintain her composure. "And yet you wanted to be the one to make the bargain with Azragul."

"With his power combined with my own, I could have become far more than Vatreus," Myrradin said, his voice steady with conviction. "I wouldn't have wasted lives like Vatreus. I'd have used that power to bring the kingdoms together. To raise the greatest army Galanor has ever seen. We would have been ready. Ready for the day the Lord of Pandemora steps onto the mortal plane, ready to stop the world from unraveling into chaos."

Myrradin tilted his head, a glint of bitter amusement in his eyes.

"When you saw the gate in your vision, did you even stop to read the inscription carved into it?" He didn't wait for her answer. "Weathered stone, etched deep, like a scar. And still, no one ever reads it."

He took a step closer, his breath hanging like mist between them.

"It wasn't meant to be opened," he said. "The spell carved there was a failsafe, a riddle with no answer. Neither god nor beast could break it. No deathless hand. Only one thing could ever unmake that seal… and even then, it was absurd. Unthinkable."

His voice dropped to a whisper, half-reverent, half-accusatory, as he recited the lines:

> *"No god nor beast, nor deathless hand,*
>
> *Shall break the seal upon this land.*
>
> *No timeless soul, nor ageless might,*
>
> *May shift the stone from dark to light.*
>
> *Yet flesh and blood, a thousand deep,*
>
> *With will as one, and vows to keep,*
>
> *By mortal hands, in toil and strain,*
>
> *Shall break the lock and loose the chain…"*

He let the words hang in the still air.

"That was never meant to happen," he said. "What army of mortals would ever willingly open that gate? What could compel a thousand hearts to work as one to this end? It was safe… until your family decided to meddle with something they didn't understand."

Selaina's eyes narrowed.

"Yes," Myrradin said, not without satisfaction. "Azragul found a loophole. Give them one by one. A hundred. Two hundred. And with each sacrifice, Azragul whispers a little louder, grants a little more power. That's not strategy, that's addiction."

He paused.

Then, softer: "Your father realized it too late. He thought one more life, his own, might undo the damage."

"All the more reason I have to stop Vatreus," Selaina said. "But don't pretend you'd be any better."

Myrradin's expression didn't change, but something in his posture stiffened.

"You're just angry that the power isn't yours," she added. "That he beat you to it."

"And you are wasting the power you have," said Myrradin. "If you had been trained as a mavin, as I and Ysadora have, it would come naturally."

"Does she know about me?" asked Selaina, her voice trembling slightly. "Being related to Vatreus."

"She only knows what she needed to know," said Myrradin. "Perhaps I was wrong to protect all of you from this knowledge, but in my experience, it is best to focus on the task in front of you. We had better get moving, the lord of chaos never sleeps. On the way, I will train you. Together, we will unlock your potential as Zhal Evurah."

"Train me? I'm not going anywhere with you!" Selaina asserted, raising her bow again. "I will continue on alone if I have to."

"That would be unwise," warned Myrradin. "With everything you know about your family, how can you trust yourself to do the right thing? How will you prevent the power from controlling you?"

"I trust myself more than I'll ever trust you," Selaina said defiantly.

Myrradin studied her, then sighed, heavy, resigned. "Must you do everything the hard way?" He straightened. "So be it. I'll leave you to your path. Now it's your burden to carry. The world's fate, all of it."

Selaina didn't flinch. "Good. I'm not turning my back to you."

He gave a slight nod. "If the need arises, use the power inside you. Call on me, with your will."

"I won't," she said.

What was once flesh and bone unraveled before her eyes, his form stretching, twisting, caught in some unnatural current. Cloak and limbs blurred as they dissolved into wind and shadow, spiraling upward like a cyclone torn from the mountain itself.

The air turned sharp. Snowflakes in his wake crystallized to shards, spinning like razors before vanishing in the updraft. His form became a phantom streak of storm and darkness, until he was gone, swallowed by the night, and the mountain was quiet again.

The world lay ahead, vast and unfamiliar. A wave of solitude washed over her, amplifying the distance between her and everything she had known. For a moment, doubt pressed on her mind.

Darian had once told her that hope was the hardest thing to carry, and that was why it mattered most. She hadn't understood it then. But now, in the quiet cold, his words came back to her like a warmth she didn't know she needed. Not a flame, but an ember, small, flickering, and stubbornly alive.

As Selaina turned to leave the plateau, her boots crunching softly over the crusted snow, something caught her eye. Half-buried near the place where she and Myrradin had fallen, a glint of blue peeked through the ice.

She crouched, brushing away the snow. A talisman lay there, its chain tangled, the pendant cold against her fingers. Her first instinct was to toss it aside. But something stopped her.

The pendant was shaped like an open circle, its delicate, vine-like engravings spiraling inward toward a gemstone. The carvings looked impossibly old, as though they held secrets from a time long before her own. The gemstone itself was a deep, rich blue, like the twilight sky right before nightfall, polished to a mirror-like sheen that glowed with a faint, ethereal light.

As Selaina stared into its surface, a steady pulse shimmered from within, subtle and rhythmic. Like a heartbeat.

She frowned. Myrradin must have dropped it when they crashed into the mountain.

Selaina held it a moment longer, the cold metal coiling in her palm. If this talisman had belonged to him, then it had to be useful, since he wouldn't have carried anything that didn't serve a purpose.

The wind answered with a howl, sharp and sudden, as if the mountain itself had seen her.

A chill traced down her spine. She glanced over her shoulder, half-expecting to see Myrradin's cold gaze watching from the mist.

But there was nothing, only silence and the vast, breathless mountain.

Could she really reach the summit alone?

CHAPTER 33

R YKAN STIRRED AS the sky softened from the velvet of night into pale streaks of gray and amber. The cold bit at his skin, but his tangled thoughts kept him numb. Selaina had filled his mind through the long, restless hours. Her face kept returning, no matter how he tried to think past it. What did Myrradin want with her? His fists clenched. Revenge, maybe. Or something darker. He had to find her.

He rose from the campfire, body aching from the night's vigil, and made his way to the base of the cliff where the waterfall thundered down like a silver ribbon. Mist stung his face as he stared upward at the sheer rock face. The trail they'd followed ended here, unless he could climb.

To the side, narrower cliffs and uneven ledges offered a possible route. Rykan scanned the stone, locked on a series of outcroppings, and began his ascent.

His boots found a shallow crevice; his fingers clutched at slick rock. Slowly, he pulled himself higher. But soon the stone turned smooth. He hesitated, heart pounding, the roar of the falls deafening. The ledges had brought him this far, but ahead, there was nothing but wet stone and a faint crease that might be climbable.

Testing a foothold, Rykan shifted sideways toward the falls. He reached for a ridge, fingers brushing a promising groove. He pushed upward, then slipped.

His balance vanished. The cliff spun. A shout caught in his throat as the world tipped and the churning pool rushed up to meet him.

With a violent splash, he plunged into the freezing water. The impact knocked the breath from his lungs. For a moment, there was only chaos, bubbles, dark water, the weight of the fall. He kicked hard, fighting the pull toward the deeper end, and finally broke the surface, gasping.

The waterfall roared beside him. Cold water streamed from his face as he stared up at the cliff again, breathing hard. The rock loomed above, smooth and impassable, daring him to try again.

The others were awake now, rushing to the edge of the pool, shouting his name, their voices barely audible over the crashing water. Rykan paddled toward the bank, his limbs heavy and cold, his mind reeling from the sudden fall. As he reached the shore, he dragged himself out of the water, collapsing onto the wet stones.

For a moment, he lay there, catching his breath, his body trembling from the cold and the shock of the fall. He had tried, but the mountain had bested him, for now.

"Rykan, are you hurt?" Nadara knelt beside him, her brow drawn tight.

"I'm fine," he muttered, pushing up on his elbows. His gaze climbed the cliffs. "But we can't go this way. I tried. There's no way up."

Garrick stood a short distance away, arms crossed. "Then maybe this is as far as we go."

Rykan's brows knit, water dripping from his hair. "That's not how this works. You don't stop just because the path got harder to see."

"Selaina's gone," Garrick said flatly. "Taken by someone we can't stop. We don't even know where they went, or why. We came this far for her, and now she's just... gone."

"We didn't come for her. We were with her," Rykan said, his voice rising. "This is still her path."

Kadin rubbed sleep from his face, glancing warily at the cliffs. "Even if we wanted to keep going, we don't know where she is. It's a big mountain."

"We get higher," Rykan said, forcing himself to stand. "From up there, we'll see more. Maybe the other village is close. Maybe someone saw something. But standing here isn't an option."

Ysadora exhaled hard, crossing her arms. "So we just chase shadows now? We don't even know where Myrradin went. What if this whole thing," she hesitated, then said it anyway, "this 'Zhal Evurah' prophecy... what if it's just a myth we've clung to because we needed something to believe in?"

Rykan stared at her. "You don't mean that."

"I do," she said. "Or part of me does. I want to believe Selaina is destined to save Galanor. But lately? It feels like everything's unraveling. And we're still wandering through it blind."

Silence fell. Even Kadin didn't offer a quip.

"You all got mad when I ran off before," Rykan continued. "Said we needed to stick together. Well, this is when that matters. When it's not easy. When someone we care about is missing, and we don't know the way."

Garrick didn't meet his eyes.

"And where exactly are you going to go?" Rykan asked, sweeping his gaze across them. "Back down the mountain? Through Iron Flood territory? You think they'll just let you stroll home? There's no going back. Standing still just means letting everything break without trying." He glared at each of them in turn. "I've watched that happen once already."

That landed. Even Ysadora's defiance softened, her arms loosening to her sides.

Kadin shifted his weight. "I'm not usually the one to say this, but... he's right."

"Selaina's the only one who might be able to stop them. You said it yourself," Rykan added. "And she trusted us to stand with her. If we walk away now, we're not just giving up on her, we're giving up on everything."

"I'm going up there," he said finally. "Even if I have to climb it with my bare hands. Better to bleed for trying than sit here doing nothing."

Nadara stepped forward. "Then I'm going too. I came to find the Dreylith Ward. It's further up. But if there's even a chance we can find Selaina, I'm not turning back."

Kadin sighed. "I swear, this mountain's cursed. But I'll climb it too. I've got nowhere else to go."

Garrick rubbed his face. "You've got a real gift for guilt, you know that?"

Rykan gave a wry smile. "Is that a yes?"

Garrick grunted. "Let's just find this path."

Ysadora was the last to speak. Her voice was quieter than usual. "Destiny or not, I don't believe Selaina would leave me behind. So I won't leave her. That doesn't mean I trust you."

Rykan turned toward the waterfall. "Then trust in her."

And for the first time since she vanished, they moved as one.

He turned toward the waterfall. "Oran said to look closely, 'the subtle ways water has carved its path through the earth.'"

Ysadora brushed her damp hair back. "Subtle ways? He must mean erosion. Water shapes the land, it's still shaping it. But where?"

The others followed Rykan's gaze. Nadara stepped to the edge of the pool, eyes scanning the rocks.

"There," she said, pointing. "See how the river left the surface exposed? The water used to be higher. It would've carved through where the cliff was weakest."

Rykan nodded, his eyes narrowing. The pool stretched wide, jagged stones jutting from the surface like bones.

"It's a path," he murmured. "Or what's left of one."

Garrick squinted. "You're telling me we're jumping across wet rocks toward a waterfall? That's your plan?"

Before Rykan could answer, Nadara ran ahead, leaping across the rocks as if she were running on the water's surface.

Rykan didn't wait any longer. He pushed to his feet, legs still shaky from the fall, and stepped onto the first rock. Slick, but solid.

"Watch your footing," he called.

"Brilliant," Garrick muttered, following with a grunt. "If I fall in, someone better fish me out."

Kadin trailed behind. "They couldn't have built a nice bridge? Would that have been so hard?"

One by one, the group made their way across. Garrick cursed every leap. Ysadora kept to the rear, gripping her staff as if it might steady the world itself.

As they neared the waterfall, the roar became deafening. Mist soaked their clothes and hair. Rykan joined Nadara as she squinted at something.

"There," Nadara said, pointing. "Behind the falls. Look."

At first, it seemed solid. Then, caught in the slant of morning light, a narrow fissure appeared, half-hidden behind the cascade. The stone around it looked darker, smoother, as if polished by centuries of water.

"That's it," Ysadora said. "Oran's clue. It's behind the waterfall."

"It's barely wide enough," Garrick muttered. "If we're wrong, we're face first into a wall."

"Then we'll be wrong, but it's better than standing here," Rykan said, leaping to the final rock and stepping into the spray. The icy water lashed him, but he pressed on. At the cliff face, his fingers found the gap. Narrow, but real.

Ahead of him, Nadara turned, soaked and breathless. "It's here! I found it!"

Kadin and Garrick reached him next, Garrick swearing with each slippery step. Ysadora hesitated.

"You think it'll collapse?" Rykan shouted through the roar.

"No," Ysadora said with a blank expression. "I'm just reviewing all my bad decisions."

Rykan laughed and ducked into the fissure. The stone walls closed around him as he followed Nadara, damp and cold. For a moment, it felt like the mountain was swallowing him whole.

Kadin's voice echoed faintly. "Would it kill someone to widen these things? Just a little?"

The passage opened. Rykan stepped into a small chamber; at its far end, a narrow staircase wound upward, carved straight into the rock. The others emerged behind him, faces flushed from exertion and relief.

"This is it," Rykan said quietly, gazing up the stairs disappearing into shadow. "Oran's hidden way."

Garrick clapped him on the back. "Well, I'll be... Can't believe you found it."

Rykan nodded, eyes lifting toward the heights. Beyond them lay answers, and Selaina.

"Then let's go," said Ysadora.

With Nadara waiting at the top, Rykan continued up the steps, ignoring the murmur of voices behind him.

CHAPTER 34

THE GAP BETWEEN the boulders widened, and as Rykan climbed the final step, he raised his head above the rocks. Before him lay a serene lake, its surface rippling with the cascade of a waterfall that tumbled from a massive dam wall.

But it wasn't the lake that held his attention.

At the lake's far edge stood an unusual wall, its surface textured like hardened mud, cracked and rippled as if sculpted by time and heat. At its gate, two figures stood as sentinels. They were tall, their forms slender and tapered, their presence somehow both serene and imposing. Each held a long spear with a carved wooden shaft and stone tip.

The guards' garments were layered and flowing, tightly wrapped linen adorned with woven reeds, while cloaks of soft fabric hung from their shoulders. Around their necks, strands of blue and silver stones coiled in intricate patterns. One wore deep blue, the other greenish-gray, the colors flowing like water.

As Rykan and Nadara approached, their spears crossed in unison, blocking the path. One guard placed his free hand over his heart, a gesture of respect, as he bowed his head.

"This path is not open to those who have not embraced the cleansing waters," he said, his voice calm but unyielding.

The second guard mirrored the motion, stepping forward. "Only those purified in the Silquaren may pass," he added with quiet authority.

Kadin, trailing behind Rykan, raised a brow. "Purified? We're already half-drowned. Isn't that close enough?"

The second guard's face remained impassive. "You carry the waters, but you have not embraced them."

"We've been in these waters," Kadin persisted, gesturing to his still-damp clothes. "Twice, if you're counting Rykan's little leap earlier."

"It is not the same," the first guard said gently. "Please understand, we do not allow entrance to those who refuse the cleansing."

Garrick stepped forward, his tone pragmatic. "Let's not waste time. They're guards, not an obstacle. Just do what they're asking, this might be our only lead to finding where Myrradin took Selaina."

Rykan glanced at the waterfall, frustration smoldering in his chest. "What exactly do we have to do?"

The guard gestured toward the lake's series of stepped waterfalls, where the water flowed gently into the larger basin below. "The Waterkeeper will guide you."

The group followed the direction of the guard's extended hand, their boots brushing through soft moss as they neared the series of basins. The air here was thicker with moisture, the mist softer, more soothing than the roar of the Serpent's Tear. Small alcoves lined the area, bundles of flowers and carved stones carefully arranged like offerings to the water itself.

Seated on a naturally smoothed stone throne above one of the larger basins was the Waterkeeper. She wore a flowing robe of pale blue threaded with silver, the fabric shimmering softly as though lit from within. Her dark hair, slicked back and wet, hung in a thick braid over her shoulder, and her gaze was calm, welcoming. She rose as they approached, her palms extended outward.

"Welcome to the Silquaren," she said, her voice clear yet serene, carrying effortlessly over the sound of flowing water. "Here, the water cleanses not only the body, but also the spirit."

Kadin squinted at her skeptically. "So how's this water any different from the rest on the mountain?"

The Waterkeeper regarded him with a faint smile. "The same way this mountain is different from any other stone. What makes it sacred is not its nature, but the meaning we give to it. Why have you come to this place?"

Kadin opened his mouth, then hesitated, a glimmer of something unreadable crossing his face. "Still figuring that out," he said again, but quieter this time, less flippant, more honest. He rubbed the back of his neck, then added, "I wasn't chasing destiny or sacred rivers. I just didn't want to stay where I was." His eyes lingered on the mist rising from the water. "But maybe there's something here I didn't know I needed."

"I came to find answers," Ysadora said, her voice carrying a faint edge. "To see if destiny really favors those who haven't earned it." She paused, her gaze drifting toward the peaks above. "Now I just want to know if any of this matters."

"I had a reason once," said Garrick. "But it seems the higher we climb, the further away I am from it." He turned to Rykan and nodded toward him. "Ask him why we're still here."

"We're all here for Selaina," Rykan said. "She was taken during the night by a Windwraith. Have you seen one?"

"There was a strong wind that passed through," the Waterkeeper replied. "But I haven't heard stories of Windwraiths in a long time."

"A strong wind!" Rykan's eyes lit up. "He must've come through this way!"

"Don't get too excited," Ysadora said dryly. "Wind's pretty common in the mountains, if you haven't noticed."

"Perhaps the waters will bring you clarity," the Waterkeeper said, "and help you find what you seek."

"Those are interesting stones," Ysadora said to the Waterkeeper. "What are they?"

The Waterkeeper lifted the chain, revealing a translucent gem that shimmered blue and silver, like captured light.

"Flowstone," she said. "It is formed over centuries, where water flows gently over the rocks of Kylinshan. The stone purifies the water, and the water, in turn, cleanses all it touches."

"And what are we supposed to do here?" Rykan asked, his voice edged with impatience.

The Waterkeeper gave him a calm look, a hint of a smile on her lips. "You speak of it as though it is a burden," she replied softly. "Water is the essence of balance in our world. Mist carries the wildness of chaos, ice the stillness of order. Yet water moves between them. It flows like fate, ever searching for a vessel to fill."

She paused, allowing the sound of the nearby waterfall to punctuate her words.

"Let your life flow like water. The harder you try to force its course, the rougher it gets. It will always find its way to its destination. Embrace the journey and allow it to carry you where you need to go."

With a pointed gesture toward Rykan, she continued, "You bear the scars of shadow, and chaos clouds your mind. Yet even this can be healed. Step into the basin. Let the water wash over you, cleansing the burdens of your journey. Stand beneath the falls and feel the purity and balance return to you, flowing like the very currents of life."

Rykan gazed down at the maugwin bite on his arm, the edges still outlined in dark crimson and black. Taking a deep breath, he closed his eyes and steeled himself as he stepped beneath the icy cascade. For an instant, he caught a glimpse of Arathain flashing in his mind, but it vanished almost as quickly as it had appeared.

As the cold water enveloped him, his body gradually adjusted to the rhythmic pounding against his skin, each drop awakening his senses. He wanted to absorb every detail of this cleansing ritual, to embrace the purity the Waterkeeper had spoken of.

In his mind's eye, he envisioned himself merging with the water, feeling the boundary between himself and the waterfall dissolve. He imagined flowing through every crack and crevice of the mountain, coursing into hidden caverns, cascading over the falls, gliding along winding rivers, and settling into serene, tranquil lakes. For a moment, he wasn't just a boy under a waterfall. He was part of the mountain itself, connected to its heartbeat and flow.

The sounds of the waterfall faded as Rykan stepped out from beneath the cascade, his clothes heavy, water streaming down in rivulets. He blinked, the world sharpening into focus, the vast sky overhead, the rugged stone beneath his boots, the glistening water pooling around him. For a fleeting moment, it felt as though he was seeing everything anew, the colors brighter, the air clearer.

But as he glanced at his arm, hope dimmed. The cursed wound remained unchanged, its jagged edges still etched in dark crimson and black. The faint hum of disappointment sank into his chest, and the clarity he'd felt drained away before he could hold onto it.

"It's still there," he muttered, more to himself than anyone else.

The Waterkeeper, watching with eyes that seemed to see far more than they should, inclined her head knowingly. "The water does not erase scars, it shows you how to carry them."

Rykan let out a slow breath, his gaze falling to the falls one last time before stepping aside to let the others approach.

One by one, Garrick, Ysadora, Kadin, and Nadara entered the Silquaren's embrace, each emerging with varying degrees of discomfort or quiet contemplation. Nadara moved with a stoic grace, her face unreadable, while Ysadora appeared to shiver at the touch of the water, as though it unsettled her more than it soothed.

"It's colder than it looks," Garrick grunted as he ran a hand through his wet hair.

"Refreshing, if you ask me," Kadin said, shaking his arms out with exaggerated flair. "I think it's brought clarity, a whole new level of charm."

Ysadora shot him a glare, though the corner of her mouth twitched. "Let's hope it cleansed some of your judgment, too."

When they returned to the gate, the guards stepped aside, their spears lifting in practiced unison.

"You may enter," one said, bowing his head respectfully.

Rykan stepped through first, the others following close behind. Beyond the gate, the ground shifted from mossy earth to a sheet of flat rock, its surface worn smooth by time and water. Small canals ran like veins through the village, carrying crystal-clear streams that flowed under the walls and into the lake they'd seen earlier. The quiet murmur of the water blended with the gentle sounds of the village, a rhythm as constant as a heartbeat.

Lining the inside of the walls, guards identical to those at the gate stood at regular intervals, their spears upright, their faces unreadable, like they'd been carved from the same stone as the village. Their tall, tapered frames and linen garments, adorned with woven reeds and shimmering stones, made them look both regal and ancient, like statues someone had forgotten to wake. The blue and greenish-gray hues of their cloaks shifted gently in the breeze, the faint sound of their sandals brushing against the stone as they moved ever so slightly to track the newcomers.

Houses crafted from reed, wood, and stone stood nestled against the land, positioned carefully to avoid the exposed stone slab that formed the village's center. The scent of fresh fish and burning wood lingered in the air, mingling with the damp freshness carried by the breeze.

A man carrying a basket brimming with silver-scaled fish passed by, his face warming with a smile. "Welcome, wanderers! May the whispers of the river bring you wisdom, and the tides of the lake grant you peace."

"Thank you," Rykan replied, offering a small nod. He lingered, turning back toward the gate as the others caught up.

"There has to be someone cooking around here," Kadin declared, sniffing the air as though it might lead him to a feast.

Garrick narrowed his eyes. "We'll find something soon. My belly is empty too."

For a moment, the village felt peaceful, almost untouched by the world beyond its gates. Yet, the weight of Selaina's absence returned quickly, heavy as a stone in Rykan's chest. Whatever tranquility this place held, it wouldn't last until she was safe again.

Two men crossing their path forced Rykan to slow. "Travelers," said one of them. "I see you have come hoping to see the Sky Serpents, to gain some wisdom and live great lives."

"Why do all of you come?" asked the other. "The Sky Serpents appear to no one. You are wasting your time. What makes you think that you are so special that the Sky Serpents will speak to you?"

"We're searching for a friend," said Rykan, his voice steady. "Did you see anything strange in the sky recently?"

"In the sky?" said one of the men. "What kind of strange things would there be?"

Garrick stepped forward. "What about a man with long gray hair and a beard? He would be wearing dark robes and may have a young Lith woman with him."

"I haven't seen anyone like that," said one of the men. "At least not in the last few months."

Before Rykan could search for someone else to ask, a voice called from the nearby wall. "You there, travelers!"

They turned as one of the guards peeled away from the line along the village walls. His appearance matched the others, tapered frame, layered reed-and-linen clothing, and sandals that brushed softly against the stone. Yet his expression was far friendlier, with a gleam of curiosity in his pale eyes. He rested his long spear casually against his shoulder as he approached, his movements confident but not threatening.

"You carry interesting weapons," the guard remarked, stopping just a few paces from them. His gaze lingered on Rykan's sword, Nadara's glaive, Garrick's worn gear, and Ysadora's staff. "We don't often see travelers so well equipped. You seem... different from the pilgrims who usually pass through."

Garrick narrowed one eye, like squinting against the sun, studying the guard harder than he likely realized. "What do you mean different?" he muttered, folding his arms.

The guard let out a low chuckle. "Don't worry, stranger, I mean no insult. I'm just curious." He tapped the butt of his spear gently on the stone before speaking again. "My name is Aresh. I serve as one of the lakewardens here, though you'll find most just call us 'guards.' What brings travelers like you this far up the mountain? Surely not just the legends of the Sky Serpents?"

Rykan hesitated, glancing back at Garrick, then answered. "We're looking for a friend. She was taken, by a man we believe may have passed through here."

Aresh's brow furrowed. "Taken? That's troubling news. We don't often have visitors who mean harm here." His gaze softened a little as he added, "Though, to be fair, most travelers who reach this village are seeking answers, not causing trouble." He gestured to Rykan's sword. "That blade of yours, where did you get it?"

Rykan blinked, caught off guard by the question. "It was... passed down."

Aresh nodded appreciatively. "It has seen its share of battles, I think. And you," he turned to Ysadora, "a staff like that doesn't belong to someone who simply dabbles in magic. You've all come a long way. Travelers like you aren't common here."

Ysadora stiffened, her fingers clenching on the staff. Her expression remained composed, but her eyes flicked briefly toward the nearby gate. Rykan saw it, that flash of guarded tension she wore whenever someone tried to size her up.

"We're definitely not common," Nadara interjected firmly, her tone sharp but not unkind.

Kadin smirked, tapping the hilt of his dagger lightly. "Speak for yourself. I think I'm delightfully average, just with sharper accessories."

Ysadora gave him a sideways glance, but didn't respond. The faintest breath of a smile tugged at her lips, so brief Rykan wasn't sure he'd seen it. But she didn't pull away.

Still, Rykan noticed the way her shoulders eased ever so slightly. The tension hadn't vanished, but something in Kadin's timing had disarmed it, if only a little.

Kadin didn't look at her again, but as they began to walk, he slowed his pace until he ended up beside her, quiet for once. For a few steps, they walked in step without speaking.

He didn't make a joke. Didn't nudge or prod. Just stayed close, like he was making sure she wasn't alone. And maybe that was the closest he ever got to comfort.

Aresh smiled, his curiosity seemingly only growing. He glanced back toward the walls, where the other guards still stood in their silent vigil. "If you're searching for someone, you'll want to speak with Liora. She knows more about the goings-on in this village than anyone."

"Can you take us to her?" Rykan asked.

"I can point you in the right direction," Aresh said, motioning with his spear toward a distant, gnarled tree at the far edge of the village. Its branches were vast and heavy with pale blossoms that shimmered faintly in the light. "The Skybloom Tree. Liora will likely be there. Follow the stone path, and you'll find her. She's… different," Aresh added, almost as an afterthought. "The kind of person you listen to, even when you don't understand why."

"Thank you, Aresh," Rykan said, dipping his head in gratitude.

The guard returned the gesture. "Be cautious, travelers. Not all answers are what we hope they'll be." He turned back toward the wall, his friendly demeanor fading into the practiced composure of a sentry once more.

As they watched him rejoin his fellow guards, Garrick muttered, "Finally, someone who doesn't glare at us like we've stolen their dinner."

Kadin snorted softly. "Give it time. We're great at making good first impressions and ruining them later."

Rykan shook his head, a small smile playing on his lips as he started toward the tree. "Come on. Let's find Liora."

CHAPTER 35

S ELAINA CREPT BEHIND a large snow-covered stone, her breath curling in the icy air like smoke from a fading fire. She watched intently as a white-haired veyu pawed at the frosted earth, its sharp nose probing patches of ground where sunlight had melted the snow. A hollow pang twisted in her stomach, a sharp reminder of how long it had been since her last meal, more than a day now, by her reckoning. Desperation gnawed at her as she scanned the barren plateau, but no useful plants caught her eye, only endless drifts of snow and jagged rocks. Myrradin's departure weighed on her like the cold itself, each moment deepening her sense of isolation and sharpening the urgency of her hunger.

Nocking an arrow to her bow, Selaina drew back the string and took aim. The chilling wind whipped around her, sending a shiver down her spine and amplifying the loneliness of this unfamiliar place. She took a deep breath, holding it for a moment before releasing both breath and arrow into the wind. She imagined the arrow flying true, but the wind shoved it sideways, spoiling her shot.

Intensifying her focus, she straightened the projectile's trajectory, guiding it as it sliced through the air as if it were unaffected by the weather. With a swift adjustment, the arrow found its mark, and she felt a moment of triumph amidst the cold isolation.

Using her knife, Selaina drained the carcass of blood and slung it over her shoulder, pressing onward through the frozen meadow toward the white canopy of the forest. Beneath the trees, she found dry ground. She laid the veyu on a large stone while she searched for flammable foliage. With fallen pine needles, shreds of bark, and tree sap, she managed to gather a good mixture to ignite.

Drawing on the techniques Jeth had taught her, she took an arrowhead from one of her projectiles and began spinning the wooden shaft back and forth against a large piece of bark to generate friction. As she worked, the end of the arrow shaft started to heat up, but the mixture refused to ignite.

Her arms began to tire, so she grabbed two rocks about the size of her palms and struck them together, hoping to generate a spark, but nothing happened. Frustrated, she returned to the drill technique, using the arrow shaft to create friction once more. Finally, she saw smoke rising from the mixture. With a gentle breath, she blew on it, and the heat ignited the dried leaves and bark, causing the fire to grow.

Staring at the flames, Selaina admired the fire she had created. She was both surprised and proud of herself for being able to do it. She prepared the veyu for cooking, skewering it and holding it over the flames. The scent of burning wood brought back memories of her life in the forest, nights spent beside the fire with Ysadora, Garrick, Kadin, and Rykan. So many evenings where both their laughter and silence had wrapped around her like warmth.

She missed them more than she ever thought she would. Especially Rykan. They had a way of communicating without words. If Garrick started on a long rant, she could glance at Rykan and know exactly what he was thinking. The thought made her smile, but the smile faltered, buckling under the weight of absence.

She turned the skewer slowly, trying to center herself in the task, but her thoughts kept drifting.

What would Jeth think if he could see her now?

Not just the girl who had followed him through the trees, learning how to find her footing on a trail no one else could see, but the one who had taken up a burden that wasn't meant for her. Zhal Evurah. The words still felt heavy, even when left unspoken. She had made the choice. She'd touched the Wishing Stone. Taken destinies that didn't belong to her, because someone had to.

But now?

The power didn't feel like a gift. It felt like a weight pressing deeper into her chest with every step. A mark some revered, some feared, but few understood. No one saw her. Not the girl who still missed her mother. Who sometimes wondered if she'd done the right thing. If she was strong enough to carry what she'd taken. If anyone would've done better in her place.

Jeth had taught her how to survive. To listen to the wind. To find fire where others would only see damp wood and cold earth. But this, this path of stars and serpents and broken prophecy, this wasn't survival. It was something bigger. Something heavier. And Selaina wasn't sure she wanted it. Or that she could carry it for long.

The fire crackled softly. Her skin warmed in its glow, but a chill curled stubbornly in her chest.

They all looked at her like she was the answer. As if her presence would mend the past. Garrick didn't say it, but he looked at her like he wanted her to be more than a symbol. Ysadora's eyes held questions she couldn't ask without it sounding like doubt. And Rykan… Rykan still believed in her. That, somehow, was the hardest part. Because she didn't know if she believed in herself.

He had a way of standing beside her that made the world feel steadier. Like, no matter what came at them, she didn't have to face it alone. Now, every decision, every step, felt heavier. Her aim had to be perfect. Her fire had to catch. Her courage had to hold, because there was no one else here to catch her if she faltered.

She hadn't noticed how much she leaned on him, until she had to carry all of it alone.

Maybe Jeth would've said that wasn't the point. That belief came later. That you start with the next step, and the one after that, until belief catches up.

As the veyu roasted, hope crept in, not a surge, but a slow ache, like the kind that comes after a long day's work. A soreness that tingled with tenderness, an homage to the effort it had taken to get here.

Selaina's mouth watered uncontrollably as the meat's aroma mixed with the smoke. It was a bit tough, but she pulled it apart into pieces small enough to chew. She couldn't wait for it to cool, scarfing it down and burning her tongue.

She filled her flask with a handful of snow and set it near the fire to melt. After a few more bites, she lifted the flask to her lips. The cold hit her throat like stone, but she drank anyway, savoring the relief.

Even alone, she had made it this far. That had to mean something.

Though she had knowledge of how to survive on her own, it had never been tested quite like this. Selaina leaned back against a tree, savoring the taste of the meat that lingered on her tongue. She really could do this. It pleased her to know that, if she had to, she could live without relying on anyone else.

There was something about being alone in the forest, something spiritual that could never take place with the presence of others around. It was a profound stillness that enveloped her, a quiet intimacy with the natural world. She couldn't quite decide what it was exactly, but it felt familiar. It was almost as if she wasn't alone, that there was some unexplainable force watching over her, guiding her in her solitude.

This sensation, a gentle whisper of connection, stirred memories of the woods near her old home, where she often found solace among the trees. There, too, she had felt this presence, a sense of belonging intertwined with the gentle rustle of leaves and the soft songs of the wind. It comforted her, and unsettled her. A reminder of how strong she was… and how breakable.

Everything that had been lost flowed through her mind. She realized now that, with all that had been going on around her, she had not had the chance to reflect. The images of finding Jeth's body by the brook came to the forefront of her thoughts, but they were quickly overshadowed by more recent memories. Elysia's face, vibrant and alive one moment, and in the next, her eyes blank and her expression locked in place. Selaina was struck by the realization that their bodies were merely shells, hollow flesh filled with living beings, each with their own hopes, fears, and experiences. Yet, she recognized that she had often viewed people more through the context of their skin, understanding so little about the essence that lay within. In many ways, she wondered how much she truly understood about herself.

She recalled Darian's last moments, and how they had contradicted everything she had come to believe about him. A sense of betrayal washed over her, yet she could also grasp the truth in it. Love, she thought, was everything. The most beautiful thing in the world. But it could still twist into something selfish. Something ugly.

With no one around, she allowed the tears to flow freely down her cheeks. Their cold trails provided a refreshing harshness against her skin, painful yet satisfying. She longed for this release; she needed to feel it. She let it pour out, grief she hadn't known she'd been carrying. Like wringing out a rag soaked too long. Every ounce of sadness and anger she had harbored began to pour out, overwhelming her mind with thoughts and memories.

And then… her father.

The memory hadn't settled until now, like a thorn snagged on cloth, catching as she began to unravel. Myrradin's words came back with a clarity that stung: He walked to the gate alone.

She hadn't wanted to believe it at the time. Hadn't had space to. But here, in the quiet, with the grief pouring loose from places she didn't know she was holding, it landed.

Her father had gone willingly. Hoping, maybe, that one last offering might be enough. That Vatreus would see it. Feel it. That something might soften inside him.

But nothing had changed. Her father had died trying to fix what her brother had become. Or maybe it was the shame of what he had begun that drove him to it.

Selaina's breath wavered. She pressed a hand to her chest, fingers pressing against the ache. She had spent so long wondering where he'd gone, if he was out there somewhere, waiting for the right time to return. But he wasn't. Not if Myrradin had told the truth. He'd been gone for a long time.

Swallowed by the gate. The thing behind the gate. Azragul.

The thought hollowed her, sharper than she expected. Not just grief, but guilt. That her father had tried to stop it, and failed. That now she was the one left to carry what he couldn't undo.

The tears came faster after that. Tears for a father she had never known. For the choices he had made. For the ruin left in his wake.

As darkness fell over the forest, Selaina gathered herself, clearing a small space to sleep. She positioned herself close enough to the fire for warmth, yet far enough away to avoid the risk of being burned. Carefully, she arranged some stones around the fire pit, creating a barrier to keep the flames contained.

As she worked, she couldn't seem to take her eyes off her bag. A faint deep blue pulsing softly with a gentle ebb and flow of barely visible light. She reached inside the bag, touching the hard, smooth metal of the talisman Myrradin had dropped. What should she do with it? It had to be magic.

Though part of her wanted to toss it as far as she could into the forest, she couldn't let it go. Taking it out of the bag, Selaina admired the craftsmanship of the pendant that surrounded the gemstone, tracing the spirals with her finger. The last thing she wanted was for it to draw Myrradin to her. But if there were any chance she might run into danger she couldn't handle, it wouldn't hurt to have a magic item if she needed it. She placed the talisman back into the bag.

Wrapping her cloak tightly around her, she settled onto a bed of grass and fallen leaves, allowing the gentle crackle of the fire to lull her into a deep sleep. The fire's warmth clung to her, and sleep pulled her under.

As the night wore on, a gust of wind rustled through the trees, sending a shiver coursing through the branches. It stirred Selaina from her dreams, but she kept her eyes closed, hoping to slip back into the soothing depths of sleep.

Yet, as she drifted in her light slumber, a soft crunching sound intruded upon her awareness, echoing through the stillness of the night. At first, it was distant and faint, like the whispers of the wind. She dismissed it, convincing herself it was merely the forest settling around her.

But the sound persisted, gradually drawing closer, the snow crunching underfoot. Her senses sharpened, each soft crackle pulling her further from the embrace of sleep. Selaina's heart quickened, a primal instinct urging her to remain alert. She opened her eyes, squinting into the darkness, where shadows danced ominously around her.

Throwing off her cloak, she reached for her bow, rising to her feet. She scanned the darkness outside the firelight, ears straining for the faintest sound of movement. Could it be Myrradin? Even though she hadn't invoked his presence with the talisman, she felt a twinge of unease for having touched it at all.

After several moments of silence, only the night birds and the occasional rustle of leaves filled her ears. Had she imagined the sounds? Feeling foolish, she curled back up in her cloak, allowing her thoughts to wander, hoping to surrender to sleep once more.

But soon after, the sound came again, the unmistakable crunch of snow pressed beneath boots, the rhythmic pattern of someone walking slowly. This time, the footsteps were louder, closer. Selaina shook herself awake, bow in hand, rising to her feet again. The forest had come alive with sound, the footsteps unmistakable.

Attempting to calm her nerves, she pushed forward, stepping out of the fire's shimmering glow and into the darkness. The shadows seemed to grip her, but she knew she had a choice: sit in fear or confront whatever lurked in the night.

Her mind raced, trying to rationalize the presence of whoever was walking around her camp. If it were Myrradin meaning to harm her, he could have done so before now. If he were merely watching her, he would keep his distance, hidden from view.

Selaina opened her mouth to call out, but the words wouldn't come. She closed her eyes, imagining the daylight, envisioning the forest as a friendly place.

"Who's out there?" she finally managed, her voice wavering. "If you mean no harm, speak now, before my arrow finds you."

Only the sounds of the forest answered her. The footsteps had ceased. Finding a dry tree limb, Selaina returned to the tree where she had gathered sap before. She claimed some of the sticky substance oozing from a knot-hole, coating the end of the stick in a thick layer. Igniting the sap-covered tip in the campfire, she held the torch in front of her, the flame flickering defiantly against the night.

She began searching the area, lighting the snow nearby to illuminate her surroundings. Her eyes scanned the ground, desperate for any signs of intrusion.

Circling the campsite, she eventually returned to her own prints in the snow. Moving farther out, she widened her search but still found no traces of anyone's presence. Was she losing her mind? The only tracks she uncovered were from some kind of hooved animal, perhaps an elk, but they appeared to be old and faded.

With a sigh, she conceded defeat, concluding it was likely just a harmless creature wandering through the woods.

Feeling the chill of the night seep into her bones, Selaina lay back down, yet sleep eluded her. Despite the absence of evidence, the initial anxiety lingered like a shadow in her mind. Every rustle of leaves and distant call of an animal sent her heart racing again, a reminder of her solitude in this vast, unfriendly wilderness.

As dawn broke, Selaina shuffled the cloak over her face, shielding her eyes from the encroaching light. Knowing what lay ahead, she wasn't yet ready to face the day. Drifting in and out of sleep, she felt the sun rise higher, its rays penetrating the fabric of her cloak.

Pulling the cloak off her face, and turning toward the remaining warmth of the embers, she froze.

There was someone sitting by the fire.

CHAPTER 36

RYKAN WOVE HIS way between weathered wooden crates, their surfaces slick with moisture, the earthy scent of damp wood mixing with the faint, soothing aroma of herbs drifting from the nearby huts. The village buzzed with quiet vitality, its life carried in the cheerful chatter of villagers and the occasional burst of laughter that rose above the gentle murmur of the morning.

Beneath his feet, water trickled softly through narrow stone channels, their paths snaking like veins through the heart of the village. His boots thudded lightly on the wooden bridges that arched over the shimmering streams, the rhythmic sound punctuating the serene harmony of flowing water and distant voices. Was this the village of Glissara that Oran had told them about?

He glanced back, ensuring that Garrick and the others were still behind him, their presence a comforting anchor in this foreign place. The sun began to rise higher, casting a warm glow on the sand-brick structures that dotted the landscape. As he continued onward, he noticed one of the channels flowing purposefully into a larger brick building, where a small group of villagers stood waiting to enter, their faces reflecting varying degrees of patience. The building itself radiated a sense of purpose, its wide door ajar, inviting yet mysterious, as though it held secrets waiting to be uncovered.

The wooden bridges gave way to cobblestone paths, their uneven surfaces worn smooth by countless footsteps over the years. Vibrant mosaics of blue and green tiles of flowstone, depicting swirling water patterns, caught Rykan's eye, glinting in the sunlight.

Up ahead, the scent of damp earth intensified, mingling with the sweet fragrance of flowers blooming in small suspended gardens, their vines trailing down from hanging pots that danced in the wind above the water channels. Rykan's gaze lingered on one of the hanging baskets, its lush greenery spilling over the edge, almost touching the surface of the stream below, as if balanced on the edge of chaos and order itself.

The large tree in the distance grew clearer with each step. Its sprawling roots stretched out, some disappearing into the water channels, while others twisted and knotted into the earth like a natural anchor holding the village together. The tree's bark was dark, weathered with age, and adorned with symbols etched into its surface. It towered above the rest of Glissara, its branches thick and reaching, casting a wide canopy that shaded much of the village's edge.

Children played nearby, their laughter soft and innocent, guiding small wooden boats along the channels with sticks, the water gently pulling them along. Rykan couldn't help but smile at their simple joy, reminded of his carefree days as a boy in the streets of Tathara.

His boots finally pressed into the mossy patch surrounding the ancient tree, feeling the temperature drop even further as its massive shadow enveloped him. There air was colder but fresher here, almost as though the tree itself breathed its own misty breath into the air. Rykan's boots crunched softly on the fallen leaves that blanketed the ground as he approached the tree's base.

The faint twinkling of chimes hidden within the branches rustled with the leaves overhead. Rykan reached out, brushing his fingertips against the tree's rough bark. There was power here—not in any way he could see or touch, but something that crept into his thoughts and wouldn't let go.

Garrick and the others arrived shortly after, standing beside him as they gazed up into the tree's towering presence.

"This must be it," Garrick muttered, his eyes scanning the twisting mass of branches above.

As Rykan's gaze pierced the veil of leaves, something caught his attention. A wooden structure, resting upon one of the thick branches, like a platform or balcony, was built onto a small house high above them, cradled by the great tree's sprawling arms.

"Where is she then?" Ysadora asked.

"Perhaps you need to climb the tree," said Kadin.

"Liora!" Rykan called out, projecting his voice up into the tree, making some birds scatter into the sky.

"I'm not sure that's the best way to gain her trust," said Garrick.

Rykan put his hands on each side of his mouth, shouting again. "Liora!"

"I suppose annoyance is one way to get someone's attention," said Kadin.

Waiting for a response, Rykan stared up at the wooden dwelling in the branches of the tree. Small birds hopped along the crooked limbs, chirping in unison.

As Rykan continued to call up to the tree, gentle laughter floated down from above, mingling with the rustling leaves.

"What a curious bird you are, shouting so loudly!" A figure emerged onto the wooden balcony, perched gracefully on the edge.

It was a woman, her gray hair cascading like soft waves of sunlight, adorned with small, woven flowers that complemented her earthy attire. She wore a simple tunic of muted greens and browns, but along its cuffs, an almost imperceptible embroidery shimmered, a looping pattern of waves or spirals that caught the light when she moved.

Around her neck hung a single drop-shaped pendant, pale blue and glowing faintly in the filtered sun.

"Surely you could sing a sweeter song than that!" she teased, her voice light and melodic as she tilted her head, revealing a youthful face framed by soft, warm features, while her bright, inquisitive eyes sparkled with mischief and depth, as if they held years of secrets. "If you're hoping to attract my attention, perhaps a bird call or a chirp would serve you better!"

"I—I can't do a bird call all that well," said Rykan.

Liora stepped to a lower branch, using only her bare feet to walk down the tree, as if the branches were stairs.

"You must be travelers," she said. "Pilgrims, seekers, hoping for a chance to see the Sky Serpents. To gain their blessing. Why have you come to me?"

"We came to ask if you had seen our friend," said Rykan. "A Windwraith took her. We were told that, if anyone might know anything about it, it would be you."

"A Windwraith?" Liora said, her brow lifting in curiosity. "Now that's something I haven't heard of on this mountain in ages. Tales of such beings were whispered long ago. But why would a Windwraith carry your friend away? Was it mischief or something more sinister?"

"Something sinister, I'm afraid," Rykan said, his expression hardening. "But yes, we did come with her to see the Sky Serpents. She was called here as the Zhal Evurah."

Liora's smile faltered, her eyes narrowing. "Zhal Evurah?" she repeated, almost skeptically. "That name hasn't carried meaning in a long time."

She turned her gaze toward the horizon.

"What makes you think a new Zhal Evurah has risen?" The mischief faded from her voice, replaced with something quieter. "Have you felt it? A change in the world's breath? The stones vibrating differently? The wind singing in a new key?"

"Nothing like that," Rykan admitted. "But she has the mark on her forehead."

"I'd like to see this mark for myself," Liora said, her eyes cutting back to him, sharp now. "I didn't think it was still possible without Ethyllion. But the Azsh Rozaht has surprising ways of weaving threads of fate."

"Can you help us find her?" Rykan asked.

"There was an unusual storm over Elyndra Bluff during the dark hours of the morn," Liora said thoughtfully. "Perhaps that was your Windwraith, stirring up trouble along its path."

Rykan couldn't hide his excitement. Finally, a clue to where Selaina might be. "How do we get there?"

"You would have to go most of the way up the mountain, near the summit," said Liora, her gaze drifting to the horizon as if envisioning the journey. "From there, you'd need to take the spur trail to the east."

"What is on Elyndra Bluff?" asked Ysadora. "Why would he take her there?"

Liora shrugged with a small smile. "A lovely vista, mostly. Aside from that, not much of significance. My guess is that he's taking her toward the temple on the summit. That's where most outsiders come, to seek the Sky Serpents."

Rykan's face brightened. "Then we should head for the bluff!"

Liora's expression grew serious as she shook her head. "It's not that simple. The only way to the bluff from here is to cut through the caverns where Azirok resides."

"Azirok?" Rykan asked, with a hint of confusion.

Liora's gaze darkened, her voice low. "The leviathan that slumbers in the mountain's heart, its scales formed of unbreakable crystal. It often sleeps in the caverns there. It sleeps a deep rest... but I wouldn't count on slipping by unnoticed."

"Myrradin wouldn't go anywhere near a creature like that," Ysadora said. "He could avoid the caverns entirely as a Windwraith."

Rykan felt a moment of relief. "Is that where Myrradin is taking Selaina?" he asked.

"Why would Myrradin take her to the Sky Serpents?" Garrick said. "That's what we were doing already."

"There must be something in it for him," said Ysadora.

"Maybe he wants to see the Sky Serpents for himself," Rykan said.

"Or maybe he just has a thing for dragging people into life-threatening situations," Kadin said. "Seems to be his style."

"He may want the chance to speak with them," Ysadora mused. "Many would give anything to be in their presence, to hear their wisdom."

"So he would take the Zhal Evurah prisoner for this chance?" Liora wondered aloud, her eyes glinting with curiosity.

"That must be it," Ysadora said.

"Would the Sky Serpents even acknowledge him?" Nadara asked.

"While they would only appear to the Zhal Evurah, I don't think they'd ignore anyone in their presence," Liora replied, a smile curling her lips.

"How is it right that someone like Myrradin would be allowed to hear their wisdom? He is only out for himself. He wants more power so he can dominate Galanor," said Ysadora.

"Then perhaps he needs wisdom more than anyone," Liora said, her voice taking on a serious tone.

"But we all could use some guidance," Ysadora countered. "Why won't they acknowledge us too? Are we nothing to them if we aren't Zhal Evurah?"

"You speak of the Sky Serpents like gods," Nadara said, her voice low.

"But I've heard some call them tyrants. What if their blessing is just control wrapped in prophecy?"

Liora looked down at the flowing water, her fingers brushing lightly across her collarbone, it might have been a reaction to the cold, or a shield for something deeper. "It's not godhood. It's burden. The serpents carry more than power, they carry regret. We just tell the stories differently." She paused, then added more quietly, "That's why the Dawnstone mattered." Her expression sobered. "We had a conduit to the celestials once, and we abused it."

"That wasn't entirely our fault, was it?" Ysadora asked.

"It's in our nature," Liora replied. "We chase what we lack and waste what we already have."

"And so now we are lost?" Ysadora asked, her brow furrowed as if weighing the truth in Liora's words. "Or is that just another excuse we tell ourselves when the world doesn't bend to our will?"

A crease passed across Liora's expression, sadness, perhaps, or something older than sadness. She didn't answer right away.

"Maybe it is," she eventually said softly. "But even so… we don't need the Dawnstone to receive wisdom." Her voice regained its strength. "The celestials may keep themselves hidden, guarding their presence from the world, but true wisdom has always come from the Azsh Rozaht. It's there for those who seek it."

Silence fell as they each considered Liora's words, a sense of unease lingering in the air.

Kadin spoke up, breaking the quiet with a thoughtful frown. "One thing still troubles me: just how vulnerable are the Sky Serpents?" he asked, glancing around at the others, who looked at him with a hint of confusion. "In trying to think like Myrradin for a moment, I wonder if he would be able to destroy them and take their power?"

"The Sky Serpents have physical forms," Liora said, her voice calm and measured. "They are not impervious, which is one reason they reveal themselves to so few. Yet they remain more powerful than any beings known in the mortal realm. It would take immense strength, and more than any single soul could muster, to pose a true threat to them."

"If someone did destroy them, what could be taken from them?" asked Rykan.

"I suppose if someone had the ability to capture their remaining essence," Liora said thoughtfully. "The same essence they would bestow upon the Zhal Evurah."

"Something like a Windwraith…" said Ysadora, her voice trailing off.

"Do you really think Myrradin is powerful enough to contend with three Sky Serpents, who used to be celestials?" Garrick asked.

"The Myrradin I knew wasn't capable of that," Ysadora said, then hesitated, one finger brushing the base of her horns as if trying to center herself. "But maybe that's the problem. Maybe I never really knew him. Maybe it's not his power we mustn't underestimate, but his ego."

"I can see this journey has taken quite a toll on you," Liora chimed in, her tone light yet sincere. "Before you go charging off in search of your friend, how about a hearty meal to revive your bodies, minds, and souls? After all, even the bravest of adventurers need a little fuel!" With a playful smile, she tied her cloak around her and beckoned them to follow her into the heart of the village.

"She's right," said Ysadora. "We need our strength if we're going to make it up this mountain."

Rykan clenched his jaw, frustration bubbling over. "We should have never come here. First, you wanted to wait until daylight; now we have to rest and eat," he snapped. "Do you even want to find Selaina?"

"The only reason I'm on this forsaken rock is for Selaina," Ysadora shot back. "We need to be in good shape when we find Myrradin. But if you want to rush off and find her yourself, go right ahead."

"Gladly," Rykan snapped, tightening his belt. "Sitting here won't find her. Every moment we wait, he gets further away. You all want to ration your strength like we've got time to waste," he added, voice sharp. "But the mountain isn't going to wait, and neither will he."

He stormed away from them, heading toward the village gates.

"Rykan, wait!" Nadara called, stepping toward him. "Charging ahead might feel right, but splitting up only makes us easier to break. The mountain is only going to get colder. And this Myrradin… he'd love to see us fall apart before we even reach him." She paused, then continued more gently, "You want to move fast? Then stay with us. We'll get to her sooner together than scattered."

"If Myrradin is moving with the same urgency you have, he would have already accomplished his goal by now," Garrick added, his tone calm yet firm. "It won't take long to eat and rest a moment before we move on. If we hadn't come to Liora, we wouldn't even know where to look for Selaina."

"Look," Kadin chimed in with a smirk, "I don't know about you, but I refuse to take on Windwraith mavins until I've had my fill. It's just common sense!"

Ysadora shot Kadin a look, but this time, it didn't carry the usual sharpness. "You're not as foolish as you sound," she muttered, and walked ahead.

Kadin blinked, lips parting like he meant to respond with a quip... but didn't. Instead, he watched her go, something unreadable in his expression. Not amusement. Something quieter.

Rykan noticed it, that unspoken weight between them, the kind that only shows when you start to care more than you intended.

Rykan sighed, a puff of smokey condensation escaping his lips. He drew in behind Garrick, frustration still simmering beneath the surface. As willing as he might be to risk his life for Selaina, he knew he wouldn't make it alone. "Are we going to stand here all day or follow Liora?"

With an exasperated roll of her eyes, Ysadora hurried ahead, forcing the others to pick up the pace to catch up with her. Liora turned around as they approached, leading them over a wooden bridge and through the line of people filing into the temple.

"What are they waiting for?" asked Rykan as they passed by.

"To make peace," said Liora as she continued walking. "This is one of four temples of the fallen. There are always things people regret saying or not saying. Even if the dead may have deserved it, we don't want anyone going into the Wellspring without tranquility."

"There are so many," said Nadara. "Is there so much animosity here among the villagers?"

"It takes some a while to come to terms with things they did or had done to them," said Liora. "Sometimes there are small things that you don't remember at first and think of later, so they return to the temple to give them more peace."

"What happens if someone doesn't remember something?" Garrick asked. "Would they be stuck?"

"All return to the Wellspring," said Liora. "But their progress in the flow can be interrupted. Their spirits must flow to Nereathe, the source of all tranquility and purity. To enter, you must be cleansed of all impurities. Some things aren't rectified until everyone they knew in life are with them in the Wellspring."

"There was a large stream flowing through the temple," said Ysadora. "Does that limit how many can be buried there?"

"They say we need water flowing over each tomb in each of the temples," said Liora. "To carry their spirit to the Wellspring and to connect the living with them there," she explained, her expression somber yet hopeful. "It's a journey we all must take, ensuring there's no animosity left behind. Only then can they flow freely toward Nereathe."

Ysadora tilted her head. "You speak of the Wellspring and Nereathe as if they are certain. But I was raised to believe in the Everdream. That, after we die, we awaken into the great dream beyond, a place of peace, yes, but not rivers and water."

Garrick grunted. "Same. My family never spoke of spirits flowing anywhere. The Everdream is what awaits, that's what we were told. Not some pool you have to earn your way into."

Kadin glanced at the water trickling through the temple. "Yeah. And if it's all real, who's to say which door you walk through?"

Liora smiled gently, unoffended. "Names and symbols change. But I believe it is all the same place. The Wellspring, the Everdream, the Netherwood, the long meadow beyond the last mountain, they are different ways of seeing the same truth. One we've only glimpsed from this side." She looked toward the stream winding around the tombs. "I speak of the Wellspring because it's what most Glissarans understand. What brings them peace."

A nearby elder, overhearing the exchange, stepped closer. His robes were damp at the hem, as though he had been tending to the tombs.

"It is more than peace," he said. "The Wellspring is the true afterlife. And Nereathe is where all spirits must go, washed clean and whole. Not a dream. Not a forest. The Sky Serpents weep not for sorrow, but for reverence. Their tears guide the dead through the current. They are the first witnesses to every soul's return."

His eyes flicked from Rykan to Ysadora, not unkind but steady.

"You may call it Everdream, or meadow, or song. But here, we name it truly. And we walk the path of water to reach it."

Rykan nodded, the elder's words echoing deeper than he expected. The Wellspring. The tears of the serpents. Perhaps the dead weren't as far away as they'd always believed.

He looked toward the summit. Selaina was still out there, and time was slipping away.

CHAPTER 37

THE STRANGER WORE a coat made of animal fur, sitting with their back turned to Selaina. Her pulse thundered, instincts kicking in as she quietly leaned over to pick up her bow. But before she could nock an arrow, the stranger spoke.

"I hope you don't mind an old man borrowing the warmth of your fire," he said, his voice carrying a knowing tone that sent a shiver down her spine.

Selaina had thought she'd been silent.

Realizing that she wasn't fooling him, she replied cautiously, "That depends. Who are you?"

"No one important," he said. "Just an old man, living out the rest of his days, enjoying the serenity of the mountain."

As Selaina met his gaze, her sight drew her into a series of quiet, unassuming images. She saw him walking the mountain trails, his steps deliberate and unhurried, the lines of his weathered face softening as he paused to watch the sun crest a distant peak. His hand brushed a pine's rough bark, lingering as though communing with the ancient tree. A breeze stirred his gray hair, carrying with it the mingled scents of wildflowers and cold stone, and she felt a profound stillness emanating from him, like the hush of the earth before a storm.

She saw him perched on a precarious ledge far above the world, at a height no trail could ever reach. The vast expanse of Galanor stretched before her like a living map, its valleys and forests revealed in breathtaking clarity. The silence was profound, broken only by the distant roar of wind weaving through unseen crags, carrying with it a sense of timelessness. For a moment, she felt an overwhelming sense of freedom, of boundless space, as if the entire world lay within his grasp.

The man before her had mastered the unforgiving peaks of Kylinshan, moving through the mountains with a quiet ease born of countless years exploring their secrets. Perhaps he was a climber, one who had spent a lifetime scaling impossible heights and seeking paths that others dared not tread.

"Why were you walking around my camp all night?" Selaina asked, her voice steady despite the unease churning in her gut.

"What makes you think I was walking around all night?" the man replied, turning to glance at her over his shoulder. "I only recently woke up."

"Well, someone was," Selaina said, crossing her arms defiantly.

"It doesn't seem that they meant you any harm," he said, a hint of amusement in his tone. "What brings you to this part of the mountain? Most travelers prefer the passage at the Serpent's Tear."

"That was the plan, but… it's a long story," Selaina admitted, her mind racing with the details she would need to share.

"I'd love to hear it," he said, his eyes twinkling. "Since we are going the same way, there's plenty of time."

Selaina felt an inexplicable pull toward the old man. There was something familiar about him, a connection she couldn't quite place. Her heart raced, though she was not entirely sure whether it was from fear or intrigue. What secrets might he hold?

Flurries of snow drifted between the trees, melting into icy rivulets as they landed on Selaina's exposed skin. The crisp air carried the faint scent of pine and the distant murmur of the wind weaving through the forest's towering branches. She quickened her pace, her boots crunching through the thin layer of snow that clung stubbornly to the rocky trail. Ahead, the old man moved with surprising swiftness, his steps sure, as if the mountain itself had etched its paths into his bones. Every stride he took spoke of years spent traversing these rugged slopes, leaving Selaina to push herself to keep up as she told the most recent parts of her story.

"There hasn't been a Windwraith on Kylinshan for ages," he mused, his voice soft but carrying the weight of years. "In fact, I haven't heard tales of them in quite a while. It's as if the winds themselves have forgotten."

"What do you know about them?" Selaina asked, intrigued.

"Very little, I'm afraid," he replied, his gaze drifting to the sky. "They were thought to ride on storms, drawn to the warmth of life. Draining it from those they came across."

"Why did they do that?" Selaina inquired.

"That's how they survive," he explained. "Instead of consuming food, they feast on the life energies of mortals. Quite the unsavory diet, if you ask me."

"Can they be defeated?" Selaina wondered.

"Ah, now there's a question," he said with a twinkle in his eye. "Anything can be defeated. But I'm afraid my advice on that matter is as elusive as a shadow in the fog."

"Do you think he is watching us now?" Selaina asked, glancing around nervously. "Following?"

"I haven't seen anything," the man said, his tone reassuring. "And I have a pretty good knack for these things. If he were close, I'd have chills running down my spine, and not from the cold."

"You never told me your name," Selaina prompted.

"My goodness, where are my manners?" the man said. "I am Caelum, pleased to meet you."

"I'm Selaina," she said, a smile breaking through her anxiety. "I thank you for your company."

"I noticed the mark on your forehead," Caelum said, his gaze becoming serious. "Of all the travelers I have seen come and go, well, I never thought I would see a Zhal Evurah in the flesh. How did it happen without Ethyllion?"

"I used the Wishing Stone," said Selaina. "It was a piece of Ethyllion that still contained destinies. I was supposed to change fate, to stop the Iron Flood from ever existing. But I saw a future worse than what we have now. But I couldn't waste the stone or the destinies that were meant to help the world. I allowed its remaining destinies to flow into me so I could do whatever I could to help make Galanor as it should be."

"How many destinies do you think were in there?" Caelum asked.

"I don't know for sure," said Selaina. "Not many, I don't think."

"Every Zhal Evurah has a path," Caelum replied, his voice softening. "Do you know yet what you are truly meant to do?"

"To stop the Iron Flood," Selaina said. "From what I understand, the role of the Zhal Evurah is to stand against the greatest threat to Galanor. And right now, that's them. They're killing villagers, destroying cities, if they're not stopped, there won't be anything left to save."

She paused, her fingers curling around the edge of her cloak. "But it's not just about stopping them. It's about how. If I make things worse… then what's the point?"

"You say that as if you're still deciding," Caelum said, watching her closely. "Is that truly what you feel in your heart?"

"What else would it be?" Selaina asked, too quickly. "It's the reason I took on these destinies."

"I believe you took them on to help the world," Caelum said gently. "Those you know. Those you've never met. It's a noble choice, but not without its dangers. You will be loved by some, hated by others. And not all your enemies will be strangers. Sometimes… your worst one will be yourself."

Selaina's brow furrowed. "I've heard the stories. Of Zhal Evurah who turned inward. Who used their power for themselves."

"Power doesn't corrupt all at once," Caelum said. He tilted his head, as if listening for an answer not from her lips, but from her heart. "It happens in small choices. On the road up this mountain, ask yourself why you seek this strength. If the answer is still for Galanor, for others, then your path is true. But if, even once, it becomes about your own glory…" His eyes met hers, steady and calm. "That's when you must let it go."

"I only want enough to keep the Iron Flood from taking control of everything," she replied. "To do what's right."

"I'm glad to hear that," Caelum replied. "I feel it in your words. But be wary, many who seek power begin with noble aims. They fight for justice, for peace, for others. Until one day they look back and realize they've reshaped the world in their own image instead."

His gaze drifted briefly to the sky, then returned to her.

"Injustice tempts us to act swiftly. But true wisdom often walks more slowly than rage. And sometimes, the hardest fight isn't against the enemy at your door, but the desire in your heart to wield power as they did."

Selaina's brow furrowed in contemplation. "What if I end up becoming like their imperion, Vatreus? What if I lose my way?"

Caelum didn't answer immediately. When he did, his voice was quieter, more solemn. "Then I pray you'll have the strength to stop yourself, or the courage to let someone else do it for you."

He paused, a distant look in his eyes, as if recalling something from long ago.

Then, quietly, he said, "Let me tell you a story. One the mountain whispered to me long ago."

Selaina stilled, her breath slowing. His tone carried a weight that made her wonder—was this truly a story, or a truth wrapped in words?

Caelum turned his gaze toward the horizon, where snow-capped ridges glowed faintly in the late morning light.

"Long ago," he began, "a lone wolf roamed the highlands, always searching, always watching."

His voice had softened, like it wasn't meant to carry far.

"One day, he followed a mighty river, a wide, slow-moving force that carved through stone and shaped valleys. Wherever it passed, life flourished. Crops thrived. Forests rose. The land grew strong under its touch."

He held his hand out, palm low, as if feeling the river pass beneath it.

"The wolf admired it. 'So steady, so patient,' he thought. 'It can even move mountains.'"

Selaina watched him closely, drawn in. There was something in the way he spoke that reminded her of Myrradin, but without the weight of hidden motives.

Caelum shifted his stance, stepping around a patch of ice on the trail.

"Further on, the wolf discovered another river," he continued. "This one was swift, restless and narrow. It darted through ravines, skipped over rocks. It couldn't shape the land, but it could keep up with the wind."

He gave a slight shrug, a half-smile forming as though he was amused by the river's reckless freedom.

"The wolf was clever. He told the two rivers of each other. 'Together, you will be strong and fast,' he said. 'You will reach the sea before the sun sets.'"

Selaina tilted her head, her expression thoughtful. "What happened?" she asked softly, already sensing that the outcome wasn't what the wolf expected.

Caelum's face turned serious again.

"The rivers agreed. They merged. And for a while… they were magnificent."

He paused there, letting the image linger before his voice dropped.

"But their speed became chaos. Their strength became destruction. The land cracked. Villages were swallowed. Trees tore from the earth like weeds."

Selaina's brow furrowed, a knot constricting her chest. The parable was beginning to sound less like a fable and more like a warning.

"The wolf stood on a ridge and howled," Caelum said. His eyes, though distant, carried the weight of that cry. "He saw what he had helped cause."

He clasped his hands behind his back and took a slow breath.

"And in his howl, he begged the rivers to stop."

Selaina imagined it, the lone creature standing against the force it had unleashed. She could feel the cold wind in the story, the ache of regret.

"The rivers listened," Caelum said, his voice turning quiet, reflective. "They parted, not from pride or anger, but understanding. And they chose a new path, not as one, but side by side. The wolf followed them both to the sea. No longer leading. No longer lost. Just walking beside them."

The silence that followed was long and heavy, but not uncomfortable.

Selaina didn't speak at first. She watched the trees sway in the wind, her heart stirring in ways she didn't quite understand yet. She recalled the vision Brali had told her in Alisaren and the similarities it shared with this story. Part of her wanted to ask if the wolf was meant to be her. Another part… wasn't sure she wanted the answer.

Caelum looked out across the ledge, then back at her.

"So you see," he said, "like those rivers, you must tread carefully. Sometimes strength and swiftness, even with the best intentions, can bring ruin. The fiercest battles often rage inside us, not on the fields we see. Seek balance, Selaina. That is where your path begins."

Selaina's gaze dropped. The weight of his words settled in like snow on stone.

"The Iron Flood stands against us," she asked quietly. "Should I not use power to stop them?"

Caelum didn't answer immediately. When he did, his voice was soft, but clear.

"In your journey, there may come times when you must use strength to overcome what is impossible to move around, you must take lives from this world," he said. "But remember, you are not only ending an existence. You are extinguishing a purpose. A path only they could walk."

Selaina looked up, unsettled. "That's… I never thought about it like that."

Caelum's expression turned grim, the firelight catching in the lines on his face.

"Taking a life leaves a bitter taste in the mouth," he said. "But you must not wash it away. Let its flavor linger on your tongue. Let it remind you, every time, of the weight of power."

Selaina hesitated, then asked, "Have you ever had to take a life?"

A shadow wavered in Caelum's eyes, old and worn.

"I have made mistakes," he said, low and even. "Once, I thought I could make things better… only to find I had made them worse."

"Is that why you live up here alone?" Selaina asked.

Caelum chuckled softly, the sound warm and inviting against the crisp air. "I enjoy solitude," he said, his gaze drifting toward the snowy canopy above. "There is something magical in the quiet. It's in those still moments that you can truly hear the world breathe around you. When you're alone, the subtle whispers of nature become clearer, revealing secrets hidden beneath the surface."

He paused, a twinkle in his eye as he continued.

"You start to notice the delicate calls of the birds as they flit through the branches, each note carrying its own story. The gentle rustle of the leaves as they dance in the wind tells of the changing seasons, and the soft crunch of snow underfoot becomes a rhythm, a reminder that you're part of something larger."

Caelum smiled, lost in thought for a moment before returning his attention to Selaina.

"In those quiet times, you find clarity. Problems that once seemed insurmountable begin to unravel. It's as if the silence speaks, guiding you toward understanding, nudging you gently toward truths you might overlook amidst the chaos of the villages."

Selaina was reminded of her walks through the forest where she once lived. After her chores were completed, she loved to wander through the trees, crossing the brook to her secret hideaway behind the hill. It all seemed like a lifetime ago.

"I like that too," she said. "But I do get lonely before long."

"Sure," said Caelum. "On occasion, I'm called to go down to Glissara or even Shadal at times."

"I've been to Shadal," said Selaina. "But not Glissara. What is it like?"

"They can be a bit odd at times," said Caelum. "Always on about purifying everything in their sacred waters."

"Why won't they let more water into Shadal?" said Selaina. "They have a shortage."

"I try not to get involved in these disputes," said Caelum. "Not anymore. They worked out their differences once, I can only hope they will again."

"The two people, Doran and Talia, they brought the villages together," said Selaina. "I don't understand how they ended up dividing again."

"That was the mistake of the Sky Serpents," said Caelum. "Often bad things happen, so that necessary growth can come from it. We as mortals, each have a beginning and an end and they are both important in many ways. As much as we don't want to face the end, it leads to new beginnings, both in this world and beyond. In the face of tragedy, the Sky Serpents questioned the wisdom of the Aszh Rozaht... and acted when perhaps they should have trusted the design. Abandoning their mandate to not interfere in the lives of mortals, they lent their power to Doran to defeat a wild beast and survive."

"Why do you think that was a mistake?" Selaina asked.

"Did you not listen to what I said?" Caelum said. "After the attack, Doran and Talia went on to be leaders of their respective villages. They were married and spent time in both villages. Both villages made compromises with each other for the good of both. They trusted both Doran and Talia."

"If only things could have remained that way," said Selaina. "I guess after they both passed on the trust faded too."

"Yes, but not in the way you might think," said Caelum. "Doran and Talia went on to have three children, two daughters and a son. They were perfect blends of their mother and father, part Shadalan and part Glissaran. They were raised at an early age to carry on the leadership of both villages. After a long rich life, Doran grew ill and he passed on, Talia's bones became weakened and she soon found it hard to travel. She spent her last years in Glissara, where her children stayed with her. They grew to consider Glissara home and had little to do with Shadal," Caelum said. "Even as they made decisions affecting both villages, Shadal felt those choices favored Glissara, not them."

"So none of them were spending any time in Shadal?" Selaina said.

"They were not," said Caelum. "Even after Talia passed on, her children considered Glissara home and had little to do with Shadal. They still made decisions, though, that affected Shadal and whether true or not, the Shadalans believed that, unlike their mother and father, their decisions were about what was better for Glissara, not Shadal. The children wanted a Flow Temple built for their mother's tomb, which constrained how much water flowed down into Shadal. Soon they were building more temples and the water for Shadal became less and less until it was the same as before Talia had taken a stand to give Shadal more water. Ironically, her children had undone the very thing that their mother was most revered for. They had only known their mother as a sort of goddess, the way everyone treated her, forgetting that she was simply a mortal like anyone else. That she was exalted for deeds not birthright. One thing mortals often forget is that the most beloved person is only a breath away from the most loathed."

"What do you mean?" Selaina asked.

"Meaning we all have the capacity for great deeds or great harm," Caelum replied. "Our circumstances and choices lead us one way or the other. We should be cautious about taking pride in our goodness. What makes someone kind today might make them ruthless tomorrow, it's not just about who we are, but where we stand when the choice comes."

"Are you saying that those who do evil are not at fault?" Selaina asked.

"I'm saying that, when our decisions don't align with the Azsh Rozaht, they can lead us to evil," said Caelum. "In some points of view, anything outside of the will of the Azsh Rozaht is evil. If the Sky Serpents had not taken it upon themselves to interfere and save Doran and Talia, perhaps both villages would have come together in the tragedy and their bonds remained strong to honor them, instead of what happened later with their children."

"One decision can have such big repercussions," said Selaina.

"Yes, like a tumbling pebble that leads to an avalanche," said Caelum.

"And Myrradin thought changing the order of fate itself would be a good idea," said Selaina. "I'm so glad I at least made the right decision on that."

"Perhaps it was the Azsh Rozaht's will… or perhaps your own," Caelum said. "The path forward depends on which one you walk."

Selaina's gaze dropped, her fingers brushing lightly across the mark on her forehead before falling back to her side. "Sometimes it's hard to tell the difference," she said. "I didn't feel like I chose, more like… something was already waiting, and I just stepped into it."

She hesitated, the memory of that moment flashing behind her eyes, not just the pull to act, but the pressure of something waiting. Ever since she had touched the Wishing Stone, there had been a strength at her core, steady, vast, and quiet. It wasn't power she could summon, not yet. It sat beneath everything, like a great current beneath a still sea.

She didn't know if it was destiny, intuition, or something else entirely. But it was there. And in the instant she reached for the stone, it had risen like breath held too long, answering her hand before her mind could form the question.

Caelum regarded her with a steady gaze. "You must be honest with yourself. Did you make that choice out of necessity for others, or for the outcome you desired?"

Selaina hesitated, her gaze drifting as she pondered his words. "For others… I think so." She shook her head. "You're making me second-guess everything, Caelum."

A staggered movement caught her eye in the shadows beneath a group of trees ahead. She stilled, squinting into the gloom. "Wait."

Caelum's voice dropped to a murmur. "What do you see?"

Instead of answering, Selaina stepped away, moving carefully between the trees to get a better angle. A dark figure shifted just beyond, blending seamlessly with the shadows, like a living part of the forest itself.

She pulled her cloak around her, tugging the hood lower to conceal her white hair, concerned about who might recognize her.

Her voice came soft, barely audible. "The Nadrok are watching us."

CHAPTER 38

A S THE SUN climbed higher in the sky, its golden rays spilled over the bustling village of Glissara, casting dappled light across the cobblestone paths and timber-framed huts. Rykan paused, letting the lively scene wash over him. The earthy scent of damp wood mingled with the rich aroma of smoked fish and freshly baked bread wafting from the market-place. Baskets of dried berries and bundles of hardy herbs added splashes of muted color to the stalls, where merchants bartered cheerfully with the locals. Laughter and spirited chatter wove through the air, punctuated by the occasional bark of a vendor advertising their wares.

Beneath it all, the gentle trickle of water meandered through the narrow stone channels, winding like veins through the heart of the village, their soothing sound a constant undercurrent to the vibrant morning. Above, the sunshimmer braided faint streaks of gold and lavender through the day-light, like the sky itself had woven a quiet blessing into the start of their day.

In the heart of the marketplace, villagers exchanged greetings and traded goods, their faces illuminated with the simple joys of daily life. Brightly colored stalls adorned with hanging baskets overflowed with herbs and produce, while the distant echo of children playing near the water channels added to the symphony of village sounds.

Shadal, for all its beauty, had felt tense and braced, like something unseen pressed at its borders. Its streets held quiet wariness. Even the wind seemed to hesitate.

Glissara, by contrast, moved freely. The air felt unburdened, untouched by fear. For a moment, Rykan envied them. And wondered how long that peace would last.

"Liora! Seren ven'thara," called a man from a long bench where fruit, fish, and stalks of water-rich plants were laid out in woven reed trays. He sat beneath a slanted awning of pale bark, its frame supported by river-smoothed stones, stacked with a craftsman's care.

"Jorin," Liora replied, her voice a familiar melody as she glided toward him. "Sere ven'thara. What has Elric caught so far today?"

"Mostly dace, but they're perfect for a stew," Jorin said, his weathered face creasing with a smile.

Rykan watched the exchange, feeling how different the village air seemed here, thick with mist and green scent, soft with the sound of water trickling beneath the stones. The buildings seemed grown from the land, their river-smoothed foundations shaped by time and tide, unlike Shadal's hard-edged stonework, carved in defiance of the earth it rested on.

"I have some hungry travelers," Liora said, suddenly grabbing Rykan's hand with a surprising firmness. Her spindly frame held unexpected strength. "They need nourishment before they leave on their quest. But they are in a hurry. Do you have anything cooking?"

"Nothing for sale; I haven't started anything yet," Jorin replied, glancing toward the others. "Your travelers in a big rush? Hoping to see the Sky Serpents?"

"They're looking for a missing friend," Liora explained.

"A missing friend?" Jorin raised his eyebrows. "That changes things. I'll gladly share my stew. I've got a pot brewing behind the tree. I'll trade you each a bowl for some neluska."

"Neluska?" Rykan asked, brow furrowed. "Where would we get that?"

"I'll take care of it," Liora replied. She reached into her cloak and pulled out five small parchment bags, setting them gently on the bench. She opened one to reveal a dense brown powder that released a warm, spiced scent into the air.

"What is it?" Rykan asked, his curiosity piqued.

"Tea spice," Liora said with a smile. "We trade it more than we actually drink it."

"For you, Liora, I'd never charge," Jorin said. "If these are your friends, they're friends of mine. We'll share the stew, it's nearly ready."

Rykan recalled the question Selaina had wanted to ask. He hated to bring it up, but for her sake, he would. "Why won't Glissara allow more water to flow into Shadal?" he asked.

"Shadal?" Jorin's expression hardened like river clay left too long in the sun. "If they weren't so stubborn, they'd have moved their village ages ago. Then they wouldn't keep hunting in our territory."

Rykan glanced at the soft moss underfoot, then to the curved stonework of a nearby structure that almost seemed to ripple like water around its corners. Shadal's buildings had been hard-edged and proud, cut from the mountain or hacked from the forest, refusing to bend. The contrast felt like night and dawn.

"Where could they move?" Rykan asked carefully.

"There are other water sources around the mountain," Jorin said, crossing his arms.

Rykan nodded slowly. "Maybe there's no solid foundation there," he offered. "Moving an entire village isn't simple."

Jorin's mouth drew into a tight line. "So you've come here as their advocate, then? To tell us how we should live?"

"It's only a question, Jorin," Liora said gently, stepping between them. "Questions from outsiders help us see our choices from a new perspective."

Jorin let out a huff, not fully mollified. "Funny how they all come here, ask questions, and end up thinking poorly of us. If they have a problem with how we live, the Shadalans should come and tell us themselves, instead of having travelers do it for them."

"They have come before," said Liora. "And it only ended in fighting."

Nadara stepped in, her voice warm as she attempted to ease the tension. "This stew smells incredible! I can't believe how generous you all are. Thank you for sharing it with us."

Jorin's face softened, but there was a lingering edge to his tone. "Well, yes, it's an old family recipe," he replied, his pride returning. "The simmering technique gives it that perfect consistency. Maybe some things are best learned from tradition."

He handed out the bowls, each uniquely shaped, though his movements were a touch more reserved. When everyone was served, Rykan took a bite, savoring the flavors. Small chunks of fish floated in the thick broth alongside hardened bits of bread, adding a delightful crunch.

"This is very good," Rykan said, sincerely appreciative. "Thank you."

Jorin gave a short nod, but his gaze lingered on Rykan, as if still weighing the conversation.

Garrick took a long, appreciative sniff of the stew, a faint smile crossing his face. "This is the meal of a warrior," he said, holding his bowl up. "A good stew like this, it's hearty, filling, easy to make for a group. Keeps the cold at bay, warms your bones for a long march."

"Ah, so that's the secret to keeping you going all these years." Kadin smirked, glancing at Garrick's bowl. "Turns out it's not grit or glory, just a hearty pot of stew. Who knew all it took to keep a warrior on his feet was fish and a few crusts of bread?"

The others echoed their appreciation, and with each swallow, Rykan realized just how hungry he was.

"I hope wherever Selaina is right now, she has food too," he said, glancing around the group.

Ysadora shrugged, her tone carrying a hint of exasperation masked by confidence. "I'm sure she's fine," she replied. "After all, she's Zhal Evurah. I doubt a little hunger could trouble someone so… destined."

Though the stew was modestly portioned, it was enough to calm the pangs in Rykan's stomach, bringing a touch of warmth to the chill around them.

"Zhal Evurah?" Jorin's eyebrows rose. "We've had plenty of people pass through claiming they were bound for greatness, but most had the sense to know they weren't Zhal Evurah. That prophecy ended a thousand years ago."

"There was one piece of Ethyllion left," Garrick said, his voice steady. "The Wishing Stone."

"Is that what she told you?" Jorin asked, raising an eyebrow.

"We were all there," Rykan replied firmly.

Jorin chuckled. "Oh sure, when you find her, and the Sky Serpents come down to bless her, have them swing by here for a chat," he said with a dry grin. "I'm sure the whole village would turn out for that."

"You don't believe the legend?" Garrick asked.

Jorin shrugged. "Most folks around here do. Some even swear they've seen wings over the peak during storms. But I've never seen anything that made me think giant flying serpents were real. It's a legend. A good one, but still a legend."

He scooped at his stew.

"Stories like that always get bigger with each telling. Makes the dead sound more important than they were, or the living feel like they're part of something grand."

Liora chimed in, her voice soft but assured. "Even if the stories aren't entirely true, they hold wisdom. Sometimes legends are vessels for deeper truths."

Ysadora stepped closer, her doubt at the waterfall seemingly gone. "The mark glows at her brow. It's written in prophecy. Whether we accept it or not, the sign is clear. The Zhal Evurah rises when balance falters." Perhaps she was trying to convince herself.

"Where I'm from," Nadara said, cutting in. "No one waits for fate to save them. You either move, or you get buried. We acknowledge Zhal Evurah not as a prophecy but as someone with the power to fight, that's what matters."

Garrick looked into his bowl, his expression thoughtful. "I used to be right there with you," he admitted. "I never put much faith in things I couldn't see or feel for myself. But recently… I've seen things that make me wonder. I'm looking forward to seeing how this plays out."

"Are you sure you're not just seeing what you want to see?" Jorin asked, his gaze narrowing.

Garrick sighed, a faint smile tugging at the corner of his mouth. "Honestly? I'd rather it weren't true. If it is, well… I'll have a lot to rethink. And life rarely gets simpler with truth."

Jorin leaned back slightly, resting a hand on the bench beside him. "Talia's the only real legend worth speaking of. She brought reason to Shadal to unite our people. But once she passed into Nereathe, that unity cracked like dry clay. Shadal broke the bond. We kept the memory." He looked off toward the center of the village, where the stream flowed beneath an arch of flowering vines. "Some of her blood still lives here, you know. Not royalty, just… quiet reminders."

After they finished their meal, Rykan and the others gathered their belongings, preparing for the journey ahead.

"Until the currents bring us together again," Jorin said, waving with a fluid motion that mimicked the flow of water.

Liora approached Rykan, her gaze settling on his arm. "That wound of yours," she said, voice laced with quiet concern. "It looks like it's festering with shadow."

"It's healing," Rykan replied. "Ysadora suppressed the curse."

Liora's eyes narrowed thoughtfully. "You're lucky to have her close by," she said. "But watch it carefully. It appears dormant now, but if it returns, it could come back stronger. If that happens... use this." She handed him a small bottle of prismatic glass.

Rykan held the bottle up to the sunlight, examining the shifting colors within. A tiny bead of water glimmered as it ran to one corner of the glass. "What is it?"

"A drop of Eluthra's Essence," Liora said. "They say it's water from Nereathe itself."

Rykan's eyebrows lifted. "How could that be possible?"

"It's probably just water, to be quite honest." Jorin shrugged dismissively. "But all water is sacred and cleansing."

"Eluthra's Essence was first recorded in the journals of the Yathran Navigators," Liora said. "They believed it could heal the most grievous wounds if applied correctly."

Rykan held the bottle up again, watching the shifting colors catch the light. "You mean it might actually work?"

Liora smiled knowingly. "Maybe. Or maybe it's just a legend, like most of the treasures I've studied. Still, objects like this have a way of surprising you when you least expect it."

"Well," Kadin interjected with a grin, "even if it doesn't work, at least it'll dazzle your enemies before they run you through. Nothing like a bit of mystic flair to keep them guessing."

Nadara stepped closer, intrigued. "You've studied treasures?"

Liora's voice softened, taking on a reverent tone. "Yes, of all kinds. I love collecting items with their own stories to tell. A fragment of the lives that touched them, shaped them. Some are mere curiosities, but others...

they carry echoes of power, remnants of the purposes they once served. I was once entrusted with two rings that were bondmarked."

"Bondmarked?" Rykan repeated, the word unfamiliar.

Ysadora interjected swiftly. "Bondmarked items are connected through magic, forming a link between their bearers. They're often used by sorcerers, particularly those venturing into dangerous situations alongside other magic users. The enchantment ensures that when one bearer is struck by magic, the effect is shared with the other. The enchantment is meant to share the impact, so neither bearer takes it all at once."

She paused, her gaze sharpening.

"But getting the bond right is difficult. Sometimes, one bearer still takes the full force of the magic. Worse still, it might amplify the pain, hurting both far more than intended."

Rykan tilted his head. "Why would anyone take that risk?"

"Desperation or arrogance, usually," Ysadora replied with a shrug. "They can give you an edge—if everything goes exactly right. But that almost never happens. That's why the Conclave forbids them, they're unpredictable and dangerous."

Kadin added, "Sounds like a love story gone horribly wrong. 'Trust me,' they said. 'It'll bring us closer together,' they said. Next thing you know, one's a charred heap, and the other's writing tragic poetry in a cave somewhere."

Liora, who had been silent, nodded slowly. "You're not far from the truth. The rings I encountered were tied to a story of betrayal. One bearer believed the bond would protect them both equally. The other... knew better and used it to shield themselves, letting their companion take the brunt of the danger."

The group fell silent for a moment, the weight of the tale settling over them. Rykan's expression turned grim. "Sounds like more trouble than they're worth."

"They often are," Ysadora said, her voice cold. "But magic always comes with a price. It's just a question of whether you're willing, or foolish enough, to pay it."

Rykan glanced at the bottle again, then at Liora. "How do you get artifacts like this?"

Liora smiled, a touch of mischief in her eyes. "They have a way of finding those who understand their worth. Some come through barter, some through discovery. But the rarest ones?" Her gaze grew distant, as though recalling a memory long past. "You don't really find them. They show themselves when you're ready. If you're listening, that is."

"How many dangerous artifacts do you keep up in that tree?" Kadin asked.

Liora laughed. "I keep the harmless ones—items with stories, or ones I just find beautiful. The dangerous ones? I hide those."

Rykan raised the vial in appreciation. "Thank you, Liora, I'll keep this close," he said.

Liora offered a gentle smile. "Nere'vate. May your path flow as strong as the rivers, and may the Wellspring guide you."

As the group turned to leave, Nadara lingered by Liora, glancing down at her hands before looking back up with a smile. "Yes, thank you both for this kindness."

Liora returned the smile, tilting her head as if reading Nadara's expression. "Is there something else, Nadara? I sense there's more on your mind."

"Oh," said Nadara. "I know everyone is anxious to find Selaina. I'll ask you on the way back down the mountain."

"It's fine, Nadara," said Rykan. "Go ahead."

Nadara took a breath. "In your collection of artifacts, have you ever learned anything about a group called the Brotherhood of the Silent Star?"

Liora's expression stayed neutral, though her eyes narrowed. "I haven't heard of them directly, but 'Silent Star' sounds familiar."

"Could there be a temple here on the mountain?" Nadara asked. "Or an old sacred tree?"

"There are many ruins," Liora said, "but none that stand out. There is an old tree, though it may not look distinct. It is further up the mountain, a little off the path."

"What about this? Would you consider it an artifact?" said Nadara, pulling out the red shard named Embryss.

"Let me see that," said Liora as her eyes widened.

Nadara turned the sharp jagged point of the shard away from Liora as she handed it to her. Liora's eyes examined the shard as she reached out to take it, its edges shimmering with an otherworldly light. Her usually serene expression faltered, just for an instant, with something Rykan couldn't quite place, surprise, maybe, or even sorrow.

Liora's hand seemed to twitch toward the shard before she stopped herself, fingers curling slowly into her palm. Her gaze lingered on the shard with a kind of reverence that pained her as much as it fascinated her.

"That's… no ordinary stone," Liora said, the usual warmth in her tone replaced by something Rykan couldn't identify, like she was handling each word with careful intent. "You hold a piece of the Heart of Entropy."

Rykan felt a shiver run down his spine at the name. He glanced from Nadara to Liora, sensing the sudden tension in the air. "The Heart of Entropy?" he echoed, curiosity mingling with unease. "What is that?"

"The Heart of Entropy is a powerful relic, crafted long ago by the Forsaken One, a celestial who defied the Azsh Rozaht, but refused to accept judgment," said Liora. "It was intended to hold the power of chaos itself, the force that unravels and reshapes. This is but a piece, though it could be enough to grant strange abilities, perceptions beyond mortal sight, the power to glimpse what lies beneath the surface of things… and sometimes, to alter them. I thought it had been lost to time or destroyed."

Nadara's fingers closed around the shard, a wary look in her eyes. "Is it dangerous?"

"Potentially, yes," Liora replied, voice grave. "It has the power to corrupt, though mortal hands couldn't harness its full power."

Nadara looked at Liora, her voice barely a whisper. "Is it safe to hold on to?"

"Keep it hidden," Liora replied softly, her tone laced with warning. "Show it to no one."

"Is someone looking for it?" Rykan asked.

Liora's gaze grew distant, as if a shadow of ancient knowledge passed over her. "Mortals have been hunting the Heart of Entropy since the dawn of civilization," she murmured, her voice barely above a whisper. "If you can find a place to hide it, somewhere unreachable, even to you, I would do so."

A chilling silence fell over them. Nadara swallowed, her fingers tensing around the shard as though it might vanish if she let go.

"How bad would it be if the wrong person found it?" Rykan asked, his voice tense.

Liora's eyes darkened, the faintest tremor in her voice. "If someone who could unleash its power ever got hold of all of the pieces and remade the Heart of Entropy, then may the Azsh Rozaht shield us from what's to come. Our faith would be tested."

CHAPTER 39

SELAINA MOVED CAREFULLY, the sharp mountain air slicing through her cloak and biting at her exposed skin. Her boots crunched softly on the gravel-strewn path, the sound swallowed by the stillness of the encroaching dusk. Jagged cliffs towered on either side, their rugged faces painted in shifting hues of amber and gray as the sun dipped lower, casting restless shadows that danced like phantom movements. She stopped, her breath curling faintly in the chill, and fixed her gaze on the solitary tree ahead. The Nadrok lingered there, their dark silhouettes barely discernible among the twisted branches. They were watching her, just as she was watching them.

"You have sharp eyes," Caelum replied. "I've seen these creatures before, here on the mountain. They're elusive, likely around us more often than we realize. When people do catch sight of them, it leaves an uneasy feeling, but there's little cause for fear. They've been written about for hundreds of years, and never once have they harmed anyone."

"That's what everyone says," Selaina countered, her tone edged with doubt. "But they led Gwenna straight to me so she could attack us. Seem harmless until they're not."

Caelum's brow lifted, intrigued. "That is… unexpected. I've never known them to behave with such intent. Perhaps this Gwenna has tapped into knowledge even I do not possess."

He glanced into the distance, his tone shifting. "Nadrok means 'neverborn.' They are not truly of this world. Shadows caught between the breaths of creation. Glimpses of lives never lived. They do not walk as you and I do, bound by stone and soil."

He turned back to her, his gaze thoughtful. "They move between the moments, where the weave of reality thins, where even light has no hold. That they would act with purpose…" He trailed off, as if suddenly wary of what that might mean.

"You're not exactly making them less frightening," Selaina muttered.

"I only meant to offer what I have learned about them," Caelum replied calmly. "No one truly knows what they are or what they are here for, but I don't believe they can harm you, at least, not directly."

"I can only hope they haven't identified me," said Selaina. "I think whatever they see, so can Gwenna."

"Curious indeed," Caelum said. "What kind of unnatural magic must she be using to gain a connection to the Neverborn?"

"I'll follow behind you," said Selaina. "Maybe she won't recognize me."

"There are Neverborn all over Galanor," said Caelum. "You think she can connect to all of them?"

"I'm not taking any chances," said Selaina.

As they moved deeper into the forest, the atmosphere thickened. The air became heavy with the scent of damp earth and the chill of the shaded sun. Caelum led the way, his steps deliberate as he navigated the underbrush.

Selaina followed Caelum through the trees, her senses heightened, aware that unseen eyes could be watching. Shadows shifted unnaturally, and she caught fleeting glimpses of the Nadrok, their forms slipping between trunks like wraiths. Sometimes they peeked from behind trees, hollow-eyed, watching, then vanished the moment she turned.

Her heart quickened. One silhouette stretched impossibly tall, its head cocked unnaturally before it flicked out of view. The sensation of being observed crawled across her skin.

The forest grew quieter. Usual sounds faded into stillness. A cold gust whispered through the branches, and somewhere in the distance, a faint, echoing laugh stirred the air.

"Can you hear that?" Selaina asked, pausing to listen.

"I hear the sounds of the forest," said Caelum.

"I thought I heard voices," Selaina said, glancing around warily.

"Your heightened senses are filling in the gaps of what you can't see or hear," Caelum replied. "That can play tricks on the mind. Slow your thoughts; let your mind wander to other things."

After what felt like miles of cautious movement, they finally arrived at a large cave opening, its dark maw gaping like the entrance to another world. The mouth of the cave was framed by twisted vines and jagged rocks, and Selaina could feel a faint chill emanating from within, as though it were a living thing exhaling cold air.

"This is where we must part," Caelum said, stopping before the dark mouth of the cave. He tilted his head, studying her with an almost wistful gentleness. "You must travel through the tunnel if you wish to reach the summit. But I must warn you, Azirok, a crystal leviathan, resides within these caverns. He will be asleep, unaware of your presence, but you must keep quiet."

"Leviathan?" Selaina felt a prickle of fear. "What should I do if he wakes up?"

"Run, if you must," Caelum said, the faintest hint of amusement in his voice. "Scream, if it helps. But if you are truly meant to reach the summit… you will."

Selaina hesitated, glancing from the mouth of the cave to Caelum. "What about you? Where will you go?"

"I've always had a fondness for Seeker's Ridge," he said, looking skyward. "When the mists part and the moon is high, the world shines like silver glass. It reminds me of home."

"That sounds lovely," Selaina murmured. "I almost wish I could go with you. Sometimes… I wish I wasn't the Zhal Evurah. It should've been someone with greater strength. Greater will."

"It is always your choice," Caelum replied. "Many have turned away from the path laid before them. They chose to make their own."

"But you said that was evil."

He gave a slight nod. "Evil or not, it is still a choice. And many still choose it, knowing full well what it means."

Selaina drew a slow breath, the chill of the cave brushing her skin. "No. I have to keep going. I've come this far."

"You have greater strength and will than you realize, and courage to go with it," said Caelum. "Perhaps that is why you received the mark of the stars."

Selaina couldn't stop a smile from cracking the corner of her lips. "Thank you, Caelum, for everything. I enjoyed your company. I hope you will consider visiting the villages more often. There are others who would enjoy your company as well. Even solitude needs a companion from time to time."

Caelum chuckled softly, a faint glimmer of warmth in his usually reserved gaze. "Perhaps you're right," he replied. "Even the mountain finds companionship in the rivers and trees that shape it. I suppose I could try to visit… now and then."

He paused, his expression growing more thoughtful. "But solitude is itself a comfort. It has a way of calling one back to quiet places."

Selaina smiled faintly, and stepped toward him. For a breath, she hesitated, then, quietly, she wrapped her arms around him. Caelum stiffened in surprise, but only for a moment. Then he returned the gesture with a quiet sigh, his arms light around her, like someone who had not been held in a very long time.

"I hope we meet again," Caelum said as they pulled apart. He gave a bow, the barest curve of a smile on his lips.

Selaina nodded, turning back toward the yawning cavern.

With that, he turned and vanished into the trees, the mist seeming to close around him as if he had never been there at all.

For a moment, Selaina stood in the silence he left behind. Then she turned to the cave. A cold draft rolled from its mouth, thick with the scent of stone and stillness. If Caelum was right about what was inside, she needed more than courage.

She scanned the forest edge until she spotted a fallen branch partially buried in the drift. Kneeling beside it, she brushed away the snow with her sleeve, testing the wood with her fingers. It was sturdy, dense, just dry enough beneath the surface.

Dragging it to a patch of exposed stone, she worked quickly. Her hands, though stiff with cold, moved with ease. She scraped the bark clean with one of her arrowheads.

From a nearby tree, she chipped away a knot of amber-colored sap, thick and tacky in the cold. She smeared it around the head of the branch, layering it with lichen and threadbare scraps from her satchel.

When the torch was ready, she crouched low and struck two of her arrowheads together. The first spark danced away. The second caught. A small flame flared to life, hesitant, then steady.

She rose slowly, the torch in her hand casting flickering light into the yawning dark ahead.

Drawing a deep breath, Selaina faced the cavern once more. The weight of her purpose settled within her like a heartbeat. The path ahead was hers alone.

CHAPTER 40

THE AIR GREW crisper as Rykan and the others trudged along the winding path, each breath clouding briefly before fading into the stillness. The lake stretched out before them, its glassy surface perfectly mirroring the rugged peaks above, their jagged edges softened by the haze of morning. Overhead, the sunshimmer moved in slow, curling ribbons, soft as smoke. The lake caught every glimmer, casting them back toward the peaks like the mountain was dreaming in light. Yet something more caught Rykan's eye, a faint iridescence shifting just beneath the water's surface, like elusive flashes of light skimming through hidden depths.

His gaze lingered, drawn to the dark, quiet waters with an almost magnetic pull, a strange yearning he couldn't explain. The air here felt heavier, weighted by an unnatural stillness that pressed against his senses. Even the faint crunch of boots on gravel seemed muted, swallowed by the peculiar hush that cloaked the area, as though the world itself held its breath, waiting for something to break the silence.

Somewhere beyond those cliffs lay Elyndra Bluff, where Liora had seen the storm. It had to be a Windwraith. If Myrradin was taking Selaina to the summit of Kylinshan, they had to stop him before the Sky Serpents answered his call. With any luck, they weren't too late.

As they followed the winding path along the lake's edge, the group moved in a steady rhythm, boots crunching over damp gravel and moss. Mist rose in lazy spirals from the water's surface, wrapping their ankles in drifting smoke. The lake stretched wide beside them, its glassy surface rippling with each breath of breeze. Beneath that calm, Rykan caught glints of movement, long, slender leaves and pale, drifting petals suspended in the depths, swaying like they were dreaming.

He slowed, fingers brushing the edge of his cloak as he found the vial Liora had given him. There was something about this place, still and watching. The vial seemed to hum with the same quiet presence as the lake, as if both were part of the same breath held in the belly of the mountain.

Beside him, Nadara kept pace, her gaze on the red shard in her hand. "If Embryss is a piece of The Heart of Entropy," she murmured, "what do you make of it?"

Rykan blinked, drawn back from the water. "Honestly? It sounds ominous." He glanced at her, the light catching on her cheek. "Liora said it was dangerous, so maybe we're better off not knowing what it does."

"I'm not planning on using it." Nadara frowned, stepping around a gnarled root as the path narrowed. "But I keep wondering... why would that stranger come back to Zalorin with it? The tree in the temple was already dead. If the Brotherhood was trying to corrupt the trees, why return to a dead one?"

"Whatever he was trying to do might've gotten him killed," Rykan said. His eyes flicked to the shard in her hand again, uneasy.

"But what was he trying to do?" Nadara pressed, lowering her voice as if the wind might carry the answer. "If we knew that... it might tell us everything."

Rykan exhaled through his nose. The gravel crunched louder beneath his feet as the incline steepened. "Liora said it could 'alter' things."

"What if the tree isn't dead?" Garrick asked from behind. "What if it's corrupted? Maybe he was trying to restore it."

Nadara slowed, her steps faltering as something lit in her eyes. "That's why he came back," she whispered. "He left his family because he thought the Brotherhood was right... but later he realized they were wrong. That the trees weren't holding the world back, they were strengthening it."

Ysadora caught the thread. "And he returned to undo the damage?"

"Yes!" Nadara's voice rose with clarity. "He was trying to put it right."

Rykan was unconvinced. "The same shard that corrupted the trees... you think it could fix them?"

"If it transforms," Nadara said, "then maybe it can reverse corruption too."

Rykan walked in silence for a beat. The path curved upward now, winding between boulders streaked with lichen.

"Someone should finish what he started," Nadara added quietly. "To repair the boundary between our world and Pandemora."

Rykan's tone hardened. "But it killed him. Don't follow him into the same grave."

Nadara didn't answer right away. Her hand closed over the shard as her gaze dropped to the shifting light in the water. "There's more we still have to learn… but maybe there's a way."

The path curved once more along the lakeside, narrowing beside a stretch of wind-battered stone. As they rounded a bend, Rykan slowed, spotting a figure crouched near a cluster of broken boulders just off the trail.

The man wore a patchwork robe, frayed and salt-stained, with feathered charms braided into his tangled hair. He murmured to himself, tracing shapes into the frost-dusted ground with a crooked finger. Small cairns surrounded him, each topped with a smooth river stone.

"Are you well?" Nadara asked carefully, keeping her distance.

The man lifted his head. His eyes were bright and unblinking, too clear for comfort. "You follow the sky, but not the rhythm. That's why they won't answer you."

"The Sky Serpents?" Rykan asked, exchanging a glance with Garrick.

"No," the man whispered. "The sky itself. The breathing beneath the mountain. The serpents ride it, like threads on a loom. You call out with noise. But they only answer with silence."

Ysadora tilted her head. "Are you saying you've seen them?"

The man chuckled, softly, sadly. "I was one once. Or maybe I dreamed I was. I fell. Landed wrong. Broke something inside. Now I only remember pieces."

He pointed toward the summit.

"You won't find them up there. You'll only find cold wind and the echo of your own fear. Unless she is the one who can unravel the threads."

His gaze landed on Ysadora, direct, intense, almost reverent.

"The mountain watches. If your shadow matches the echo, maybe they'll return. Maybe they'll sing again."

Then, just as suddenly as he had placed his attention on them, he turned away and began to hum, a soft, tuneless sound that disappeared into the mist like smoke.

The group stood in silence a moment longer.

"Well," Kadin muttered, "that was unsettling."

They walked on in silence, the strange man's words clinging to them like mist. The path narrowed as it climbed, stone giving way to slick roots and scattered gravel. Mist rolled in thicker now, curling around them like breath from the mountain itself.

"Are we still on the path?" Garrick asked, voice low.

"It's hard to tell," Nadara murmured.

The trees thinned. The slope steepened. Then the earth simply fell away.

Rykan stopped just short of the drop, boots skidding in loose rock. A sheer cliff stretched below, the valley sprawling into a gray haze. The wind rose suddenly, cold and biting.

"This… definitely isn't the trail," he said.

Garrick stepped up beside him, jaw tight. "We must've been following runoff."

"And none of us know the way without it," Ysadora said, her eyes scanning the ridgeline. "We need to go back. Now."

They turned, moving faster this time. The mist pressed close, and every tree looked the same. Rykan kept his eyes low, searching for their own boot prints in the mud, until finally, the sound of water returned.

The lake came into view again through the fog, its glassy surface a cold kind of reassurance. A moment later, the true path emerged beneath their feet like a memory resurfacing.

They had found it again. But none of them spoke. The silence felt heavier now, not just with the weight of the strange man's words, but how easily the mountain could let them vanish.

Beneath their feet, the path turned rocky as they continued. The mist began to lift, and the shadows cast by overhanging trees danced across the trail like moving brushstrokes.

"You're looking glum, Ysadora," Kadin said, glancing over. "What's weighing on that genius mind of yours?"

Ysadora didn't smile. "I'm not sure we should even confront Myrradin. We don't know what he plans or how powerful he is. If we act too soon, we might make it worse."

"You think he can take all of us?" Garrick asked as he scratched at his beard, the motion slow, like he was weighing something heavier than the words themselves.

Ysadora's brow furrowed. One hand absently drifted to the silver chain wound through the base of her horns, fingers catching on the delicate metal as if grounding herself. "Most of his magic…" Ysadora paused, pressing her lips together. "The magic I've seen is mostly defensive. But that was before I knew he was a Windwraith."

Rykan stepped over a moss-covered root. "Then we don't go for him. We go for Selaina. Free her first. Then, he'll have to dodge her arrows while we box him in."

The group pushed on, the silence around them gradually returning, broken only by the faint sound of wind through the trees and the soft lap of water against the stones.

"You think she still has her bow?" Ysadora said. "He would have taken any weapons from her."

"We'll figure something out," said Rykan. "Our strength is our ability to adapt to the situation."

Ysadora snorted. "Is that what we're calling it now?"

"If he needs her to get to the Sky Serpents, he can't afford to harm her," said Nadara. "That may give us an advantage."

"If we are somehow able to defeat Myrradin, we'll have to kill him," said Ysadora, closing her eyes. "He would be too dangerous to allow a moment of mercy."

"She's right," said Garrick. "No matter what he says, the moment we have him, we must end it."

"He brought this on himself," said Rykan. "I'm prepared to do what we must."

"I wish we knew a bit more about Windwraiths before we go into this," said Kadin.

"Next time we stop and rest, I'll read through some of my books," said Ysadora.

They came upon ruins quietly nestled in the snow, where shattered stone walls stretched upward like ghostly relics of another world, draped in vines brittle and browned by the winter chill. Snow had softened their edges, blanketing the scattered stones with a muted, ethereal glow as if each fragment held memories of a world long lost.

The sky had begun to darken, casting the scene in deepening shades of twilight. The foundation remained mostly intact, but patches of it had crumbled into shadowed hollows, while other parts seemed to disappear beneath the earth, as though the mountain itself were drawing them back. A faint mist clung to the ground, swirling around the stonework in slow, almost reverent patterns, and the air felt heavy with the quiet of something timeless and unseen.

"There's no tree here," Nadara said, her voice barely a whisper. "I was hoping this would be the tree temple marked on the map."

"I'm sure there must be another temple around here somewhere," Rykan replied softly.

"We should make camp here," said Garrick, glancing up at the darkening sky. "No reason to go any further now."

"As long as there are no restless spirits that linger," Nadara said.

"I don't think they'll mind," Garrick said.

"I should look around and make peace," Nadara said. "Let any spirits who remain know we will not desecrate their temple."

"It's already been desecrated," Garrick said. "If you can make peace with time, let me know."

Ysadora knelt beside a broken arch, her fingers trailing the edge of the weathered stone. She pressed her palm to the surface, and her eyes grew distant. "There was grief here," she said quietly. "But not for a battle. This place... it held someone precious. A child, I think. No. Someone who chose to stay behind when others fled."

Her eyes fluttered shut.

"I see a circle of stones. People gathered, laying tokens down, fragments of carved wood, feathers, bits of colored cloth. They weren't mourning just a death. They were mourning a choice. A sacrifice."

A moment passed.

"One woman stayed long after the rest had gone. Her hand rested on the stone, just like mine. She whispered, 'We'll carry it forward. Even if it breaks us.'"

Ysadora opened her eyes.

"This wasn't just a ruin. It was a promise someone tried to keep."

Rykan tried to picture what Ysadora had seen. A woman who had stayed behind, not to win but to remember. To carry something forward when the rest had already let go.

His jaw tensed. It wasn't that he admired the sacrifice. It was that he understood it. That quiet, stubborn kind of strength. He wondered if Selaina would do the same, no, he knew she would. That was what terrified him.

Because she wouldn't hesitate. She'd kneel in the ashes and bear the memory if no one else could. She'd let it break her if it meant saving someone else.

Once the fire was made, Rykan ate a handful of the nuts Liora had given them, just enough to take the edge off his hunger while saving the rest for the climb ahead. Kadin and Ysadora chatted quietly nearby, their voices low and companionable, but Rykan's thoughts drifted elsewhere.

He stared into the shimmering flames, wondering where Selaina was now, what she was facing, and how far Myrradin had taken her. He didn't imagine her as helpless. If anything, she was probably fighting, resisting in whatever way she could. That was who she was. But still… he hated the thought of her facing it alone.

If there were any way he could comfort her, he would do it without hesitation. No matter how far apart they were, part of him would always be with her. He hoped she felt that now. He had been so focused on finding her that he hadn't allowed himself to think about how this might end. Could they really bring her back from Myrradin's power, safe and unharmed? The thought felt fragile, like breath on glass. But he couldn't bear to linger on the alternative.

Instead, his mind drifted to that last day, the way Selaina's eyes had brightened as she stared up at the Serpent's Tear. The light had caught the mark on her forehead, the glow soft against her skin. He hadn't realized it might be the last time he'd see her standing freely beneath an open sky, wind in her hair, fire in her eyes.

Now all he had was that moment, suspended in memory like frost that wouldn't melt.

He almost wished they had never set out to save the world, that they'd let it crumble and decay around them, for even a hollow, broken world would hold beauty with her in it. With her beside him, he could weather any darkness, find light in the shadows. But without her? Even if they vanquished every foe and restored all they'd dreamed of, the world would be a bleak, empty shell, lifeless, cold, and stripped of grace.

He felt the air thin in his throat, as if he were standing on the brink of utter despair. A part of him longed to give in, to let the darkness consume him and numb the pain, to extinguish all hope and burn his senses until he felt nothing. It would have been easier than fighting back against the anguish tearing at him. But he didn't give up. Leaning back against one of the broken temple stones, Rykan let his eyes drift closed. The mountain air was still, but his thoughts pulled him far from it, back to the city where he'd first seen her.

Selaina had been standing at the edge of a stone bridge, the chaos of the marketplace humming behind her. Her white hair caught the golden light slanting through the alleys, stirring in the breeze like a banner in still water. She was alone, yet utterly composed, her gaze fixed on something distant, above the rooftops, beyond the smoke and noise.

He hadn't known who she was. Only that she looked like someone who didn't belong to the noise. There'd been a calm about her, a quiet gravity that drew his eye before he even heard her speak. When she finally turned, her eyes, storm-gray and searching, met his with a silent challenge, like she was daring him to matter.

He hadn't spoken to her that day. But something had sparked in him anyway.

Now, the silence around him felt heavier. The memory didn't warm him, it ached, because she was gone. Taken. And whatever thread had drawn them together was stretched thin, nearly invisible.

But not broken.

There had been a gleam of curiosity in her eyes then, an innocence that saw the world not as it was, but as it should be. So much had changed in such a short time. That look had transformed into a sharp, unwavering resolve, the gaze of someone who had taken on the burden of setting things right. She now carried a purpose no one should have to bear, a task that only the strongest could face without succumbing to the very darkness they sought to undo.

Without realizing it, his thoughts began to unravel, drifting like clouds in a silent, aimless sky. His mind floated, weightless, slipping quietly into an unknown space where time lost meaning. Slowly, he felt himself descending, drawn down from the safety of light into the dark below. A heavy, red glow blinked like distant lightning, casting shadows that danced with strange intensity. An oppressive force pulsed against him, thickening with each breath, as if the very air weighed him down, holding him in place.

Then he saw it. The portal.

It pulsed from the heart of a massive, dead tree, its bark twisted and blackened, roots gnarled like the limbs of a dying god. The trunk had split open unnaturally wide, the hollow interior yawning like the mouth of some ancient beast. Within it, the portal churned. Not with flame, but with something heavier, something hungrier.

The once-burning heart of the gate had collapsed inward, as if molten light had been sucked through the hollow of the tree and replaced by rot. The surface rippled like blood stirred by a distant pulse, deepening to a bruised red that throbbed with something almost alive. Shadowy tendrils slithered from the edges, weaving through the inner bark, feeding on the tree from within.

And the tree allowed it.

Roots stretched along the cavern floor like veins, pulsing with the same sick crimson glow. The cries Rykan heard were no longer distant, they echoed from the roots themselves, a chorus of muffled voices that had no mouths. The tree was not merely housing the portal. It was becoming part of it.

"We are watching the path, my lord," said a voice through the haze. Rykan knew it, Arathain. "The girl will not reach the summit."

The portal trembled.

From within the hollow of the dead tree, its roiling surface compressed, then expanded outward with a sudden pulse, as though breathing. When Nociferon's voice came, it cut through the air like a blade drawn across metal.

"You've said that before."

The portal warped, rippling violently. The red light deepened to a bloodier shade, and for a moment, the shape of a twisted crown, antlered, burning, flared across its surface like a reflection in still water disrupted by a scream.

"I've rounded up a pack of maugwins bound fully to me now," Arathain said quickly, his voice tense. "The bloodshadow runs deep in them now, it thickens their shroud. They should be able to endure sunlight's blaze longer than before."

"Fail me again," Nociferon growled, "and you surrender your life force. All your borrowed power will return to me."

The shadows lashing from the portal recoiled with a hiss, like smoke sucked into a vacuum. Arathain's form shimmered, half-translucent, as if the threat had burned through the dream itself.

"It won't come to that," Arathain muttered.

Nociferon turned his gaze elsewhere, and the portal responded, its surface swirling inward like a whirlpool of red ink dropped in water. "Iravane. What of the Sullen?"

A different figure emerged, cloaked in shadow. "The girl has sealed her fate by climbing the mountain," said Iravane. "We gather near the base, if your beasts don't reach her, we will. One way or another, she won't leave Kylinshan alive."

"And Gwenna?" Nociferon's voice darkened, the portal vibrating with his command.

"My spies are watching," came the reply, her voice like smoke. "They always are."

Suddenly, Arathain's head snapped toward Rykan as if he could see him in the dream.

"Someone else is here," he hissed. "Listening."

The portal buckled inward, its surface tearing. Red cracks bloomed like veins across the bark of the old tree, pulsing with a sick light. Deep within the roiling chaos, the suggestion of a face began to press forward, not fully formed, but hinted at in the shifting folds of shadow and light. Features stirred like reflections in disturbed water, almost surfacing, never solid.

"Ah. The bitten one," came Nociferon's voice, curling through the air like smoke from a dying star.

The portal pulsed in sync with Rykan's heartbeat.

"Why do you resist the shadow?" Nociferon asked him. "You struggle in the dark, believing in a world that has abandoned you. Bring the girl to us and all of this can be avoided. You must not let her reach the summit. The Sky Serpents will never accept such an abomination. One not born of fate, but who stole the power of the Wishing Stone. They will destroy her. Bring her to us. Let her be repurposed. Let the wild breath return."

Rykan kept silent as his heart pounded. He wanted to run away, but there was nowhere to hide inside this dream. His throat caught. He felt exposed, cornered.

"She is an abomination in their eyes," Nociferon continued. "But in our hands, she can serve a purpose. The conflict of order will end. Together, we can decide what this world becomes, and shape it into something better." His voice thickened with quiet certainty, as if unveiling a universal truth. "Choice is illusion. True freedom is the absence of structure."

The words slithered under Rykan's skin like a second heartbeat, too calm to be a threat, too seductive to ignore.

Rykan remained still, but his heartbeat thudded in his ears.

"I see you," Arathain whispered. "I can feel your pulse. You're only a breath away. Give us the girl… and I'll hold back the maugwins."

Rykan clenched his fists. He wanted to scream, to vanish, but there was nothing but darkness beyond. The tree creaked, roots shifting beneath his feet.

"Bring her to us, Rykan," Nociferon said, his voice calm now, like something ancient and final. "And you'll both have a place in the world we are making."

Rykan abandoned all doubts and reason. He turned and ran, through shadows, through smoke, toward the frayed edge of the dream. The darkness fractured around him, the nightmare collapsing like ash in wind.

A sound followed him.

Not from the dream, but from beyond it.

A low growl, distant but rising. Footfalls, soft but many. Wet, heavy breaths rasping against the night.

Rykan jerked awake with a gasp, heart pounding in his chest like a war drum.

The crackle of the campfire replaced Nociferon's voice, but not the sounds.

They hadn't stopped.

Beyond the ring of firelight, something moved. Leaves rustled where no wind blew. The ground trembled, subtle, rhythmic, like paws pressing into the earth.

Nadara and Garrick slept nearby, cloaked in their bedrolls, while Ysadora stirred at the sound of Rykan bolting upright. Ysadora scrambled to her feet, staff already half-raised.

Kadin stepped between her and the shadows, his dagger flashing into his hand. "Stick close to me," he muttered, eyes sweeping the dark.

"They're coming!" Rykan shouted, scrambling to his feet. His eyes locked onto the trees just beyond the flickering light, where shadows shifted like wolves circling the edge of flame. "The maugwins, wake up! They're here!"

CHAPTER 41

SELAINA STEPPED CAREFULLY over the splintered remnants of wooden beams scattered at the cave's mouth, relics of a long-forgotten structure now claimed by time. In her hand, the torch she had crafted quivered and sputtered, its flame casting a warm, shifting glow across the jagged stone walls. Shadows leaped and twisted with each step she took, as though the darkness itself recoiled from the light. The faint scent of charred wood mingled with the damp, mineral scent of the cave air, every breath heavy with the weight of the unknown. The firelight moved in rhythm with her cautious stride, a fragile shield against the vast, waiting blackness beyond.

The torch's heat was a small comfort against the chill that seeped from the stones. Without it, she doubted she would have ventured far. Shadows stretched and shifted along the walls, hinting at shapes that weren't there, their silent movements a constant reminder of how isolated she was.

The stone floor stretched before her, littered with crystalline formations that gleamed even in the shadows. The crystals in the flame's glow reflected in fragmented rainbows, creating fleeting constellations on the ceiling above.

Deeper into the cave, the air grew heavier, tinged with an earthy, metallic scent. The crystalline formations began to grow larger, their surfaces refracting the light into patterns so intricate they seemed alive. Selaina paused to inspect one, her breath momentarily stolen by the iridescent veins that pulsed faintly within, as if the crystal itself were alive, echoing the lifeblood of the mountain.

She pressed forward, the path narrowing into a jagged corridor where stalactites hung low, dripping water into unseen pools. The flare of the torch began to falter, its flame sputtering against the damp air.

"No, no, no," Selaina whispered, holding the torch upright as if coaxing it to stay alight. The fire clung stubbornly for a few moments longer, then guttered out, leaving her in suffocating darkness.

Her pulse quickened, the void around her pressing in from all sides. She fumbled in her satchel, her fingers brushing against the cold, smooth surface of the talisman Myrradin had dropped.

The moment her hand closed around it, a soft, silvery glow emanated from the object, illuminating the cavern with an ethereal light. Shadows twisted and fled as the talisman's radiance filled the space, casting the crystalline formations in shifting hues of blue and violet.

Selaina hesitated, holding the talisman at arm's length. Its glow pulsed steady and strange, otherworldly, as if it came from somewhere just beyond the edges of this realm. She glanced around the cavern, half-expecting something to stir in answer. A glimmer of doubt crept in. Would using it call out to Myrradin? Would he feel it? But the silence around her remained unbroken, save for the faint hum of the cavern itself.

As she moved deeper, the glowing talisman illuminated the path in ways the torch never could. The stone walls seemed to shimmer with new life, their patterns now resembling flowing rivers frozen in time. The crystals absorbed the talisman's light, their cores pulsing faintly in response, creating a dazzling interplay of shadow and luminescence.

Her steps slowed as the tunnel opened into a vast chamber, its size impossible to gauge as the talisman's light struggled to reach its boundaries. A gentle wind whispered through the space, carrying with it a sense of age and weight, as though the cavern itself were a living memory.

Then the light fell upon the formation, a massive, gently curving surface that didn't look quite like stone. It caught the light strangely, the light didn't bounce—it softened, bleeding through like it was passing behind clouded glass, or some vast, slumbering crystal. Selaina drew closer, her steps slowing. The texture was smooth but not uniform, as if shaped by time, or something else.

She reached out, her hand trembling, and brushed the formation lightly. It was cold, but beneath the chill was a pulse, a slow, steady vibration that climbed her arm and sent a shiver down her spine. The talisman's light shifted across the surface, revealing the gentle arc of something vast, smooth, and impossibly curved, disappearing into the dark like the limb of some ancient statue half-swallowed by time.

Her breath caught as she stepped back. The shape extended farther than she could see. This was no stone. This was something else, something alive. The still air stirred faintly, and with it came the subtle rise and fall of a breath too large to belong to anything natural.

The talisman in her hand flared slightly, as if responding to the creature's presence, casting Selaina's shadow across the cavern like a wraith. She stared, her heart racing, as the realization settled over her.

This had to be the crystal leviathan, Azirok, that Caelum had warned her about. If he had described it like this, she never would have set foot in these caves. Selaina froze, heart hammering in her chest as the sheer scale of the creature settled over her like a weight.

Every instinct screamed for her to turn back, to flee toward some illusion of safety. But there was no going back now.

Her friends had risked everything to bring her this far. Their sacrifices echoed in every step she took. All she could do was move forward, into the dark, into the unknown, into whatever fate waited ahead.

She swallowed, her gaze drifting along the monstrous form that filled the cavern like a living wall of crystal. Pressing forward seemed impossible; getting past this creature and back to the light of day felt like a distant dream.

But she couldn't turn back. If she failed here, everything her friends had done, their sacrifices, their belief in her, would be for nothing. And worse, the Iron Flood would continue its march unchecked. Vatreus would grow stronger. More cities would burn. More innocents would vanish into silence.

She took a shaky breath, feeling the weight of the choice before her, knowing each step could either lead her closer to her destiny, or into the jaws of a sleeping giant.

If only she had Rykan's fearlessness. But she was Selaina. She was Zhal Evurah. Were any before here afraid of anything? Not in the historical accounts anyway, but Selaina reasoned that they probably were at times, like anyone else. She found that being Zhal Evurah alone had not given her any newfound courage, it was more of a push to face the fear and doubt and press through the darkness despite what your sense of self-preservation might tell you.

A large wall of rock in front of her blocked the path ahead. As she drew closer, it became apparent that the shape was the large clawed foot of the creature. She tried to go around it, but its claws edged against the walls of the cavern.

The only way through was to climb over its clawed toes and hope she wouldn't wake the creature. She was Zhal Evurah, she kept telling herself, she feared nothing.

"I had a shape once. Then they peeled it off my bones."

Selaina staggered, hand pressed against the cold stone. The words weren't sound. They slid into her thoughts like water seeping under a door. Too old to belong to her. Too heavy to be anything human. She wanted to turn back. Her legs almost obeyed. But turning back would mean admitting this place had unmade her, and she would not give it that power.

I am Zhal Evurah, she reminded herself, teeth clenched. Not because she felt worthy. Not because she felt brave. But because she had to be.

Taking a deep breath, Selaina put the talisman chain around her neck to free her hands. She tested the creature's awareness by touching the scaly surface of its nearest toe.

"Stone remembers. The cold is full of voices. They whisper backwards."

She tried to focus, to push forward, but the voice, or whatever it was, kept surfacing like a memory she'd never lived. It was in the walls, in the breathing stone, in the dark vastness around her.

It had to be the creature. What else could dream like this?

The hide of its toes was unlike that of its body, rough and leathery. It didn't move, other than the reverberations of its breathing. Selaina pressed more of her weight against the toe, ready to run if the creature woke.

After a long moment, satisfied that Azirok was in a deep, unbreakable hibernation, she began climbing, each scale offering a foothold as she hoisted herself over the ridge of its toe to reach the top of its massive foot.

Selaina crested the top of the leviathan's foot and paused, steadying herself on a jutting ridge of scale.

"They built me from the scream beneath the scream. It had teeth."

She tried to ignore the words, whatever they were. The cavern opened wider ahead, revealing a strange glow pulsing faintly from deep within the shadows.

Rising from the heart of the cavern like a jagged wound in the world stood a towering red crystal, fractured and immense, as though it had been struck by some divine force but had refused to shatter entirely.

"The sky was wrong. I bit it. It bled. It bled."

The crystal's surface shimmered like glass soaked in blood, veins of pulsing crimson light twisting through it with slow, rhythmic flickers. A silent heartbeat.

And coiled around it, resting like a beast guarding its core, was the leviathan's tail.

It wrapped the crystal tightly, protectively, as if the creature had been bound to it, or perhaps born from it. The tail's massive coils shimmered with embedded fragments of the same red light, glowing faintly where flesh met crystal.

Selaina froze mid-step, her muscles locking for a heartbeat. Whatever the crystal was, its presence chilled her more deeply than the cold of the cavern. It felt… wrong. Like it had no place in the world of the living. Like it wanted to change everything it touched.

But she couldn't look away.

Moving with deliberate care, she took shallow breaths, fearful that even the faintest exhale might carry enough warmth to rouse it. Prickly crystalline hairs lifted between the scales with each of her steps, responding to her weight with slow, eerie elegance.

The hairs shimmered faintly, catching the light from her talisman and refracting it in sharp angles that cast eerie, needle-thin shadows across her path. They looked deceptively fragile, yet as they lifted higher, they gave the impression of thorns or jagged shards, like defenses bristling to life in response to her presence. She imagined they could prick her skin at the slightest misstep, or worse, alert the leviathan beneath to her touch.

"Still falling. Still. Still. The hole has no bottom. I've checked."

She didn't know if the voice was speaking to her, or just bleeding through its own madness. Either way, she didn't answer.

Navigating the spaces between these crystalline spines, she felt the incline of the leviathan's foot grow steeper, forcing her balance to shift. Her foot pressed into the skin near the base of one of the hairs, and suddenly, the creature's flesh twitched, a ripple of movement that threw her off balance and sent her tumbling down the groove between two massive, clawed toes.

"The dream folded. I folded with it. Then it kept dreaming."

The leviathan's toes began to flex, squeezing together with a force that pressed her on all sides. Selaina's heartbeat pounded, her arms straining against the constricting space. Each pulse of the creature's breath thudded through her bones, the pressure mounting.

She twisted, teeth gritted, scraping her shoulder against the slick wall of flesh. The cavern echoed with the faint rumble of the leviathan's shifting body. Her fingers found the rough edge of a crevice near the joint, just wide enough. With a burst of strength she didn't know she still had, she shoved her weight sideways and wriggled free, landing hard beside the creature's massive foot.

Scrambling up over the curve of its limb, she staggered across the stone, her breath ragged. Her hands trembled, scraped and raw, and she stared at them for a long moment, not in awe of some unexpected power, but in disbelief that she'd made it.

"You bleed like the bright ones. But softer. Quieter."

Pressing onward through the chamber, the air grew warmer, thickening with the creature's breath. It smelled of damp earth and minerals, like rain-soaked soil with a sharp, metallic tang that clung to her senses, sending her pulse pounding loudly in her head, yet her heartbeat felt calm and steady, despite her fear.

Ahead, her talisman's light revealed an enormous shape looming in the dark. The leviathan's long neck curved inward, its colossal head resting on its front claws. The jagged points of its teeth peeked out from under its lip, gleaming like ice. The slow, deep thud of its heartbeat echoed through the cavern, and Selaina felt her own heartbeat falling into sync, as though the creature itself controlled the rhythm of her pulse. Panic prickled at her spine, but she couldn't shake the eerie calm in her chest.

"There was a song once. It sang itself out. It broke its own throat."

Selaina crept carefully around the leviathan's immense snout, feeling the warm gusts of its breath wash over her like waves. A mineral scent clung to the air, rich and tangible, sinking into her skin with every step. Its head lay partially turned, resting on one claw, with only a single closed eye facing her. Her gaze shifted over its features, hoping for a clear path forward. But then, just as she moved past, a faint shift caught her attention, and a crackling, grinding sound, like stone scraping over stone, echoed through the silence.

"I was made for the end. But the end did not wait. It left me here."

Her breath caught, and she half-stumbled a step backward, instinct warring with awe as the leviathan's eye peeled open. Light broke from beneath it like a wound reopening. Then the full weight of the leviathan's eye locked onto her.

She should've run. Should've screamed. Instead, her hand moved on instinct.

Selaina drew her bow.

Arrow notched, string pulled taut. Her hands shook, the tip aimed between eyes vast enough to swallow stars. The creature began to rise, muscles pulling against themselves like stone strained past its breaking point. The air thickened with violent expectation.

"So small… But your shadow comes first. I've been waiting in it."

Not a thought. Not a guess. A knowing, cold and sudden, like breath drawn too deep. The voice hadn't come from the stone, or the crystal, or the dark. It came from the thing she'd stepped around like it couldn't see her.

It had been dreaming her the whole time she had been here.

Selaina's hand trembled on her bowstring. But beneath the fear, something deeper coiled, recognition, like a name whispered through her bones.

Their eyes met.

Something deep stirred inside her. The moment stretched, breathless and still. Her sight, the strange gift she barely understood, reached out, uninvited, instinctual. The connection hit her like a pulse of heat through ice. She blinked, and suddenly she wasn't just seeing the creature, she was inside it.

A great depth opened in her mind. Ancient sorrow. Unyielding patience. The cold memory of centuries spent beneath stone and time.

The leviathan halted.

Its breath came slow and thunderous, fogging the air. The aggression that had swelled in its frame softened, as if the connection had stilled some primal instinct. Its eyes narrowed, not with anger now, but with recognition.

Recognition of something older. Something buried in her that she herself did not yet understand.

Her vision blurred for a heartbeat, and then snapped into painful clarity.

The familiar pressure of her gift flared in her mind. But she had never experienced a consciousness like this. The moment their eyes met, her "sight beyond seeing" surged forward unbidden, pulled across a great distance, like a tide drawn toward the moon.

Her surroundings faded. She was sinking like a stone into an ocean. Memories, not hers, but the leviathan's, flooded over her, vast and ancient, each one imbued with the creature's timeless consciousness.

Its breath came slow and thunderous, fogging the air. The aggression coiled in its frame began to ease, stilled not by fear, but by something older, recognition. Its vast eyes narrowed, not in fury, but in knowing.

Selaina felt it then, deep and sudden. Her vision blurred and snapped into sharp clarity. The familiar pressure of her gift flared behind her eyes. But this was no ordinary connection. This was not a mind, but a vast sea of memory, and she was already falling into it.

She didn't fight it.

Her surroundings vanished. She was sinking, slow and heavy, like a stone dropped into a dark ocean. The crystal leviathan's memories rushed over her, ancient, endless, flooding her senses with something more than thought. This was not recollection. This was becoming.

It began in stillness. The weight of stone above. Silence pressed in from every side. Then came the cold, deep, unmoving, primeval. Not winter's chill, but the unmelted breath of time itself.

Something stirred. Pressure built, pulling inward, pushing outward. Sensation formed before thought, and from that sensation, awareness. A self, unnamed, buried beneath the earth. Its limbs were not yet limbs. Its eyes had not yet opened. It did not know what it was, only that it was becoming.

Then pain. A pulse of red light tore through the dark.

Above, a figure emerged, tall, cloaked in shifting shadow, one arm raised high. In his hand burned a jagged crystal, blood red and alive with inner fire, as if carved from the marrow of the world itself. It pulsed with terrible intent.

Selaina stiffened. Something inside her recoiled, even as her gaze locked on the crystal. It looked just like the fractured shard wrapped in Azirok's tail, only this one was whole.

A wisp of memory smoked through her mind, weightless, inescapable, whispering the crystal's name. The Heart of Entropy.

Its light pulsed, not merely with power, but with intent. A command to rise.

And the creature obeyed.

Stone cracked. Limbs broke free from the depths. A spine twisted upward through ancient rock. Lungs pulled in their first breath. Crystalline veins fused with flesh as molten light bled through bone. The creature, once something simpler, something wilder, was being remade.

Not born, but reforged.

Selaina felt the transformation like it was her own. She watched through the leviathan's senses as crystal grew through its body, an evolution forced upon it. It had once been beast. Now it was purpose.

The Heart of Entropy pulsed again, and the world shifted in answer. Mountains bowed. Rivers reversed. Forests tore themselves apart, roots twisting like veins. Chaos was not a flaw. It was the plan.

The figure above remained still, the Heart raised high. The leviathan's mind, newly shaped and cruelly awakened, burned with a rage that wasn't its own. A hatred for all that resisted change. A loathing for order.

It marched.

Towns disappeared beneath its tread. Lives, small and fragile, vanished in the quake of its passing. Their cries were muffled by the roar of the world breaking apart.

Then, another light. White, piercing, and righteous.

From the heavens, celestial beings descended, radiant figures like stars wrapped in form. They confronted the wielder of the Heart, and the earth trembled under their fury. The Heart of Entropy blazed brighter, and the chaos it commanded deepened, its influence digging into the very roots of creation.

Another memory surged forward.

A canyon, carved from obsidian stone and rimmed with black glass. There, beside the leviathan, moved another, a second creature, leaner, swifter, terrible in her elegance. They moved as one, shaped by the same will.

Selaina felt their bond. Not just force or instinct, but something else. A love twisted into servitude. They had not been born for violence. They had been forged into it.

Above them hovered the Chaos Lord. The Heart of Entropy burned in his hand, reshaping the world according to his will.

And then came war.

A figure appeared on the battlefield, radiant and marked with the emblem of Zhal Evurah. The symbol burned on their brow, unmistakable even across time. Mortal armies surged at their side, humans, Liths, giants, all wielding weapons forged in defiance of chaos.

The battle shook the heavens.

The female leviathan fell first.

Selaina felt the shattering grief pierce Azirok's core. The loss echoed deeper than flesh, something vital torn away. It howled, not with fury, but with sorrow, then turned and vanished into the earth.

Not in defeat, but in mourning.

Stillness returned.

Selaina's vision began to blur, pulling her back to the present. As she returned to herself in the cold, dark cavern, she felt an ache unlike any fear she'd known before, this creature she'd been so wary of was no mere monster. It was a being alone in a world it was no longer part of, cursed to wander its silent prison with no purpose but survival.

She took a shaky breath, her hand instinctively brushing against the cool rock of the cavern walls as she moved forward, keeping as quiet as she could. A newfound kinship flared in her heart, an understanding she couldn't ignore. The cavern felt heavier now, weighted with the respect this place commanded.

A pang of sorrow struck her as she thought of the leviathan's fate, a creature bound to an endless, solitary existence as the last of its kind. The weight of its isolation echoed in the silence around her, lingering in the cavern's depths. Selaina turned to the cavern walls ahead, the vast chamber receding into shadow as a narrow tunnel lay waiting beside her, winding between jagged crystal formations.

As she gazed upon Azirok, he slowly rested his head back on its bed of stone. He closed his eyes, breathing a deep sighing breath as if preparing to return to hibernation. She felt as though he was as aware of her mind as she was of his. Maybe he felt her empathy, her understanding, and was allowing her passage. Selaina moved carefully around him, not wanting to disturb his slumber again.

Carefully, she moved forward, her fingers grazing the cool rock, grounding her as she rounded a bend in the tunnel. As she walked deeper into the dark, her resolve solidified. She was not just passing through; she had felt the presence of a life bound by chaos and marked by tragedy. It was one more reason to continue, to ensure that her own purpose, to restore balance to this fractured world, would not go unfulfilled.

A circle of faint, silvery light glimmered at the far end, casting an ethereal glow over the cavern walls. She took a deep breath, her heart swelling with relief and determination. The journey through darkness was nearly over; she had reached the tunnel's end, and beyond it, the mountain awaited.

CHAPTER 42

RYKAN UNSHEATHED HIS sword, the steel catching a fleeting glint of light before the shadows swallowed it again. The maugwins' bellows grew louder, guttural roars that rumbled through the trees like a storm tearing through the forest. Nadara was already on her feet, her glaive spinning in precise, defensive arcs, the blade catching faint embers of light as it moved. Ysadora clutched the Sunkeeper crystal tightly, her trembling hands brushing its smooth surface as its golden glow pushed feebly against the encroaching darkness.

Garrick rose methodically, his sword gleaming in the dancing light, his deliberate movements a stark contrast to the chaos around him. Kadin, crouched low, fanned his daggers with a practiced flick, their edges flashing briefly before he stilled, his sharp gaze fixed on the shifting shadows ahead. Tension crackled in the air, each of them poised as the first stirrings of the creatures' approach sent a ripple through the underbrush.

The maugwins burst through the forest like swaths of living ink, their shadowy forms writhing with bloodshadow energy. Tendrils of darkness lashed out from their bodies, stretching toward the group like living whips. The tendrils hissed and twisted, aiming to ensnare and crush anything in their path. Ysadora thrust the Sunkeeper crystal forward, bathing the clearing in brilliance. The shadowy tendrils withered and burst under the searing light, leaving trails of ash in their wake.

Enraged, the maugwins recoiled, their liquid-like bodies smoldering at the edges. Their focus shifted to Ysadora, and with a collective, feral snarl, they charged. They clustered together, forming a mass of living shadow. Some hurled themselves forward, taking the brunt of the Sunkeeper's light so the others could press on.

Rykan stepped forward, slashing at the oncoming maugwins. His blade carved through one, but the wound sealed almost immediately, leaving only a thin red scar where the steel had landed. He struck again, harder, and this time the creature burst into red ash and mist. He barely caught his breath before another lunged toward him.

Kadin's crossbow thudded beside him, each bolt finding its mark. The maugwins staggered with each hit but didn't fall. Instead, their shadows stretched, melting into the ground, only to rise again, twisted and whole.

"They just won't stay down!" Kadin shouted.

Nadara's glaive flashed in the snowlight, cleaving one creature nearly in half. The dark ichor that spilled sizzled on contact with the frozen ground, but the wounded maugwin pressed forward with mindless ferocity.

"We can't hold them like this forever!" she shouted, spinning low and slicing clean through a second tendril that reached for Kadin. Her movements were swift, practiced, a dancer's precision with a warrior's strength.

Another maugwin lunged, aiming for Ysadora. Nadara pivoted, stepped into its charge, and drove her glaive upward in a brutal arc. The blade pierced the underside of its jaw, lifting the shadowy creature off its feet before she slammed it back into the earth.

A tremor rippled through the ground, sudden and violent. Rykan risked a glance past his opponent. The earth behind Ysadora cracked open, jagged stone spears erupting upward. Several maugwins were caught in the surge, impaled and thrashing, but even skewered, they writhed, snapping the stone and dragging themselves free.

More were coming. Rykan ducked a slicing tendril, driving his blade up into the creature's gut. It burst in a spray of black mist, already replaced by another clawing its way toward him.

To his left, Garrick stepped into the fray without hesitation. His sword flashed in clean, brutal arcs, one creature fell, then another. Rykan caught a glimpse of him slamming a beast off balance with his shoulder, then dropping it with a bone-deep strike that split its head like timber.

Garrick didn't flinch. He planted his feet wide again, daring the next wave forward, and wiped a streak of ichor from his chin with the back of his hand, then scratched his jaw like it was just another day's work.

Rykan gritted his teeth and turned back to his own fight, matching Garrick's momentum. If the old soldier could still move like that, Rykan sure as hell wasn't about to fall behind.

Rykan adjusted his grip. His pulse thundered in his ears. Every swing of his sword felt heavier, his body fighting not just the enemy, but the growing weight of dread. They couldn't hold like this forever. The creatures kept coming, faster, hungrier, eyes locked on Ysadora like hounds on the scent.

They were losing ground. And if they broke here, there'd be no coming back from it.

Two maugwins slipped past Garrick while he was entangled with another. Rykan lunged, driving his sword into one before it could reach Ysadora. But the second creature leaped at her, knocking her to the ground. Before Rykan or anyone else could intervene, the maugwin's shadowy mouth engulfed Ysadora's hand. Her scream tore through the air, raw and visceral, freezing Rykan in place for a heartbeat. He saw her crumple as the crystal flared, its light scorching the maugwin even as it ripped the Sunkeeper from her hand. Her body tumbled like a broken doll across the clearing, smoke rising from her twisted fingers.

"Ysadora!" Rykan shouted, slashing desperately at the shadows blocking his way.

Nadara and Garrick fought beside him, but the sheer number of maugwins kept them at bay.

The maugwin carrying the stolen Sunkeeper crystal bolted away, trying to envelop the light with its shadows, but the brilliance of the crystal burned through, causing the creature to melt and break apart even as it attempted to flee. With the Sunkeeper now out of reach, the remaining maugwins regenerated their tendrils. Shadowy appendages snaked toward Rykan and the others, forcing them to fight desperately to avoid being ensnared.

Ysadora lay sprawled on the ground, her broken staff just out of reach. What remained of her hand trembled violently, blackened at the edges, slick with a mix of blood and something darker, something that shimmered like oil and smoke where it touched the snow. The fingers, or what was left of them, twitched unnaturally, as if the wound pulsed with more than just pain. Steam curled up in ghostly wisps, carrying the scent of scorched flesh and old magic. Her lips moved, whispering something too quiet to hear. Rykan saw Kadin glance toward Ysadora, saw the shift in his stance, the way he broke free without hesitation.

Rykan, Garrick, and Nadara fought to free themselves from the web of tendrils as Kadin reached Ysadora. A maugwin lunged at him, one dagger slashed through a tendril, severing it, while another plunged deep into the nearest creature, forcing it back.

"Kadin, get away!" Ysadora gasped, struggling to sit up. "You can't—"

His shoulders squared sharply, exaggerated like a caricature of confidence, the kind that's meant more to steady others than himself.

"Save your breath," Kadin snapped. "You've talked enough for three lifetimes anyway." He flashed a crooked grin. "Let me handle the stabbing."

The creatures roared, surging forward. Kadin moved like a shadow himself, dodging and striking with precision. He severed more tendrils, buying precious seconds, but the maugwins pressed closer. Kadin's movements slowed, his limbs heavy, breath ragged, but he didn't stop. Another tendril cracked across his ribs, dropping him hard into the snow. He coughed blood, still rising, still fighting. For her.

"Kadin!" Rykan screamed, his sword cutting through the tendrils with renewed desperation.

Nadara's glaive carved a path, and Garrick roared as he tore through the shadows, but they were still too far away.

Kadin pushed himself up, blood dripping from his mouth. His daggers fell from his hands as his strength faltered, but he didn't retreat. With trembling fingers, he seized a shard of Ysadora's staff, the last piece of her strength. And with a wordless cry, he drove it into a maugwin's heart. The creature convulsed, screeching in fury as it dissolved into ash around the weapon.

Another tendril lashed out, wrapping around his torso. With a cry of pain, Kadin tore it free, but the effort left him open. The remaining maugwins surged forward, their tendrils piercing and tearing into him.

"Kadin, no!" Ysadora screamed. She crawled forward, her mangled hand dragging behind her, her face contorted with pain and grief.

He lay bleeding in the snow, half-buried in red. He turned his head just enough to see her. Blood trickled from the corner of his mouth.

Rykan had never seen Ysadora unravel like this. For all her sharp retorts and cold logic, she'd always kept her distance. But now, crawling through blood and snow to reach Kadin, something raw and real broke through. Maybe Kadin meant more to her than she ever let on. Maybe she'd never dared to find out, until it was too late.

"Don't you dare give up," Kadin said, voice strained. "I expect nothing less than legendary vengeance for this. Something in the range of tenfold would be sufficient."

Garrick swung his blade furiously, each strike meeting with a sickening crunch as tendrils recoiled, only to reform and lash out again. Rykan fought beside him, his sword moving in tight, controlled arcs to keep the shadowy limbs from advancing. The battle was relentless, a blur of motion and darkness that felt endless. Nadara stumbled backward, her glaive slipping in her grip as a tendril knocked her to the ground. Rykan stepped in front of her, his heart hammering in his chest, as he slashed at the encroaching shadows. He continued to hack at the appendages as Nadara pushed herself up beside him.

Rykan's stomach twisted when he saw Embryss in her grasp. Its crimson light pulsed ominously, casting sharp shadows across her face.

"What are you doing?" he demanded, his voice raw with disbelief. "We agreed it's too dangerous!"

"We don't have a choice," Nadara said, fire flashing behind her words. "Fear's no excuse for freezing. Move or die." She gripped Embryss tighter, her gaze locked on the advancing threat. "If we don't end this now, they'll kill us all."

Rykan clenched his teeth, bracing himself as she lifted Embryss. The tendrils recoiled, hissing and retreating. For a brief, heart-stopping moment, silence fell over the ruins and Rykan thought Embryss had worked.

Footsteps broke the stillness. Arathain emerged from the shadows, his presence chilling the air. He surveyed the scene, his eyes gleaming with cruel amusement. Arathain tapped Kadin's lifeless body with his boot.

"How noble," he said, with a sickening smooth voice. "But ultimately pointless."

"You'll die for this," said Rykan. "I swear it."

"Fear not," Arathain said, his gaze sweeping over the group. "I've only come for the Lith."

Rykan gripped his sword tightly, his heart pounding with rage and grief. "You'll have to get through us first."

His eyes swept over them, narrowing as they landed on Nadara. "Hiding, is she? Perhaps she isn't as special as Nociferon thought."

Rykan's jaw clenched. He glanced at Nadara, whose hands trembled as she clutched Embryss.

Arathain's gaze shifted to the crystal, a cold smile spreading across his face. "What have we here?" he mused, stepping forward. The shard trembled in Nadara's grip, then wrenched itself free, flying into Arathain's waiting hand. "I've been missing a few of these," he sneered, tucking the shard into his belt. "I doubt you even know the true power of this, but I must thank you for returning it to its rightful owner."

Rykan's mind raced, dread settling in his gut. Arathain now had the Embryss.

"But that's not why I'm here," Arathain continued smoothly. His gaze swept over the group, a glint of cruel amusement in his eyes. "All you have to do is tell me where she is, and the rest of you are free to go."

Then he turned to Rykan, voice dripping with mockery. "I never did thank you, my bitten one," he said, smiling like a knife. "That wound of yours has been… most helpful. My beacon."

"That's a lie!" Rykan snapped, his voice tight with anger and fear. The accusation cut deeper than he wanted to admit, but he couldn't afford to show any doubt.

Arathain chuckled. Shadows curled tighter around him. "Don't sell yourself short. It was your blood that opened the nether gate. Your trail that led me straight to your camp."

Rykan's knuckles went white around his sword. "And we sent you crawling back!" he roared, lunging forward.

The world twisted violently, and shadows swallowed him whole.

When Rykan could see again, he stood beneath a massive, dead tree, its branches skeletal, its roots sunk into cracked stone. At its base, dark red flames coiled, not burning, but bleeding from a split in the bark. The wound pulsed like a heartbeat, and from it churned a portal, slick and thick as congealed blood.

It wasn't housed in the tree. It was the tree, grown around the wound like scar tissue. Shadowy roots pulsed outward, feeding on the darkness. A low groan echoed from within, as though the tree remembered what it had once been, and hated what it had become.

As the disorienting haze faded, a chilling sound reached Rykan's ears: the familiar, bone-chilling cries of the maugwins, not too far away. His friends were still fighting, desperately trying to hold their ground against the shadowy creatures. The realization twisted in his gut, a bitter mix of guilt and helplessness.

Before he could compose himself enough to rise to his feet, Arathain stepped close. "We are far enough away from your friends now," he said. "You can tell me where Selaina is."

Rykan forced himself to stand, his body trembling with the effort. "I don't know," he said, his voice steady through the fear.

Arathain tilted his head, a sinister smile playing at his lips. "You're not a bad liar," he said. "Now tell me the truth."

"For all I know, she may have reached the top of Kylinshan by now," said Rykan.

Arathain's eyes narrowed. "I've been watching the pass. She hasn't come through here. It appears she sent the rest of you into my trap. Is that how she cares for you? Dangling you in front of me as bait while she slips away to the summit?"

Was he lying, or had Selaina gotten past him unseen? As much as it pained him to not know where she was, Rykan found himself amused that he couldn't be used to give away her location. He couldn't hold back a weary grin. "I really don't know where she is."

Arathain's smile faded, his voice growing cold. "Tell me where she is now, or when I find her, I'll make her suffer in ways you can't imagine. Even the faintest heartbeat is enough for Nociferon to consider her alive. I'll make sure you see every tear she sheds, every scream she tries to swallow. Your dreams will be filled with her torment until madness takes you."

Rage burned through Rykan's fear, and he charged, swinging his sword with reckless abandon. Arathain raised a hand, shadows swirling around it, and the blade struck an invisible field of darkness. Rykan watched in horror as his sword's steel began to waver and wisp, turning immaterial as it pressed deeper into the shadowy force. The harder he tried to push, the more his weapon dissolved into smoke.

With a sneer, Arathain stepped forward, his hand radiating the shadowy field. Rykan pulled his sword back, and it solidified in his grip once more, but he felt his confidence waver.

"Your weapons mean nothing to me," Arathain said, his voice echoing with dark amusement. "Shadows bow to me, and soon, you will too."

Rykan gritted his teeth, his mind racing as he circled Arathain. The shadowy force emanating from Arathain's hands had made every attack so far useless, turning his sword into smoke whenever it got too close. But Rykan wasn't giving up. Not when this monster had come for Selaina. Not after what he'd done to Ysadora. To Kadin.

"You're wasting your energy, Rykan," Arathain taunted, his voice echoing like a thousand whispered curses. "Every swing only feeds the darkness."

Rykan steadied his breath, anchoring his resolve with the familiar weight of his sword. He narrowed his eyes, and feinted to the left. Arathain's hands shifted, moving the shadowy field in anticipation of the strike. Seizing the opening, Rykan pivoted sharply and swung low and wide, aiming for the mavin's midsection rather than his head.

The blade cleaved through the swirling shadows, tearing into Arathain's cloak. For a fleeting moment, Rykan's strike seemed destined to land a fatal blow, but the sword dissolved into shadows, reforming mere inches away. A flash of red light erupted as something slipped from Arathain's belt, a shard of dark, crystalline energy, its malevolent glow pulsing like a heartbeat. Embryss struck the ground with a sharp clatter, releasing a ripple of dark energy that reverberated through the ruins.

Arathain's eyes widened with fury. Shadows writhed and pulsed around him. He stretched out a hand and the shard began to shake loose from the snow.

Rykan's heart pounded as he lunged forward, stretching out his hand. The shard shot through the air toward Arathain, but Rykan intercepted it, his fingers closing around the cold, pulsing crystal. The sudden surge of dark energy coursed through him, burning the wound on his arm but he gritted his teeth and held on.

"You don't know what you're dealing with," Arathain sneered, his voice dripping with contempt. "I am the shadows, I am power itself. You are nothing." His eyes gleamed with dark confidence as he summoned every ounce of his strength, shadows coiling around the shard.

Rykan's grip faltered. The darkness nearly tore the shard from his hand.

Then, an idea. Reckless. Desperate. As Arathain pulled with everything he had, Rykan let go.

Embryss shot forward, driven by his own power, embedding itself in his chest.

For a heartbeat, he stood still. Then he laughed, low and breathless, triumphant. But the shard pulsed.

Shadows burst from his body, but they didn't flee, they clung to him, coiling tighter. His scream cut through the mountainside, not of pain alone, but of something deeper, resistance.

His form began to shift, too fast, too wrong. Limbs lengthening, spine warping, his features distorting as though Embryss were trying to perfect him, dragging him into some higher form he could not contain. His power fed it, and it fed on him.

"No, no!" he howled, clawing at his chest. "I command you!"

But Embryss only had one master.

"Nociferon!" Arathain cried. "Stop this!"

Rykan could only watch as Arathain's triumph twisted into a grotesque transformation—one that cracked under its own weight. Flesh split. Shadows shrieked. And in a final blinding pulse of red light, the figure that was Arathain came apart.

What remained fell to the snow, steaming, not ashes, but something unrecognizable. The shard rolled from the ruin of him, still pulsing.

Rykan had dreamt of killing him. A thousand different ways. But none of them had felt like this. No shout of triumph. No satisfaction. Just cold air and silence. Not with Kadin's blood still soaking the snow. Not with Ysadora's broken hand, and the screams that still echoed in his mind. Not with Selaina out there in Myrradin's grasp. Justice hadn't made it right.

The wound in his arm throbbed violently, opened wider by the effort, oozing bloodshadow in dark, pulsing veins. It reminded him, this wasn't over. Not completely.

He glanced up at the last flutter of raging shadows where Arathain had once stood. In the snow, Embryss still pulsed. Waiting.

CHAPTER 43

THE MOONLIT SNOW shimmered with a ghostly iridescence, casting fleeting, spectral hues across the rugged mountainside as Selaina stepped out of the cavern into the vast, open expanse. The crisp, untouched mountain air rushed into her lungs, carrying with it an invigorating clarity that seemed borrowed from the ageless wilderness. Each breath tasted of frost and distant pine, a sharp, clean burn that anchored her to the present. Around her, the trees swayed in unison, their snow-laden boughs murmuring secrets to the breeze, their whispers blending into the soft hiss of falling snow. The world was cloaked in an exquisite stillness, a silence so profound it felt alive, absorbing even the faint crunch of her footsteps as she ventured forward.

Despite the purity of the night, a sharp pang of loneliness stabbed through her, planting seeds of doubt that took root. What dangers awaited her now? Could she really face them alone? The thought gripped her like the bitter cold, making her wish, if only for a moment, that she could surrender to the snow and let the ages pass her by. The image of her friends, though, of their lives withering in a world left to decay, left an emptiness deeper than she had ever known.

She thought of Darian, of how he'd tried to protect her, even when he was falling apart under the weight of his own grief. The way he'd looked at her sometimes, like she was all he had left of Bellaria. In the end, he'd made the wrong choice, trying to use the Wishing Stone to bring her back. He'd betrayed them… and yet, she couldn't hate him for it. Not when she understood that kind of pain. She had forgiven him. But the ache of it lingered, sharp as the mountain wind. She missed what they'd had before it all fell apart, even if she could never have it back.

Determined, Selaina knew she needed to find a place to rest, to calm her mind and prepare her body for the final ascent at dawn. First, she needed to locate the road; the unknown gnawed at her nerves, making any sleep impossible until she knew her direction. Quickening her pace, she wove through the thinning trees until she reached a peculiar rock formation that loomed like a guardian of forgotten times.

It was a weathered statue, carved from stone. The features of its face had been nearly erased by the passage of centuries, leaving only vague hints of humanity. Was it a man or a woman? Selaina couldn't tell. She brushed away the snow clinging to the statue, her fingertips tingling as if the stone held some lingering essence. When she looked up, a shadow in the distance caught her eye, a Nadrok, standing in the gloom, barely visible beneath the trees. Its cold, unwavering gaze rooted her to the spot, intensifying the isolation that weighed on her spirit.

With a shiver, Selaina pressed on, moving across the clearing until she discovered a winding path threading through the forest. Relief glimmered inside her, though it was faint and fleeting. Even with the path guiding her steps, there was no comfort to be found in the deep, whispering woods.

The forest twisted around her, the trees seeming to shift and breathe with a will of their own. Shadows lengthened and coiled, dancing at the edge of her vision like living things. Selaina halted, her pulse pounding in her ears as she scanned the encroaching darkness. A silhouette flitted behind a gnarled oak, vanishing before she could focus. The Nadrok were everywhere now, their ghostly forms whispering in and out of the moonlit gloom, their presence oppressive and suffocating.

A narrow wooden bridge arched over a stream, its surface dark and icy, and Selaina crossed it quickly, feeling the weight of unseen eyes upon her. The woods parted, and she emerged into a wide clearing where a frozen lake stretched out like a mirror of polished obsidian, reflecting the pale moonlight. The air was crisp, almost brittle, and carried a crackling, unnatural energy that set her nerves on edge.

Beyond the lake, the cliff walls rose like towering sentinels, splitting into two jagged peaks that loomed ominously close together, as though the mountain had been wrenched apart by some ancient force. One peak soared higher than the other, its summit veiled in cloud, while the lower peak cast sharp shadows across the frozen expanse. A faint outline of a winding path etched its way up the nearer peak, disappearing into the darkness of the craggy ascent.

Selaina stumbled back, desperation driving her back toward the trees. But before she could vanish into their cover, a voice cut through the stillness, lilting and sinister, sending a chill down her spine.

"Oh, come now, dear. Where do you think you can hide?" Gwenna's voice was sweet as poison, and her eyes glinted with cruel amusement. "The night has eyes, and its gaze is mine."

The forest seemed to twist and warp as Gwenna stepped out of the dark gateway, her silhouette framed by the restless, swirling shadows. She strode around the edge of the frozen lake, her boots cracking the thin layer of frost that formed along the shore. The Nadrok hovered at the lake's edge, their unblinking forms an ominous presence fixed on Selaina's every move.

With a wave of Gwenna's hand, the air itself seemed to ripple, and the frozen lake groaned under an unseen, oppressive weight. The Nadrok remained motionless, silent and watchful, their forms almost merging with the shadows that stretched across the clearing. Gwenna's smile deepened, her predatory eyes locking onto Selaina.

Selaina's breathing turned shallow, each inhale thin and strained, knowing that running would only delay the inevitable. Her heart pounding, she pulled her bow from her sling, plucking one of her few remaining arrows and taking aim at Gwenna. The wood of the bow creaked under the strain, echoing the tension that filled the air.

"I have no plans to harm you," Gwenna said, her smile widening. "You've made yourself far too valuable for that."

The Nadrok began to spread out, forming a loose circle around Selaina and Gwenna. Selaina's fingers trembled on the bowstring, and she steadied herself with a deep breath, knowing that an arrow alone would not defeat Gwenna. She had to wait, bide her time for the right moment to act.

"I only wish for you to meet someone," Gwenna continued, her voice as smooth as silk. "Someone quite powerful. Someone who can help you achieve everything you've ever wanted."

Selaina held her ground, her gaze never wavering from Gwenna. The Nadrok began to break their circle, closing in behind her, their forms a creeping, silent threat.

"Will you come willingly?" Gwenna asked, her eyes widening in a mockery of innocence.

Selaina pulled back the bowstring even further, the strain making her arms ache.

"I see you need a little motivation," Gwenna said, her voice turning cold. Flames erupted around them, branching off in chaotic patterns.

The fire hissed and cracked, melting the snow beneath Selaina's boots. Heat pressed in on all sides, stifling and thick. She released the arrow, watched it vanish in a burst of flame before it ever touched Gwenna. Ash drifted down like cursed snowfall.

Gwenna didn't even flinch. She brushed the soot from her cheek, smiling like a cat that had already won.

Selaina lowered her arms, her breath shallow. Around her, the Nadrok moved, silent shapes gliding closer through the smoke and firelight. Her every instinct screamed at her to run, to fight, to do something, but her body felt heavy, paralyzed by the weight of doubt. She had imagined that being Zhal Evurah would come with power, with clarity. But right now, all she had was a racing heart and a bow that achieved nothing.

She backed up a step, flames curling high behind her. Gwenna calmly waited. The Nadrok closed in, gliding like smoke across the ice.

Selaina's hand slipped to the talisman Myrradin had left behind. It pressed against her chest through her cloak, cool to the touch. She didn't know what it did, didn't know how it worked, or if it even would, but it was the only thing she had left.

A sudden gust of wind tore through the clearing, snuffing out the nearest flames and carrying Selaina into the air. The world spun as dark clouds gathered above, the sky roaring with newfound fury. Gwenna sent bursts of flames that spidered through the air in all directions, igniting the Windraith. Myrradin emerged from the wind, his robes aflame, and they both plummeted toward the frozen lake. Ice cracked beneath them as they crashed into the frigid water. The flames hissed as they met the lake's frozen crust, steam rising in ghostly tendrils that blurred the line between fire and ice.

Selaina gasped as the icy cold pierced her skin, her limbs heavy and numb. Her limbs felt as heavy as stone, the icy water stealing the last of her strength, and the burning flames stung her face, the heat searing through the thin fabric of her clothes. She clawed at the ice, her fingernails scraping against the slick surface, but she kept slipping back into the water. Gathering the last of her strength, she braced herself for one final push to pull herself up. A sudden force from behind shoved her upward, and she slid onto the frozen crust.

Her chest heaving, Selaina crawled across the ice, the Nadrok moving through the wall of flames, advancing toward her.

"Myrradin!" Gwenna's voice rang out, sharp with disdain. "How nice of you to join us."

Myrradin lay flat on his back, his robes still smoldering from the fire. He sucked in deep, ragged breaths, his face etched with pain. Gwenna stood at the lake's edge, her eyes narrowing as she assessed the situation, but she did not dare step onto the ice.

Selaina's eyes locked onto her bow, lying on the ice, and a fragile, wavering hope ignited in her chest. She forced herself to stand, every movement weighed down by her sodden clothes and the cold that was seeping into her bones. Her breath came in shallow gasps, and she fought the urge to collapse. On the shore, Gwenna waited, her gaze unyielding, as the Nadrok began to shift, moving to encircle Selaina once more.

"Myrradin…" Selaina called out, her voice cracking with desperation.

Only the sound of his ragged breathing came in reply, weak and fading. Panic clawed at her stomach, threatening to shred the last scraps of her courage. What could she do? Her arrows were useless against Gwenna's flames, and every second she wasted felt like a step closer to ruin.

Selaina reached into her quiver, fingers trembling, her breath shallow with panic. Nothing. Just the biting touch of cold air and the scratch of empty fabric. The last of her arrows were gone, lost to the lake, to fire, to futility. Her heart clenched as the weight of helplessness crushed down on her chest. No more weapons. No more chances. Gwenna was rising again. Myrradin still lay motionless on the ice. And Selaina, she was out of time.

But something in her refused to accept that this was the end.

She lifted her bow anyway.

Her hand moved by instinct, drawing the string back with no arrow to nock, the creak of the bow like a cry of defiance against fate itself. She imagined the shot, felt it, her body remembering the rhythm even as logic screamed it was pointless. Maybe Gwenna wouldn't notice. Maybe this one bluff would buy a breath more time.

Then the air around her changed.

It thickened, crackled, shivered. A blue light sparked at her fingertips, small at first, like the glimmer of starlight. But it grew. It gathered.

Power flowed into the space between her fingers and the drawn string, an arrow made not of wood or steel, but of shimmering energy, radiant and humming with unseen force. It pulsed in rhythm with her heartbeat, resonating with something ancient inside her. Her eyes widened as she stared down the shaft of a weapon born not from the world, but from within.

A tremor of awe passed through her.

She released the bowstring.

The arrow of energy exploded forward, pure light against the cold, slicing through the clearing like a streak of divine vengeance. Gwenna's eyes snapped wide as she conjured flames to intercept it, but too late. The arrow tore through the fire, untouched by the heat, and struck her open palm.

There was a burst of light, sharp and blinding.

Gwenna cried out, stumbling back as smoke curled from her fingers. Her flames sputtered, momentarily broken. Her expression, once amused and composed, twisted into something raw, human. Pain and disbelief. She clutched her hand, staggering. Selaina didn't even have time to marvel at it. Myrradin was stirring.

She reached again for that power, for another arrow of light, but the glow in her hands wavered and failed. Nothing came. She was drained. Empty.

Across the ice, Gwenna's face contorted with fury. Her flames roared back to life, billowing in great arcs around her. With a scream of rage, she thrust her hands forward, unleashing a wall of fire that surged toward Myrradin, molten and fast.

Selaina's voice caught in her throat as she watched the inferno race toward him, certain the ice beneath would give, that he'd be swallowed whole by fire and freezing water.

But she'd tasted the power now.

And something had changed.

Myrradin gathered his strength. Hope surged like a storm inside her. She had to strike again.

She drew back the bowstring, her breath shaky, heart pounding. This time, the glow came faster, less hesitant. Another arrow of blue energy surged into being, brighter than before. She released it with a cry, the shot streaking through the air like a lance of light.

But Gwenna was ready.

Snarling, she thrust both hands forward and caught the energy bolt in mid air, focusing her flames into an intense burst of crackling shadow and heat. The arrow shattered in a burst of sparks against her spellwork, its remnants hissing as they scattered across the ice.

Her lips curled into a sneer, fingers still smoldering from the earlier wound.

"Clever," she spat, voice thick with malice. "But tricks like that only work once."

A sudden flare devoured Gwenna's sleeve, her own fire turning against her. She cried out, staggering, but the sound twisted, rising into laughter, wild and jagged. Flames curled back into her hands like tame serpents, and she cradled them with reverence, her eyes gleaming with madness.

Around Selaina, the Nadrok began to close in, silent and fluid, their forms sliding between shadow and shape. They circled her like wolves, their movements nearly imperceptible but utterly inescapable.

With a savage flick of her wrist, Gwenna hurled another wave of fire toward Myrradin. It roared across the lake, but his wind met it head-on. The clash erupted into a vortex of heat and cold, fire spiraling into air that screamed across the ice, shattering and steaming beneath their fury.

Selaina seized the moment. She bolted across the slick surface toward the edge of solid ground, her boots skidding, breath burning in her lungs.

The Nadrok surged to follow, their shifting bodies gliding like liquid shadow.

She raised her bow and loosed a shot of blue light at the nearest one, but even the arrow of energy passed straight through, slicing empty air. The Nadrok's form rippled, unaffected. Panic flared in Selaina's chest.

No more tricks. No more power.

She dropped her bow and tore a knife from beneath her cloak, gripping the hilt with trembling fingers. The cold metal felt heavier than it should, weighted by fear. Her back to the ice, shadows creeping in, Selaina braced herself.

With a focused swing, Selaina slashed at the nearest Nadrok. Her blade vanished into its shadowed form as though striking mist. But it wasn't mist, it was absence. The void swallowed her arm up to the elbow, cold racing along her skin like fingers of frost threading through her veins.

She jerked back, but something, some echo, held her fast. Not physically. Inwardly.

A pulse stirred within the darkness.

It aligned with her heartbeat for one sharp instant, then slipped out of rhythm, rippling like a memory dropped into deep water. And in that ripple came a sensation she hadn't felt since the Wishing Stone: a weightless pull, vast and ancient, stretching far beyond her body or mind. It wasn't pain. It wasn't warmth. It was recognition, a pressure behind the eyes, a strange ache in the chest, as though her soul had touched something outside of time.

Her breath held. Her vision fractured.

No eyes to meet. No mind to read. And yet her sight, her strange, gifted sight, reached. Not outward, but inward. Not into thought, but into possibility. It wasn't just a connection. It was a collision.

Was the Nadrok aware of this too? Did it feel the same pull? Or was she alone in this sudden fracture of time and meaning? She had connected with others before, but this felt... older. Deeper. Stranger.

Why had she never felt this before, the other times she'd seen them? What had changed? Was it her power? The Wishing Stone? Or something inside the Nadrok themselves?

Suddenly, the world around Selaina fractured like glass. Time itself seemed to splinter and slow, and she stumbled into a landscape that defied reality, a swirling chaos where light and shadow coiled together in an eerie dance. The sky was a shattered canvas of drifting stars, each fragment glowing with spectral light, while the ground was a patchwork of reflective shards, mirroring memories that shimmered and twisted in the void.

Her mind tensed as she took a hesitant step forward. Before her, a young woman knelt in a halo of ghostly light, cradling an infant in her arms. The mother's lips moved in a silent lullaby, her eyes brimming with love and longing. Selaina could almost feel her desperation, the sheer force of a mother's will to comfort her child. The woman's form fluttered, and then she vanished, leaving behind only the lingering ache of an unfinished song.

The vision shifted. Selaina found herself amidst a swirling mist on a spectral battlefield. Ethereal warriors charged into battle, their armor gleaming with a pale, ghostly sheen. One soldier, a noble ferocity etched on his face, raised his sword high, his movements confident and full of purpose. Yet, as his blade descended, his body dissolved into vapor, as if he had never existed. The battle around him unraveled, the warriors fading like a dream dissipating at dawn.

Scene after scene unfolded, each more haunting than the last. A scholar hunched over an ancient tome, the glowing text slipping between his fingers like sand. His eyes widened with unspoken knowledge, but before he could grasp the truth he sought, he vanished, leaving only the echo of his yearning imprinted on the air.

Selaina's mind reeled. The visions surrounded her, fragments of lives that had almost been, souls flaring like fireflies trapped between worlds. The weight of their loss bore down on her, and she stumbled forward, her heart aching. The echoes of those never-lived moments whispered to her, pulling her deeper into the enigma of their existence.

Then, she stood in a crystalline hall, its walls pulsing with a blue, living light. At the center, a cloaked figure hovered over the Wishing Stone, its jagged form glowing with an almost sentient energy. The figure reached out, and Selaina felt the force of a wish, so powerful, so desperate that it reshaped reality itself. Time twisted, paths were rewritten, and destinies were unmade. For every wish granted, a ripple of erasure followed: a child never born, a hero never needed, a life unlived.

The souls she had seen, the mother, the soldier, the scholar, were undone again and again, their potential snuffed out with each change. Selaina clutched her chest, the truth crashing over her like a wave. The Nadrok weren't just shadows; they were the cost, the remnants of those rewritten by the Wishing Stone's power. They were the neverborn, lives erased in the wake of selfish desires and altered fates.

As the vision splintered, the crystalline ground cracked beneath her feet, and Selaina tumbled back into the icy reality of the frozen lake. Her knees struck the ice, and she gasped, each breath a desperate gulp of cold air.

She looked up at the Nadrok with new eyes, understanding and sorrow entwined in her heart. These weren't mindless phantoms or agents of darkness. They were lost souls, chained to the whims of fate and bound by magic they never chose. And somehow, Selaina knew she carried a piece of that power inside her, the Wishing Stone's legacy burning like a brand against her skin.

CHAPTER 44

RYKAN'S HAND TREMBLED as it hovered above Embryss, its crimson glow pulsing in time with a sinister, unspoken rhythm that seemed to resonate in his chest. The shard sat nestled in the snow, its light casting faint, jagged shadows that flickered like dying embers. Around him, drops of bloodshadow from the remains of Arathain bled into the ground, the dark liquid pooling into inky tendrils that crawled with an unnerving, purposeful motion.

His gaze dropped to his arm, where the jagged wound left by the maugwin wept its own dark ichor. The viscous liquid mingled with the fresh snow, the flakes hissing softly as they melted on contact, leaving faint trails of steam curling into the cold air. Each heartbeat sent a dull, throbbing ache through his arm, as though the shard's malevolence was already reaching for him, waiting for him to take it.

Gritting his teeth, Rykan snatched up Embryss and slipped it into his satchel. The shard's cold energy surged through the leather like a current, but it was the searing jolt in his arm that made him gasp. His wound, where the maugwin had bitten him, flared with pain, the bloodshadow pulsing as if answering the shard's call.

It wasn't just heat or cold. It was recognition. As if Embryss knew the wound, had touched it before, and now sought to reclaim it. The sting was deep and strange, like fire spreading inside the bone.

He clenched his jaw and forced the satchel shut.

He twirled the pommel of his sword in his grip, readjusting his hold and willing strength back into his weary limbs. Snow crunched beneath his boots as he forced himself forward, but as he drew closer, the cacophony of the fight began to shift, the maugwins' cries dwindling into a tense, unsettling quiet. Panic surged in Rykan's chest, was it over, or were they running out of time?

He dug his feet into the snow and pushed himself into a sprint, heart pounding, the cold air biting at his face. The campsite loomed ahead, and dread twisted his gut as he prepared for whatever awaited him.

When Rykan arrived, he found Garrick, Nadara, and Ysadora finishing off the last of the maugwins. Ysadora, despite her ruined hand, fought fiercely, her broken staff channeling her magic to force jagged rocks through the snow, trapping one of the shadowy beasts. Garrick stepped in with a clean slash of his sword, and before the creature could regenerate, Nadara thrust her glaive into it, ending its existence.

"Rykan!" Nadara called, her eyes lighting up with relief. "What happened?"

Rykan reached into his satchel and pulled out Embryss, holding the pulsing crystal aloft.

"You got it back!" Nadara said, a mixture of awe and disbelief on her face. "Does that mean… is Arathain dead?"

"How did you manage to defeat him?" Ysadora asked, her voice tight with exhaustion but laced with curiosity. Her uninjured hand rested over her withered one, as if shielding it from the cold or the gaze of the group.

Rykan's grip on Embryss stiffened. The image of Arathain's transformation, the twisting, the rupture, the light, seared itself into his mind. "He won't be coming back," he said softly.

Using their weapons, the four of them worked together to dig a grave for Kadin. The frozen earth fought back, but their determination held firm. When the hole was finally ready, they lay Kadin to rest, his daggers crossed over his chest as if he were still guarding them in death. Ysadora raised a slab of stone through the snow with trembling hands, wincing as the injured one twitched involuntarily. She shaped the stone into a rough but sturdy tombstone.

They stood around the grave in reverent silence, the icy wind biting at their faces. Each of them offered their own quiet farewell, the weight of loss heavy in the air. Kadin's sharp wit and courage had been a constant presence, and now, his absence left an aching void.

"I keep waiting for Kadin to make some clever remark about all this," Ysadora said softly, her voice breaking the silence. She looked down at the freshly turned earth, her expression distant. "Only to remember... he's really gone."

"I wonder what he would say right now, if he could see us?" Nadara asked, her voice quieter than usual.

"Probably something about how bad of a job we did on his grave," Garrick said, a faint smile tugging at his lips.

Ysadora let out a breathy chuckle, her lips trembling. "Yeah, that sounds about right."

"In Zalorin, we say that every weapon carries the soul of its maker," Nadara added quietly. "If you forged with anger, the blade would be cruel. If you forged with care..." Her voice trailed off, then steadied. "I think Kadin's soul would have made a clever sword."

Garrick shifted his stance, arms crossed tight. "For someone who was always pretending he didn't care about anyone, he died proving otherwise."

No one replied. The ache in the silence said enough.

Rykan nodded silently, his gaze fixed on the grave. Even thinking about Selaina, usually a source of hope, brought him no comfort. She was still in Myrradin's clutches, and every passing moment made the weight of their task feel heavier. The only thing keeping him upright was the determination to find her and set her free, before it was too late.

After a few moments, they turned away, their steps slow and heavy as they prepared to continue their journey. They couldn't stop now. Elysia and Kadin had both died to get them this far. Even Darian, in his own way, had been sacrificed for their cause. To falter now would dishonor their memory.

Nadara extended her hand, her gaze meeting his with silent pleading. Rykan hesitated only a moment before passing Embryss back to her.

"Be very careful," he murmured. She nodded solemnly, tucking the shard carefully into her bag.

Rykan sheathed his sword and collapsed into the snow with a weary exhale, the bloodshadow still seeping from the wound on his arm, staining the pristine white beneath him.

"That bite will never heal, will it?" Nadara said, concern clouding her features. "Are you ever going to use that stuff on it?"

"What stuff?" Rykan asked, trying to catch his breath.

"The water from Nereathe. The stuff Liora gave you," Nadara reminded him.

Rykan's brow furrowed. "I'd almost forgotten," he admitted, pulling out the small vial from his satchel. "It's only a single drop. I hate the idea of using it up."

"If Arathain is gone," Nadara said hopefully, "maybe we won't have to worry about the maugwins hunting us anymore."

Rykan's gaze drifted to Ysadora. She sat with her knees pulled up, staring vacantly at her ruined hand. The withered, shadow-twisted limb hung uselessly at her side, her blank expression laced with a quiet, defeated pain. The sight stirred something heavy and unresolved in Rykan's chest. He knew how strong she was, how much she'd overcome in her life, but seeing her like this, so broken, it struck a chord he couldn't ignore.

He held the vial, feeling the cool glass press into his fingers. The water from Nereathe held mysterious power, but he had no way of knowing if it could truly restore her hand. Maybe it wouldn't change her fate at all. But if it could at least cleanse the bloodshadow, ease her pain, even a small relief would be something. The idea of using it on himself felt selfish, a pang of guilt twisting in his gut. Without further thought, he rose and stepped toward Ysadora.

"Let me see your hand," he said softly.

Ysadora's head snapped up, anger flashing in her eyes. "No," she snapped. "What are you doing?"

Rykan knelt beside her, his eyes conveying conviction and concern. "Just trust me," he insisted.

Gently, he reached for her wrist, feeling her resistance tense through her skin. When her eyes met his, her posture softened, slumping with reluctant resignation.

He tilted the vial over her mangled hand, feeling a tangle of emotions: a fragile, quiet hope countered by biting, nagging uncertainty.

"You're supposed to use it on your wound," she murmured, her voice cracking, as if she could barely hold back her own pain.

Ignoring her protest, Rykan tilted the vial and let the drop fall onto the shadow-tainted flesh of Ysadora's hand. It shimmered like liquid starlight, vanishing into her withered skin. For a heartbeat, nothing happened, just the cold, empty stillness of the snowy clearing.

Then, a molten silver glow began to spread from the point of contact, radiating outward like quicksilver vines creeping over the gnarled surface of Ysadora's hand. The dark, twisted flesh seemed to melt away under the metal's touch, dissolving into shimmering light. The silver overtook the corruption, searing away the bloodshadow tendrils as though purging an ancient curse.

The transformation wasn't smooth but rippled like molten metal poured into a mold, reshaping bone and muscle into something beautiful yet otherworldly. The reflective surface captured the pale moonlight, gleaming with an ethereal brilliance. Her remaining two fingers uncurled, molding back into their normal shape.

Ysadora's eyes widened in shock, her breath caught in her throat. "It doesn't hurt anymore," she whispered, awe and fear lacing her voice. She flexed the fingers and what was left of her thumb. "Stronger than ever," she said.

A tentative smile broke across her face, her expression a mixture of wonder and disbelief. She wiggled her metallic fingers, the silvery surface catching the light, and her joy bloomed in the wake of so much loss.

Rykan watched with a sense of wonder and hope, feeling a warmth spread through his chest at the sight of her amazement and newfound strength. Ysadora touched her new hand, grasping it with her other one, testing it.

Garrick, who had been tending to a wound on his arm, let out a low whistle. "Now that's something you don't see every day," he said, eyes wide with awe. "Is it… really metal?" He took a hesitant step closer, marveling at the way Ysadora's new hand gleamed in the light.

Nadara's eyes lit up as she approached, her glaive still in hand. "Incredible," she murmured. "We needed some good for a change." She gave Rykan a meaningful look, her gratitude clear.

Garrick paused in wiping the bloodshadow from his sword, his hardened expression softening. "You've given her hope," he said, his voice rough with unexpected emotion. "But what are you going to do about your wound?"

Rykan glanced down at his arm, the skin stretched and broken around it. He wiped away some of the strange thick dark blood oozing up to the surface. "Keep it clean, I guess," he said.

He took a breath and turned to Nadara, a new sense of urgency settling over him.

"There's something else," he said, his voice low. "Something I need to show you real quick before we get back on the road. It's where Arathain took me… it's not far."

Nadara's smile faded, replaced by a look of concern. She straightened, gripping her glaive. "Show me," she said with a steady voice.

Rykan led the way, his steps crunching through the snow, his mind still racing from the events that had just unfolded. As they climbed a gentle slope and wove through a grove of snow-laden trees, he could feel the tension building. The air grew colder, heavier, as if something unseen was pressing down on them, and a faint, acrid scent lingered in the air, like burnt wood mixed with iron.

At last, they emerged into a small clearing where the single dead tree stood like a sentinel over the snow. Its branches reached skyward like brittle bones, its bark cracked and gray as if all life had been drained from it long ago. At its base, dark red flames coiled, not burning, but bleeding, from a split in the bark that pulsed like a living wound. The flames licked upward in slow, sinuous patterns, casting twisted shadows that danced like serpents across the snow.

It wasn't just surrounded by magic, it was fused with it. The portal churned from the wound itself, thick as congealed blood, its surface reflecting streaks of broken color and light. It wasn't housed in the tree, it was the tree, grown around the corruption like scar tissue feeding on rot.

A low groan echoed from within, and Rykan felt it in his bones, as though the tree remembered what it had once been… and despised what it had become.

Nadara's breath caught. "That tree…" she whispered, her voice conveying disbelief. "It looks dead, like it's had all the life drained from it, just like the one in my village." She turned to Rykan, a chill of understanding dawning in her eyes. "This is one of the Dreylith Wards."

Rykan nodded, the unease he'd felt earlier returning full force. "I thought it might be," he said.

"What is this… this magic on it?" Nadara asked, her gaze locked on the dark red flames that shifted and crackled with a life of their own.

"I'm not sure," said Rykan, recalling his experience with the burning tree in the mountains. "But don't touch it." Ever since he had reached out to that tree, he had been having nightmares. He had been connected to Nociferon and Pandemora.

Nadara frowned, her hand moving toward the satchel at her side. "If it's been corrupted, maybe we can undo it." She pulled out Embryss, its crimson glow pulsing like a heartbeat in the gloom. "Like the stranger wanted to do."

"No… Nadara, I told you how dangerous that is," Rykan warned, stepping closer. "Liora said the same thing. You should have seen what it did to Arathain."

Nadara's jaw tensed. "When I was taken by the Iron Flood, all I thought about was how I had wasted my life," she said, her voice thick with remembered pain. "How I was going to die and no one would remember me. Once those who knew me faded, my existence would never have mattered. Every thought I had would be gone, as if they were all pointless, as if life was pointless. But when you freed me, I got a second chance, a chance for purpose, for my life to mean something. I have to try. To see if this can be my purpose."

"Nadara, of course you matter," Rykan said earnestly, his voice cracking as his fingers fidgeted at the leather wraps on his wrist, not daring to look directly at her. "We wouldn't have made it this far without you."

She shook her head, determination hardening her features. "That is Selaina's destiny, not mine. I believe that I, and you as well, both have our own destinies, not just as part of Selaina's." As she spoke, her fingers moved to the edge of her satchel, checking its contents with a sharpness that had nothing to do with organization, like she was preparing for a fight that might never come.

"But the man you took Embryss from, the stranger," Rykan countered, his concern deepening. "He died from whatever he was trying to do with it. We need to know more before you try to use it."

Nadara's eyes narrowed, a faint smile playing at her lips. "Since when are you so cautious? It's my choice, and I choose to try it."

Rykan's stomach clenched as Nadara moved toward the tree, Embryss clutched in her hand. The flames around the trunk flared wildly, reacting to her presence, twisting and writhing like serpents ready to strike. As she approached, Rykan's gaze drifted to a hollowed knothole in the tree. Inside, something strange and unsettling stirred. Jagged formations, like mountainous spires, shifted and ground together as if struggling to align, only to collapse and reform. Colors of deep red bled into vivid purples, with streaks of gold that crackled and forked like chaotic lightning. Dark skies fractured like splintered glass, and shadows seeped through the breaks, bleeding into a void of swirling chaos.

A voice emerged from the swirling ash within the tree, distant at first, a roar that softened into a chilling whisper that seemed to breathe right into Rykan's ear.

"Rykan, my faithful servant," it breathed, each word a tendril wrapping around his mind. "Keep her from the tree. This is your final chance to prove your worth to me."

Before he could process the command, his hand inched toward the hilt of his sword, compelled by a darkness that felt like an extension of his own shadow. The voice of Nociferon clenched down on his thoughts, relentless.

"She must not touch it," the voice insisted, laced with a promise of ruin. "Think of your father, your precious city, Selaina, the things you crave most. They hang by a thread, and only your obedience can keep them from falling away."

The voice deepened, echoing with a note of finality. "Fail me, and you will have nothing. When my victory comes, you will drift for all eternity, lost and formless in the endless void, a soul without purpose, trapped in the darkness you fear most."

Images of the past ignited through his mind, choices that had always seemed unavoidable. The weight of his past mistakes pressed on him, and he gripped the sword's hilt. But then, Nadara's voice broke through the storm of fear and doubt. A memory of her words from a moment ago.

I believe that I... and you as well, both have our own destinies, not just as part of Selaina's.

Rykan hesitated. If what Nadara said was true, what did he truly want his destiny to be? To become a puppet of chaos, serving a power that only promised destruction, or to blindly uphold order at any cost? The tension in his arm eased. His fingers, wrapped around the hilt, slowly released their hold. The blade slid back into the sheath, and the pull of Nociferon's voice weakened, dissipating into the frigid air.

Nadara stepped closer to the tree, Embryss glowing in her hand. The flames around the trunk surged, sensing its presence, not like a weapon, but like a long-lost piece returning to the whole.

She hesitated, her breath catching. "I don't know if—"

Before she could finish, the shard tugged her forward, as if drawn by something inside the tree. Her hand clenched instinctively, but it was no use, Embryss pulled itself from her fingers and slammed into the bark with a low, resonant thud.

The response was immediate.

A deep groan rippled through the tree, followed by a surge of energy that spilled outward in waves of pulsing light. Rykan staggered back, shielding his eyes as color bled into the cracked bark, ashen gray turning rich and vibrant, as if the very blood of the world were flowing back into it.

Then, with a slow, pulsing breath, the tree released Embryss.

It slid from the bark as if exhaled, tumbling into the grass below.

Where it landed, the grass curled unnaturally, coiling in tight spirals, its color deepening into shades of crimson and violet. The blades shimmered with a faint, oily sheen, as if something in the shard's essence had rewritten their nature, not growth, but mutation. A reminder that, while the tree had healed, Embryss was still a fragment of something far more dangerous. Something not meant for mortal hands.

Rykan turned to Nadara, stunned. She was unharmed, wide-eyed, trembling, staring at the transformed giant before them.

"The tree used it," she whispered. "It took Embryss." Her voice was filled with awe, and fear.

The branches above swayed as if exhaling for the first time in centuries. Beneath their feet, the ground pulsed once, faint but certain. Something had returned. Something that had been sleeping... and no longer was.

Rykan turned his head, his hand inching toward his weapon as a chill crept up his spine. "Did you feel that?" he whispered.

Nadara's fingers clutched Embryss. "Yes," she replied, her voice barely audible, as if afraid to disturb the quiet. "It feels like… we aren't alone."

And from deep within the woods, a whisper, too faint to be real, curled through the air. A whisper of something waiting, something that had been disturbed and was now stirring in the shadows.

CHAPTER 45

THE NADROK CIRCLED closer, their spectral forms swirling in tighter arcs around Gwenna, their movement like a noose slowly constricting. Selaina's chest tensed, her heart aching with the weight of what she now understood about their existence, a shadowy half-life tethered to forces they could not escape.

The Nadrok closed in, forming an eerie circle around Gwenna, their shadows moving in tight synchronization, silent, soulless, obedient. Selaina braced herself, trembling. She could feel their presence now in a way she never had before, not just as figures in the mist but as something deeper.

Around her, the world had not gone silent, but it felt removed, distant. Myrradin and Gwenna battled nearby, his spiraling winds clashing with her arcane fire, but to Selaina, their movements seemed slowed, suspended. As if time itself was holding its breath.

Something was happening. She was still tethered to the Nadrok, not just their shadows, but their absence, their lost place in the world. Somehow, in reaching for what they could have been, she had stepped into the empty space where they should have existed. Time frayed at the edges around her. Not broken, but uncertain.

Then, something caught her eye, just beyond normal sight. Threads.

Faint as spider silk, strands of dark magic shimmered in the air, tethering each Nadrok to Gwenna's outstretched hands. Not literal strings, but something older, something binding. Gwenna's will ran through them like puppeteer threads, anchoring her command deep into their formless bodies.

Selaina's pulse quickened. This wasn't just power. It was control.

And maybe… maybe it could be undone.

She drew in a breath and reached out, not with her bow, not with her blade, but with the same part of her that had once seen into the Wishing Stone. The same part that had touched a Nadrok's shadow and glimpsed what it could have been. A child. A soldier. A mother. A poet. A soul never allowed to be born.

She closed her eyes and pulled that vision forward, not memory, but potential, and pushed it through the tether like a flood of light pouring into an old wound. The thread snapped.

The Nadrok halted, its form wavering. For the first time, it didn't move. It didn't obey.

One tether broken.

Selaina cried out softly and reached for the next. Each connection fought her, since Gwenna's magic wasn't just embedded, it was entangled. But Selaina shoved the weight of possibility through it, pouring into them what they might have been, what they should have been, until the thread burst into light and dissolved.

Two. Three. Four.

Sweat beaded on her brow. Her limbs shook. Every snap of a thread sent pain lancing behind her eyes, like her soul was being stretched too thin. But she kept going. Not with hatred. Not with violence. With recognition.

Across the ice, the Nadrok had stopped moving.

Gwenna's arms tensed, her lips parting in disbelief. "What are you doing?" she hissed, her control slipping like water through clenched fists. "They are mine!"

"No," Selaina said, breathless, "they were never yours."

The last tether snapped, and the final Nadrok froze. Slowly, it turned, not to Gwenna, but to Selaina. Then another. Then all of them.

They weren't her shadows anymore.

They were something else.

As Gwenna continued to engage Myrradin, she staggered, sensing her power slipping away. Her eyes blazed with fury and disbelief, wide with the horror of realizing she had lost her hold. The web of magic she had woven so carefully unraveled before her, each thread snapping under Selaina's influence. Shadows blustered wildly around her as the Nadrok turned to face her, their spectral forms closing in.

"No!" Gwenna shrieked, her voice cracking. Panic twisted her features, and she stumbled back, her hands raised as if to ward them off. "Take the girl as I commanded!" she roared, desperation leaking into her tone.

But the Nadrok paid her no mind. They glided closer, no longer heeding her will, no longer enslaved by her commands.

The Nadrok began to meld together, forming a massive, shapeless shadowgate that twisted and bent around Gwenna. The gateway pulsed with an ominous energy, its edges curling inward like a monstrous jaw about to snap shut. For the first time, Gwenna seemed truly afraid, her eyes darting about as she realized the Nadrok were no longer under her control.

Gwenna's eyes went wide, terror replacing fury. "Not me! The girl!" she screamed, her voice rising in desperation. The shadowgate loomed around her, its darkness creeping in with a will of its own. "Where are you taking me?" she demanded, her voice breaking. "I command you—"

But her words faltered as the gateway closed in. This time, it was the Nadrok choosing where to take her, the silent, vengeful will of those who had once been her unwitting tools now directing her fate.

Myrradin didn't move. He only watched as the Nadrok delivered their judgment, the shadows swallowing Gwenna whole.

The Nadrok dissolved from their collective form, returning to their individual shapes. They turned to Selaina, their gazes lingering, full of something deeper than menace, an understanding, a gratitude, or perhaps a silent farewell.

Then, without a sound, they melted back into the forest shadows, their presence fading until only the stillness and the faint scent of magic lingered. Myrradin's shoulders slumped, and his breath came in ragged gasps, as though the weight of Gwenna's power had pressed the strength from his very bones. He tried to sit down gracefully, but ended up collapsing to the ground. The blanket of snow caught most of the impact, but prompted Selaina to hurry to his side.

"What was that?" Myrradin asked. "What did you do?"

"I gave them a choice." Selaina's voice wavered, her heart heavy with the sorrow of what she had seen. "I saw what they are. Shadows of a fate that never came to pass,' she whispered, haunted by the faces of those unfulfilled lives. "Consequences of those who dared to wield the Wishing Stone to change what fate had written. They were never given a chance to live. They had no will. I saw their potential and returned it to them."

"Very interesting," said Myrradin. "If only we could measure the times the Wishing Stone has been used and all it changed."

"And you would have had me use it," said Selaina. "What else would it have changed that you didn't understand?"

Myrradin's eyes narrowed, a shadow of regret rippling across his features. "We do the best we can with what we are given," he said. "The last Zhal Evurah wielded the Wishing Stone out of necessity. When Azragul shattered Ethyllion and broke into the mortal realm, that power was the only way to undo his devastation. Without him being sealed within the mountain, none of us would be here today." He paused, his voice dropping. "Sometimes there are no right choices, only necessary ones. You haven't yet faced the kind of difficult choices that others have had to make." His voice edged on something between accusation and regret.

Selaina's gripped the talisman hanging around her neck. "My life has been nothing but difficult choices since I met you," she retorted. She pulled the talisman from her neck and tossed it at him. "Did you come back for this?"

Myrradin dug the talisman out of the snow. Rising to his feet, he offered it back to her. "Keep it for now," he said, his tone gentle but firm. "We must see you to the summit, the world depends on it."

Selaina reluctantly took the talisman from Myrradin's hand, its cold, engraved surface pressing heavily into her palm.

"The Keeper and the Throne," said Myrradin as he turned his focus to the two spires that walled the other side of the lake.

Selaina looked past him to the sloping path ahead, which twisted its way upward along the sheer cliff face of the nearer spire. The trail hugged the jagged rock wall, clinging precariously to the mountain as it climbed toward the summit of this lower peak.

"You act as though you are forgiven," said Selaina. "I'm not going to the summit with you."

"You don't have to walk with me," said Myrradin. "But I am following you regardless. If anything happens to you, all hope is lost."

Selaina grabbed her bow from the snow, aiming it at Myrradin. She expected the energy to form an arrow in her hand like before, but nothing happened.

"We need to work on that," he said. "The Sky Serpents will need to see something in you. Or else they will never appear."

"I'm leaving," Selaina said flatly. "Do what you will."

She didn't look at him. Just turned and started up the path, her fingers locking around the talisman like she might crush it. Frost cracked beneath her boots as she moved, steady and alone in spirit, even if Myrradin trailed behind. He said nothing, his breath misting the air in slow clouds, his footsteps falling in deliberate silence.

The trail was narrow and unforgiving, zigzagging up the mountain's sheer face, forcing their focus on each step. Loose rock crumbled beneath their weight. The cliffs beside them gave way now and then to open sky, offering fleeting views of the world below, endless trees, ribbons of frozen river, the glinting shard of the lake where Gwenna had vanished.

Selaina stopped, her chest rising with sharp, controlled breaths. She turned just enough to catch a glimpse of the landscape behind them, distant and cold, like a life she'd stepped out of. Ahead, the jagged ridge-line loomed, close now. Too close to back out.

She didn't want to speak to Myrradin, but the question burned, and silence had never been a refuge for her.

"You mentioned before," she said, not looking at him, "that we'll have to face the Lord of Pandemora. Once I receive the Sky Serpents' blessing, how will we be ready to fight him?"

Myrradin's steps slowed beside her. "The blessing will strengthen what is already inside you—what you need, what you've sacrificed. Until you face your first battles with it, we won't know its full shape."

Selaina frowned, eyes narrowing at the ice-fringed ledge ahead. "I've already had moments. When I've been in danger… things happened. I didn't mean for them to."

"And you didn't control them," Myrradin said, almost smug. "Power without mastery is a danger to yourself and others."

Selaina turned her gaze forward again, but her jaw tensed. She didn't trust his tone, or his agenda. She kept walking, but a thought tugged at her, urgent and half-formed. That arrow she'd conjured during the fight with Gwenna… It had come from something deep inside her.

Not power. Not will. Something else.

She drew her bow without a word. No arrow waited in her quiver, only the memory of that moment. Her fingers tingled, the cold string beneath them pulsing with possibility.

She closed her eyes. Nothing came at first. Her breath stilled, the world around her quiet and unyielding. Then, somewhere below thought, she remembered Wekenwild, not its trees or its silence, but the way her feet had found the path before she knew it was there.

A rhythm.

A pattern beneath the chaos, pulling her like music carried on the bones of the earth.

That same pulse lived now at her core, quiet, steady, waiting. Not something she could summon. But something she could follow.

Her breath synced to it. Her grip adjusted. The bowstring felt like the next note in a melody already playing through her skin.

She exhaled and drew.

A flash of light. A pulse.

A blue arrow shimmered into being, no command, no force. Just alignment. It loosed as she released the breath she'd held too long, striking the cliff wall with a burst of energy, crackling across the stone like lightning frozen in place.

Selaina lowered her bow slowly, breath caught in her throat. She hadn't forced it. She'd simply remembered the song.

Behind her, Myrradin's voice was cool, unreadable. "Interesting," he said. "If you cannot find it yourself, you'll never control it. What matters isn't that it answers you once. It's whether it listens again."

Selaina felt the glow at her brow throb in response. She looked away, unsettled. She wasn't sure what disturbed her more, his answer, or how much he had seemed to enjoy withholding it.

She shook her head. "I don't crave power the way you do," she said, her voice quiet but firm. "I only wish to help save this world and its people."

Myrradin's eyes softened with something that might have been pity or understanding, or perhaps both. "Everyone craves power, my dear," he replied. "Only the reasons differ. You must be prepared for when the Sky Serpents bestow their gifts. You'll need discipline, mastery, or you risk becoming like Vatreus."

"I have to stop him," Selaina said, resolute. "And I still need to find my mother."

Myrradin's gaze hardened, a somber look settling over him. "If you had wisdom, you would let Vatreus continue to unite the kingdoms," he said. "Let him build his army. When the Lord of Pandemora rises, you could fight alongside him, brother and sister, wielding the power of Archeinor. It's the only way we stand a chance."

Selaina's eyes widened in disbelief. "You can't be serious," she said. "I'm not joining him. I made a promise to stop him and the Iron Flood. He's not uniting kingdoms, he's tearing them apart. What about all those who have been crushed beneath his boot? I fight for them."

Myrradin gave a weary sigh. "Perhaps you're not ready to hear the truth," he said. "I pray that, when you receive the blessing, it grants you the vision to understand what must be done."

Selaina stood, the weight of the conversation pressing heavily on her. She slipped her bow into the sling on her back and picked up her satchel. "I hope for the same," she said, her voice defiant. "But I doubt the outcome will align with your expectations."

With that, she turned and began walking up the path, the wind whispering through the mountain peaks. She almost wished Myrradin wouldn't follow, though she knew he would. She continued up the incline, pretending not to notice his presence, the things he had said still swirling in her mind. Seliana tried to clear those ideas, not wanting to cloud her thoughts with his confusion.

She paused mid-step, her heart pounding as a faint rumble reached her ears. The sound was distant but unmistakable, a low, growling vibration that made the ground feel momentarily alive beneath her feet. She glanced up at the towering cliffs that loomed over the winding path, dusted with snow and lined with jagged edges. The rumble grew louder, like a monster stirring from a long slumber.

"What is that?" she whispered, her voice barely carrying over the deepening noise.

Myrradin, who had been following close behind, immediately tensed. His eyes darted to the cliffs above, and his expression grew grave. "Avalanche," he said, the word like a stone dropping into the silence. "Move, now!"

Snow began to cascade from above, small streams turning into thundering waves. For a heartbeat, Selaina's breath froze in her lungs, her muscles locking as if the avalanche had already buried her. Myrradin grabbed her arm, pulling her into action. But as the snow roared down the mountainside, Selaina knew there was no way they could outrun it.

CHAPTER 46

THE WHISPER HUNG in the frigid air, unraveling slowly until it melted into the faint rustle of newly awakened leaves, their edges trembling in the faint breeze. Rykan's heart hammered in his chest, each beat reverberating in his ears like a distant drum, mirroring the restless energy that pulsed through the forest. The light from the revitalized tree spilled across the snow in strange, fluid patterns, casting shimmering ripples that danced like ghostly specters. Shadows stretched and coiled around the tree's base, their movements unsettlingly deliberate, as though the forest itself were alive and watching.

From the shadows emerged a being of awe-inspiring presence, tall and statuesque with an aura of timeless power. Its body appeared almost sculpted from living stone, but it wasn't entirely solid. Shimmering veins of blue and silver light pulsed through it like a heartbeat, and parts of its form seemed to waver, as if the being belonged to another plane of existence, only partially manifesting in the mortal realm. Its face was serene yet commanding, with eyes that glowed like twin stars, holding both ancient wisdom and an unyielding sense of duty.

But it was the wings that truly captured the essence of the creature's otherworldly nature. They unfolded in a mesmerizing display, stretching wide and shimmering with an ethereal brilliance. The wings appeared as if sculpted from translucent glass, with veins of glowing energy pulsing and swirling through them like liquid starlight. As the wings moved, they refracted the surrounding light, casting rainbow shards across the clearing. Each motion emitted a soft, resonant hum, a sound like the echo of a distant cosmic song. The being exuded a perfect blend of fragile grace and immense, otherworldly power, as if forever caught between realms.

Rykan and Nadara instinctively took a step back, Rykan's awe mingling with a primal fear that twisted deep in their chests. Rykan's hand curled around the hilt of his weapon, but he made no move to draw it, as if knowing that steel and strength would be useless here. His breath caught in his throat, and he could feel his pulse pounding, each beat echoing in his ears.

Nadara clutched Embryss closer to her chest, her hands trembling despite her attempts to appear strong. Her eyes were wide, reflecting the guardian's otherworldly glow.

The guardian's luminous eyes regarded them with an almost compassionate intensity. Its voice resonated through the air, deep and otherworldly, but somehow soothing.

"Be not afraid," the creature said, its voice deep and melodic, resonating in Rykan's very bones. "I am Orithar Razalorn, a guardian of this boundary, of this world and others. But my form is not meant for mortal eyes. As much as I am able, I will shield you from the full intensity of my presence as some have perished from merely beholding it." His gaze, like pools of starlight, softened. "Yet... here I stand before you, awoken from a slumber I do not understand."

Razalorn's luminous eyes shifted toward the shard clutched tightly in Nadara's hand. His gaze sharpened, a ripple of light coursing through his wings as he seemed to register the significance of Embryss.

"That stone you carry," he said, his voice deepening, "is a splinter of great consequence, imbued with the raw chaotic power of transformation."

Nadara flinched, her grip on Embryss tensing. "We used it to restore the tree," she explained, her voice wavering. "We didn't know it would awaken you."

Razalorn's wings pulsed, the energy swirling within them shifting to a deeper hue. "Embryss is no mere trinket," he said, his voice resonating with gravity. "Its essence is intertwined with the forces that shape existence itself. Be mindful, for wielding such power often demands a greater price than you know."

Nadara's hand trembled around Embryss, her eyes wide with both amazement and fear. "We were only trying to heal the tree's corruption. Her voice wavered, but she held Razalorn's gaze. "You said be mindful," she said. "I am. But I won't flinch from doing what needs to be done, no matter what power it takes."

Razalorn's wings pulsed gently, their light shifting as he tilted his head, an almost thoughtful gesture. "Corruption?" he echoed, the word carrying a note of deep disquiet. "This tree was never meant to falter, and I was never meant to rest. If I have slept, it is because the balance I was sworn to guard was compromised."

His radiant eyes narrowed, as if he was contemplating something from deep within the fabric of reality. His shimmering wings flared briefly, casting dancing lights across the clearing, and his expression shifted to one of dawning realization.

"There is only one who could disrupt the balance of realms so precisely..." Razalorn continued, his voice now tinged with a solemn dread. "Has the Fallen Star returned?"

Rykan stiffened, the name sending a chill down his spine. "The Celestial who defied the creator... but hid from punishment?" His voice barely held together. "We've heard the story. But that's all it was."

"His true name is Nociferon, Lord of Pandemora." Razalorn's wings flared wide, a halo of light spiraling around him. His gaze became piercing, as if searching the very depths of their souls. The air around them grew heavy, almost crackling with an invisible energy, and the ground seemed to tremble beneath their feet.

Rykan took an involuntary step backward, his eyes wide. The very air felt alive with tension, pressing against his skin and making his pulse race. "Nociferon is the Fallen Star? He was a Celestial?" he asked, disbelief warring with fear. "But... how could he become what he is now?"

"Nociferon's fall began not with a hunger for power, but with a hunger for freedom," Razalorn said, his voice low, reverberating with ancient sorrow. "He believed the Celestials had fixed the world too tightly, locking time in sequence, binding matter in rules, caging life in predestined paths.

He longed to return creation to its wild beginnings, where existence could evolve through unfettered change."

A hush fell across the clearing. Snowflakes drifted, weightless in the charged silence. And in the far corners of his mind, Rykan remembered the voice again, low, vast, unshaken:

No beginning. No end. Only will.

It wasn't just a dream. It was a philosophy, a force, still reaching.

"He wanted to experiment freely," Razalorn continued, his wings drawing inward. "To let chaos run where order had drawn borders. But when he broke the barriers between realms, the chaos did not obey him, it consumed him.

"His essence unraveled. What remained fled into the wound he had torn, where he forged Pandemora. There, chaos reshaped him, not into a god of frenzy, but into a force that could no longer create… only unmake."

Rykan's breath came faster, the cold air biting at his lungs. "I have heard him in my dreams," he said, his voice almost a whisper. "He spoke to me."

Razalorn's gaze fixed on him, and a gust of wind swept through the clearing, carrying with it the faint scent of magic.

"Then his reach is greater than I feared," he said, his tone grave. "If he can now speak through dreams and manipulate the will of mortals, it means the wards protecting this world's balance are crumbling. If you find other Dreylith Wards, rekindle their strength, for I am bound to this one and cannot aid you beyond its nexus point."

As Razalorn finished speaking, the light surrounding his wings began to dim, and his form shimmered, as if retreating into another plane. The radiant energy that had allowed him to be seen by mortal eyes blinked, growing thinner and more ethereal with each passing moment. His voice thundered, softer now, as if coming from a place far away.

"Remember," Razalorn said, his words lingering in the frosty air. "Restore the balance, and guard yourselves against his corruption. Do not let any fragment of the Heart of Entropy fall into the enemy's hands." His luminous eyes, once filled with compassion and intensity, became pinpoints of light before vanishing altogether. The wind rustled once more, carrying his final whisper like the last note of a fading song.

Rykan and Nadara stood in stunned silence, the clearing now empty save for the newly revitalized Dreylith Ward. The vibrant energy of the tree pulsed quietly, as if breathing life into the world around it. Yet the absence of Razalorn's presence left a cold void, a reminder of the immense task that lay ahead.

Nadara took a shaky breath, still clutching Embryss. "Did… did that really just happen?" she asked, her voice unsteady.

Rykan nodded, still processing what they had seen and heard. "We woke something ancient," he said. "And the war's already begun. If we're going to stop Nociferon… we'll need Selaina. Whatever the Sky Serpents are meant to give her, we can't face what's coming without it."

Nadara and Rykan returned to the camp near the other set of ruins. Sitting with his back to one of the broken walls, Rykan gave his feet a chance to rest. Nadara leaned against the wall nearby.

"Rykan, you're back," said Garrick. "There's something I wanted to show you."

"What is it?" Rykan said.

"You'll have to come and see," Garrick said.

"Can't you bring it here?" said Rykan.

"Get up and come with me," Garrick ordered.

Rykan took a deep breath and made it back to his feet, following Garrick along the path, away from the camp and into the forest.

"I did some scouting while you were gone," said Garrick as he hurried ahead.

The path took them further into the snowy trees until they came to an old statue carved of stone. Some of its details had chipped away. Rykan moved in for a closer look, but was unsure what he was supposed to find so interesting. Tracing the shape of the figure, he tried to place its significance.

"Not the statue," said Garrick. "Look at the ground."

Rykan's eyes searched the snow, uncertain what he was looking for. After a few moments, he noticed the blanket of white was disturbed. In some spots, the wet blue grass was exposed under the snow, but in others, the imprints of boots could be seen.

"Those are her footprints," said Garrick. "I'm certain of it."

"Selaina?" Rykan's eyes grew wide, his pulse quickening with a surge of hope. "Come on! We have to find her!" Without waiting for Garrick,

Rykan dashed through the forest, the snowy branches whipping at his face as he ran.

Rykan pushed forward, his boots crunching through crusted snow, breath rasping in his chest. The cold tore at his lungs, but he didn't slow. He couldn't. Behind him, he heard Garrick's footsteps lagging, heavier, trying to keep up. The forest stretched on like a white maze, every bend in the path revealing only more shadow, more silence. It felt endless.

"Please be well," Rykan whispered, the words almost swallowed by the whispering wind. His chest ached, not from the exertion but from the gnawing fear that he might be too late, that she might slip through his grasp just as she always seemed to.

He paused as the forest opened, the snow-covered ground glistening in the first rays of morning. Rykan's eyes scanned the expanse, his hand drifting instinctively to the hilt of his sword, heart pounding. Somewhere ahead, Selaina was out there, moving, surviving, fighting her way toward the summit. And he had to reach her before it was too late.

"Selaina!" he called, his voice echoing through the trees.

The silence that followed was deafening, and Rykan's heart pounded with the weight of all the things left unsaid, the desperate need to reach her before it was too late.

CHAPTER 47

THE AVALANCHE ROARED like a monstrous beast roused from its slumber, devouring everything in its path with a deafening cascade of snow and ice. The ground beneath Selaina's feet trembled violently, each tremor reverberating through her as if echoing the thunderous descent. Her heart pounded in rhythm with the rumbling stones hurtling toward them, a frantic beat against the inevitability of the chaos.

Myrradin's grip on her arm was unyielding, his fingers digging into her sleeve with an iron-like strength that betrayed a desperate edge. Yet, even his grip felt tenuous, a fragile defiance against the unstoppable force consuming the mountainside. The icy wind stung her cheeks, and shards of snow pelted her skin, carried on the avalanche's breath as it bore down on them.

"Myrradin!" Selaina's voice broke, a desperate cry as the ground trembled beneath her boots.

The snow was upon them, a white tempest that blurred the world into chaos. Myrradin's eyes narrowed, and a sudden ferocity took hold of him. With a shout, he raised his hands, summoning a powerful gust of wind that swirled around them, creating a barrier.

The storm winds howled, pushing back the avalanche with every ounce of Myrradin's strength. The wall of snow crashed and heaved, battering against the whirlwind but failing to bury them alive. Selaina watched in shock as the wind fought against the snow, her breath coming in bursts, a cloud of fear in the freezing air.

She saw the cost etched on Myrradin's face. His skin paled, and sweat beaded along his brow, despite the cold. The effort was draining him, leaving him trembling with exhaustion. The wind barrier wavered, and the realization struck Selaina like a blow: Myrradin couldn't hold out forever.

Finally, the avalanche's fury began to subside, leaving a suffocating silence in its wake. The wind barrier collapsed, and Myrradin stumbled, nearly falling into the snow. Selaina lunged forward, catching him under his arm and helping him stay upright. His breath came in ragged gasps, his whole body trembling with exhaustion.

Selaina steadied him, but her grip was tense. Her voice came sharp, laced with emotion she hadn't prepared for. "Myrradin… are you all right?"

She hated that she cared in that moment, hated that he had saved them.

He nodded weakly, his face pale and drawn. "Not… for long," he rasped. "I used too much power."

His eyes flicked toward the edge of the forest, restless, almost feral. "I need… living essence to recover."

Selaina felt a chill crawl down her spine, deeper and sharper than the snow around them. The old tales of Windwraiths echoed in her mind: creatures who fed not on flesh, but on the essence of life itself.

Myrradin's eyes locked onto a cluster of snow-laden bushes nearby. Without a word, his hand extended, pale tendrils of light, thin as breath, soft as smoke, unfurled from his fingertips and reached toward the plants.

A faint green glow flared at his fingertips, and simultaneously at the heart of the bush. Then, like threads unraveling from the fabric of the world, fine wisps of green light drifted from both, snaking toward one another. They met in the space between them, braiding together into a pulsing strand of energy.

The bush shuddered. Its leaves shriveled, darkened, then crumbled to ash in the snow.

Color returned to Myrradin's cheeks. His breath steadied, and some of the tremble left his hands. But Selaina couldn't look away from the place where life had just unraveled, drawn into him like water down a drain.

Selaina watched, frozen, both horrified and captivated. It was like witnessing a secret the world wasn't meant to show, life being rewritten, reversed, undone.

"I'm sorry you had to see that." Myrradin turned back to Selaina, his eyes filled with an unspoken sorrow. "This is what it means to be a Wind-wraith," he murmured. "A necessary evil, one I can never escape."

As they climbed the piles of snow and rock left by the avalanche, Selaina couldn't help but stare at Myrradin. She realized the depth of the unknown in him.

"How often do you have to do that?" Selaina asked. "Take life."

"I try not to use too much of this force at a time," Myrradin said. "But this time, it couldn't be helped."

"Have you ever used it on a person?" Selaina asked.

"I suppose you wouldn't believe me if I said no," Myrradin said. "And you'd be right. I've used it on people before, enemies, of course. I try not to use it often… to preserve what's left of my humanity. But in a fight, it keeps my powers fueled."

Selaina's lips narrowed. "It seems like a foul thing to do."

"I'm sure your enemies would say the same of your bow," Myrradin replied, his voice calm but needling.

She didn't answer right away, her eyes narrowing. "How many Wind-wraiths are there?"

"To my knowledge in this present age," said Myrradin, "only me."

"What happened to the rest of your family?" Selaina asked.

Myrradin tugged at his beard. "I wasn't born this way, if that's what you think."

"What happened then?" Selaina said.

"Do you think I'm going to share all my secrets with you?" Myrradin stiffened, his eyes narrowing, but Selaina pressed on.

"You carry this power, this burden, all alone. I know what that feels like." She hesitated, then added, "You said earlier that there are no right choices, only necessary ones. Maybe I'm trying to understand the choices you had to make, and why."

Myrradin's defensive posture faltered, and he looked away, as if seeing something from a long-buried past. The cold wind tugged at his cloak, and for a moment, he seemed less like a powerful sorcerer and more like a man who had paid too high a price.

"Fine," he said at last, his voice low and haunted. "If you really want to know… I'll tell you."

Selaina slowed her steps to match his, watching as he wrestled with the words. It was clear he hadn't spoken of this in years, if ever.

"When I was a young man, around your age," Myrradin began, "I was consumed by a relentless hunger for knowledge. I wanted to uncover every mystery, to pull every hidden truth into the light. No secret, no ancient text, no forbidden spell was beyond my reach, or so I thought."

He let out a wistful sigh. "I spent years studying the oldest magic texts, the ones scholars use to prove their worth to the Conclave. But it wasn't enough. I wanted more, something untouched, something even the greatest minds had overlooked."

He looked at her briefly before his gaze wandered back to the horizon.

"When I exhausted those avenues, I set out across Galanor. I joined expeditions, aided those in need, but not for noble reasons. I was no selfless hero. I did it for the books. Hidden scrolls, forgotten tomes buried in abandoned keeps, ramblings of madmen scrawled on crumbling pages, I sought them all. Anything that might hold the knowledge I craved."

He paused, his voice dropping as if to emphasize the gravity of what came next. "One day, I stumbled across a merchant whose wares were… eclectic. Among the usual trinkets and baubles, he carried an old, tattered book. Its cover bore a symbol I didn't recognize, and the pages were filled with strange notes and cryptic entries, like a journal left behind by a traveler who had glimpsed something extraordinary."

"What was in it?" Selaina asked, her curiosity pulling her closer.

"It spoke of a gathering place," Myrradin continued, his voice hushed as if he were sharing a forbidden secret. "A temple carved into cliffs overlooking the ocean. A place where a secret sect once met, a brotherhood that claimed to protect the innocent, to rid Galanor of bandits and oppressors."

He stopped walking, his eyes narrowing.

"But the further I read, the darker their story became. They weren't merely heroes; they were manipulators. They used their magic not just to protect but to shape kingdoms, amass wealth, and pull strings from the shadows. The sect's ambitions grew, and as their power intensified, it began to consume them. The book described how they dissolved into nothingness, lost to the mortal plane."

Selaina frowned. "Why would they risk such power if they knew the cost?"

"Because they believed it wasn't the end," Myrradin said. "A belief that their gifts and knowledge were never truly lost. According to their code, these powers were to be passed down to chosen heirs, ensuring their mission would endure. But more than that, they believed one of these heirs would someday find a way to restore them to this world. The book alluded to this, though it gave no details about how, or where, this so-called vault of power could be found."

His expression darkened further.

"I became obsessed. I spent years tracking down fragments of information, talking to travelers, questioning sailors, and digging through old records. Until finally, I found it. The temple."

"What was it like?" Selaina pressed.

"Desolate," he said, his voice hollow. "The air inside was heavy, thick with centuries of stillness. Dust lay undisturbed on the floors, and cobwebs draped over the statues of the sect's members, their faces frozen in expressions of... something between triumph and torment. It was clear no one had set foot in that place for centuries, and the sect that once thrived there seemed to have vanished into history. Walking through it was like moving among the dead, a hollow remnant of what they once were."

He paused, as if deciding how much to share. "I approached one of the statues, studying its details, when the air shifted. A wind began to stir, soft at first, then rising to a howling gale. It felt alive, as though it had been waiting for me. The statues hummed with resonance, and before I could pull away, the wind consumed me."

His voice faltered, and he clenched his fists. "It was overwhelming. Every sense heightened to the point of pain. My body felt as though it were being unmade and rebuilt all at once. When it was over, I was... changed."

"Changed how?" Selaina asked, her voice barely a whisper.

"I became what you see now," Myrradin said. "A Windwraith. The power I sought, the knowledge I craved, it came at a price. I learned to control it, to wield it, but it's always there, an endless torrent coursing through me. A curse as much as a gift."

He paused, his expression darkening as if he was wrestling with a private torment.

"If I had it to do over again…" His voice trailed off, and he shook his head. "I'm still not sure what choice I would make. The cost has been great, but so has the power. I don't know if I'd be strong enough to walk away from it, even knowing what I know now."

He met her gaze, his eyes shadowed with the weight of his past. "That's how I became what I am. Not born of destiny but forged by my own hubris."

"But what have you done with it?" she asked quietly. "All that power, has it been worth the cost? Have you used it for something greater than yourself, or has it only served to fuel that hubris?"

Her words hung in the cold air between them, unflinching and raw. She took a step closer, her voice softening but carrying a sharp edge. "I ask because… I've seen what power does to people. It consumes them, twists them. I've felt its pull, too. The mark on my forehead isn't just some symbol, it's a weight I carry every day."

Her words hung in the cold air between them, unflinching and raw. She stepped closer, not out of trust, but because she refused to flinch away.

"I ask because I've seen what power does to people like you. How it can twist them, consume everything good they used to be."

Her hand brushed against her chest, over the talisman she wore.

"You had power. You had purpose. And you let it hollow you out. If I become what you are… then all of this will have meant nothing. If the Sky Serpents' power would twist me into someone who's drunk on power, then I don't want it. I'd rather lose everything than lose myself."

Myrradin's lips thinned, his tone sharp with unspoken frustration. "It is the path you chose, Selaina. If you reject it now, there is no other. Galanor will fall. Or do you think your defiance alone can save it?"

She held his gaze, unwavering. "Whatever happens, it can't be worse than the world I saw in my vision, the one ruled by you." Her voice softened, laced with irony. "That vision is my constant reminder that I made the right decision."

Myrradin's expression hinted at irritation and something deeper, harder to place. "Perhaps," he said slowly, with a quiet intensity, "in the coming fight, I will prove my worth. I will stand with you against Nociferon, as your most powerful ally."

The narrow path they followed finally opened into a vast expanse, and Selaina's breath caught in her throat. They stood atop a plateau, its edge a sharp line against an endless sea of clouds below. The world felt suspended, as if they had climbed beyond the reach of Galanor itself. Only the faintest whispers of wind broke the stillness, carrying with them an ethereal hum that seemed to emanate from the air.

Selaina stepped forward cautiously, her boots crunching on the frost-covered stone. Myrradin remained a step behind her, taking in the view.

"There it is," he said, his voice barely above a whisper.

She followed his gaze.

An ancient bridge stretched across a chasm in the cliffs, narrow, weathered, its stone etched with symbols that shimmered faintly, like veins of magic still alive beneath the surface. Beyond it, another cliff rose steeply, crowned by a structure that stole her breath.

The Temple of the Sky Serpents.

Its spires reached skyward like the teeth of some forgotten god, gleaming pale beneath the morning light. Carved arches wound through the stone like threads of motion frozen in time, each etched with serpents coiling in an eternal, silent dance. The air around it felt thinner, charged.

Selaina's heart pounded. Her fingers brushed the talisman at her neck.

"It's beautiful," she murmured.

"Beautiful," Myrradin echoed, though his tone held caution. "And dangerous."

The bridge beckoned. The temple loomed.

Selaina stepped closer, the stone beneath her foot colder than the snow. The mark on her forehead pulsed once, softly, as if in answer.

CHAPTER 48

S ELAINA STEPPED ONTO the arching stone bridge, her breath catching as she dared a glance at the chasm yawning below. The air was thin and sharp, laced with the faint metallic taste of frost, and carried the echoing howl of winds weaving through the abyss. The bridge stretched between the two peaks like a relic of a forgotten age, its stone bricks darkened by centuries of storms that had battered the mountainside.

Each block bore the marks of a master's hand, intricate carvings of faded sigils and swirling patterns hinting at long-lost artistry. Time had softened their edges, cracks spiderwebbing across the surface, while moss clung stubbornly to the crevices, as if defying the elements. The structure's weight pressed heavily against the silence of the peaks, now standing as both a marvel and a risk beneath her cautious steps.

Her boots struck the stone with a hollow, rhythmic sound as she advanced, the noise swallowed quickly by the vast emptiness around her. There was no one at her side with whom she wanted to share the awe or fear. Rykan's face would've lit up at the sight of this. She could picture it so clearly it hurt. Selaina wished more than anything that she could see him now.

She'd never realized how much lighter the path felt with him beside her. Until now, when every step landed like a stone.

The sheer drop on either side made her stomach lurch, a dizzying expanse that seemed to pull at her with invisible hands. Clouds churned below, their shifting currents hiding the true depth of the fall, but the occasional break revealed jagged rock spires far beneath, glinting faintly in the dawn light like the teeth of some ancient beast.

The bridge arched steeply at its center, and as she climbed, the winds grew stronger, whipping at her cloak and forcing her to lean into each step. She placed a hand against the waist-high stone railing, its surface cold and rough, and felt a sense of unease as flakes of stone crumbled beneath her fingers. The structure was ancient, and though it had stood for ages, it felt as though even the mountain itself might betray her.

Behind her, Myrradin's footsteps echoed against the stone. His voice, steady but laced with urgency, reached her through the howling wind. "Selaina, keep moving. Keep looking straight ahead."

"I know," she called back, her voice tight with concentration. "I'm not stopping."

The precipice they had climbed from loomed behind them, dark and jagged, its cliffside path now a memory of precarious turns and sheer drops. Ahead, the crown of the Kylinshan rose in silent majesty, its summit veiled in swirling mists that glowed with the colors of the sunrise. The final ascent awaited, but first, Selaina had to complete crossing the bridge.

A gust of wind surged up from the abyss, throwing her off balance. She staggered, her hand gripping the stone railing tightly as her heart leaped into her throat. The bridge shuddered beneath her, a groan emanating from its ancient foundations. For a fleeting moment, she imagined the stones giving way, crumbling into the endless void.

Myrradin stepped up beside her, his cloak snapping in the wind. "Steady," he said, his voice calm despite the tension in the air. "The stones will hold. They always have."

"How do you know?" Selaina shot him a quick glance, her knuckles white against the railing.

"Because otherwise they would have broken by now," he replied simply.

Summoning her courage, Selaina pushed forward. The bridge's curve began to slope downward, and the stones felt more solid beneath her feet as she neared the far side. When her boots finally touched the rocky ledge of the greater apex, she exhaled a breath she hadn't realized she'd been holding.

Then her gaze drifted higher, toward the sky. Above them, the sunshimmer unfurled like a living ribbon across the heavens, painting the day with luminous streaks of violet and pale blue.

Turning, she watched Myrradin finish the crossing, his steps deliberate and unhurried despite the fierce wind. As he joined her on the ledge, she looked up at the summit path that wound its way into the clouds. For a moment, she allowed herself to marvel at the bridge they had crossed, an ancient testament to the ingenuity of those who had come before, and a reminder of the peril that still lay ahead.

The path took them along the outer edges of the peak, the world below nothing but clouds and mist. They seemed to be the only two creatures here, at this height where even eagles dared not fly. Finally, they came to a view between two ridges, and saw the temple nestled into the rock surrounding it.

"From here you must go alone," said Myrradin. "The Sky Serpents may not present themselves to anyone but Zhal Evurah."

"For once I agree with you," said Selaina. "I hope you won't be here when I return."

Myrradin's expression barely shifted. "I am still a part of your destiny, don't forget that."

Selaina didn't answer. She turned and moved toward the temple. She walked slowly across the snow, and soon felt as if she had stepped over some magical threshold as the air around her warmed. Her feet no longer crunched on snow, as the white landscape vanished into green grass and rose-colored flowers. Trees stood tall near the temple, blooming with violet colors amid their green leaves. She felt as though she were encased in a bubble, a perfect world inside the frigid landscape of the mountain.

Making her way toward the temple, she thought of Jeth, of the stories he used to tell about the Sky Serpents. He always left the endings open, letting her decide what to believe. Now she stood where myth and truth blurred, and all she could do was carry the lessons he had given her like a lantern through the fog.

The materials making up the temple were smooth and shiny, like stone from another world. Serpent statues cradled the cornerstones, carved with painstaking detail. The stone columns hummed as if they were bells, vibrating in different tones to the melodies of the will of the wind.

Selaina cautiously took the steps leading to the foundation of the temple, leading her to a courtyard surrounded by dome-shaped structures. As she glanced over the statues and carvings, she saw many symbols and numbers etched along geometric shapes on the floor, and she realized that the answers to many mysteries were likely contained here, if only they could be understood.

The lines and shapes on the floor led to a luminous point of white crystal, its surface sparkling as Selaina approached. Its intricate design mirrored the three-starred mark of Zhal Evurah on her forehead, as if the very temple recognized her destiny. She stepped onto the glowing crystal, her hand hovering unconsciously near the mark on her forehead as the ancient energy stirred beneath her. It wasn't the kind of awe that stirred the heart, it was the kind that stilled it. Like the silence before a truth made itself known.

The air around her grew heavy, thick with the weight of something ancient awakening. Light spilled upward from the crystal, casting shifting patterns across the walls of the temple. Selaina's heart thundered in her chest, excitement and fear twisting together in a symphony of anticipation. Unlike the many seekers who had come before her, she was Zhal Evurah, the first in a thousand years, and the Sky Serpents would answer her call. They had to.

She stood motionless, watching the skies with bated breath, waiting for a sign. Any sign. Minutes stretched into an eternity. Her legs began to tremble, her determination eroding as doubt crept in. Nothing stirred. The skies remained silent, unyielding.

Selaina paced the floor, her fingers clutching at the talisman around her neck as despair began to take hold. Finally, her strength gave out, and she sank to the ground, burying her face in her hands. Hot tears spilled onto her cheeks as the truth clawed at her heart, this had all been for nothing. The Sky Serpents were a myth, a cruel story whispered to those desperate for hope. She had braved fire and ice, dragged her friends across the mountain into danger, only to fail them again.

Her sobs echoed through the temple, but as they subsided, something shifted in the air.

The sunshimmer, once steady and elegant above the peaks, suddenly fractured. Its soft ribbons of color twisted sharply, like a melody struck out of tune. The flowing hues of violet and pale blue bled into streaks of crimson and gold, flashing across the sky, as though some great hand had disturbed the fabric of the heavens. Where once the shimmer had breathed in slow, living waves, it now pulsed with erratic brilliance, like the sky itself had forgotten how to move.

A ghostly wail rose from the wind, ancient and mournful, reverberating through the hollow halls. A shadow fell over Selaina, vast and all-encompassing, as though the very sun had been swallowed.

She looked up, her breath stolen by the sight. A colossal winged creature soared overhead, its form aglow with golden radiance. Its scales shimmered like liquid sunlight, casting cascades of warmth over the temple. Each beat of its immense wings sent ripples of wind through the air, carrying a sound like a thousand whispered prayers.

"Zhal Evurah must carry a humble heart," intoned the golden-winged serpent. He lowered his crown, wings folding close to his body, a judge ready to pass sentence. "For the weight you seek is not measured in glory, but in restraint."

He hovered above the temple, wings casting long beams of golden light across the stone. "I am Auronia, the bearer of light and truth. You have called, and I have answered." His voice felt like that of someone Selaina had heard before, in a dream.

Selaina's body nearly buckled beneath the pressure of his gaze. His scales shimmered with hues that refused to settle, sunlight one moment, molten gold the next. She had imagined the Sky Serpents in stories, but this was different. This was judgment incarnate, and she knew he could see her entire soul.

He descended slowly, divine brilliance pouring from his form as he filled the temple space. When he came to rest above the domed structure, his glowing gaze fixed on her. The glint in Auronia's eyes shimmered like twin stars, ancient and unblinking. Selaina's heart felt as though it would burn through her skin.

"You fear me, and you should," he said, with a blend of warmth and command. "For only the foolish approach fire without knowing it burns. Fear is the beginning of reverence. But tell me... Does fear weaken you, or does it lead you?"

Selaina tried to speak, but her words faltered, lost in the overwhelming presence before her. The light of Auronia's form dimmed slightly as his gaze held hers.

"Speak, Zhal Evurah. Not to convince me, but to know yourself."

"I don't know," Selaina admitted, her voice trembling. "I can't always still my heart, but even though I have fear, it hasn't stopped me yet. I've faced every challenge, fear or not."

The air shifted again. A low, thrumming vibration sounded through the temple, like the resonant hum of a thousand strings plucked in unison. Emerald light pierced the air as another Sky Serpent descended in a graceful spiral, its shimmering green scales reflecting the sunlight like a living jewel.

Selaina froze mid-breath, her chest constricting as the other presence joined Auronia's. The depth of their stare prickled at the back of her neck.

"To fear is to have wisdom, to persevere is to have courage," the second serpent intoned, his voice deep and resonant, vibrating through her very bones. "I am Verantis."

In his presence, her pulse slowed. Not from calm, but from the sense that every breath, every word, would be measured.

Verantis's golden eyes lingered on Selaina, piercing yet gentle, as though seeing past her outer strength to the doubts she carried within.

"You fear losing yourself to the power you seek." The great emerald serpent tilted his crown, as though weighing her words more by instinct than judgment. "And yet you are here. Tell me, Zhal Evurah, what would you sacrifice to protect the lives below? To restore balance to this world?"

Selaina faltered, her hand clenching into a fist at her side before her breath caught. She fought the impulse to flinch under the pressure of their gaze. "I... I would give anything. But how can I do that without losing who I am?"

Verantis's wings shifted, his movements rippling the air with a sound like rustling leaves. "The path of Zhal Evurah is not to seek power for oneself but to bear it for others. Look beyond your reflection in the crystal floor. What do you see? What is it you fight for?"

Selaina hesitated, but not just out of fear of what she'd see. Deep down, part of her wondered if she'd already strayed too far. Not because of what she'd done, but because of how she'd begun. She hadn't been chosen by fate or called by prophecy. She'd taken the destinies from the Wishing Stone because she was afraid. Not afraid of power, but afraid no one else would take it. Afraid that the world would fall if no one stepped forward. Maybe that made her brave… but maybe it also made her reckless. And if the Sky Serpents could see that truth in her… would they ever truly accept her?

Her gaze dropped to the crystal floor at her feet, its surface shimmering as though it held the light of the heavens within. The emerald glow of the green serpent's wings reflected on the floor, mingling with the golden hues of Auronia's light. Slowly, the shimmering surface began to shift, rippling like water, and Selaina caught her breath as the first images emerged.

At first, she saw her own reflection, but it wasn't the Selaina she knew. Her face was etched with pain and doubt, the mark of Zhal Evurah glowing on her forehead. Then the image distorted, giving way to flashes of the world below. She saw the frozen lake far beneath them, the forests beyond, and the distant villages. Faces she recognized, Rykan, Ysadora, Garrick, appeared in fleeting glimpses, their expressions heavy with hope and desperation.

The crystal rippled again, the images becoming darker. A barren wasteland stretched before her, villages consumed by fire, rivers choked with ash. In the distance, a looming figure appeared, herself, but not the person she wanted to be. Her face was hardened, unfeeling, her hands raised to command forces of destruction. The power of Zhal Evurah radiated from her, but there was no balance, no harmony, only domination and isolation.

Selaina's chest drew inward as the image fractured once more, splitting like shards of glass. She saw herself crouched on a hilltop back in the forest of her home, her hand reaching toward a glowing blue light. The sensation was as vivid now as it had been then, an overwhelming sense of connection, as though the world itself was alive, and she was a part of something vast and beautiful. In that moment, she had believed that goodness existed beyond the forest, beyond herself. She had felt it.

From the fragments emerged a final vision. This time, she stood not as a conqueror, but as a protector. Her hands reached out, not to wield power, but to heal. Around her, the land flourished, forests regrew, rivers ran clear, and people thrived in harmony. Her friends stood beside her, their faces bright with hope, and the mark on her forehead glowed brilliantly, not as a symbol of control, but as a beacon of unity.

As the images faded, the crystal floor returned to its original state, smooth and radiant. Selaina felt her heart steady, the weight of the visions settling into a quiet resolve. The choice had always been hers. Power was not the enemy, it was what she chose to do with it that mattered.

She exhaled slowly, lifting her eyes to Verantis. His golden eyes seemed to soften as he regarded her, the weight of his question now answered.

"I fight for them," she said, struggling to keep her voice steady as her heart filled with emotion. "For the people below. For those who can't fight for themselves. I will bear this power, not for myself, but for them."

A gust of wind swept through the air, carrying with it a deep, resonant hum. The sky darkened and the air grew thick with the charged energy of a thunderstorm. From the clouds came a haunting, harmonious sound that seemed to resonate in Selaina's chest. The temple floor trembled slightly as a massive shadow passed over them, circling above.

Selaina looked up to see a third serpent descending with a feminine grace. Her body shimmered like a ripple across deep water, never quite still, her wings trailing motes of stardust that faded into memory even as Selaina watched. There was something unsettling in her beauty, as if time itself bent around her.

The serpent's voice was haunting and soothing, a lilting cadence that seemed to shimmer and ripple like sunlight on water. "I am Zaryneth. Auronia and Verantis have shown you humility and selflessness. But the path of Zhal Evurah demands more. Can you embrace power not as a means of control but as a burden, a weight that may never ease? Can you wield it without losing your humanity, even when it feels like it will consume you?"

"I don't know what the future holds," Selaina admitted, her voice trembling but steadying with renewed resolve. "But I know this power is not for me, it's for the people of Galanor. And if I must carry it alone, I will."

"She is burdened by doubt," Auronia said, his tone quiet, but no less sharp. "And perhaps that is well. But doubt alone does not make one worthy. I have watched her. She falters. She second-guesses. This gift is not a salve, it is a blade. If she wields it uncertainly, it will cut more than just her enemies."

He turned, his wings folding in, light glinting across the temple walls. "Once, I hoped she might rise above. But hope, untested, is the seed of ruin. I do not grant power for dreams, I weigh it for judgment."

"No Zhal Evurah has ever been without flaws," Verantis countered, his golden eyes glowing with steady conviction. "Courage is not the absence of doubt, but the ability to overcome. She has climbed to this peak, endured trials that would have broken most. Is that not proof enough that she is worthy?"

"Worthy?" Zaryneth's voice rang out, not in accusation, but inquiry. Like a ripple cast across still water, subtle, inevitable, spreading into silence. "She was not born Zhal Evurah. She claimed the name through the Wishing Stone, an artifact never meant for mortal hands."

Her wings folded in, luminous and still.

"So I ask: is this truly her path? Or one she carved against the grain of time itself?"

Selaina let their words settle in the silence that followed, felt the heat of the crystal beneath her boots, the weight of destiny like a chain around her chest.

Then she raised her head.

"You're right," she said, her voice quiet but growing steadier. "I do doubt myself. I am afraid. I question whether I'm strong enough, whether I deserve this, whether I'll fail the people who are counting on me."

She took a breath, her hand brushing the talisman at her chest.

"But if you're afraid of power being misused, then isn't that exactly why someone like me should carry it?"

Auronia's light flared, the sky quieted. Selaina pressed forward.

"If I weren't afraid, if I charged into this power thinking I deserved it, thinking I was above the cost, then that would make me dangerous. That would make me reckless."

She turned, meeting each of their gazes in turn.

"It's the fear that keeps me in check. The doubt reminds me what's at stake. I don't want this power for myself. I never did. But if I can carry it so no one else has to, if I can use it to shield instead of destroy, then I will. Even if it breaks me."

The temple fell silent.

And for a moment, all that could be heard was the wind, gentler now, like the mountain itself had paused to listen.

"The Azsh Rozaht works in ways we cannot comprehend," Verantis replied firmly, his wings flaring. "Who are we to deny its will? The blessing we give is no trivial matter. It cannot be given lightly, nor repeated for another century. Even now, I sense the power she carries, untamed, raw, yet undeniable. If not her, then who? If not now, then when? Galanor cannot afford hesitation."

Auronia's eyes flashed, his golden glow casting long shadows across the temple. "And that very power is what gives me pause. She is already so full of potential, more than any Zhal Evurah in memory. Is it wise to burden her with more? What if it consumes her?"

"She has already defied fate once," Zaryneth interjected. Her wings coiled with restless energy, the silver-blue light around her dancing like cold fire. "By taking the destinies from the Wishing Stone, she disrupted the natural order. How can we trust that she will not make such a decision again, swayed by emotion or pride?"

"She bears the weight of her people already," Verantis argued, his voice steady. "Her companions, even her enemies. She does not seek power for herself but to save others. It is her flaws, her humanity, that give her strength. Without the blessing, the risk of failure is far greater."

Auronia's jet-black eyes narrowed, his voice measured. "And yet, the question remains: will she rise above her flaws, or will they consume her? That is for her to prove, and us to judge."

Selaina lifted her head, meeting their combined gaze. "I understand why you doubt me," she said, her voice steady. "I wasn't born to great kings or wealthy nobles. I spent most of my life in the forest, knowing nothing of the world beyond it. I came here because I heard a call, and I believed it was what I was meant to do. But if I am not worthy of your blessing, then I beg you, help us. The Iron Flood marches across Galanor, swelling its ranks and razing all who resist. If you have the power to set things right, then please, do so."

"We do not interfere in the affairs of mortals," Auronia replied, his voice carrying the weight of countless ages. "You've heard the tales of our punishment."

"The punishment where you were made mortal?" Selaina pressed, her own audacity surprising her. "What if being mortal isn't a punishment at all? Maybe it was a gift, a chance to be among those you once only watched. A chance to actively participate in the world, the way mortals do."

Auronia recoiled, his golden light flaring. "Madness! You speak as though our punishment were privilege, as though watching the world slip through our fingers was mercy."

Selaina didn't flinch. She met his glow with steady eyes. "Maybe that's exactly why it wasn't a punishment," she said. "You felt the world slipping, and it hurt. That pain, that closeness, isn't weakness. Maybe it's what the world needed from you."

She stepped forward. "You speak of balance and purpose, but what if real balance comes from standing with us, not watching from above?" She gestured around the temple. "You place the weight of the world on my shoulders. But what of yours? You expect mortals to act with courage while you remain silent. How is that balance?"

"She speaks a truth we've long tried not to face," Zaryneth said softly. Her sapphire light shimmered with something close to sorrow. "We have walked among mortals. Watched their pain. Witnessed their perseverance. Many have shown me kindness, and I've returned it in ways I never thought I would."

She paused, her silver eyes lifting toward the sky.

"But this is not the slow shaping of destiny. This is fracture. Collapse. And if we do nothing… what will be left to observe? We are part of this world now. And yet… we would withhold even the hope of a blessing from those who still believe in us." She turned toward the glowing sky. "Perhaps we haven't upheld the will of Azsh Rozaht. Perhaps we've misunderstood it."

"This is not the time for sentiment, Zaryneth," Auronia said, his golden light flaring. "You would have us abandon our mandate based on the hopes of one mortal girl?"

"Our time as watchers has long been over, Auronia." Verantis's emerald light flared brighter, steady as his tone. "As Selaina said, we are part of this world now. Yes, the blessing is our purpose. But to ignore Galanor's ruin would be to deny that purpose entirely."

Auronia fell silent, his light dimming as he contemplated their words.

"If the only gift we have left is our blessing… then let us give it," Verantis continued. "And if she proves unworthy in the end, she won't be the first Zhal Evurah to fall."

At last, Auronia inclined his great head. "Very well," he said, his voice resonant and solemn. "May the will of Azsh Rozaht be done."

Zaryneth's voice followed, low and clear. "We are not here to preserve the past, we are here to carry it forward. Let the blessing flow."

"May the will of Azsh Rozaht be done," she and Verantis said, their voices carrying the weight of an oath.

Verantis's golden eyes settled on Selaina, his tone both grave and encouraging. "This blessing is no gentle gift, Selaina. It will tear through you. But I have seen your strength, quiet, forged in sacrifice. To endure it is to face your truest self… and come through whole."

Selaina swallowed hard, her heart pounding like a drumbeat in her chest. She nodded, forcing her voice to steady as she spoke. "I'm ready."

But was she? The thought echoed in the back of her mind as she positioned herself on the glowing crystal floor. Her legs felt like stone, her fingers curling into tight fists despite her effort to stay calm. She planted her feet firmly, bracing herself against the unknown, her hands clenched at her sides.

The temple fell into a heavy silence, broken only by the faint hum of the crystals beneath her feet. Selaina lifted her chin, watching the majestic Sky Serpents circling above, their forms casting shimmering patterns across the sacred space. She felt the weight of their presence, the enormity of the moment pressing down on her like the summit's icy air.

"I'm ready," she repeated, softer this time, reminding herself that doubt was part of her strength, that courage wasn't the absence of fear, but the will to face it. She stayed her ground, awaiting whatever was to come, determined not to falter.

CHAPTER 49

THE SHARP BITE of the mountain air clawed at Rykan's lungs as he sprinted along the winding pass, his boots skidding on patches of frost-glazed rock. Overhead, the pale sun hung high above the jagged peaks, its cold light refracting off the snow-capped cliffs in a blinding brilliance that made his eyes water. He squinted against the searing glare, his breath burning in short, ragged gasps as he pushed forward, the urgency in his stride unrelenting.

The icy wind that had been his constant companion earlier had faded, replaced by an unsettling stillness that pressed heavily against his senses. Each step sent loose shards of ice scattering across the trail, the sound unnaturally sharp in the silence, as though the mountain itself were holding its breath. Rykan's heartbeat thundered in his ears, each beat amplified by the eerie quiet, making the narrowing path ahead feel all the more precarious.

He couldn't slow down now, Selaina was close, he could feel it. Or was he only telling himself that to push himself on?

His pulse quickened as he rounded a bend and caught sight of a figure standing on the narrow path ahead. A dark cloak stood out stark against the snow, the figure's long robes swayed lightly in the wind. Myrradin. The sight of the mavin sent a surge of anger through Rykan, his hand flying to the hilt of his sword.

"Myrradin!" Rykan bellowed, closing the distance. "Where is she?"

Myrradin turned slowly, his expression calm yet unreadable. His presence exuded an eerie stillness. "She is where she needs to be," he said evenly. "Do not disturb her now."

"Tell me now!" Rykan demanded. "Where have you taken her?"

"I brought her to where she has been trying to get to," Myrradin said. "The Sky Serpents."

Rykan's breath hitched as his gaze moved past Myrradin. Ahead, through the thinning mist, the temple emerged, a marvel of stone and light. Towering domed structures rose against the rocky peaks, their ancient surfaces shimmering with an ethereal glow that seemed to pulse in time with the mountain itself. But it was what perched atop them that stole the air from his lungs.

Enormous, winged creatures loomed like living monuments, their immense forms both terrifying and breathtaking. One's golden scales caught the sunlight, refracting it in radiant arcs, while another shimmered with a deep emerald sheen, its every motion exuding controlled power. Their long necks arched with a grace that defied their size, and their wings stretched wide, casting rippling shadows over the stone below, as if the very temple bowed beneath their presence.

Rykan's heart pounded, the weight of the sight pressing against his chest. These were no mere legends. The Sky Serpents, the fabled guardians, were real. But would they welcome Selaina as Zhal Evurah, or destroy her as a thief of the destinies of the Wishing Stone, as Nociferon said?

His eyes locked onto the lone figure standing before them, dwarfed by their magnificence yet unyielding in her stance. Selaina. Her silhouette was stark against the temple's radiant backdrop, her form both fragile and resolute. In that moment, Rykan couldn't tell if she was confronting destiny or being consumed by it.

"Selaina!" Rykan shouted, taking a step forward.

"I cannot allow you to interfere," Myrradin said, his voice low but commanding. With a swift motion of his staff, he erected an ethereal barrier around Rykan, encasing him in a translucent, shimmering shield.

Rykan slammed his fist against the barrier, fury igniting in his chest. "Let me out!" he roared, his voice a mix of rage and desperation. "She needs me!"

Myrradin stood firm, his gaze fixed on the distant temple.

Rykan's eyes widened as he looked back toward the temple. The Sky Serpents loomed over Selaina, their immense forms radiating an otherworldly power. He could do nothing but watch, helpless, as she stood before them, her shoulders squared yet trembling under their piercing stares.

"Well, well…" A new voice rang out, cutting through the charged air.

Rykan spun around within his confines, his eyes landing on Ysadora approaching from the mountain trail. Behind her, Garrick, and Nadara appeared, fanning out to encircle the mavin.

Ysadora's face was pale with fury, her sharp eyes locked on Myrradin. Behind the shimmering veil of the Aedavaris, her voice reached Rykan in blurred fragments, muted, warped, like shouting through water.

Her voice rang sharp as she stepped into view, the strands of jewelry threaded through her antlers swaying with each motion. "You thought you could leave me behind?" Her words bled through the shield, distorted but sharp with betrayal. "That you could use me up… and throw me away like I was nothing?"

"Oh, Ysadora," Myrradin said, his tone dripping with condescension. "Ever the ungrateful one. If you had shown an ounce of loyalty, I would have taken you with me. But no. After everything I have done for you, you remain blind to your purpose."

Ysadora let out a harsh laugh, shaking her head. "Blind to my purpose? That's rich coming from you. What a great father figure you were, Myrradin. All those nights you disappeared without a word, leaving nothing more than a scrap of parchment telling me where to find you the next day, if I was lucky."

"You wouldn't have survived without me," Myrradin countered, his voice hardening. "Who do you think taught you magic? Who protected you from the dangers of this world? You owe me your very survival."

"You didn't protect me," Ysadora snapped, stepping closer, her eyes burning with years of pent-up frustration. "You used me. You taught me magic because you needed me for your schemes, and when I wasn't useful anymore, you left me behind like yesterday's trash."

The icy wind whipped between them, carrying tension like a physical force. Rykan strained behind the Aedavaris barrier, heart pounding as he watched the standoff unfold. Selaina was still alone with the Sky Serpents, and every second here felt like a stolen one.

Ysadora's staff crackled to life, magic swirling around her as the ground trembled. Jagged rocks erupted beneath Myrradin's feet, but he reacted instantly, his form blurring into wind, vanishing in a burst of movement as he vaulted into the air with ghostlike agility.

But his flight faltered.

Mid-leap, his Windwraith form wavered, and he crashed hard into the snow. Garrick and Nadara seized the opportunity, lunging toward him from opposite flanks.

Myrradin rose on one knee, frost clinging to his robes, and thrust his hand into the air.

A violent wind surged outward, not toward them, but toward the mountain slope above.

The blast cracked through the snowpack like thunder. Ice fractured. Snow groaned. A sheet of white broke loose and cascaded down with a roar. Nadara shouted, trying to dodge, but it was too late, the wave of snow swallowed her and Garrick, burying them in a flurry of blinding white.

Rykan's eyes widened in horror. "No!"

Myrradin turned, still panting, and flung his hand toward the Aedavaris shield. It unraveled from around Rykan, and instantly reformed around Ysadora.

She screamed in frustration, but no sound came from inside the Aedavaris. She slammed her staff against the barrier as it shimmered around her like glass made of starlight.

Then came the sound.

A terrible screech, low and resonant, tore through the mountain air. It wasn't a cry of fury, it was the sound of the sky being pulled inside out. Rykan turned, his blood running cold as the Sky Serpents coiled high above the temple, their massive forms bending the light as they moved. Their jaws opened wide. They inhaled, not breath, but essence, drawing in the energy of the world itself.

Light shimmered along their bodies, radiant and terrifying, reflecting across the crystal floor in a kaleidoscope of color and motion. The whole temple seemed to breathe, the air thick with shimmering heat and holy pressure.

Rykan's heart thundered. *Nociferon was right,* he thought. *They're going to destroy her.*

No beginning. No end. Only will.

He had no idea how to stop celestial beings older than empires, but he knew one thing: Selaina needed him. Without thought, he sprinted toward her, the world narrowing to the sound of his footsteps on stone.

"Selaina!" he shouted.

She turned just as he reached her. Her eyes widened, startled, and then he threw his arms around her, shielding her with his body.

The Sky Serpents released their power.

The world exploded.

A storm of blinding light surged from above, searing through the air in a roar of colorless fire. It struck Rykan like the judgment of the stars. His scream was swallowed by the sound, his body suspended in a pillar of light so bright it erased the edges of reality.

He could feel the energy pouring into him, not consuming, not killing, but transforming. It crashed through his body like molten lightning, twisting around his bones, threading into his soul. His thoughts shattered. His name disappeared. For a heartbeat, he wasn't Rykan. He was open.

Visions poured in. Not memories. Histories. Stars being born. Cities rising and falling. The cries of battle. A serpent diving into the sea of creation. The world before time, when fate was a river and choice had yet to be carved.

He was floating in the breath of something ancient, being rewritten.

"Rykan! No!" Selaina's voice reached through the light, distant and warbling, as if it had traveled from a different world. She reached for him, but the magic burned between them like a wall.

And then, it broke.

The light collapsed inward, folding into him like a dying star.

Rykan crumpled to his knees.

His breath tore through his lungs, ragged and sharp. The cold stone beneath him was real, grounding. He lifted his head, vision swimming, and saw Selaina's face, tear-streaked, bathed in the afterglow of the storm, her eyes wide with anguish.

"Rykan…" she whispered. "What have you done?"

She reached for him, but the moment had already begun to fade. His vision blurred, the glow of the temple receding into shadows. Her voice echoed once, then again, smaller each time.

Then, silence.

Darkness took him.

CHAPTER 50

SELAINA DROPPED TO her knees beside Rykan, the last threads of light still fading from the air. Her hand hovered inches above his chest, afraid to touch him, afraid not to.

"Rykan," she breathed. Her voice cracked, torn between disbelief and raw emotion. "Why would you do that?" Her fingers brushed his hair back from his face, already clammy with sweat. His skin was warm beneath her fingertips, but not with the reassuring heat of a living body. "That was meant for me."

Tears welled again, this time not from pain or awe, but betrayal, the kind born not of malice, but of love misused.

"I was ready," she whispered, pressing her forehead to his. "I was *chosen*."

Her hands shook as she gripped his tunic, the weight of the moment finally crashing down. The blessing, the thing she had climbed so far for, fought so hard to earn, now lived inside him. And yet, as she looked down at his unconscious face, pale and slack with exhaustion, she realized the truth:

He hadn't taken it for power. He had taken it for her.

Selaina closed her eyes, letting her tears fall freely. "You fool," she whispered. "You beautiful, reckless fool. What if it kills you?"

She cradled him gently, holding him like something fragile and liable to break. "I was supposed to be the one to bear this. Now we both will… one way or another."

Her stomach churned, the strange rhythm setting her nerves on edge, as if something just beneath the surface was struggling to break free.

The sword still clutched in Rykan's hand pulsed with a brilliant white light, so blinding that its details were lost, leaving only the outline of the blade. She tried shaking him gently at first, calling his name. When there was no response, her movements grew more desperate, her voice cracking as she pleaded, "Rykan, wake up. Please."

"This was not his place," Verantis said, the weight of sorrow in his voice. "And yet... the courage it took cannot be ignored."

"He chose love over fate," Zaryneth murmured, her wings trembling with quiet awe. "Even in the face of power beyond him... he didn't flinch. But love alone does not spare us from its price."

Selaina lifted her gaze. "Then help him," she said. "You gave the blessing. Can't you guide it safely through him?"

Verantis's golden eyes glowed steadily in the gloom. "The blessing is not something we direct," he said. "It chooses how to take root. If he lives, he will never be the same. If he dies..." He didn't finish the thought, his pause speaking louder than words.

"That's not good enough," Selaina said, rising to her feet, trembling. "You're mortal. You feel. You care. Don't pretend you don't."

"He saw the light and leaped into flame," Auronia said, voice low. "It was not wisdom—but it was untainted by ambition." Auronia's golden wings flexed, casting shifting light over the snow. "Caring is not the question," he said, voice heavy with purpose. "The Crown of Breath demands more than love or sorrow. It requires strength. Will. The resolve to survive the blessing and bear its weight."

He looked down at Rykan's still form. "If he cannot endure it, he cannot carry it. That is not cruelty. It is law."

Selaina leaned over Rykan, pressing her ear to his chest, desperate to detect a heartbeat. The vibrations beneath her hand were erratic, like the surge of the power coursing through his body, making it impossible to tell if he was truly alive.

Zaryneth tilted her head toward Rykan's still form, her wings drawn close, sapphire light fluttering like a heartbeat in snow. "Is this what the

Azsh Rozaht intended?" she asked softly. "To guide them to the edge of greatness… only to watch them break?"

Verantis hovered beside her, his emerald glow pulsing steady and low. "We are not meant to see the whole design," he said. "Only to uphold its thread where it frays."

Auronia's golden radiance dimmed as he cast his gaze toward the horizon, unreadable. "The blessing has been given," he said, voice clipped but heavy. "We do not steer the tide. We are the weight it must carry to know its strength."

"Do we abandon them now, when they are so vulnerable?" Zaryneth questioned, her wings twitching with restrained energy.

Verantis remained calm, his wings barely moving. "To linger would be to shape what should be chosen," he said. "They must rise on their own strength… or be changed by the trying."

Auronia's jet-black eyes lingered a moment longer on Selaina. His voice, when it came again, had lost its edge. "Perhaps… it is not weakness that draws mortals to the edge of ruin," he murmured, more to the wind than to them. "Perhaps it is there they remember what strength is truly for." Auronia's golden wings flexed, casting shifting light over the snow.

With those final words, the Sky Serpents rose into the sky, their colossal forms fading into the clouds, leaving Selaina and the others behind. "The blessing burns brightest in those closest to ruin. May he not cross that line," said Verantis as they flew, disappearing into the clouds.

CHAPTER 51

"NOTHING HAS CHANGED!" A frantic voice cut through the tense stillness. Myrradin came sprinting up the mountain pass, his robes billowing in the cold wind. "Why didn't it work?" he demanded, his tone bordering on hysteria. "Were you wearing the talisman, Selaina?"

Selaina ignored him, brushing Rykan's hair away from his face with trembling fingers. Myrradin, however, was relentless. Reaching down, he grabbed the back of her cloak and yanked her roughly to her feet.

"Answer me!" he barked, pulling her close, his eyes wild with fury.

Selaina's fury boiled over. She ripped the talisman from her neck, snapping the chain with a sharp tug. "Here's your precious talisman!" she spat, shoving it against his chest. "Now leave me alone!"

Myrradin recoiled, staring at the talisman as if it had betrayed him. His expression shifted from shock to anger. "Why didn't it work?" he muttered, almost to himself. "Did you not receive the blessing?"

Selaina's voice cracked as she answered. "He tried to protect me." Her gaze darted back to Rykan's still form, her eyes brimming with tears. "Is there anything you can do to help him?"

Myrradin's expression darkened, his anger sharpening. "He took it," he growled, his voice low and venomous. "He took the blessing that was meant for me!"

Selaina's head snapped toward him. "Meant for you?" she said, voice rising. "You were going to steal it. Twist it for yourself. All you care about is power." She took a step closer, fury radiating off her like heat. "Get away from me, Myrradin. If I ever see you again, I swear, I'll end this. I'll end you."

Myrradin didn't flinch. Instead, his eyes narrowed, lips curling in something too smooth to be a smirk. "Perhaps… there's still something to be salvaged," he murmured, almost to himself. "If the energy hasn't rooted too deep, I may yet extract it from his body—"

"No," Selaina said, cutting him off. She stepped between Myrradin and Rykan, her stance protective, unshakable.

Undeterred, Myrradin stretched out his hand, the faint shimmer of his life-draining ability starting to pull at Rykan's essence. A thin, wavering beam of light rose from Rykan's chest, glowing faintly as it moved toward Myrradin.

Selaina's fingers closed around her bow as if summoned by instinct, the motion fluid, unthinking, born of rage and resolve. Without hesitation, blue energy coalesced along the bowstring, shimmering like lightning. She didn't warn Myrradin. She didn't speak. She fired.

The bolt of energy streaked toward Myrradin, the air crackling with its force. Myrradin countered instantly, his hands raised as his Windwraith power slowed the arrow's momentum. The bolt shimmered and wavered as it inched forward, losing speed until it hovered, frozen, just before him. With a contemptuous flick, Myrradin unraveled the bolt in mid air, its light shredding into strands of raw magic that vanished on the wind like dying embers.

"You think you can stop me?" Myrradin sneered, his voice laced with venom. "You're no Zhal Evurah. Just a hollow vessel, shaking under a power you were never meant to hold."

Selaina's grip on the bow hardened, her fury blazing in her eyes. "Lay a finger on him again," she growled, drawing another arrow of blazing blue, "and I'll show you what a Zhal Evurah is truly capable of."

Myrradin launched a burst of windforce at Selaina, lifting her feet from the crystal floor. The air hit her like a tidal wave, slamming into her chest and sending her tumbling down the steps outside the temple. She landed hard, her knees thumping into the grassy meadow in the area around the temple, breath knocked from her lungs. Dirt and debris scattered around her, and for a moment, the world spun.

Gasping, she scrambled to her knees, her fingers digging into the cold dirt. Pain radiated through her ribs, but she pushed it aside.

Selaina's arm burned from the strain of drawing another arrow, but the fire in her chest eclipsed it. After everything she had lost, she would not let Myrradin claim Rykan as well. The energy sputtered, unsteady, but she forced it into shape and loosed it with a cry of defiance.

The arrow streaked through the air like a comet, blazing with furious light. Myrradin's wind rose to meet it, his hands trembling as the force of the arrow pushed against his barrier. His teeth clenched, the veins on his temples bulging as he poured everything into stopping the attack. Finally, the arrow exploded into particles of fading light.

As a new arrow coalesced in Selaina's grasp, Myrradin extended his hands, siphoning the living essence from the grass and flowers outside the temple. Grass curled in on itself like burning paper. Flowers blackened to ash in seconds. The very breath of the mountain recoiled from him as he drank its vitality to stoke his own. His aura brightened, glowing with stolen vitality. His gaze locked onto Selaina, and with a sharp motion, he unleashed another powerful gust of wind.

The air slammed into her like a wall of hammers, lifting her bodily and hurling her through the temple arch. A cry was torn from her lips as she crashed into the earth below, skidding through shattered stone and frost-laced grass. She cried out, her back slamming against the uneven ground at the edge of the summit. Rocks and dirt crumbled beneath her, tumbling into the abyss below. The cold, biting wind howled in her ears as she struggled to regain her footing.

The pain was blinding, but beneath it, something clearer stirred. The strike hadn't just hit her. She'd felt the shape of it, how the wind curved and compressed before it struck. Her ribs ached, but her thoughts held the echo of the spell's rhythm. Like a melody she hadn't realized she'd heard before.

Standing at the temple's edge, Myrradin exuded a terrifying calm, his form wreathed in a shimmer of power. His voice carried over the mountain, smooth and sharp as a blade. "You can't win, Selaina. You were never meant for this. The blessing is mine to claim, and I will twist his body and soul until it yields."

Selaina gritted her teeth, forcing herself to stand. Her bow trembled in her hand, her chest burning with defiance. "It was never meant to be held by you," she spat. "You are unworthy."

Myrradin's expression darkened, his voice chillingly calm as he strode toward her. "I wish it hadn't come to this," he said, his tone heavy with feigned regret. "But you leave me no choice."

He raised his hands, the air around him rippling with a surge of energy. The winds coiled and twisted, gathering at his fingertips in a deadly storm. He began forming the final strike, a concentrated blast that hummed with destructive intent.

Before he could release it, the sky darkened, and a low rumble echoed across the summit. The air grew electric, a sharp tang of ozone filling Selaina's lungs. Her heart pounded as a jagged bolt of crimson lightning tore through the clouds, streaking down with an ear-splitting crack. The world seemed to pause as the lightning struck the temple, its raw energy illuminating the summit in an eerie red glow.

The bolt hit Myrradin directly, slamming into him with a deafening explosion. He cried out in pain, his body convulsing as the chaotic energy tore through him. The ground trembled, loose stones clattering against each other as the shockwave rippled outward.

The force drove him to his knees, a guttural cry escaping his lips as the red lightning burned across his body. His wind barrier faltered, and for the first time, Myrradin looked shaken.

Selaina's breath caught in her chest as she looked past him, her eyes widening in disbelief. A silhouette emerged from the heart of the maelstrom. Rykan.

He stood at the temple's edge, wind rippling his cloak, his sword aglow with red and black light that licked up the blade like fire tasting air. The glow cast jagged shadows across his face, his stance unsteady, as though the power coursing through him was too vast to control.

"Rykan…" Selaina whispered, her voice thick with both relief and fear.

Myrradin twisted to face him, his narrowed eyes filled with fury and fear. "Chaos," he spat. "You've turned the serpents' blessing into chaos. An abomination!"

Rykan leveled his blade, chaotic energy crackling along its length, but Myrradin's voice cut through.

"Do you even understand what you're playing with, boy? That power will consume you. Chaos doesn't serve. It twists, unravels, hollows out everything it touches."

The red and black lightning arced through the air, wild and unrestrained, splitting into jagged forks that tore through the ground and walls around them. The force of it sent rocks flying and churned the air into a frenzied vortex, but the energy veered off course, missing Myrradin entirely.

Instead, the blast struck a nearby column, shattering it in an explosion of stone and sparks. The ground shook beneath them, and a spray of debris rained down, forcing Selaina to the ground to shield herself. Myrradin stood untouched, a mix of triumph and disbelief flashing across his face.

"Do you see?" Myrradin sneered, his voice cutting like a blade. "Chaos is a beast that cannot be leashed. It does not obey its master, it destroys indiscriminately. The blessing was meant to fight the chaos that threatens this world, not to empower it. You cannot fight chaos with chaos!"

Rykan's sword blazed brighter, the chaotic energy swirling and pulsing around him as though the weapon had a will of its own. He raised it high, his face contorted in a mixture of determination and pain, ready to unleash another devastating strike.

Myrradin's eyes widened as he raised his hands. "No!" he shouted, his voice laced with urgency.

A shimmering shield erupted from his palms, but instead of defending him, the barrier surged outward, encasing Rykan in a translucent, shimmering dome of light.

The chaotic energy clashed violently against the shield, sending ripples of distortion cascading across its surface. Rykan roared in frustration, slamming his sword against the barrier. Each strike sent shockwaves through the dome, but it held firm, containing the wild energy within.

"You're reckless!" Myrradin spat, his voice a venomous growl. "You wield chaos as if it's a weapon, but it will turn in your grip. It always does. It feeds, and then it devours. You will lose everything if I don't find a way to take the blessing from you."

Inside the shield, Rykan staggered, the chaotic energy swirling erratically around him, battering him as much as it did the shield. Selaina's heart clenched as she watched him struggle, his movements growing more desperate with every passing moment.

She seized the opening, conjuring another arrow of light. She loosed it without hesitation, then another, and another, the air filling with streaks of blue energy. For a moment, it felt like time itself slowed, each arrow hurtling toward its target like a promise unfulfilled.

Myrradin lashed out with bursts of wind, scattering Selaina's arrows as they streaked toward him. But the relentless assault overwhelmed his defenses. One arrow slipped through, piercing his shoulder with a searing crack of energy. He staggered, snarling in pain, his hand clutching at the wound, but his grip on the shield around Rykan did not waver.

Selaina paused to catch her breath, her chest heaving as she steadied herself. But Myrradin struck back with a furious torrent of windforce. Selaina didn't move. The wind slammed into her like a tidal roar, meant to crush, but instead of bracing herself, she stepped into it. The current wrapped around her, not striking, but spiraling, uncertain.

She'd felt this before. Not just in Wekenwild, where she learned that magic moved like ripples in water, like breath through a song, but again, when Amera had tried to bind her with that same unnerving precision. Selaina had slipped through it then, not with power, but with understanding. This was no different.

She let herself fall into the pulse of the wind, reading its intent like music on a stave, every surge a note, every shift a beat. Then, she moved with it. Not by force. By resonance.

The gale faltered, twisted, and folded back on itself. It spun out behind her like a snapped tether, then hurled itself straight toward Myrradin.

He reeled, his boots skidding across the stone, heels digging furrows in the earth as he fought to stay upright. His cloak snapped behind him like a banner in a storm.

"How?" he hissed, eyes narrowing.

Selaina's bow snapped up, already humming with energy. "You're not the only one who's learned how to wield power."

She fired without hesitation. The bolt screamed through the air, a crackling streak of blue-white light that carved through the smoke between them.

A second burst of magic slammed into the ground nearby, earth split, rock fountained, and through the rising haze strode Ysadora, cloak rippling, her eyes glowing with a dangerous clarity.

"You freed me for him? How insulting," she said, voice edged like glass. Her gaze cut to Rykan, still trapped in the glimmering sphere. Then she looked back to Myrradin, a cold smile forming as she raised her staff. "I thought I rated as more of a threat than that."

Without waiting for a response, she slammed her staff into the ground. The earth cracked with a deafening roar, and jagged spikes erupted beneath Myrradin in a spiraling wave. He twisted away, already shifting, his form unraveling into the spectral swirl of a Windwraith, barely clearing the strike as the stone splintered upward like spears.

Selaina fired another volley of arrows, their radiant blue streaks illuminating the battlefield as they hurtled toward Myrradin. His Windwraith form swirled and twisted, the spectral winds slicing through the air. But with a sudden, forceful gust, he shed the form, returning to his corporeal body. The arrows scattered wildly as the winds redirected their paths, sparking harmlessly against the stone.

Breathing heavily, Myrradin straightened, his robes billowing in the residual gust. Though his stance was steady, a crease of weariness crossed his face.

Selaina's focus remained unbroken, her sharp gaze fixed on Rykan's encasement. She pressed forward, her steps deliberate despite the chaos around her. Behind her, Ysadora wasn't finished. With a commanding gesture, Ysadora drove her staff into the ground, summoning roots and vines from the earth's depths. They surged upward, twisting and coiling around Myrradin, seeking to ensnare him.

The vines locked around Myrradin, but only for a moment. A green glow flared at his hands, mirrored by a shimmer at the roots themselves. Wispy tendrils of energy stretched between them, meeting in mid air like threads weaving a fatal connection. The vines withered, crumbling to dust as their essence was drained away, and the light pulsed up Myrradin's arms, steadying his stance and sharpening his breath.

Selaina approached the barrier encasing Rykan, the Aedavaris, woven from pure order. She'd shattered it once from within. Could she do the same now from without?

Her fingers met the smooth curve of the shield, its cold shimmer humming beneath her skin. Her thoughts burned with Rykan, how he'd stepped into danger without hesitation. She couldn't fail him. Not now.

The energy surged into her, not violently, but with structure, layered and precise, like Wekenwild. It didn't resist her; it sought alignment, testing her ability to match its pattern.

The resonance deepened. A tremor raced up her spine as her power clashed with the shield's rhythm. She gritted her teeth. Then screamed.

A pulse of blue erupted from her palm, a harmonic shockwave that rippled outward, cracking the structure at its core. The shield didn't just break. It unraveled, each thread collapsing in perfect sequence until only silence remained.

But the silence lasted only a breath.

From the space the shield had held, a violent pressure burst outward, chaotic, untethered. Rykan's sealed power, compressed too long within the grip of order, exploded free.

Black and red lightning arced into the sky like veins through storm clouds, raw and aimless. It struck without pattern or mercy, tearing across stone, rending the sky, and slamming into Selaina.

Pain cracked through her as the force hurled her backward. She hit the ground hard, air ripped from her lungs. Sparks danced in her eyes. The world spun, thunder in her ears and lightning still pulsing beneath her skin.

She gasped, tasting blood, but pushed herself up on trembling arms.

Above, Myrradin's Windwraith form buckled as the blast slammed into him in mid air. The winds tore free from his shape, his body twisting as he tumbled down, crashing behind a shattered pillar and vanishing from sight.

Rykan stood at the center of the storm.

Selaina's heart thudded. That power, it didn't move like anything she'd ever seen. It writhed, it surged, it wanted.

Ysadora staggered to her feet beside her, brushing ash from her cloak, eyes wide. "Rykan, stop! You can't control chaos," she hissed. "You're going to kill us all."

Rykan's face tensed. "I'm trying to hold it in," he said.

Selaina, still on one knee, felt the hum of shattered magic vibrating through her bones. The remnants of Myrradin's Aedavaris drifted in the air like scattered starlight, shards of pure order, fractured but still alive, buzzing with echoes of their original purpose.

She reached for them. They answered, not with resistance, but recognition.

The fragments surged toward her, orbiting in a widening spiral, blades of blue fire spinning around her like the rings of a newborn star. Myrradin's magic, once a prison, now bent to her will.

From behind a cracked pillar, Myrradin stepped forward, his form still fraying at the edges, spectral, wrathful, unraveling and reforming. His voice tore through the air like broken glass.

"I'll take the blessing, if I have to kill every last one of you!" he shouted.

Selaina stood. The shards circled her in a storm of light and memory, each one a broken piece of order, a promise turned into a blade. She raised her hand. And unleashed them.

The shards screamed through the air, no longer passive threads of containment but instruments of defiance. Memory forged into weapon. Magic with purpose.

Myrradin's eyes widened.

He lashed out, summoning a wall of shrieking wind. Most of the shards disintegrated against the gale, flitting out like dying stars.

But not all. A few slipped through, clean and precise. They sliced across his cheek and brow, carving red lines that welled and ran like blood mourning its origin.

He flinched. Grimaced. Staggered. But did not fall.

Then, without warning, he changed, becoming wind and shadow. His spectral form surged like a storm breaking loose, wisps of Windwraith essence trailing behind him. Tendrils of pale green and silver snapped through the air, latching onto Rykan. The red-black lightning that had coiled around Rykan faltered as Myrradin's essence plunged into his chest.

Rykan staggered, folding forward with a strangled gasp.

Myrradin fed, greedy, relentless, not just on life, but something buried deeper. The blessing itself. He clawed at it like a drowning man clawing for air, trying to rip it from Rykan's core. Could it even be done? Or was it the madness of a sorcerer unraveling?

Selaina's bow ignited, not with fire, but with memory.

She loosed a streak of light, a flash of will and fury. Myrradin felt it coming. He wrenched away from Rykan, spun, and met the arrow mid-flight with a cyclone of wind, shredding it to glowing fragments.

Ysadora slammed her staff into the earth. Stone answered. The ground rose in jagged spears, a cry of the mountain itself. Myrradin surged into the air like a rising maelstrom, wind coiling around him in violent spirals, then turned his fury on her.

A gale screamed down, catching Ysadora in its teeth and flinging her toward the broken edge of the path.

Selaina drew again, but too slow.

Tendrils of pressure and cold burst from the vortex, not wind exactly, but something pulled from within her. They struck her chest and spine; she gasped, her arms locking, lungs frozen mid-breath. It wasn't pain at first. It was a leeching, her energy unspooling thread by thread, unwoven from the inside out.

The tendrils pulsed in rhythm, subtle, buried, but deliberate. It wasn't truly wild. It followed a rhythm, just one few could hear. Even this magic had rules. Not like the crystalline logic of Wekenwild. This rhythm was harsher. Cruder. Like a storm. Patterned enough to endure. Savage enough to devour. And with every glimmer of stolen strength, she was learning it.

She was learning its language with every fading heartbeat.

Then, the sky cracked. Rykan's chaos exploded across the stone in a jagged spear of red and black, striking Myrradin mid-draw. The tendrils shattered. The storm recoiled. Myrradin's body slammed back into physical form, his shape snapping together like broken bone forced into place.

But even as he hit the ground, he turned, wind surging from his palm, raw and furious. It caught Rykan in the chest and hurled him against the temple steps, where he crashed in a sprawl of red sparks.

Selaina dropped to one knee, breath sharp, skin raw with cold, but her hands moved with fierce intent. It wasn't pain that drove her now, it was purpose.

The magic that had tried to unravel her now swirled in her grasp, torn from ruin and reshaped into rhythm. She no longer resisted his drain. She commanded it.

An arrow coalesced between her fingers, threads of luminous green, the same spectral hue that had siphoned some of her energy moments before. But now it pulsed with her will, synchronized to the beat of her heart. No longer a wound, now a weapon.

This wasn't vengeance or wrath. It was understanding, reclaimed and sharpened. A closed circuit. A reckoning. She fired.

The arrow tore from the bowstring with a low, resonant chord, half thunder, half music, ripping through the air like a blade drawn across a cathedral bell.

Myrradin turned, his form half-shadow, half-flesh, the wind weaving through him like a living shroud.

Wind shrieked from the vortex, a cyclone of pressure and fury, but the arrow met the storm, and drank it.

The sound deepened, richer and darker, as the gale curled inward. The battlefield trembled, the ground, the stones, the mist around Myrradin's shifting form, all shivering under the weight of the sound.

A single note pulsed through the air, tightening like a drawn wire, rising until it throbbed through marrow and mist alike. Then the cyclone shuddered. Shivered. And collapsed into the arrow like a scream swallowed by silence.

His magic didn't deflect it. It fed it. And the arrow sang as it struck.

There was no explosion, only stillness. Then a sharp recoil, as if the world itself exhaled. Myrradin's body convulsed. His hands clawed at the air around the wound, but there was no blood, only light pouring out, coiling into threads that reversed course and streamed back toward Selaina.

The stolen vitality returned to its source. Selaina's body surged with heat. Her breath steadied. Her limbs steadied. Her vision cleared. The cold in her blood fled before the returning fire.

Myrradin staggered, eyes wide with disbelief. "I could have saved us…"

He reached for another spell, but all his power was gone.

The arrow's magic continued to drink him down, unraveling every thread he had siphoned, every tether he had twisted. His form cracked, split, fractured like frozen glass struck by a single, perfect note.

The remnants of the storm collapsed inward, falling away in spiraling shards of mist and dust, each fragment fading like the last echo of a dying song.

The Windwraith came undone. Not just in death. It was disintegration, like a spell being undone.

Myrradin dissolved into ash, a gray smear pulled into the wind he no longer controlled. Only his robes remained, folding into the silence like a flag lowered at the end of a lost war.

Selaina stood in the stillness, breath calm, skin warm with the life energy she'd reclaimed. The battlefield was silent, but the arrow's pattern still thrummed through her bones, humming to a rhythm only she could hear.

She exhaled slowly, the bow in her grip warm and alive. The mountain pulsed beneath her feet. For a moment, everything felt weightless, effortless.

Selaina felt alive in a way she had never known.

"Your eyes…" Ysadora's voice broke through, sharp and quiet. "Like blue flame."

Selaina stiffened for a heartbeat, her hand twitching up toward her face. Then she blinked, the world snapping back into focus. "What?" Her voice came low, distant even to her own ears.

Rykan stepped closer, his expression twisted with something more than concern. "Just like Vatreus…"

Selaina looked away, her hand on her face, as if to hide something that couldn't be hidden.

"I'm not him," she said, but there was a tremor beneath the words. "I won't be him."

Neither of them answered. The wind moved around them, quiet now, as if even the mountain was waiting.

"Ethyllion's power is awakening in you," said Ysadora. "Perhaps you don't need the Crown of Breath after all."

Without another word, she knelt beside the rubble, brushing aside the dust. Two metal trinkets lay exposed in the pile.

Selaina moved closer and crouched beside her. Her fingers hesitated for a moment, then closed around the objects. Two necklaces: one the talisman she had thrown back at him, its chain now broken, and another identical, untouched, its chain gleaming faintly in the dim light.

"Bondmark relics," Ysadora said, her tone sharp with disdain. "A magical copy, made to bind two people together. Unnatural, dangerous magic. I wonder what he planned to do with this."

Selaina turned the intact talisman over in her hands, her expression darkening. "Just like the one I was wearing," she murmured.

Rykan stepped forward, his voice cutting through the tension. "Why would he want to bond with you?"

Ysadora's eyes narrowed. "The Crown of Breath," she said, the realization dawning in her expression. "He was hoping to receive the blessing through the bond of these talismans. Were you wearing it when the Sky Serpents gave their blessing?"

Selaina nodded slowly, her voice edged with frustration. "Yes, but I didn't receive the blessing. Rykan did."

"What?" Ysadora's brows knitted together in confusion. "How is that possible? Why would they give it to him?"

"It wasn't meant for me," said Rykan. "I reacted. I thought Selaina was in danger."

Selaina's fingers dug into the talisman. "Myrradin left this behind on the mountain, knowing I would take it."

Ysadora exhaled sharply. "That sounds exactly like something he would do."

"A deceiver to the bitter end," Selaina muttered, tossing the talisman to the ground. Her eyes flicked to the temple, its glow fading now, and then to Rykan, still standing as though holding the weight of all that had transpired. "Was it all worth it?"

Rykan glanced around, tension still thrumming in his voice. "What about the others? We need to help them!"

CHAPTER 52

Tʜᴇ ɪᴄʏ ᴡɪɴᴅ howled through the pass, carrying flecks of snow that stung Rykan's face as he hurried to get back to Garrick and Nadara. The jagged peaks loomed above them, casting long shadows over the frozen ground. Ysadora stood at the edge of the path, her silhouette rigid against the white expanse beyond.. She kneeled near fresh mounds of snow.

"Ysadora!" he called, his voice straining against the wind.

She straightened abruptly, her staff tapping the frozen ground with a sharp, echoing crack as she turned back toward him. "They're alive but buried in ice. I can't get them out on my own."

Rykan's chest ached at her words. The thought of Garrick and Nadara trapped beneath the frozen weight sent a surge of urgency through him. They'd fought too hard to lose anyone else now.

He dashed toward Ysadora, and Selaina quickly followed. The blue flame had faded from Selaina's eyes, bringing comfort that she was still the same Selaina he knew. A pile of snow covered the path, where it had slid from the rock terrace of the mountain. Ysadora had already dug through the snow, uncovering Nadara's hand sticking out from a sheet of ice. It appeared the snow had been heated and frozen again as it melted.

Rykan crouched, pressing the tip of his sword against the ice, testing its resilience. Selaina and Ysadora dug furiously at the surrounding snow, trying to uncover more of the bodies beneath. He focused on the power in the blade, willing it to rise. For a fleeting moment, it answered, a faint surge of heat pulsing through the weapon. But as soon as he became aware of it, the energy ebbed like a receding tide.

The snow shifted as Selaina dug with her hands, uncovering the outline of Garrick's arm. Rykan's frustration deepened. The power flashed again, bubbling up unpredictably. Too much of it, and he risked harming them. Too little, and he would be no help at all.

Ysadora unearthed Nadara's glaive, buried beneath the snow, and began using it to chip away at the ice. Their progress was painfully slow. At this rate, hours might pass before they freed even one of them. Hours they might not have.

Rykan's hold stiffened on the hilt of his blade. He couldn't hold back anymore. The time for caution had passed. If he failed, they would suffocate before they saw the light of day.

Taking a deep breath, Rykan pushed into his connection with the blade, searching for the storm of energy that simmered within. He coaxed it carefully, but the power teased him, flaring just beyond his reach before retreating again. He clenched his jaw, his frustration mounting.

Then he stopped holding back.

Focusing every fiber of his will, Rykan forced the energy to rise, pushing it to the brink. It boiled up, violent and uncontrollable, until it surged through the blade like lava. A crackling storm of red and black lightning erupted, tearing through the air.

"Rykan, stop!" Selaina shouted, raising her arms instinctively.

The lightning froze mid-arc, its chaotic tendrils spiraling harmlessly upward into the sky. The blade in Rykan's hand shifted, its fiery glow softening as it turned a deeper, darker red. Steam hissed from the ice as the power within the sword pulsed, focused now, but not by his hand.

He glanced at Selaina. "What... what did you do?"

"I felt it," Selaina said, lowering her arms. "The power inside your blade... it has a wild rhythm, like a broken pattern." She paused, eyes narrowing. "I didn't control it. I just... kept it steady."

Rykan blinked. The sword still pulsed in his hand. The chaos had stilled, circling now like a tide drawn by moonlight. "You did that?"

She nodded. "Try it again."

He turned back to the ice and swung the blade.

The ice melted away under the blade's touch, hissing as steam rose in thick clouds. Within moments, Nadara broke free, coughing and shivering but alive.

Rykan nodded slowly. For now, it was enough. But a part of him wondered how much longer he could walk the line between wielding this power and being consumed by it.

Before long, he had freed Garrick as well. Ysadora began catching them up on recent events.

"If Rykan got the blessing," Nadara said, curiously, "does that mean he's Zhal Evurah now?"

"No," Ysadora replied firmly. "It only means he received the blessing."

"So what will happen?" Garrick asked, his voice heavy with doubt. "How will Selaina defeat Vatreus without the blessing? Did we come all this way for nothing?"

"Maybe I can help," Rykan said, sheathing his blade. The red glow died instantly as his fingers left the hilt, like a breath held too long finally exhaled. "I have some of this power now. I can use it."

"Is that why you did it?" Garrick asked, his tone suddenly accusatory. "Wanted some power for yourself?"

"What? No!" Rykan snapped, his frustration boiling over. "Did you not hear anything Ysadora said?"

"If he hadn't taken it, Myrradin would have," Ysadora interjected, her tone measured but firm. "We're fortunate things went the way they did."

"Are you sure Myrradin is dead?" Garrick pressed.

"His body dissolved into nothing," Selaina said softly, her expression dark. "It blew away with the wind." As everyone prepared to leave, Selaina glanced around, her brow furrowing. "What about Kadin? We haven't gotten him out yet."

Rykan froze, closing his eyes briefly. The weight of her words pressed against his chest. He took a deep breath, knowing he couldn't shield her from the truth. "Selaina," he began, his voice low and pained. "Kadin never made it this far... he's gone."

For a moment, Selaina didn't move. Her face remained still, unreadable. Then, like something inside her gave way, she dropped to her knees. Her hands sank into the dirt, fingers trembling.

Silence stretched around them, heavy as stone.

Rykan glanced at the others. Nadara had turned away, arms crossed, her gaze fixed on the horizon. Garrick stood rigid, fists clenched at his sides, the muscles in his jaw tight.

Rykan didn't need words to know the grief wasn't just his.

"It's my fault," Ysadora said, breaking the silence. Her voice was quiet, raw, trembling as she forced the words out. "He died to save me. All the time I've spent perfecting magic… and telling everyone about it to make me feel important. I guess he believed it."

Selaina looked up, tears streaking her face. "Ysadora, you are important," she said, her voice steady despite the crack in it. "Without you, none of this would be possible."

Without hesitation, Selaina reached out, pulling Ysadora into an embrace. For a moment, Ysadora stiffened, but then her arms found their way around Selaina, holding her tightly.

"Kadin didn't care about your magic," Garrick said, his voice rough but earnest. "He saved you because you're one of us."

Ysadora's hold on Selaina tightened as a sob escaped her, unbidden and raw. She pulled back slightly, raising her silvery hand around Selaina. Her lips curved into the smallest smile as she glanced up at him, fragile yet genuine.

For a moment, the group was united in silence, the weight of Kadin's absence pressing heavily on them. Yet within the quiet, there was an unspoken understanding, a need to keep moving forward, for each other and for those they had lost.

As the sky deepened into dusk, they made camp near the frozen lake. The stillness of the water mirrored the somber mood, broken only by the soft hiss of the fire Garrick started. Selaina crouched by the lake's edge, filling a vial with water from a narrow break in the ice. Nearby, Ysadora passed around some of the food they had gathered in Glissara, her movements careful but steady, her gaze distant yet present.

Around the fire, Selaina shared stories of what had happened to her since Myrradin took her, her voice a mix of sadness and determination. Rykan followed, recounting what the group had seen in her absence. As he spoke, their shared struggles came into sharp focus, the moments of despair, the small victories, and the unyielding bonds that had brought them this far.

They fashioned a shelter as best they could and gathered beneath it.

Most of them huddled around the fire, using the warmth of each other's bodies to guard them against the cold.

Selaina left the firelight behind, her silhouette swallowed by the night. Rykan hesitated, but only for a moment. He followed, finding her leaning against a stone, her eyes tracing the sky above.

The three stars, once clustered in a perfect triangle the night the Wishing Stone stirred, had drifted apart. Scattered now, each shone alone in the vast dark. The sight unsettled him more than he expected.

"Do you mind if I join you?" he asked softly.

She didn't answer, but she didn't say no. That was enough. He settled beside her, but not too close.

"You took the Crown of Breath," she said at last, her voice barely more than a whisper. "The blessing that was meant for me."

The words struck deeper than he expected.

"I thought…" Rykan began, but trailed off. "I thought they were attacking you."

"I know," she said gently, cutting him off. "You stepped in to protect me. You didn't know what would happen. I'm not angry at you for that."

"But something else?" he asked.

"At first I was… I was angry at the world," she said. "At the Sky Serpents. At whatever this destiny is supposed to be. I have this mark", she touched her brow lightly, "but I was still just a girl who grew up in the forest. I thought the blessing would make me believe I was Zhal Evurah. That without it, I was just pretending."

"You stopped Myrradin," Rykan said. "You did things I don't even understand. Even without the blessing."

Selaina exhaled, her breath curling in the cold air. "I'm still sorting it all out. But tonight…" She paused. Then added, quieter still, "Tonight I wonder if I never needed the blessing. Maybe I just needed to understand what's inside me."

She turned to face him, her eyes reflecting a pale silver glint from the sky. "Caelum told me a story. About two rivers, one swift, one strong. A wolf convinced them to merge, thinking they'd be better together. But when they did, they became too powerful. They destroyed the land. It was only when they ran side by side, separate, but in harmony, that they brought peace."

Selaina looked away. "Maybe the blessing and the power in me were never meant to belong to one person. Together, they might've ruined everything." Her voice dropped. "Even with good intentions."

Rykan was quiet, struck by the image. Then Selaina gave a small, rueful smile.

"You have the breath of the Sky Serpents. I have the spark of the Wishing Stone. We're different, but maybe that's what makes us stronger."

Rykan swallowed. "You really believe that?"

"I do," she said. "Because now I don't feel like I'm pretending anymore. I don't feel like I have to prove something. Zhal Evurah isn't just a title. It's who I am. And not even you can take that from me."

He froze, then saw the curve of a smirk at her lips.

"Don't be too sure," he said, trying to match her tone. "There's no one better at messing things up than me."

She gave a quiet laugh. "You haven't always given me a reason to trust your judgment," she said, her tone growing serious. "But your heart? I trust your heart more than anything."

He looked at her, his throat tight. A long silence passed between them, but it wasn't uncomfortable. Not anymore.

"You should get back to the camp," she murmured. "Get some rest. I'm going to stay out here for a little while longer."

Rykan returned to the camp, finding a place between Nadara and Garrick. He replayed everything from the previous day in his mind over and over until the thoughts wandered free, no longer aware they were even thoughts at all.

As some sense of awareness found him again, Rykan saw a dark space filled with shards of broken glass floating in the air. Some pieces barely moved, while others flew haphazardly around a central point. Each shard was of a different size and shape, reflecting a red light that had no source.

Moving through the floating dust of the smallest particles, Rykan saw the reflections of one shard that revealed the misshapen forms of The Sullen. They were gathering in the forests under a pale moon, even now as he and his friends slept.

"Rykan…" said a voice. "You have done well."

Rykan turned to see a shard of mirrored glass behind him. Its surface shimmered with an oily, dark sheen.

"You have taken the blessing… and in doing so, you have made it a vessel for chaos. My gift flows through you now. Whether you realize it or not, you are already mine. You could be the greatest servant of chaos I have ever produced," Nociferon said as the reflection swirled in a mass of black and red, colors bleeding into one another like ink in water. "Chaos does not stumble blindly, Rykan. It chooses. No beginning. No end. Only will."

The words hung in the air, reverberating through the space like a death knell. Rykan opened his mouth to speak, but no sound came at first. A glimmer of doubt coursed through him, could he really stand against this force? The power within him burned like an uncontained storm, and he briefly wondered if Nociferon's words held a sliver of truth. Was he already losing control? Was he already on the path to becoming exactly what the Chaos Lord wanted?

The shard nearest him reflected another version of himself, twisted, consumed by chaos, his features distorted by malice. His chest tensed as fear whispered insidiously: *What if this is who I am meant to become?*

The faces of his companions flashed in his mind, Selaina's unwavering commitment to helping free the world, Garrick's steady loyalty, Ysadora's and Nadara's fierce will. They were his anchor, his light against the storm. He couldn't falter, not while they believed in him.

"I am not your servant," said Rykan. "Taking the blessing was not my intent, but for as long as it is mine, I will only use it to fight against you."

The voice of Nociferon came again, smooth yet jagged, layered with countless tones. "Fight me? Foolish mortal. Chaos cannot be fought. It consumes all, even its wielder. Do you think you can wield its power without succumbing to it?"

The shard's surface trembled, and Rykan felt a faint pull, as though the Lord of Pandemora's presence was reaching for him. Within the swirling chaos, brief wisps of form appeared, twisted faces, screaming mouths, and gleaming eyes that watched him with malice before dissolving back into the formless void. The shard began to hum, its vibrations sharp and resonant, cutting through the stillness of the space like a blade.

"The forests surrounding the mountain are filled with the Sullen," said Nociferon. "Take the girl to them. She carries the last spark of the Wishing Stone, and through it, I will take form. Then the mortal realm will not resist. Chaos will no longer whisper, it will thunder. Together, we will shape Galanor into a realm unshackled by fate. Even the stones remember. Beneath every law, every border, the wild breath stirs, waiting to reclaim what was tamed."

Through the shards of glass, Rykan saw reflections of himself, some as he once was, some as he was now, and others that disturbed him. He saw himself standing in the middle of a fiery battlefield, his sword raised high as the world burned around him.

"You cannot escape it, Rykan. You cannot fight fire with fire, nor chaos with chaos," said Nociferon.

The formless presence in the shard coalesced and expanded, an ever-shifting vortex of grotesque shapes. Tendrils of darkness spiraled outward, only to dissolve and reform as jagged spires or gaping maws.

Rykan reached out to touch one of the reflections of himself, but it exploded into dust. A low, rumbling laugh emanated from the shard, shaking Rykan to his core. The swirling mass within the shard surged forward, pressing against its surface as though trying to break free. Rykan thought he saw something deeper within the chaos, something ancient and immeasurably vast, a presence that stretched beyond the shard, beyond him, beyond the very concept of form.

A crack split the air, and the shard nearest him shattered, its pieces scattering into the void. The low, rumbling laugh of Nociferon echoed in his ears, shaking him to his core.

The shards began to spin faster and faster, blurring together into a vortex of red light. The voice of Nociferon spoke one last time, fading as the space around Rykan began to collapse. "You cannot fight chaos with chaos..."

With a jolt, Rykan awoke, the echoes of Nociferon's laughter still buzzing in his ears, like a whisper that refused to die. His breath came sharp and ragged, and his heart pounded in his chest as if he had carried a fragment of that storm back with him. The blade beside him seemed to hum, its crimson glow flickering like a dying ember. For a moment, he questioned if he had truly escaped Nociferon's grasp, or if the storm within him was merely lying in wait.

CHAPTER 53

SOMETHING STIRRED SELAINA from her sleep, a pull in the night she couldn't explain. She rose from the shelter as the others slept, not even bothering to cover her feet. The snow met her bare skin, unexpectedly warm, almost welcoming, as though the earth itself called her forward. Outside, the air was unnaturally still, the stars hidden behind a thin veil of mist. The forest around the lake seemed alive, not with the rustle of leaves or the distant cries of animals, but with a profound, watchful presence that prickled her senses.

Shadowy forms emerged, slipping from behind trees, rising from the mist, and even stretching forth from the darkness of her own shadow. The Nadrok gathered silently, forming a semicircle. Their featureless shapes rippled and shifted, caught between solidity and nothingness, as if the very act of existing was tenuous for them. Their presence pressed against Selaina's mind, not with words, but with the raw weight of their intent.

Selaina froze, unsure whether to run or to stay. But then, the closest Nadrok stepped forward, its movements impossibly fluid. It stretched out a hand, or something like a hand, its shape indistinct, trailing wisps of shadow that dissipated into the night.

In its palm was a glimmering light, faint and fragile, like a dying ember suspended in a void. The light pulsed gently, each glow a heartbeat that resonated within Selaina's chest. The Nadrok leaned closer, not menacing but deliberate. The light in its palm shifted, stretching into a slender thread that spiraled slowly toward her. Selaina's breath caught as the thread wove itself into the air, connecting her to the Nadrok. She felt it sink into her skin, like a chill that settled deep within her chest, cold yet not unpleasant.

Her vision fractured into countless fragments, each shard showing a different place. She saw the vast plains of Galanor, where the Iron Flood's armies marched with mechanical precision, their banners cutting stark lines against the horizon. Beneath Kylinshan, shadows stirred, the Sullen whispered in hidden depths. And yet, in every scene, the Nadrok were there: silent, watching, sentinels of a world teetering on the edge of change.

As the vision faded, Selaina's sight returned to the quiet of the lake. The Nadrok had not moved, their forms still and unreadable, though she sensed their gaze lingering on her. She touched her chest, feeling the faint cold radiating within and understanding the gift they had bestowed, not stolen, but freely given. She could see through their eyes, connected to their silent watch across the world.

Her heart raced as the vastness of their gift settled over her. The closest Nadrok inclined its head, a subtle motion that seemed to seal their bond. One by one, they dissolved into the night, fading into the shadows from which they had come. Selaina stood alone beneath the misty sky, the enormity of her new awareness both exhilarating and humbling.

As dawn broke, Selaina helped everyone take down the shelter, packing things into Garrick's backpack before gathering her own bag, along with her bow and quiver. For a moment, she wondered if she even needed the quiver anymore. It was empty and she hadn't bothered to make any new arrows. For now, she felt confident in her ability to harness the energy of order to form bolts when she needed them, but picked up the quiver too, perhaps for sentiment if nothing else.

They marched through forests and past ancient ruins until the waterways of Glissara came into view. Selaina stopped, marveling at the sight before her: a lake that gleamed like polished glass, fed by waterfalls cascading from jagged cliffs. Twisting streams and rivulets crisscrossed the landscape, their currents flowing toward the river ahead.

Rykan walked up beside her, his gaze following hers.

"This is incredible," she said as she turned to face him.

"Makes you wonder how much of this world could be like this if we weren't so busy tearing it apart," Rykan said.

Selaina glanced at him, a small smile forming. "Not tearing it apart, putting it back together."

Ysadora stepped closer, her gaze analytical. "The waterways here are ancient. The way the streams interlock… this place should be in complete harmony with everything around it, but something feels off," she said. "The Glissarans' damming might've disrupted it, but if the balance can be restored here, maybe it's possible elsewhere."

"Maybe," Garrick said, his tone skeptical. "But it's going to take a lot more than balancing nature to change minds, people are messy."

Above the village walls rose a massive tree, its ancient branches stretching skyward as though seeking the heavens. Rykan led them to the village gate, where two guards eyed him with recognition and opened the way. Inside, villagers bustled about, but many turned to stare as the group passed. Selaina could feel the weight of their gazes, whispers rising in her wake like wind through the trees.

A warrior approached, his long spear glinting in the fading light. His armor, battered but well kept, marked him as someone of importance.

"Well, you don't look too disappointed, finding out there's no Sky Serpents up there," he said to Rykan. "You're taking it better than most."

"Aresh! I'm not disappointed," Rykan replied, his tone firm. "We saw them! The Sky Serpents appeared!"

The warrior Rykan called Aresh stiffened. "Don't mock us. Making light of our beliefs won't go well here."

"But I'm serious," Rykan insisted. He rested a hand on Selaina's shoulder. "This is Selaina, the Zhal Evurah I told you about."

Aresh squinted, his gaze narrowing on the glowing mark on Selaina's forehead. He reached out, then hesitated, his hand falling back. "The mark is convincing. But the Whisper Beyond the Stars is a legend, nothing more. No one is coming to save us."

"You have to believe me," Rykan said, stepping forward. "The Sky Serpents gave me their blessing."

Aresh replied. "Why would they give it to you and not her? At least she is marked, whether by destiny or some other magic."

Selaina interjected before Rykan could respond, her tone steady. "Maybe the Sky Serpents don't follow a strict path like we imagine. Maybe they act as they see fit for the time and place." She glanced at Rykan, her gaze softening. "Perhaps they give their blessings where they are needed."

Aresh's eyes shifted back to Selaina, skepticism hardening his features. "What would either of you do for us then? Will you guard our lands against Shadal and force them away once and for all?"

Selaina felt the weight of the crowd's attention pressing on her. She stepped closer, meeting the Aresh's gaze. "I would ask why you dam the waters and leave so little for Shadal."

The people around them gasped, whispers rippling through the growing crowd like waves. The warrior's jaw tensed, and he crossed his arms over his chest.

A gray-haired elder pushed through the crowd, his presence commanding. "What is this?" he asked.

"This one claims to be the Whisper Beyond the Stars," someone muttered.

"We give Shadal more than they deserve," the warrior said sharply. "We cannot forgive them for the betrayals of the past. Even now, they hunt sacred creatures like the moondrakes, guardians of the rivers and protectors of the balance."

"You speak of what you do not understand," the elder said. "The waters are not merely rivers to us. They carry the spirits of our ancestors, ensuring their peace. To let the tombs go dry is to forsake them, to condemn them to unrest."

An older woman with youthful eyes stepped forward, her voice soft but clear. "Glissarans believe that the flowing water connects the living and the dead, ensuring the spirits' journey to the Wellspring. It is a tradition as old as this village itself."

"Liora!" Rykan called, his voice cutting through the rising murmurs.

Heads turned toward the older woman, some with subtle nods of respect, others with furrowed brows. She acknowledged him with a brief nod, her expression calm but distant, as though she was weighing her words carefully before speaking.

Selaina frowned, searching for the right words. "I didn't know," she admitted. "But… if that is the only way to prevent suffering for the living, wouldn't your ancestors want you to do so? Weren't some of them alive when Glissara and Shadal were friends? Would they not want you to honor them by protecting their descendants?"

As the conversation continued, Ysadora stepped in, addressing the elder. "You said the waters connect the living and the dead," she said, her voice measured. "But if the living fall, what happens to that connection? Does it fade, or does it survive through those who are still here to honor it?"

Selaina turned to Garrick, who had been watching in silence. "You've seen more battles than any of us," she said.

Garrick's thumb tapped once against his belt before he sighed and stepped forward. "When people are too proud to band together, they lose…" he said simply, his voice heavy with the weight of memory. "I've seen it before, villages that thought they could stand alone, only to fall one by one. If we don't fight together, there won't be anything left to fight for."

"You speak of peace with Shadal?" a woman shouted from the crowd. "There can never be peace with those we cannot trust."

Selaina stepped forward, wind catching the edge of her cloak. "We must find a way to work together, not just Glissara and Shadal, but all of Galanor. The Iron Flood won't stop at the foot of the mountain. If we do not stand together, we'll fall alone."

Laughter, bitter, tired, broke from an elder near the front. "When has anyone ever come to help us? We bury our own dead. We bleed alone. We won't give our lives for those who'd never mourn us."

"This isn't about what they deserve," Selaina said. "It's about what we become if we don't rise now. The city beneath the mountain is already lost. Do you think they will spare Glissara, your water, your children, your songs?"

The crowd murmured, doubt and anger sparking like dry leaves in wind. Faces were drawn, voices tense, trust brittle as glass. Among them stood a woman too still to be ordinary. Rykan had called her Liora.

"If they come," the elder said firmly, "we will fight. We will defend Glissara."

"It will be too late," Selaina replied. "Defense means you've already been broken. We must act now, while we still can."

The murmurs swelled into something like thunder, doubt, tradition, pride all clashing in a storm of uncertainty.

"Our ways are not easily cast aside," the elder added, voice hard but not unmoved. "The dead cannot speak. And yet…"

He glanced toward the temple waters, and something in him, barely, briefly, wavered.

Liora raised her hand. "I can," she said softly, but her voice cut through the crowd like wind over water. "I've seen the Wellspring. The spirits do not cling to a single stream. They flow with the world's heartbeat."

Aresh scoffed, stepping forward. "And what does that mean, Liora? You've seen nothing but your tree and your rambling dreams. Go back there and leave us to reason."

But Liora didn't retreat. She glanced at Selaina, then at the crowd, and exhaled, as though releasing something long kept secret.

Her skin began to shimmer, water threading beneath the surface of flesh. A silver glow lit her eyes. The murmurs of the crowd turned to gasps as the light spread through her limbs, her outline blurring, then dissolving.

She burst into streams of radiant liquid, swirling upward in luminous arcs.

People staggered back instinctively, cries of alarm rising as they stumbled and scrambled to clear the square. Awe and fear rippled through the crowd like shockwaves. Children were pulled behind parents. Elders pressed against walls. Space opened, wide and reverent, as something far too large for the moment began to take shape.

The streams of light stretched, elongated, coalesced.

Wings unfolded like curtains of starlit mist, casting rippling patterns on the snow-dusted ground. Her scaled form shimmered with the colors of deep ocean and stormlit sky. She rose above them, vast and majestic, the air around her thrumming like the breath of the sea before a storm.

"I am Zaryneth," her voice rang out, not shouted, but resonant, carried on some deeper current. "And I have watched too long."

Above her, the sunshimmer pulsed in sync with her form, each motion of her wings drawing another wave through the heavens. The villagers looked up, open-mouthed and unblinking, tears glinting in more than one eye, not from fear, but from something deeper. Wonder. Memory. Recognition of an ancient truth returned.

Her tail curled through the mist below, the silvered scales catching each glimmer of light as she hovered.

"As a Celestial, I was forbidden to intervene. I failed once, and paid for it. But this rift, this feud between your people and Shadal, is a wound that festers. It poisons the rivers, weakens the land. It is my failure as much as yours. Now I choose to make it right."

She dipped her massive head, the great frill along her neck shifting with the movement, stirring the air into eddies around the gathered crowd. "Selaina is your Zhal Evurah, not by fate alone, but by the strength she's shown when no one was watching."

Selaina's breath caught. She hadn't expected this, not here, not now.

Zaryneth's luminous wings arched upward, framing her against the swirling sunshimmer above. "I have seen this one choose mercy when vengeance would have been easier. I have seen her stand alone when even her friends doubted her."

The air around the serpent vibrated with power, each beat of her wings sending shimmering gusts through the stunned silence. "She was worthy of the Crown of Breath, yet she did not cling to it. When the Sky Serpents came, it was Rykan who stepped between, believing we meant her harm, and so it was he who received our blessing."

She circled once over the square, her vast shadow sweeping across the villagers like the slow arc of an ancient memory returning to roost.

"Selaina bore no anger. No envy. She did not seek power for herself, but stood ready to protect others. Even when fate turned from her hand, she chose to lift others up instead of grasping for what was lost."

The sunshimmer pulsed overhead, answering the soft beat of Zaryneth's wings.

"She needed no blessing from us. Only that we open our eyes… and walk beside her."

Her words rang like a bell through the square, the resonance deepening in the bones of the earth.

"That is the heart of Zhal Evurah."

A ripple passed through the gathered villagers. Murmurs hushed.

Somewhere, a child took a step forward to see better, wide-eyed beneath the pale arc of Zaryneth's tail.

"She is not perfect. That is why she is worthy. She will not lead you as one above, but as one among you, bearing a weight too great for one heart alone."

Selaina lowered her head, not from shame, but from the sheer weight of the truth behind the words. Zaryneth's massive form coiled in the air, the mist around her spiraling in reverent shapes.

"Listen to her. Stand with her. For the time has come." The serpent's form shimmered once more, folding in on itself until Liora stood among them again, her face pale with the effort but unshaken.

"Liora…" Aresh's voice cracked. "You… you're a Sky Serpent?"

"I am one of you," she said. "And I choose to remain one. But even I cannot save this world alone. You must do what even the stars cannot."

Another man stood frozen, staring at Liora like he was trying to see her with new eyes. He shook his head once, slowly, more in wonder than disbelief.

"All this time…" he murmured. "I sat across from you. Talked with you. Shared stew with you. And still, I doubted."

He looked toward the temple, then the streams beneath their feet, as though everything familiar had just shifted beneath him.

"I thought the Sky Serpents were just old stories. Even while looking you in the eye, I never really believed." His voice dropped lower. "I thought if they ever had walked among us, they'd left long ago… but they hadn't. We just stopped looking for them."

Liora smiled at him, her gaze warm and steady. "Doubt is not failure, Jorin. It's the shadow cast by longing." She looked toward the temple and the flowing stream beyond it. "I never needed you to believe in me. Only to remember what we were meant to be."

Her eyes found his again, softer now.

"The serpents never left. But belief… belief has to walk its own path. I have shone too long in silence. Now, let the people speak."

Selaina stepped forward, her voice quiet, but firm as stone. "I know what your rituals mean to you. I know what it is to honor the dead. But if we lose the living, who will remain to carry their names?"

She turned slowly, meeting as many eyes as she could. The mark on her forehead hummed faintly.

"Do you think your ancestors would ask you to watch your children die just so their tombs remain untouched? Would they want silence... or survival?"

The crowd held its breath.

"The Iron Flood doesn't care about your rites or rivers. It will trample your temple, silence your songs, drown your prayers in blood. Unless we stop them. Together."

She pointed toward the dam.

"Opening it isn't just survival. It's a signal. It's the first thread in a braid we must weave together. If we work together here, we can unite the peaks. And the valleys. We can win. But not if we pretend this dam can hold back what's coming."

The silence afterward was not the silence of uncertainty.

It was the silence of something breaking, then beginning.

An older woman stepped forward, her silver-threaded hair catching the last gleam of twilight. Her voice was rough with age, but steady with conviction. "And what of the spirits?" she asked. "Without the water, how will they find peace in the afterlife? The currents are their guide. Are we to abandon them now?"

Selaina's expression softened, but her voice rang clear as bells over still water. "The peace of the dead does not lie in ritual alone. It lives in you, in your memory, your grief, your love. You honor them with every act of courage, every choice that defends the living. Their legacy flows not only in water, but in you."

Liora raised her head toward the stream below. "The Wellspring flows in many forms. It is not bound to stone or channel. Let the rivers flow freely, and the blessing will carry, not just to Shadal, but to the mountains, the valleys, the children who do not yet know what is coming. The balance of the world is deeper than we understand, and far harder to break."

A younger man stepped forward, uncertainty shadowing his brow. "If we do this... will Shadal stand with us? Will they fight, shoulder to shoulder, when the Iron Flood comes?"

Selaina didn't hesitate. "I will go to them myself. I'll tell them what you've done. I'll call them to meet us not as strangers, but as kin. And when the battle comes, we will stand together."

Another voice rose from the crowd, thick with fear. "But what if you're wrong? What if the spirits turn away? What if we lose both the living and the dead?"

Selaina stepped into the center of them all, her gaze sweeping across faces marked by time, by loss, by hard-won survival. "Then let me be the one who is wrong," she said. "But let it not be said that you stayed silent while the storm gathered. Trust is not born in ease. It begins here, now, in risk, in sacrifice, in hope. We do not forsake the past. We fight for the future."

For a long moment, no one spoke.

Then, like the first drop before a flood, a voice whispered, "Let the water flow."

Another called out, louder. "For Glissara! For Shadal!"

"For Talia and Doran!" someone cried, and Selaina's breath caught.

She turned toward the voice, her heart swelling. "They believed unity was more than a dream. They proved it. They showed that love could span rivers, that blood could be thicker than water, but compassion runs deeper still." She lifted her chin. "We honor them not with stillness, but with action."

The elder who had challenged her earlier stepped forward again. But now, his gaze held something new, respect. Resolve.

"You have my support, Zhal Evurah," he said, his voice solemn. "Let the waters rise. Let them run together."

He turned to the crowd and lifted his hand. "Send word to Shadal. If they will stand with us, then we will stand with them."

And like a dam breaking, voices rose in answer, one after another, until the summit echoed with the sound of unity. The mountain winds carried the chant like a promise written in the bones of the world.

CHAPTER 54

Aﬆer a night of uneasy rest in Glissara, the time had come to move on to Shadal. The morning air was heavy with unspoken tension, and the muted clatter of preparations filled the village square. The elders and most of the Glissaran warriors gathered near the path, their steely expressions leaving no doubt about their resolve. Their leader's words had been firm: they would accompany Selaina and her group, not just to lend their strength but to witness firsthand if the Shadalans could truly set aside their animosity.

Selaina stood at the edge of the gathering, her gaze fixed on the distant peaks that marked their next destination. Would freeing the waters really be enough to bridge the chasm between these villages? Her stomach twisted with unease. The history between Glissara and Shadal ran deep, and mistrust was not easily thawed. As much as she wanted to believe in their mission, doubt lingered like a shadow, gnawing at the edges of her resolve.

She glanced back at the line of soldiers marching behind her. Their armor caught the morning light, gleaming like shards of ice as they moved in single file along the narrow path between the rocks. Their presence felt like both a reassurance and a gamble.

"What if they think it's an invasion?" Selaina had asked Liora the night before.

Liora's response had been calm, as always. "I will be with you."

"Soldiers or not, we can't afford another misstep," Ysadora had added, her tone sharp but thoughtful. "When you speak, focus on what they gain by uniting with us, not just what they lose if they don't."

Selaina clung to their words as they approached the end of the river, where the water dropped below, forming the Serpent's Tear. The roar of the waterfall grew louder, a thundering symphony that filled the air and drowned out her racing thoughts. One by one, they descended the hidden narrow pathway to the bottom. With the reservoir now filled with water, they each had to swim to the shore. As she looked back toward the cliffs, the sight took her breath away.

The Serpent's Tear cascaded with newfound force, torrents of water crashing into the basin below and spilling into the river. The water raced through from the basin, carving a shining path through the rocky forests ahead. The wild beauty of it made Selaina's heart ache with a strange, bittersweet joy. This was what the world was meant to look like, alive, thriving, unbound.

Garrick stepped up beside her, his expression unreadable. "Beautiful," he said gruffly, though there was a softness in his voice. "But don't let the sight fool you. Peace like this doesn't last if we don't make it."

Selaina glanced at him, his words grounding her thoughts. Garrick's bluntness was often harsh, but she had come to value the steady practicality behind it. She nodded, drawing strength from his presence. The snow had receded in this part of the mountain, giving way to lush plants and green trees. Before they reached the village, darkness fell over them, forcing them to camp for the night.

"You made this happen," Rykan said, stepping up beside her. His voice was low, reverent. "The river flows because of you."

"We all did," Selaina nodded, but the weight of what lay ahead tempered her pride. "Let's hope Shadal sees it that way."

The landscape changed as they descended further. The snow that blanketed Glissara had melted into rich green undergrowth, the air thick with the scent of damp earth and budding leaves. As the sun dipped behind the horizon, they set up camp by the river. The sound of rushing water lulled Selaina into a fitful sleep, her dreams filled with visions of what might await them.

At dawn, they continued. The river guided their path, its currents reflecting the morning light. As they neared Shadal, Rykan stepped forward, his posture calm but purposeful. He turned back to address the Glissaran warriors.

"When we reach the village, hold your ground, but stay silent. Let them speak first. No raised voices, no reaching for weapons. You're not here to fight. You're here to prove that we're stronger together."

One of the soldiers frowned. "And what if they don't see it that way?"

Rykan's gaze hardened. "Then we give them time. This isn't about winning an argument, it's about planting a seed. Unity takes time to grow, but it won't start if they think we're here as conquerors."

Selaina watched him, a glimmer of surprise and admiration reflecting in her expression. This wasn't the impulsive Rykan she had once known. His words showed thoughtfulness and consideration.

"You're right," she said quietly. "They need to see this as an offering, not a demand."

When they reached Shadal, Selaina's breath caught. The once-empty watering pool had swelled into a vast lake, its edges crowded with villagers who stared in awe at the transformation. Their wonder was palpable, a quiet reverence that rippled through the crowd like the water itself.

"They look at the water like it's a miracle," Nadara murmured, stepping beside Selaina. "That's how we felt in my village before the Iron Flood came for us. They'll need more than water to believe we're here to help."

Their awe quickly turned to alarm when a Shadalan man stationed at the edge of the village spotted the approaching Glissaran warriors. His eyes widened, and he reached for the horn slung across his back. Without hesitation, he raised it to his lips and blew a deep, resonant note that echoed through the valley. The sound carried far, reaching the heart of the village.

Before anyone could react, Nadara stepped forward, her voice cutting through the air. "Wait!" she called, holding her hands up. "Look at the river. This isn't an invasion, it's a gift. Let us speak before you decide."

An elder stepped forward, his face etched with lines of distrust. His staff struck the ground as he spoke. "I might have known this was a trick," he said. "You send the waters, then march an army to our gates. Do you think we'll welcome you with open arms?"

"We've come to make peace," said Aresh. "We have broken our dams to share the water with you. We want to join with you to defeat the Iron Flood controlling the city below the mountain."

The Shadalan elder's eyes narrowed, his hand closing on the staff he carried. "When have the Glissarans ever gone to war, but to fight against us?" His tone was sharp, laced with years of distrust. "How can we trust them now? What's to stop them from rebuilding the dams the moment it suits them?"

"You are," Aresh said. "Not just to keep us honest, but to stand with us. If we're going to survive what's coming, it has to start here. This time, we don't need more walls. We need to see each other. Fight for each other."

"Anyone can talk. Even liars can promise," said the elder.

Garrick stepped forward, his grizzled presence commanding attention. "You're right to question us," he said bluntly. "I've fought for men who made promises they never meant to keep. But I've seen the Iron Flood firsthand, and if we don't stand together, none of us will have a village left to argue about."

Selaina looked over at Garrick, surprised by the raw honesty in his voice. The elder's suspicion clearly lingered, but he said nothing.

"What is the meaning of this, Selaina?" Oran's voice rang out as he stepped forward from the crowd. His piercing gaze bore into her, sharp with disapproval. "If you have what you came for, why drag Shadal into it?"

"The Glissarans offer hearthshare," said Selaina. "Opening the rivers is their good deed for the day. Do you offer anything in return?"

"We will return this good deed," said Oran. "But we won't fight others' wars."

"You think you can wait until the Iron Flood is at your gates?" Nadara said, her voice trembling with anger. "I thought the same. But when they came, we were too late to stand together. Don't make the same mistake."

"My city, Tathara, made that mistake too," said Rykan. "We underestimated the Iron Flood."

Selaina stiffened, Oran's words cutting deeper than the elder's skepticism. "This isn't just Glissara's fight or Shadal's fight," she said, meeting his gaze. "The Iron Flood threatens everyone. If we don't stand together now, none of us will survive."

Oran folded his arms, his expression unyielding. "How often has Galanor united without devouring itself from within? Even now, the scar between Shadal and Glissara bleeds beneath your feet."

Liora, standing nearby, spoke up, her tone calm but firm. "Oran, you of all people should understand the stakes. This isn't about old grievances, it's about the survival of Galanor."

Oran's eyes flicked to her, his jaw clenching. "I understand the stakes better than you think, Liora. But this path will always lead to ruin. We've seen it before, and we'll see it again." His arms remained folded across his chest, his expression set like stone. "We've guided enough. Light forced too early blinds more than it guides."

"And what have they learned from us?" Liora stepped forward, her voice steady but filled with sorrow. "When we interfered, we didn't guide them, we disrupted them. Do you not see? We interfered with the Aszh Rozaht's design."

Oran's frown deepened, but he didn't argue.

Selaina blinked, her head tilting. The way Liora said we, not they… it wasn't just rhetorical. She knew now who Oran was.

"I've come to understand that the Aszh Rozaht had a plan for Doran and Talia," Liora continued. "Their love was meant to end in tragedy, a sacrifice that would unite Glissara and Shadal, binding the villages in shared mourning and giving them a foundation to build lasting peace."

Selaina's heart thudded once. The way Liora spoke to him, so deliberate, so personal.

Oran's eyes flashed with something between pain and anger. "And we were supposed to let them die?" His voice cracked, betraying a rare glimpse of emotion. "To stand by and watch them perish when we had the power to save them?"

Selaina turned to him, startled by the raw emotion. That wasn't the voice of a village elder telling a story. That was someone who had lived it.

Liora's gaze softened, but her tone remained firm. "What we wanted doesn't matter, Oran. What mattered was the balance. By saving them, we thought we were sparing them pain, but we didn't see the ripples of our actions. Their children grew up favoring one village over the other, twisting their parents' legacy into a cause for division."

Selaina's mind raced. Suddenly, so many things Oran had said came flooding back with new weight. His questions, his warnings, even the way he had looked at her when no one else was watching. It hadn't just been curiosity. It had been caution. Judgment. A test.

"You speak of meddling," Liora continued, her voice sharper now. "But we meddled first. We let our hearts decide, when wisdom told us to wait, and the result was generations of pain. If we refuse to act now, Oran, we're not protecting mortals from our interference, we're abandoning them to the consequences of our mistakes."

Oran turned away, his jaw tight, his gaze fixed on the villagers of Shadal and the Glissaran soldiers waiting just beyond. "They were meant to pass, so the story could endure. But how could we stand by, knowing we had the power to stop it? How does a heart that still feels… choose silence?"

Selaina's breath quickened, she stared at Oran, her voice trembling as she took a step closer. "You… you were there," she said. "You're not just speaking about the past. You're part of it."

Oran stiffened, his shoulders rising as if bracing for a blow.

Selaina's eyes widened. "You're one of them. A Sky Serpent."

Gasps rippled through the crowd, and Oran turned back to face her, his expression weary and guarded.

Liora stepped forward, her gaze steady. "Yes," she said softly. "He is Auronia, the golden Sky Serpent. And like myself, he's been among mortals all this time."

The elder beside Oran staggered back, his face pale. "What… what is this?" he stammered.

A mix of shock and betrayal flooded through Selaina. "Why didn't you tell me?" she asked, her voice trembling. "Why hide who you are?"

Oran exhaled slowly. "Because I've seen what grows from our interference, pride, division, ruin. Remaining among mortals wasn't exile. It was a sentence. I wasn't a guide returning. I was a watcher paying penance."

Liora stepped closer, her voice calm but firm. "And what has your penance achieved, Oran? Has it healed the wounds we caused? Or has it let them fester? When we interfered, we may have robbed Glissara and Shadal of a long-lasting peace. Now, maybe we can help fix what we've broken."

Liora turned to the crowd, her voice carrying over them.

"Perhaps all this time, being among mortals wasn't punishment, it was purpose. And now we have the chance to fulfill it."

Oran's shoulders sagged, the tension bleeding out of him. For a moment, he looked older, wearier, as though carrying the weight of centuries. Finally, he turned to Selaina, his voice low but steady. "If we give this gift, it must not be squandered again. Promise me, Zhal Evurah, lead them not by flame, but by restraint."

Selaina stepped forward, meeting his gaze, her voice steady despite the storm in her chest. "I'll do everything I can."

A sudden gust of wind tore through the camp, scattering leaves and sending cloaks whipping in the air. Heads turned upward as a shadow passed over them, and gasps rippled through the crowd. Emerging from the clouds, an enormous emerald serpent descended, its wings shimmering like sunlight on water. The ground seemed to hum with the force of its presence as it landed in the clearing, its massive form dwarfing the gathered villagers.

The serpent shimmered, light cascading from its scales, and began to shift. In its place stood an old man with kind eyes and a knowing smile.

A sharp breath knifed into Selaina's chest. She stumbled back, then forward again. Her legs faltered, trapped between the urge to run and the awe rooting her in place.

"No…" she whispered, eyes wide. Her gaze darted between the man and the sky, searching for proof she hadn't just imagined it. "Caelum?" The name barely made it past her lips. Her pulse thundered. "You're… Verdantis?"

He chuckled, his voice as warm and steady as a hearth fire. "I am," he said. "Sometimes, it's better to observe before revealing the truth."

Selaina hesitated for only a moment before stepping closer and embracing him. The tension in her shoulders eased, his presence filling her with a sense of unexpected hope. Around them, the crowd remained frozen in stunned silence. Slowly, many of the Shadalans dropped to their knees, some bowing low to the Sky Serpent.

Caelum's gaze swept over them, his expression soft but firm. "Do not bow to us," he said, his voice carrying gently but with unmistakable authority. "We are only creations, same as you. You carry your own light, no less sacred than any written in the sky."

He looked to Oran, then to Liora, then to Selaina.

"It's time. Let what was broken begin to mend."

↝

Selaina stood at the overlook, her hand resting on the weathered stone ledge. Her shoulders ached from the day's labor, and dust clung to the folds of her sleeves like the day itself didn't want to let go. Below, the river now flowed freely for the first time in ages, carving its way down the valley, swelling what had once been a shallow water hole into a growing lake. The sun had bled into the horizon, leaving a bruised purple sky above the mountain peaks, and with it came the hush, soft, expectant, like the world had paused mid-step, listening for what might come next.

The last clangs of hammers rang out like punctuation, then faded into memory. The soldiers of Glissara and Shadal laid down their tools not with ceremony, but with quiet reverence, as though the mountain itself had asked for silence. One by one, they drifted into the village center, drawn by something older than habit, something carried in bone and breath. Heads tilted upward. Eyes searched.

The light shifted. It didn't grow darker. Just… deeper. Like the light had folded inward. As if the evening had pressed its palms over the day, gently guiding it to rest. Above them, the first star waited, just out of reach.

Selaina didn't look away. She watched the sky the way the Nadrok watched the world, still, distant, bearing witness.

Their thread still pulsed faintly inside her, a cold weight tucked beneath her ribs. Since accepting their sight, she'd glimpsed too much: distant cities already slipping toward ruin, villages marching to a war they hadn't chosen.

Behind her, a step crunched lightly in the gravel. Not hurried. Familiar.

Rykan came to stand beside her, the warmth of his presence settling just close enough to feel. For a moment, he said nothing. Just looked out with her, his arms crossed loosely, silence lingering between them, familiar and frayed like old fabric.

Then, gently, "They're all gathering. Why aren't you down there?"

Her gaze lifted to the sky, where a single star had appeared, bright and steady over the darkening peaks.

Selaina nodded toward the sky. "They must be gathering to see Aelara."

Rykan followed her gaze. The first star gleamed above the peaks.

"They are," he said. "Same way they did before. Even now…" He hesitated. "Why keep the ritual, with battle so close?"

Selaina's voice was quiet. "Because it reminds them who they are.

What they're fighting to protect." She exhaled, the sound barely more than breath. "They stop. They look back on the day. What they gave. What they learned. How to walk forward better tomorrow."

Rykan studied the star, then glanced back toward the quiet circle forming below. "It's strange," he murmured. "This feeling in the air... it reminds me of the night before the Iron Flood attacked Tathara."

Selaina turned toward him.

"We sat around fires. Celebrated in taverns. Talked about what we'd do after," Rykan said. "There was this calm... like misplaced confidence had settled over us. But it wasn't peace, it was the stillness before a storm." His voice quieted. "Things didn't turn out so well."

"No," Selaina said softly. "But that doesn't mean this will be the same."

They stood there, silence filling the space between words. His hand hovered near hers. She noticed, and didn't move away.

Rykan's fingers brushed against hers, hesitant, not because the touch was new, because of what it carried with it, all the words they hadn't said. When she didn't pull away, he laced his fingers with hers, gently but firmly.

"Let's make sure it's not," he said.

The wind brushed her cheek, cool and knowing. Somewhere far above, past the veil of clouds, the Sky Serpents waited, watching. She could almost feel their gaze, like a thread pulled through time. She had thought their blessing would change everything.

She looked up at Rykan, and thought, maybe it had. There was something different in his gaze now. His eyes hadn't hardened. They'd settled, like someone who'd found a reason to stay still.

As if the boy who had once danced through firelight and dared the world to break him had quietly vanished when the Sky Serpents' blessing touched his skin. A shadow of purpose had settled there instead, sharp and steady, like something sacred he could never put down again.

The power she carried from the Wishing Stone was changing her, too. It stirred beneath her skin like a gathering wind, quiet but insistent. The more she bore it, the farther she drifted from the girl she'd been. And sometimes she wondered, quietly, guiltily, if the destinies she carried were slowly overwriting her. The closer she came to becoming what the world needed, the less of her there might be left to save.

She wondered if the stars wept for those who carried such fire. Or if they simply watched, as they always had, while another name burned its way into legend.

Together they stood, side by side, as the first star burned brighter above them. Below, the murmurs of the camp faded into reverent stillness. The villagers of Shadal and Glissara lifted their eyes to Aelara, the mountain winds brushing past.

Hope lingered beside memory, resolve tangled with dread, all suspended in the hush that may not outlast the dawn.

THANKS FOR READING!

If you enjoyed *The Legacy of the Sky Serpents*, I would be incredibly grateful if you could take a moment to leave a review on Amazon (or your preferred platform). Your feedback not only helps other readers discover the book but also means the world to me as an author.

Thank you for your support, and I hope you'll join me for the next book with the thrilling conclusion of *Fates of Galanor*. Book 3 is in the works, and I can't wait to share it with you soon!

Stay Connected!

Authorkevincox.com

Want more stories and updates? Join my newsletter and receive a free short story as a thank you for subscribing!

Sign up now at www.authorkevincox.com to get your free story and stay updated on upcoming releases, exclusive content, and special offers.

Thank you again for your support, and I hope to connect with you soon!

KEVIN COX
BEWILDERNESS
BOOK ONE

KEVIN COX
SHADOWSPHERE
BEWILDERNESS
BOOK TWO

KEVIN COX
NEVERSCAPE
BEWILDERNESS
BOOK THREE

KEVIN COX
STORMWAKER
BEWILDERNESS
BOOK FOUR

KEVIN COX
ETERNIUM
BEWILDERNESS
BOOK FIVE

OTHER BOOKS BY KEVIN COX

If you are enjoying the *Fates of Galanor* series, be sure to explore the *Bewilderness* series, a thrilling blend of fantasy, sci-fi, adventure, and mystery. In this series, you'll journey through multiple worlds and encounter alien races while battling against the Shadows, with characters facing challenges that will test their strength and determination.

The *Bewilderness* series includes:

Book One: *Bewilderness*

Book Two: *Shadowsphere*

Book Three: *Neverscape*

Book Four: *Stormwaker*

Book Five: *Eternium*

Available on Amazon:

https://www.amazon.com/dp/B09J3Z9J2F

Copyright © 2024-2025 by Kevin Cox

ACKNOWLEDGMENTS

I would like to begin by expressing my deepest gratitude to God for the strength, guidance, and inspiration that made the completion of this book possible. His blessings have been the foundation of this journey.

To my family, who have been my unwavering pillars of support and encouragement, thank you for standing by me at every turn. Your belief in me has fueled my perseverance and driven me to push through challenges.

To Amber and my friends, I'm truly grateful for your constant support, your kind words, and your invaluable feedback. Your presence in my life has enriched me in more ways than I can fully express.

A special thanks to Emily Katzenberger, whose steadfast support and encouragement as an editor played a pivotal role in bringing this book to life. Her thoughtful insights and unshakeable belief in my abilities pushed me to pursue excellence and ensure this book reached its fullest potential. Emily, your inspiration and motivation have been a guiding light.

A heartfelt thank you to Annie Percik, whose keen eye as an editor helped refine the manuscript. Her attention to detail ensured that the story was as polished and coherent as possible.

Finally, to everyone who has contributed, whether through encouragement, insight, or support, your help has meant more to me than words can express.

ABOUT THE AUTHOR

Kevin Cox burst onto the literary scene with his debut novel, *Bewilderness*, which was honored as one of Kirkus's Best Indie Books of 2022. Fascinated by the splendor of the universe and the mysteries it holds, Kevin uses his imagination to explore the vast unknown, crafting stories that captivate readers with their emotional depth and vivid worlds.

Though he never planned to be a writer, Kevin often found himself imagining stories and characters, ideas sparked by long drives and the music that inspires him. When he finally sat down to write a single chapter, he discovered a passion he didn't know he had. His writing draws inspiration from growing up in the 80s, immersed in the golden age of fantasy and science fiction books, movies, and music.

Kevin believes that great stories are driven by relatable characters, each facing struggles and finding the strength to overcome them. Through his work, he hopes readers will see reflections of their own journeys and feel inspired to grow, connect with others, and embrace their potential. Themes of friendship, resilience, and self-discovery are central to his storytelling.

Kevin lives in Leesburg, a small town in southwest Georgia, where he enjoys playing guitar and video games when he isn't writing. With a track record of delivering critically acclaimed stories, Kevin continues to create adventures that resonate with readers of all ages.

For the latest news and updates on the next book in the *Fates of Galanor* series, follow Kevin on social media or contact him via email.

Email: authorkevincox@gmail.com

Instagram: @kevincoxauthor

Twitter: @authorkevincox